MW01633494

GREAT IRISH STORIES OF
MURDER AND MYSTERY

EDITED BY PETER HAINING

For
Ray Bradbury
to stir a few Irish memories
—murderous or otherwise!

CONTENTS

INTRODUCTION

One of the earliest examples of Irish prose fiction written in English is a dramatic short story of murder and mystery, 'Wildgoose Lodge' by William Carleton, which is today acknowledged as a classic of its kind. This particular genre began early in the nineteenth century with Maria Edgeworth's trio of Irish novels, *Castle Rackrent* (1800), *The Absentee* (1812) and *Ormond* (1817), but when it comes to short stories in the genre, the honour of 'founding father' more accurately belongs to Carleton and his collection *Traits and Stories of the Irish Peasantry*, first published in 1830. The youngest of fourteen children of an Ulster tenant farmer, his tales of the oppressed and often violent lives of the people amongst whom he grew up have deservedly earned him comparison with Dickens and Dostoevsky who also drew inspiration from crime and mystery. 'Wildgoose Lodge' in particular, with its description of a mysterious gathering and the brutal killing that follows, has frequently been singled out for special praise, most recently by William Trevor who called it 'a chilling tale of multiple murder and one of [Carleton's] finest stories.'

The influence of 'Wildgoose Lodge' can be seen in the work of many subsequent writers of fiction and there are perhaps two main reasons for this. First, it was based upon *fact*, and second, it was related in the same timeless manner as the old Irish sagas and folk tales in which the protagonists sprang, living, from the pages just as they had done for centuries in the oral tales of the *seanchai*. The narrator of the story describes being summoned to a midnight meeting in an isolated and gloomy old country house. A sense of evil begins to oppress him even as he walks towards the building, and inside he finds a group of over a hundred men sitting in apprehensive silence. As the storyteller also waits uneasily, he notices about him 'some of the most malignant and reckless spirits in the neighbourhood' and begins to suspect his worst fears are about to be realised. The man next to him whispers that they are awaiting the arrival of 'The Captain' to begin a 'project of vengeance'. At this moment, both we, the readers, and the man himself, realise we are present at a meeting of the infamous secret society of Ribbonmen.

After the men have all committed themselves to the task by drinking a tot of whiskey and striking a Bible, they are led out into the night by 'The Captain', each brandishing a gun or flaming brand. Following a lengthy walk, the mob surrounds the home of its victim and sets light to it. During the appalling scenes that follow, the Ribbonmen use bullets or bayonets to prevent *anyone*—men, women or children—from escaping the blazing pyre. Standing in a silent, merciless circle, they remain until the house and everyone inside have been reduced to ashes.

'Wildgoose Lodge' has seemed to many readers to come straight from the realms of nightmare. But in the original edition of *Traits and Stories of the Irish Peasantry*, William Carleton added a final paragraph in which he related the source of the story.

'The tale of terror is, unfortunately, too true,' he wrote. 'The scene of hellish murder detailed in it lies at Wildgoose Lodge in the county of Louth, within about four miles of Carrickmacross and nine of Dundalk. No such multitudinous murder has occurred, under similar circumstances, except the burning of the Sheas in the county of Tipperary. The name of the family burned in Wildgoose Lodge was Lynch. One of them had, shortly before the fatal night, prosecuted and convicted some of the neighbouring Ribbonmen, who visited him with severe marks of their displeasure in consequence of his having refused to enrol himself as a member of their body.'

This 'pitiable tragedy', as the story has been described by the Irish writer Benedict Kiely, who included it in his anthology, *The Penguin Book of Irish Short Stories* (1981), can equally be seen as a forerunner of many of the tales of murder and mystery in this book. The ingredients of the unexplained, of casual violence and brutal death, which Carleton blended with such effect, are still very much those employed by Irish writers today.

Stories of murder and mystery are not confined to the rural areas of Ireland, for crime and death are just as much a part of city life, too. Nor are they a subject exclusive to literature. In the field of cinema, for instance, Conor McPherson's *I Went Down* (1997), about two convicts who run foul of some big-time Dublin gangsters, has enthralled audiences on both sides of the Atlantic; so, too, has *The Boxer* (1998), written by Terry George, in which Daniel Day-Lewis starred as a fighter trying to rebuild his life after 14 years in prison. And, perhaps most notable of all, *The General* (1998), based on the true-life story of Martin Cahill, the Republic's most notorious criminal of the twentieth century, who was shot dead in Dublin in 1994. This movie won the coveted Best Director award at the Cannes Film Festival for its director, John Boorman, who has lived in County Wicklow for almost a quarter of a century.

A number of Irish playwrights have also been exploring the same themes. Frank McGuinness's *Mutabilitie* (1997) is about three travellers attacked in an Irish forest after the Munster atrocities of the 1580s, and Gary Mitchell's contemporary drama, *In a Little World of Our Own* (1997), depicts the murderous extremes to which clannishness and bigotry can go on a Belfast housing estate. Even greater acclaim has greeted Conor McPherson's tragic, haunting mystery, *The Weir* (1998), which has deservedly earned several awards. The trend is equally evident among Irish novelists—for example, *The Butcher Boy* by Patrick McCabe, short-listed for the Booker Prize in 1992, in which a young boy's desire for revenge on a busy-body neighbour turns to murder; and Hugo Hamilton's *Headbanger* (1998), featuring *Garda* policeman Pat Coyne, whose one-man battle against the Dublin gangland bosses involves torching cars, kidnapping a top criminal's girlfriend and generally dispensing his own version of what he calls 'Coyne's Justice'. Carlo Gebler's powerful *How to Murder a Man* (1998) turns back the clock to recount the terrible events which envelop a group of nineteenth-century villagers in

County Monaghan when they become the targets of the Ribbonmen who featured in William Carleton's story.

The Celtic imagination is rightly famous for the special way it has of approaching stories of murder and mystery: sometimes focusing on the killing, sometimes on the inexplicable events behind a death, but always making it evident how narrow the divide can be between the two. In *Great Irish Stories of Murder and Mystery* I have attempted to bring together a representative cross-section of the best of such tales, all written in the twentieth century although in many of them the reader will find echoes from the past, back to Carleton's time and beyond.

When discussing the special affinity which Irish writers appear to have with such stories, I am reminded of a very strange event recounted in the *Daily Mail* in 1981 by the Irish-born columnist, Mary Kenny:

'In April 1912 a neighbour of my mother's—in a small town in the West of Ireland—had a strange experience. Around midnight there was a knock on her cottage door. She opened it— and found her 20-year-old son standing there. She embraced him, he came into the kitchen, and they sat together for several hours. In the morning he was gone.

'The woman was puzzled by the visit because her son was supposed to be on his way to America. He had been. On the *Titanic*. At the moment of the visitation—midnight—the great ship was sinking. His was among the 1,500 lives lost.'

While there are some who consider that what happened on the *Titanic* that dreadful night amounted to murder, there is still a great deal of mystery about what actually *did* befall the ill-fated liner. It therefore seems to me that regardless of whether they occur at times of great historical importance or during moments of everyday normality, violent deaths and mysterious events may always be just a heartbeat away.

Peter Haining
January, 1999

1

DEATH SENTENCES

Tales of Killers

THE SNIPER

Liam O'Flaherty

Not only is Liam O'Flaherty (1896–1984) regarded as one of Ireland's most important twentieth-century writers, but few other literary men could claim a closer acquaintance with violence and death. While still a young student at University College, Dublin, he abandoned his education to join the Irish Guards, 'tired of waiting for the Revolution' as he later put it. During the First World War he served in the army and was blown up and shell-shocked at Ypres in 1917, as a result of which he was invalided out of the army.

After a period of recuperation in which he began to write, O'Flaherty plunged into the Irish troubles and in 1921 led a group of unemployed workers who seized the Rotunda in Dublin and held it against the forces of law for several days. When the Civil War broke out in earnest, he joined the Republicans against the Free Staters and was involved in many actions. But with the chances of arrest growing ever more likely, he escaped to London and there began publishing the books that would make him world-famous. Thy Neighbour's Wife *(1923) and* The Black Soul *(1924) were followed by* The Informer *(1925), the story of an IRA informer fleeing from Republican vengeance, which was filmed ten years later by John Ford and earned an Oscar for its star, Victor McLaglen.*

O'Flaherty's early life on Inishmore, the largest of the Aran islands, was, by contrast, one of rural tranquillity. The second son of nine children of a local farmer, he was destined for the priesthood, and for a time was educated at Rockwell College, Tipperary, and the Dublin diocesan seminary. It was here, however, that he abandoned the idea of taking orders and went instead to University College. After the success of The Informer *he travelled extensively, had two breakdowns and for a time succumbed to alcoholism, though never completely stopped writing. O'Flaherty spent the period of the Second World War in the Caribbean, South America and the USA before returning to Dublin in 1946. Here he became increasingly reclusive and wrote no more new fiction after the early Sixties—although his reputation was already assured. In 1976, on his eightieth birthday, he received the Irish Academy of Letters award.*

'The Sniper', which O'Flaherty wrote for The New Leader *in 1923, is a story undoubtedly created from his own experiences of killing and has a finale of horror and poignancy that has rarely been equalled anywhere in literature.*

*   *   *

The long June twilight faded into night. Dublin lay enveloped in darkness but for the dim light of the moon that shone through fleecy clouds, casting a pale light as of approaching dawn over the streets and the dark waters of the Liffey. Around the beleaguered Four Courts the heavy guns roared. Here and there through the city, machine-guns and rifles broke the silence of the night, spasmodically, like dogs barking on lone farms. Republicans and Free Staters were waging civil war.

On a roof-top near O'Connell Bridge, a Republican sniper lay watching. Beside him lay his rifle and over his shoulders were slung a pair of field-glasses. His face was the face of a student, thin and ascetic, but his eyes had the cold gleam of the fanatic. They were deep and thoughtful, the eyes of a man who is used to look at death.

He was eating a sandwich hungrily. He had eaten nothing since morning. He had been too excited to eat. He finished the sandwich, and, taking a flask of whisky from his pocket, he took a short draught. Then he returned the flask to his pocket. He paused for a moment, considering whether he should risk a smoke. It was dangerous. The flash night be seen in the darkness, and there were enemies watching. He decided to take the risk.

Placing a cigarette between his lips, he struck a match, inhaled the smoke hurriedly and put out the light. Almost immediately, a bullet flattened itself against the parapet of the roof. The sniper took another whiff and put out the cigarette. Then he swore softly and crawled away to the left.

Cautiously he raised himself and peered over the parapet. There was a flash and a bullet whizzed over his head. He dropped immediately. He had seen the flash. It came from the opposite side of the street.

He rolled over the roof to a chimney stack in the rear, and slowly drew himself up behind it, until his eyes were level with the top of the parapet. There was nothing to be seen—just the dim outline of the opposite housetop against the blue sky. His enemy was under cover.

Just then an armoured car came across the bridge and advanced slowly up the street. It stopped on the opposite side of the street, fifty yards ahead. The sniper could hear the dull panting of the motor. His heart beat faster. It was an enemy car. He wanted to fire, but he knew it was useless. His bullets would never pierce the steel that covered the grey monster.

Then round the corner of a side street came an old woman, her head covered by a tattered shawl. She began to talk to the man in the turret of the car. She was pointing to the roof where the sniper lay. An informer.

The turret opened. A man's head and shoulders appeared, looking towards the sniper. The sniper raised his rifle and fired. The head fell heavily on the turret wall. The woman darted towards the side street. The sniper fired again. The woman whirled round and fell with a shriek into the gutter.

Suddenly from the opposite roof a shot rang out and the sniper dropped his rifle with a curse. The rifle clattered to the roof. The sniper thought the noise would wake the dead. He stopped to pick the rifle up. He couldn't lift it. His forearm was dead.

'Christ,' he muttered, 'I'm hit.'

Dropping flat on to the roof, he crawled back to the parapet. With his left hand he felt the injured right forearm. The blood was oozing through the sleeve of his coat. There was no pain—just a deadened sensation, as if the arm had been cut off.

Quickly he drew his knife from his pocket, opened it on the breastwork of the parapet, and ripped open the sleeve. There was a small hole where the bullet had entered. On the other side there was no hole. The bullet had lodged in the bone. It must have fractured it. He bent the arm below the wound. The arm bent back easily. He ground his teeth to overcome the pain.

Then taking out his field dressing, he ripped open the packet with his knife. He broke the neck of the iodine bottle and let the bitter fluid drip into the wound. A paroxysm of pain swept through him. He placed the cotton wadding over the wound and wrapped the dressing over it. He tied the ends with his teeth.

Then he lay still against the parapet, and, closing his eyes, he made an effort of will to overcome the pain.

In the street beneath all was still. The armoured car had retired speedily over the bridge, with the machine gunner's head hanging lifeless over the turret. The woman's corpse lay still in the gutter.

The sniper lay still for a long time nursing his wounded arm and planning escape. Morning must not find him wounded on the roof. The enemy on the opposite roof covered his escape. He must kill that enemy and he could not use his rifle. He had only a revolver to do it. Then he thought of a plan.

Taking off his cap, he placed it over the muzzle of his rifle. Then he pushed the rifle slowly upwards over the parapet, until the cap was visible from the opposite side of the street. Almost immediately there was a report, and a bullet pierced the centre of the cap. The sniper slanted the rifle forward. The cap slipped down into the street. Then catching the rifle in the middle, the sniper dropped his left hand over the roof and let it hang, lifelessly. After a few moments he let the rifle drop to the street. Then he sank to the roof, dragging his hand with him.

Crawling quickly to the left, he peered up at the corner of the roof. His ruse had succeeded. That other sniper, seeing the cap and rifle fall, thought that he had killed his man. He was now standing before a row of chimney pots, looking across, with his head clearly silhouetted against the western sky.

The Republican sniper smiled and lifted his revolver above the edge of the parapet. The distance was about fifty yards—a hard shot in the dim light, and his right arm was paining him like a thousand devils. He took a steady aim. His hand trembled with eagerness. Pressing his lips together, he took a deep breath through his nostrils and fired. He was almost deafened with the report and his arm shook with the recoil.

Then when the smoke cleared he peered across and uttered a cry of joy. His enemy had been hit. He was reeling over the parapet in his death agony. He struggled to keep his feet, but he was slowly falling forward, as if in a dream. The rifle fell from his grasp, hit the parapet, fell over, bounded off the pole of a barber's shop beneath and then clattered on to the pavement.

Then the dying man on the roof crumpled up and fell forward. The body turned over and over in space and hit the ground with a dull thud. Then it lay still.

The sniper looked at his enemy falling and he shuddered. The lust of battle died in him. He became bitten by remorse. The sweat stood out in beads on his forehead. Weakened by his wound and the long summer day of fasting and watching on the roof, he revolted from the sight of the shattered mass of his dead enemy. His teeth chattered, he began to gibber to himself, cursing the war, cursing himself, cursing everybody.

He looked at the smoking revolver in his hand, and with an oath he hurled it to the roof at his feet. The revolver went off with the concussion and the bullet whizzed past the sniper's head. He was frightened back to his senses by the shock. His nerves steadied. The cloud of fear scattered from his mind and he laughed.

Taking the whisky-flask from his pocket, he emptied it at a draught. He felt reckless under the influence of the spirit. He decided to leave the roof now and look for his company commander, to report. Everywhere around was quiet. There was not much danger in going through the streets. He picked up his revolver and put it in his pocket. Then he crawled down through the sky-light to the house underneath.

When the sniper reached the laneway on the street level, he

felt a sudden curiosity as to the identity of the enemy sniper whom he had killed. He decided that he was a good shot, whoever he was. He wondered did he know him. Perhaps he had been in his own company before the split in the army. He decided to risk going over to have a look at him. He peered around the corner into O'Connell Street. In the upper part of the street there was heavy firing, but around here all was quiet.

The sniper darted across the street. A machine-gun tore up the ground around him with a hail of bullets, but he escaped. He threw himself face downwards beside the corpse. The machine-gun stopped.

Then the sniper turned over the dead body and looked into his brother's face.

THE DEATH OF STEVEY LONG

Sean O'Faolain

Sean O'Faolain (1900–91) went through experiences that were as violent and bloody as those of his great compatriot, O'Flaherty, with whom he is often bracketed as one of Ireland's greatest twentieth-century short-story writers. He was born John Whelan, the son of a Dublin policeman, and changed his name to its Irish equivalent at the age of 18 when he became enmeshed in the Irish troubles. For some years he served on the Republican side in the Civil War and had several brushes with killings as well as risking capture and imprisonment. Unlike O'Flaherty, however, once he had become a student at University College, Cork, he completed the course and graduated, thereafter becoming a schoolteacher for several years. Subsequently, he went to Harvard on a scholarship and there took an MA in English literature. However, he never lost his fierce championing of civil liberties and the rights of workers which he expressed in a number of the short stories and books, notably Come Back to Erin *(1940), which made him famous. His collected short stories are now widely regarded as among the gems of twentieth-century Irish literature.*

Memories of his wilder younger days surface in several short stories, and 'The Death of Stevey Long', written in 1932, may well be based on personal knowledge resulting from his years with the Republican forces in Ireland. Certainly in its picture of a young man inexorably caught up in events that lead him to a tragic destiny, it is an example of the Irish story of murder and mystery at its finest.

*   *   *

Macroom Castle was built somewhere in the sixteenth century by the MacCarthys, a building of great height raised on a solitary outcrop of rock and with a moat and a demesne reaching down to the river-edge. As Macroom is the last town on the western road through the mountainy divide of Cork and Kerry the castle has always become a barracks in troubled times, the last outpost for the wild, disaffected country beyond. It has a long history: it suffered at least one siege, and passed through several hands. The O'Sullivans lost it in 1606 to the Earl of Cork and in 1675 the crown confiscated it and put troops in it to overawe the rebels to the West, that broken land impenetrable to everyone but tories and raparees. It had its dungeons and its secret passages, and in fact when the Tans took it over as a barracks, in their time, they thought it best to close up several doors that, it seemed to them, led nowhere. But it was not a suitable place to imprison anyone; the river bred too many rats and moles and beavers, and when the mountains sent their rain-water churning down the rocky valleys the floods rose so high that they overflowed into the basement, and from the later-built cells a little higher up a prisoner could see the trees and the hedges growing out of the water almost on a level with his eye.

In one of these cells, his elbows resting easily on the window-sill, stood Stevey Long gazing westward to where the faint blue of the mountains was barely discernible against a white sky. Beside him was a little man whose finger-tips barely clutched the stone edge on which Stevey leaned, and as he strained up to peep at the mountains Stevey looked down at him with amusement.

'They'll shoot you tonight, Fahy,' said Stevey suddenly.

'Ah, shtop that talk now, Long,' said the little man with an imploring upward glance.

'Oh, but I hear them saying it,' said Stevey. ' "Bring out that fat murderer of a teacher," they'll say. Or they'll say, "Bring up that assassin of a teacher, and we'll teach him".'

'Oh, suffering Heart!' wailed the teacher. 'Me nerves is all upsot. Shtop it now, Long. It's not fair.'

As Stevey gazed off contemptuously at the mountains the teacher defended himself.

'Anyway,' he said, 'I never let on to be a fightin' man. And it's all very well for you. You haven't a wife and seven children.'

'Seven children?' asked Stevey. 'Is that all you have, teacher? You ought to be ashamed of yourself.'

'Isn't it enough? You're mocking again, Long. Saying your prayers would befit you better. That dirty tongue of yours will bring the wrath of God on us.'

'My tongue,' said Stevey vehemently, 'is our only hope.'

'Then why,' said the teacher peevishly, 'don't you get round that bastard of a jailer for us?'

'Oh! Oh! Bastard? Naughty word, teacher. Naughty word!'

'Go to hell,' said the little man in an agony of anger and fear, and he retired to a corner of the cell, by now almost in tears.

Stevey went to the iron door of the cell and listened for any sound in the passage-way. Then in one of his sudden rages he stooped over his companion.

'Haven't I told him enough lies to drown a cathedral? Said I was at Festubert? Said I had an English wife? Said I knew Camden Town and Highgate like the palm of my hand? Told him every dirty story I ever read or heard? And what have you done but sit there and cry?'—and he raised his hand as one might to a child—'you long-faced lubber!'

Stevey returned to the window.

'And after all that,' he continued, 'all he says is, ''Aow! How interesting!'' God, how I despise the English!'

'It's no use, Stevey,' said the teacher. 'We can't get round him.'

The teacher would have been secretly pleased if Stevey would believe it. For two weeks he had had to sit in that unsanitary cell listening at all hours of the day and night to Stevey and the Tan who had been on cell-fatigue since they came, exchanging indecent stories. Stevey poured them out without an effort of memory: stories he had heard in the pubs and garages and lavatories of Cork, stories he had read in the *Decameron*, the *Heptameron*, French joke-books, Maupassant, the Bible—at first to the amazement, and gradually to the horror of the little teacher. He had read nothing since he left his Training College ten years

before, and he still talked of Dickens on the strength of the one
novel he was obliged to read there. What horrified him most of
all was to find himself gradually inveigled into listening to these
stories, and (with a start) he would find himself grinning with
delight before he realised that the sewer-stream had been let loose
once again. Stevey was a plumber by trade—he was always
saying how proud his father was of 'the profession'—and he
would begin to talk of red-lead or three-inch pipes, and proceed
slowly via lavatory-traps, the sewers of Paris, chronic consti-
pation, tablets for anaemia, or cures for impotency, to the brothels
of the world or the famous courtesans of history—all with great
seriousness and a show of modest indignation—and he would
illustrate with a vast amount of inaccurate, and even for his
subject, defamatory detail at which the teacher's eyes would
swell and his fat head would shake with wonder and sudden
enlightenment. Or he would spend a whole night hinting at his
affairs with the loose girls of the city, returning quickly to the
cess-pools of chloride-of-lime if the teacher showed disapproval,
or to Margaret of Navarre or Boccaccio as if his life, too, were
one long legend and romance. But he could pollute even the
sweetest women of literature, and the teacher would find himself
trapped again when Stevey would fling Madame Bovary or Boule
de Suif or Tess into the same bawdy-box as Mata Hari or some
creature out of the *Rat Bleu et Jaune* or some local beshawled
laneway light-o'-love just previously removed to the city mad-
house. To the Tan he was as the Shahrazade to her Persian king.
The Englishman heard such stories from him as he had never
heard in tap-room or barrack-square—even an old story would
become fresh and vivid in Stevey's mouth, and weak with laughter he would scarcely have enough strength to turn the key in
the door as he staggered off roaring with delight to retail what
he had heard to his comrades upstairs. Then Stevey would, as
now, return to the window muttering contemptuous curses under
his breath and appeal to Fahy for something to add to his stock
of bawdry. When Fahy would reply with an apologetic wail that,
'I was always on the althar, Stevey,' or, 'I was a great Confra-
ternity man, Stevey,' the gunman would lose himself in gazing

at the pale, far-off horizons, wave after wave of land, paling into the all-but-invisible peaks of the real hinterland fifty miles away. Since the days of the Earls of Cork a hundred rebelly Irishmen must have gazed just as longingly at those changeless mountain-tops, thinking first of the misfortune of their capture, then of wives or friends, then of the fate in store for them, but soon reduced, as they looked out on the unattainable freedom of the hills, to thinking of nothing at all, waiting only for the dusk and the dark and the forgetfulness of sleep. None can have spent his hours, as Stevey did, thinking to coax his English jailer with bawdry, but few, if any, can have been as cruel, and as cunning, and (it must be admitted) as fearless, as Stevey Long.

Suddenly steps clanked down the passage-way and the cell began to taint of gas—the jailer had turned on the tap outside the door, and the little blue flame leaped up on the shelf above the lintel, and the circle cut in the centre of the door was filled by an eye.

'Hey!' whispered the Tan.

'Yes,' said Stevey, at the door in a flash.

'You two blokes are to be moved.'

'Where?' asked Stevey while the little teacher crowded up against him to listen.

'Cork Male Prison,' said the Tan.

Stevey groaned. There was an end to his hopes of escape from the castle, and he knew Cork Jail well enough not to like it. The eye disappeared and was replaced by a pair of lips.

'But you ain't goin'!' they whispered cautiously.

'Why not?' asked Stevey, excited with hope.

'Cos' I 'ave other plans for you,' said the Tan, blinking a wink at them. 'I won't 'ave it. 'Ere's the order,' he said curtaining the circle for a moment with a buff paper. 'There's two deserters here from the Wiltshires, higher up than you, right upstairs, and I'm jolly well going to run them out on this order. They came in an hour ago and they're blind and blotto with Irish moonshine.'

'Oh,' said Stevey, 'but you can't . . .'

'See if I don't,' said the Tan, and he opened the door and

entered the cell. He cornered Stevey by the window and prodded his chest with his finger as if it were a revolver or a knife.

'Hark at me!' he said.

'Yes?' said Stevey and the little teacher put in his fat face to listen.

'Go away, you,' growled the Tan, and Fahy retired like a kicked dog. 'Go and stand by the door and hear if anybody's coming.'

He turned to Stevey.

'You know about my wife?'

Stevey did indeed know about the wife. She had been, he always knew it, his main hope. She was London-Irish and a Catholic, and it was she who made Stevey declare his wife was London-Irish and a Catholic too, by Heaven.

'Yes,' said Stevey.

'She keeps on nagging at me in her letters,' complained the Tan. 'She's delicate, and she has nerves, and she's a Catholic.' (This last seemed to be a great grievance with him.) 'I was proud of all that when I married her. It's so romantic, I think to myself, to have a delicate wife that's a Catholic into the bargain. But now! She says I'm earning blood-money. I told her about you, and she writes and says she weeps to think of you. But that's all right. She weeps to think of anything, she does. I don't mind that. But now she says such things about leaving the kids and going to live with her married sister that I don't trust her.'

'I wouldn't trust her,' says Stevey.

'How I 'ate married sisters,' said the Tan; and then, 'Why wouldn't you trust her?'

'She's all alone in London,' said Stevey in a gloomy voice.

'She's got her kids. She's got her married sister.'

'Ah,' said Stevey in a hollow voice, 'but where's her husband? From what we know of women,' he continued seriously, 'and especially married women,' he added with an air of sad wisdom, 'you can't trust a woman that's separated from a man that she thinks isn't fond of her.'

'Nor I don't trust her,' said the Tan. 'And I'm goin' home. That's where you come in.'

'Yes,' said Stevey like a shot. 'I could get you out of this country within ten hours, without anybody knowing it—if I were free.'

'You've said so. Dozens of men—deserting, if you like to put it that way.'

'It's my job,' said Stevey. 'City of Cork Steam Packet to Liverpool. Think you were travelling first-class. Easy as that.'

'I'll chance it,' said the Tan. 'Back to London I must get. To tell you the truth I'm sick of this bloody place.'

From inside his uniform he pulled a hacksaw and a length of stout rope. Stevey took them in a grab.

'After dark,' said the Tan. 'I'll bring supper as usual. Now get to work and quietly. If that blade cracks I can't get you another one.'

As he opened the door to go Stevey's mind flamed; as fast as a bullet it flew to the old coach road south-west of the castle where they would probably begin their trek west or east.

'Sst,' he called.

The Tan turned.

'Take a message for me to the village,' said Stevey.

'No,' said the Tan.

'You must,' said Stevey. With a stub of pencil he wrote on a sheet of paper from the Tan's pocket-book, and gave it to him. The Tan read it and winked back at Stevey.

'It's the little bicycle-shop just across the bridge,' said Stevey.

'You're a clever fellow,' said the Tan. 'Of course we must have bikes.'

When he was gone Stevey wound the rope round the belly of the teacher and put him with his back to the door so as to cover the spyhole and listen for approaching feet. Then he began, stealthily at first, to saw at the first of the three bars in the window.

'This scratching,' he said, 'will be heard all over the town of Macroom.'

'If we only had a bit of grease for it,' said the teacher like a fool.

'I once read about Casanova,' said Stevey, and then he stopped talking and hacked away.

'By God,' cried the teacher, 'I once heard a story about that fellow . . .'

'Eat it,' said Stevey, working like a madman.

The evening was now falling, and as Stevey worked the interior of the cell grew dark. Away to the south-west the sun was sinking over the distant mountains and as she sank they grew first a rich, deep brown, and then purple, 'their very peaks became transparent', and lastly they paled into an unreal mist. The last level rays threw Stevey's shadows on the iron door and the limed wall, and the little teacher's face was warmed to a ruddy glow. As the air grew cold and rarefied they heard all the sounds of the village life, the children that cried out in their play and the cart that lumbered over the cobbles of the bridge.

About half-past six o'clock the teacher, weary and stiff for so long standing in a fixed position, was almost glad to announce the approach of footsteps. By that time Stevey had cut to within a feather's breadth the top and bottom of two of the bars, filling with clay from the floor the shining track of the saw through the steel. The clanking steps came to the door—it was their friend the Tan. He laid their supper on the bench and bent his head to whisper.

'I'm going with you,' he said to Stevey. 'Mind you promise to get me out of it safe and sound.'

'I swear to Christ,' said Stevey like a shot.

The little teacher was like a kettle on the hob with excitement.

'Naow!' said the Tan. 'No swearing. Parole. Give me your parole, word of honour.'

'Word of honour,' said Stevey, without a thought.

'Oh, God, yes, word of honour,' said the teacher heatedly.

'Shut up, you,' said the Tan angrily, and the little fellow piped down miserably, fearing to be left behind if he angered either of them.

'The Tommies are gone to Cork,' said the Tan with a grin. 'There'll be hell to pay when they get in with the Shinners in Cork Jail. When will we go?'

'When is sundown?' asked Stevey. 'Is there a moon?'

The Tan consulted his diary.

'Six forty-six, sun sets. Full moon, eight-ten.'

'It'll be dark at eight,' said Stevey. 'We'll go then.'

'Is he coming?' said the Tan, pointing to the teacher.

'We'll bring him,' said Stevey.

The Tan looked at the teacher and then he went away without a word. They ate but little that night and Stevey kept going and coming in a corner of the cell.

'God,' he said nervously, 'I'm like a cistern tonight.'

'Will we go wesht?' asked the teacher, stuttering with terror.

'You'll go wesht if you're not careful,' said Stevey. 'Remember that bastard has a gun in his hind-pocket. And we have none.'

They kept watching for the faint moon but the reflected glow of the village and the fluttering light of the gas-jet confused them. All the country to the west was now wrapped in night and the mountains could no longer be seen. With the fall of darkness their ears became sharper and they could hear now the last cries of the children quite plainly and the murmur of the river far below. A mist spread itself over the land before their window, and a faint mooing of cattle occasionally came out of the darkness. As he peered into it Stevey made up his mind that he would not go west—he was sick of that wild, broken country where, as he used to say, 'they ploughed the land with their teeth', sick of the poor food, the dry bread and jam, the boiled tea and salted bacon, sick of the rough country girls. He was pining for the lights and gaiety of the city and he decided he would do a little 'deserting' of his own. When the Englishman came down, sharp at eight, he had donned a civilian's coat over his green-black policeman's trousers and a wide-brimmed bowler hat that pressed his two ears out like railway signals.

'Ready?' he whispered.

Stevey nodded. From outside he extinguished the jet and plunged the cell in darkness. Stevey unwound the rope from the belly of the teacher, and the Tan pressed with all his might on the cut bars. They would not give. Stevey dropped the rope and threw his weight on them and still they held. The Tan swore, the teacher entangled himself in the rope, and Stevey searched in the dark for the saw. At last he found it and with a few sharp rasps the blade broke through the steel. It was easy then to bend the bars up on a level with the higher coping, and when the rope had been tied to the uncut bar and flung out into the dark they were ready.

'I'll go first,' said Stevey, 'and signal with one pull on the rope if everything is clear below. Send him after'—pointing to the teacher. 'And come last yourself.'

'Oh,' moaned the teacher, as he looked at the aperture, 'I'm too fat to get through that.' But they paid no heed to him.

Stevey wriggled out first, his feet scraping the wall as he was pushed behind by the other two.

'I'll never get through them bars,' wailed the teacher in a deep whisper to nobody in particular.

Stevey vanished downward, swaying as he went, hand over hand. He landed in a great bed of stinging nettles and resisting an impulse to turn and run for it he listened for a second. The little river gurgled noisily below him; he could distinctly hear the quiet munching of cattle just beyond the mound where he stood. He pulled the rope once and stood looking up. A faint white radiance was beginning to appear where the moon was rising on his left. Stevey saw the teacher's fat legs waving in the air and his fat bottom squirming skyward. But there he remained, not advancing an inch, and after a long pause he was pulled in again, and Stevey saw the bare shins of the Tan, then his black trousers dragged up to the knees, then his body following after. In a second he too was among the nettles.

'Where's Fahy?' asked Stevey in a whisper.

'Come on,' said the Tan fiercely.

The fat pale face of the teacher appeared at the window.

'I can't get out,' he wailed in a loud whisper.

'Use the saw,' said Stevey. 'We can't wait.' And he clambered down the mound, grinding his teeth as a pile of loose stones rumbled after him down the slope.

'Ssh!' said the Tan. 'The sentries will hear us.'

'Lie still,' said Stevey, and they dropped on the dew-wet grass. They heard a sentry's voice call to his mate, and the mate's reply. They heard the grounding of arms, and then the noisy river, and the wind in the willows above them shivering and whispering incessantly by the river's edge. After a while they rose and in a stooping posture they half-walked, half-ran along by the edge of the river through the grass, feeling the ground (when they left the river) rise steeper and steeper, and when they fell panting again on the ground, there below them was the black pile of the castle and the hundred eyes of the town.

'That bloody teacher nearly ruined us,' said the Tan.

'He'll never get out,' said Stevey.

But he soon forgot him, and he did not in fact live to know what happened to him in the end. They were now standing on the soft dust of the old coach road, below them the next valley, and, as if it were standing on the tip of the distant ridge beyond, the great ruby moon. To Stevey it was all familiar and congenial, but to the Englishman it was cold and desolate.

'We're out of it,' said Stevey gaily, and he slapped the Englishman on the back.

'I'm in it,' said the Tan gloomily. 'Well, where are the bikes?'

At that Stevey squared his shoulders and clenched his fists. He looked up and down the narrow, shaded road, and then at the Tan. He looked down at the far-off lights of the town and at the Tan again. Then he jerked his head onward.

'This way,' he said. 'They should be here.'

He went on ahead, peering right and left, whispering in a low voice as he went 'Jimmy? Jimmy?' When he passed a blasted oak a bicycle fell clattering on the road at his feet. He peered up and there was a gaitered leg and the tail of the inevitable trench-coat. Everything was happening just as he expected it.

'Here's one,' he shouted. 'Try is the other there,' and he pointed backwards to the opposite side of the lane. As the Tan groped in the far ditch Stevey whispered madly to the hidden figure.

'Have ye the skits?'

'Yes.'

'Get 'em ready.'

'How many are there?' said the voice.

'One.'

Then Stevey shouted back to the Tan.

'Have you got it?'

'No.'

'Here,' called Stevey. 'Hold this one.'

The unsuspecting man came forward to hold the bicycle, and as he took it Stevey passed behind his back. The bicycle crashed as Stevey leaped like a tiger at his neck, roaring at the same time to 'Jimmy' to give a hand. Two trench-coated figures leaped from the hedges at the cry and fell on the struggling shouting soldier, and in two minutes he was bound with Stevey's trousers belt and his kicking legs held and tied with a bit of cord. Finally his yelling mouth was stoppered by Stevey's handkerchief and then, except for their panting and an occasional squirm from the helpless man at their feet everything was deadly quiet again.

'Gimme his skit,' said Stevey.

The captive looked up with the light of terror glaring in his eyes. Stevey stood over him for a second with his finger wavering on the trigger.

'Here,' he said then to one of the two. 'You do it. I gave him my word I wouldn't.'

He made for the bike, dusting himself as he went, and threw his leg over the saddle. A horrible double sound of a revolver being discharged tore through the night.

'Gimme that,' said Stevey.

The revolver was handed to him, and he thrust it in his pocket.

'Are you sure he's finished?' he asked.

'Sure,' said the other.

'Good-bye boys,' said Stevey, and he pedalled swiftly along the dark lane.

Presently he freewheeled on to the lower road and came to a dimly-lighted pub. An old cart and a sleepy horse were tethered outside the door. This was the pub known as The Half-way House, and Stevey decided that he needed a free whisky. First peering through the glass door he entered. There was nobody inside but the bar-girl and an old farmer leaning in the corner of the counter and the wall; the girl said nothing, and the old farmer merely nodded. Those were tough times, and they had heard the double shot.

'Any Tans about?' said Stevey when he had ordered his drink.

The girl only shook her head silently and poured the drink, watching him as he swallowed it. The farmer lowered his eyes to sip his porter whenever Stevey looked at him, raising them slowly whenever he felt he was not being watched, nodding and smiling foolishly whenever Stevey's eyes caught him. A tiny clock among the whisky bottles ticked so loudly in the silence that Stevey looked up at it startled. It was nearly nine o'clock.

'By God, it's late,' he said.

The girl nodded and said nothing, and when Stevey looked at the farmer he was turning his glass round and round in its own wet circle, his eyes shooting side-glances towards Stevey all the while.

'Christ,' swore Stevey, 'you are a talkative pair!' And putting down his empty glass he strode out between the swinging doors and walked to his bicycle. Then it occurred to him to return on tip-toe and listen at the glass-doors. The old farmer was speaking:

'Aye,' he was saying, 'a bit o' money is a great thing.'

'Yes,' said the girl listlessly.

'Sons how are ye!' said the farmer.

'Aye,' responded the girl. There was a pause, and then:

'Money is betther than sons any day,' said the farmer.

'Yes sure,' said the girl with a sigh.

With a superior grin Stevey mounted and rode away.

Had Stevey kept his word with the Englishman he might be alive today. He would certainly have avoided Cork that night. But now, knowing nothing of what awaited him and with nobody to warn him, he covered, in less than four hours, the forty-odd miles that separate Macroom from Cork. He had cycled along the winding roads among the bogs where the mountains come down to the plains, and when the mountains vanished from sight he pedalled over a bare, high plateau where he measured the distance not by prominent hills or valleys but by a tree here and a tree there, or a cross-road, a familiar house, or a school. At last he came to the valley of the city river and for miles he cycled above it, straight as a crow's flight to the edge of the city. It was about one o'clock when he stood looking down over all its sleeping roofs as over a vale of quietness, a slight drizzle of rain beginning to fall, a gentle wind blowing it in his eyes as he peered across to the uttermost farthest light that marked the remote side of the city to the north where his father lived. He might have made a long detour to reach Fair Hill, but why should he? Had he known the city was under curfew he would never have dared to do anything else, but his two weeks in Macroom Castle were two weeks cut off from the world, and now, flinging his bike into the ditch, he dropped downhill into the danger of the streets.

After his three long months in the mountains it was sweet to feel the ring of the pavements instead of the pad-pad of the mud roads, to see the walls and the gas-lamps all about him, so sheltering after the open darkness of the country nights. But as he went on the streets were so strangely empty, even for one o'clock in the morning—there was not even a wandering dog abroad—that Stevey became worried and ill at ease. As he approached the open business section of the city especially he began to realise what a grave risk he was taking in coming back into the city at all where he was well known for a gunman; but to come late at night, with no crowds to mingle with, and the police on the alert for late wanderers, was doubly dangerous. Still, as the mist thickened, became heavier, finally changed into a wind-blown downpour, it did not occur to him that any reason other than bad weather was required to explain the strange emptiness of the streets, until suddenly, not more than a few blocks away, a dozen rifle-shots broke through the hiss of the falling rain, loud above the river purling in its narrow bed. Stevey halted in his stride. Then as there was no repetition of the sound he went on, down to the quays that shone under the arclights webbed with moisture.

The rain hissed into the river, cold and spearlike, and his calves were now wet, and his face and shoulders and he could feel his coat was sodden through. Then, in and out of the glow of the lamps on the pathway in front of him he saw a girl racing in his direction, calling as she ran to another girl to hurry, the other calling to her to wait. It was a relief to Stevey to meet somebody, but when the first girl, who ran against the rain with lowered head, rushed into his arms and then screamed and cowered away from him into the wall—he stood angry and astonished.

'Oh! Sir, sir!' she wailed. 'I'm goin' home.'

'Hello, hello!' said Stevey. 'What's up with you?'

'I'm goin' home, sir,' she said again, trying to cower past him. 'I am, honest.'

'Well, go home!' cried Stevey exasperated, and passed on. The other girl, he found, had turned and fled from him as from the devil.

Stevey now observed that the houses towering about him were almost pitchy black. All the erect oblongs of light had long since moved up nearer the roofs, wavered there for a while, and then vanished suddenly; the sitting-rooms had become bedrooms and then been blotted out, and now only red eyes of light showed bedroom walls where one could no longer see bedroom windows. Once a moving candle-flare showed the turn of a stairs, a landing, a high window. Bare boards, thought Stevey, under bare feet unheeding the silver of hammered nails in the white wood, long white neck-frilled night-dresses bending over the balustrade to call to a tiled hallway for surety of locked doors. A blind sank down, squares walking up its yellow ground. A pair of gold parallelograms disappeared, and then began to reappear and vanish, faint or defined, but never steady for a moment, and to Stevey's thought a woman curved over the flames, her fingers slipping her shoes from her feet, silken stockings falling after. All the while the rain lashed the shining pavement—a real mixture of March wind and April shower—and the spouts poured their overflow across the cement flags. Everyone was asleep in bed but he. He possessed the whole city, as if it had been made for him alone.

Again the rifle-shots rang out and this time they were followed by a rattle of machine-gun fire and a few isolated explosions. Again Stevey halted, drawing into a door and peering along the quays. He felt that after his fortnight in prison and his three months in the hills he was become a stranger to this city-world in which he had once moved so easily and safely, and he wished he had made a call in some friendly house before entering the city—it almost seemed to him as if something strange and unusual were occurring around him. He left the quays at this thought, and began to dodge among the side-lanes and the back-streets, but to cross the river he finally had to come into the open. As he crossed the railway bridge he saw on the opposite quay, spread across the street, a squad of soldiers whose accoutrements and arms glinted in the rain and the arclights, and seeing their weapons at the ready he drew back behind a girder and waited. They were approaching gradually and he knew that he would certainly be discovered if he remained there. He moved in quick bird-like leaps across the bridge, from the shelter of one girder to the shelter of another, peeping all the time at his enemy. Then he had to leave the bridge and cross the street. His heart beat faster; he breathed quickly. He heard a cry of 'Halt' and he took to his heels. Over his head, by his very ears it seemed to him, whistled the bullets. At once he took to the side-lanes, up and down and in and out until he had lost his pursuers and himself thoroughly, and exhausted he fell back into a doorway to think. It did not take him long to realise this time that it was Curfew, long threatened even while he was in the mountains, suddenly clapped on the city while he was in jail, and he had walked like a fool into the net. His hand stole to the revolver in his pocket. If he had been caught with that it would have meant anything. Now completely unnerved he left the door, halting at the slightest noise, looking around every lane-corner and down every passage-way before he dared pass them by. Gradually he began to recog-nise where he was—in the network of lanes between the river and the fish-markets, an isolated quarter to leave which would bring him into the open streets once more. A lecherous pair of cats made him leap for an arched alley-way. He laughed at himself the next minute but he realised that he could never hope to reach Fair Hill in this way, across the other bridge and along another set of naked quays. Over his head Shandon boomed out two o'clock—there would be at least three hours more of Curfew. He wiped the sweat of fear from his forehead and peeped cautiously out of his alley-way, thanking his good-fortune that he did so, for the next instant the heavens seemed to open with light and every cranny and crevice of the lane was flooded by a powerful searchlight. At the same moment he heard the soft whirring of a car and low voices. He was taut and trembling like a string that has been made to vibrate by a blow. He thought he heard steps approaching and he slunk backwards down the alley, halting in doors and watching the flooded light of the lane, beyond the tunnel of the arch. He came to the alley-end and his feet crunched on the head of a dead fish, the guts oozing under his heels. He glanced about the great pitch-dark square—he was in the markets. In the limelight of the arch far down the alley he saw two khaki figures who turned towards him and entered the arch and faced the wall. It was enough for Stevey—he turned and crouched his way along the markets, slipping on the rotting vegetables and the slime of fishgut, resting in door after door with something of the feeling that he had walked into the wrong region, that here were troops of men, that in any other part of the city it would have been far different if not entirely safe. But he felt his last turn taken when a whirring lorry roared suddenly around the corner and its floodlight poured into the street, lighting the very pavement at his feet, where he stood with his back to a door; and as if to give him no possible chance he saw, and cursed as he saw, that the jambs and lintel and panels were pure white. With the instinct of the trapped man he crushed back against it and the nearer the car came the more he crushed. Slowly, as he pressed against it, the door swung open behind him. He passed in and closed it behind him and listened, not even breathing, while the car passed slowly by. Then he began to breathe tremblingly, and panting, and with his hand to his heart, he laughed quietly to himself. Trust Stevey, said he to himself, to get out of any corner.

The hallway was blackness unbroken, and with his two hands out, one grasping his revolver, a crucified gunman, he groped his way in. His feet struck the first knee of the stairs, and he began to climb. A window-sill and an empty pot—he passed it by. A lead-lined sink and a dripping tap—he moved on upwards. A door. Was this a man or a family, or a lone woman? Damn dangerous business this, thought Stevey to himself; but not half so dangerous as the streets. What should he do? Sleep in the hall? Clear out? Neither. Was it Stevey Long not to get himself a good doss for the night? As his father would say, he must think of 'the profession'. He moved up higher and came to a landing window. Through it he could see Shandon dark against the glowing sky of the city. Across in another house he could see a back-window all lit up, and framed in it two men, both in pants and shirts. He could hear their quarrel, see the bigger of the two crash his fist into the face of the other, see a ragged-haired lane-woman drag them apart. Then the light vanished as she moved away upstairs with the candle, and the small man wiping the blood from his cheeks stumbled downstairs out of sight. Looking up diagonally Stevey saw a landing; looking down, the dark well of the stairs; through the window a tin roof on which the chutes above dripped and dripped. He went up to the landing and here he noticed a streak of yellow light at the base of the door. He tapped softly, hardly knowing what he was doing. He knocked again and still there was no reply. He peeped through the keyhole and there before a warm fire he saw an old woman sitting bolt upright in her chair.

Even to Stevey the old woman was a touching sight, her corrugated hands clasping her crucifix, her mouth all wrinkled and folded, her eyes lost in the firelight. He was moved by the peace of this room high above the markets and the river, warm after the rain. How cosy she looked!—no, not cosy, but how calm, and yes, how holy! How holy! Stevey smiled and shook his head at her. He looked at her more closely. Then he entered, closing the door softly behind him. He laid his hand on her shoulder— on her face—on her left breast. She was dead.

He looked around him slowly, and slowly he removed his wet coat, hanging it on a chair before the glowing fire. Then he sat quietly warming his hands to the flames, stretching his long legs, and drying his face. He chuckled quietly to himself. Here was joy!

He awoke before dawn and thinking he felt a little cold he

threw fresh coals on the fire. Feeling thirsty he drank half the milk in the glass beside him. Then he fell asleep again until a church bell tolling faintly in the distance gradually percolated through to his senses. For a full two minutes he stared sleepily and in wonder at the corpse seated beside him, and then, as the cries of the market-girls came to his ears his mind reverted to the city. He realised at once that he was back among his own people, as safe as a house.

He rose stretching his stiff shoulders and began to move through the house. As for the old lady, he did not trouble himself about her—heart disease no doubt or a sudden stroke, and he remembered the warm fire and the fresh glass of milk. One room was full of strange lumber, and as he peeped at the markets through the drawn blinds his hand fell idly on an old album. When he opened it and it began to ping-pong out its little tune he shut it with a fright and hoped nobody heard. The back-room was an ordinary sitting-room. He saw a chess-board and wondered cunningly who played chess in that seemingly empty house. Surely there must be a man somewhere he thought, and he felt certain of it when his eye fell on a great brass-horned gramophone, every inch of its dark maw pasted over with foreign postage stamps. He felt it best to get out of the house as soon as possible and hearing Shandon bells strike eight he decided that now was the best time—it was Monday morning and he could mingle with the crowds going to work; they would be too preoccupied to notice his wet, wrinkled clothes, his dirty boots, his unshaven face. First, however, he returned to the dead room to look for food. He found bread, and a pot of jam, and milk that was only just a little sour. He was raising the milk to his lips when his eye caught a black-japanned tin box by the window and the glint of silver in it. He strode across and looked down at the wad of notes and the loose pile of florins and shillings and half-crowns and little worn sixpenny pieces. The lock, he noticed, had been broken at some time previously. Without a thought he put his hand on the thick roll of notes and filled a fistful of silver into his pocket. Then, abandoning the food he had prepared for himself he turned and tramped down the stairs, opened the hall door and walked right into the arms of a raiding patrol as it alighted from a lorry. He looked right and left and made one step as if to attempt an escape, but in a second a dozen rifles were pointed at his heart. In another second he was seated high on the car with a crowd of market-people gathered wonderingly about him.

In a dream he found himself smoking one of a bundle of cigarettes handed him on all sides from the sympathetic fish-women. All they knew was that he was a 'Shinner' and they cheered him repeatedly for it. As he sat there in a daze one woman actually put a little tricolour rebel flag into his hand, and he waved it feebly from time to time, and the fish-wives and the onion-girls cheered him wildly as he was driven away. As they turned the corner of the markets one of the guards smiled grimly and said 'Good-bye-ee,' and Stevey smiled weakly in return and stuffed the flag into his pocket.

It was the last smile Stevey Long smiled on this earth. The search of the house discovered, hidden under the stairs, a con-glomeration of explosives, bombs and grenades and incendiaries, finished and unfinished. It took the military an hour to remove them all, and to crown the amazement of the market-folk, they then brought up a coffin, carrying it in lightly, carrying it on four bending shoulders. At his court martial, which they held an hour later at drumhead—martial law was in force—question after question was fired at Stevey and he dodged and twisted like a hare, but he was a hare in a net. By degrees they wearied him, and finally cowed him.

'Where did he get that revolver?'

'I found it,' said Stevey.

'Where?'

'In the fields.'

'There were two bullets discharged?'

'Were there?' said Stevey innocently.

'When did you find it?'

'Last night.'

'Where did you come from last night?'

At that Stevey paused, feeling that these questions were leading back to Macroom Castle, realising that he could not substantiate any statement he might make as to his whereabouts the evening before. The President repeated the question testily.

'Where did you come from?'

'East Cork.'

'Where in East Cork?'

'Midleton.'

'What were you doing in that house?'

To this Stevey replied truthfully, and though it was the only true thing he said that day, they did not believe him.

'Do you mean to say,' asked the president, 'that the people of Midleton didn't know a curfew order was in force in Cork?'

A few such questions drove Stevey to the wall, but it was when they told him that the woman was shot by a point four-five bullet, of the same calibre as the gun found on him, and charged him with the murder of the old lady that he paled and grew thoroughly confused and realised the danger in which he stood. His advocate did his best for him but it was no use, and when in the end Stevey was asked if he had anything to say he grew excited and began to talk foolishly, leaning forward and waving his hands, swearing that he would tell the whole truth this time, and contradicting almost everything he had previously said. His advocate tried again to save him but the president intervened; he had caught his man and now he would have a little sport with him.

'Let the prisoner speak,' he said, and leaned back in his chair and glanced at his colleagues. They, in turn, glanced back at him and drew their fingers over their mouths and looked down at the table—the old man, they thought, was in a good mood today

The truth was, said Stevey, that he was coming from East Cork and he was ambushed by Sinn Feiners. He fired two shots at them . . .

'At your own people?' asked the colonel.

'Well they fired at me,' cried Stevey with an oath.

'Go on,' said the colonel politely.

'The bastards fired at me,' said Stevey in a towering rage at his imagined enemies.

'One moment,' said the president. 'Where did you really get this revolver? Do you admit possessing it?'

'Ain't I telling you?' said Stevey. 'It was a Tan that gave it to me.'

'Indeed?' said the colonel politely. 'Go on.'

'I fired at them, once, twice. And then, I'm sorry to say, I ran.'

'To Cork?' asked the colonel sarcastically.

'I got a bike,' said Stevey sullenly.

'Where?' asked the president, leaning forward. 'Can we substantiate that?'

'Well, to tell the truth,' said Stevey, 'I—I stole it.'

'Like this money we found on you? You admit you stole that, too?'

'Yes, I stole it, I took it,' admitted Stevey.

'Can we even confirm that you stole the bike?' asked the president. 'Where did you steal it? Where is it now?'

Stevey told six more lies in his efforts to avoid admitting the bicycle was in a ditch on the wrong side of the road. The old colonel lost his patience here.

'Where did you steal the bike?' he roared.

'It was in the dark I stole it,' muttered Stevey and the court rocked with laughter.

'It's true,' wailed Stevey.

'Remove the prisoner,' said the old colonel in disgust.

In order to disgrace him as well as punish him he was sentenced for murder and robbery under arms.

AFTERMATH

Rearden Conner

There are often innocent victims in a killing as Sean O'Faolain has just demonstrated, but few more poignant than the central figure in this next story. It is a tale that mixes human savagery with animal terror in a series of events set against the background of divided Ireland in the Thirties. It is certainly one of the most unforgettable stories in this collection.

Rearden Conner was the pseudonym of Patrick Reardon Conner (1907–91) who was born in Dublin, educated in Cork, and worked for some time as a landscape gardener and broadcaster in London. He began to write short stories in the late Twenties and in 1933 completed Shake Hands with the Devil *(1933) which in 1960 was made into a very popular film starring James Cagney, Michael Redgrave and Richard Harris. Ireland was a recurring theme in a number of his later books, including* Rude Earth *(1934),* Wife of Colum *(1939) and* Hunger of the Heart *(1950). 'Aftermath' first appeared in* Lovat Dickson's Magazine *in 1934 and was later selected as one of the 'Best British Short Stories of the Year'. It has lost none of its power to touch the reader's heart in the intervening half-century.*

*　　*　　*

The foal stood beside the body of its mother and sniffed the wine-like air guardedly. The sun blazed down on its glistening back and flanks, making it look as though it had been carved from black marble. It was mid-afternoon on an August day. Butterflies flew from cornflower to clover head in this wide field of lush grasses. White and yellow butterflies they were mostly. Occasionally a Red Admiral came to flutter its gorgeous wings gracefully on a wide marguerite.

A wasp droned around the foal's head. It threw up its muzzle and snorted, shaking its long mane as delicately as a woman shakes the fringe of a costly shawl. It stood with head erect and looked around the deserted field. Then it bent and nuzzled the warm body at its feet. It could not understand why its mother did not respond to the feel of its sensitive nose. She lay there with a tiny hole in her side from which a red trickle meandered down to stain the emerald grass beneath.

The firing had ceased at last. No bark of revolver or crack of rifle now shattered the peace of the brooding day. The men who had raked the field with lead from the gate beyond had gone. The sky was as blue as the mid-ocean. Clouds sailed across it like yachts dipping before a stiff breeze. A halcyon sky and a halcyon scene. The only indication of man was this bleeding body of a black mare with legs bunched up in the last paroxysm of death.

The foal lifted its head and whinnied. It ran a little way up the field, then ran back again. Now the stain on the grass had grown larger and deeper. It whisked its short tail agitatedly as it pawed at its mother's carcass with a long, shank-like leg. Froth was oozing from the parent's mouth and glazing on the lips which were drawn back from the gaunt teeth.

The foal ran along the low ditch towards the gate in the far corner. Every few minutes it halted in its hesitant trot to stare back at the spot where its mother still lay. It listened eagerly as it ran for the sound of welcome hoof-beats, ever hopeful that the black heap over in the field would spring up and chase after it.

In the mornings and at evening they always raced around the field, mother and son. Their tails streamed out and their ears lay back as though much depended upon victory. Their black bodies shone and flashed above the waving mat of green. Their limbs moved with the grace and force of pistons in a perfectly tuned engine. Many a farm lad leant upon the gate to watch them at play with a glow of admiration in his heart.

But today the black figure lay as still as a boulder. The foal glanced back from time to time and whinnied loudly. It reached the gate at the top of the field, but no one came to stroke its neck or to offer it a lump of sugar. Some days ladies on their way to the little chapel beyond leant on the top bar of the gate and proffered a titbit with many caresses of light warm hands and soft words of endearment. Today no one came. Everything was strangely quiet. As still as death itself after the bedlam of an hour ago, when even the very lark had been scared back to its nest.

The foal trotted down by the far ditch towards the high grove of laurels which backed on to the chapel. Horseflies followed it relentlessly and stung its sweating flanks viciously. It scarcely heeded them, so desperate was its loneliness. When it came abreast of the laurels, it paused in its trot. A human voice had reached its sharp ears. It listened intently, hardly daring to blow breath through its nostrils. The voice came again, ceased, then droned once more. The foal stepped primly up to the wire fence which bounded the laurel grove and gazed into the dense mass of spear-headed leaves.

The three men sat stiffly in the centre of the grove. They wore trench coats blackened with oil and muddied all over. One had a cap pulled down almost to his eyebrows. The others had soft hats with down-turned brims.

Two of them held revolvers in their hands. The one with the cap had a Thompson gun resting across his knees. A half-loaded drum of ammunition was in position.

The three men had the hunted look of escaped convicts. Their hands and faces were torn. One had a red weal across his left cheek, caused by a swinging branch. They were all smoking furtively, holding half-Woodbines cupped in their free hands and inhaling deeply.

'They're gone by now,' one said at last. 'I heard the armoured car drive away twenty minutes ago.'

'Don't ye be too sure!' answered the one with the cap. 'They're cunnin' beggars, them 'Tans.'

'Why the hell didn't Gallagher say there was an armoured car bein' sent out, anyway?' groused the third.

'Probably he didn't know,' observed the man with the cap laconically.

'Yah! Not much *he* don't know! He's runnin' with the hare an' huntin' with the hounds, that fella!'

'This is the first time an ambush has failed in these parts,' remarked one of the hatted men.

'An' it'll be the last time we'll take a tip-off from Gallagher!' snarled the man with the cap viciously. 'I'll plug him meself for this!'

'It's a miracle we're not all plugged, Shamus, with that car turnin' up the way it did!'

'It is that, b'God!'

One by one they finished their cigarettes and crushed the glowing butts into the soft leaf-mould.

'Let's get out of here!' said the man who seemed to be the leader.

The two hatted men pocketed their revolvers. All three made a move towards rising to their feet. Then a sound like someone brushing against leaves came to them from the fence at the edge of the little grove.

They crouched down and peered through the overcrowded branches. They were about thirty yards from the fence, and they could not see clearly owing to the dense mass of leaves which made the centre of the grove almost sunless. The revolvers were drawn cautiously from the trench-coat pockets. Over at the fence there was movement and a glint such as a highly polished police belt would make in the sunrays.

Beads of cold perspiration sprang out on the brow of each man. 'A blasted 'Tan!' hissed the one with the cap. He lifted the Thompson gun to his shoulder as though it were a rifle and pressed the trigger. 'Cha-cha-cha-cha-cha!' said the gun.

The foal threw up its head as the bullets ploughed into its chest. It whinnied softly with wonderment. It did not understand this thing that barked so quickly, nor this burning pain which stabbed it through and through. It tried to back away from the fence, but it found that its limbs were powerless. It made an attempt to raise its head once more, but now the long muzzle sagged down like a weighted sack. It saw red streaks on its chest and forelegs. Its eyes glazed over and a delirious blinding pain drove up to the top of its skull. It crashed against the fence. The field and the grove and the whole world spun round and round and round. Then the sun went black.

THE EXECUTION

Brendan Behan

Writer, wit, rebel and rake, Brendan Behan (1923–64) was recently described in The Observer *as 'the Jack Kerouac of Irish literature—a man whose alcoholism, advancing diabetes and inability to deal with fame drove him on a path of self-destruction.' Behan was born in Dublin to a strongly Republican family and by his own admission was making bombs for the IRA when only just into his teens. His ingenuity in this resulted in him being sent on a bombing mission to Liverpool at the tender age of 16. However, his 'mission' got no further than the docks where he was arrested in possession of bomb-making equipment and charged with 'complicity in acts of terrorism'. Because he was still a juvenile, he was sentenced to three years in an open Borstal, and it was there that he first discovered literature and began to develop his ability to write. Back in Ireland, he was soon in prison for shooting at a detective during an IRA commemorative ceremony in Dublin—an act for which many believe he was lucky to escape being hanged—and served five years. In 1947 he was arrested in Manchester for helping in the escape of an IRA prisoner and served four months.*

The result of these years 'inside', which Behan liked to refer to as his 'University', were the plays The Quare Fellow *(1956) and* The Hostage *(1958) and his literary sensation,* Borstal Boy *(1958), a brilliant account of his confinement and the motley collection of prisoners he encountered, all of them living in a world based ultimately on brute—occasionally brutal—force. In the years that followed he was lauded as one of the most celebrated writers of his day, while at the same tune gaining notoriety for his drunken and disorderly lifestyle which could only have one inevitable ending.*

Behan published his first work in 1946—a poem, Filleadh Mhic Eachaidh, *about an IRA hunger-striker. More verse followed, as well as several short stories and a detective serial,* The Scarperer, *which appeared in* The Irish Times *in 1953 under the pen-name 'Emmet Street'. 'The Execution', published posthumously in 1978, with its final act exposing a man's confusion in political deed and fervour, has been compared to another classic Irish short story about 'the Cause' (as Behan liked to call it), Frank O'Connor's 'Guests of the Nation'.*

*   *   *

We got Ellis into the car fairly easily—we told him we were shifting him to a new house.

God forgive me, I told the poor devil mock-confidentially that I had it from a good source that the Army Council had decided against execution and that the Battalion Staff was having him shifted to a new house because the one we were leaving had become unsafe.

We drove out to the southern outskirts of the city and when we reached a *bona fide*, Kit, who was driving, suggested a drink. We all more or less welcomed it, even Gerry Dolan (and he being a TT disapproved of Army men drinking whether on a job or not). Now he was on the job I don't think Gerry fancied it much.

We went in, Ellis between Kit and myself. The poor devil wouldn't have run if we'd let him. He was telling me how it wasn't his fault giving the dump away. He had never been picked up before and the cells had got in on him. Smiling contentedly to himself he was, and saying that maybe the boys wouldn't think too badly of him when he took his tar and feathering like a man. Real wistfully he said to me, 'I'd sooner get an awful beating than a tar and feathering because that'd be a terrible disgrace, my old man being a '16 man an' all.' God help him. My father was a Dublin Fusilier in 1916, but that's the way.

I squeezed his arm in a friendly way. I'd never liked him much before but I felt sorry for him and sorrier for his people. He had been fond of boasting about the Fenian tradition of his family. Still, we couldn't let people give away dumps on us or there'd soon be no respect for the Army.

We entered the snug.

I'd my hand through the pocket of my mac and on my skit. It was a Police Positive .38 in a slip-holster, a nice small skit.

Gerry Dolan, I knew, had either a Lüger, Parabellum, Walther or a Browning. They were the only automatics in the company dump, except a few Colt-autos and a 9mm Peter that was too big to lug around. And Gerry dearly loved automatics, especially ones with queer names. I never saw the day he'd be satisfied with a Smith or Webley.

You can sometimes judge a fellow by his taste in skits.

Now Kit, I could swear, would be carrying a Colt-auto. He liked a Smith but held that it was bulky for work like this. Although he didn't love automatics as a rule, he'd a *grá* for the Colt. Mainly, I think, because when he went round checking dumps with the Batt. Q/M he could pinch a few rounds of Thompson stuff to bang off in it. A wild lad Kit, but dependable. A bit of a boozer. He used to drink with Mickey Horgan and Connie.

For all that I'd nearly had them dismissed for using Army stuff on an unofficial job, I thought the three of them the best suited of the five of us in tonight's work. Connie and Mickey would be carrying short Webleys.

I ordered drinks—four pints, a mineral for Dolan and a glass of whiskey for Ellis. They give a condemned man a glass of rum and a cigarette in France. I wished Ellis had asked for a bottle of stout. Connie, Kit and Mickey were drinking abstractedly. The frothy rings on their glasses were equi-distant.

I wasn't used to drink and was sorry I hadn't ordered an ale, a pint seemed even more unmanageable tonight.

Ellis knocked back his whiskey and asked what we were having. I didn't want to stop there all night and said we'd better be going. I was surprised when Gerry Dolan said it was his round.

He ordered three pints, ale for me, and two whiskeys. His face reddened when I looked at him.

When we got in the car again Ellis's spirits seemed even further improved, the liquor I supposed. He offered me a cigarette and struck a match; his face was very young looking.

About three miles further was the spot. It would be my job to tell them to get out of the car. Ellis would see the loneliness of it. There wasn't a house in sight of it. It didn't seem so easy a thing now.

It was a frosty night and my legs were getting a bit cramped. I hoped Ellis wouldn't start crying or anything. I'd sooner he put up a fight. It would be easier to let him have it.

'Let him have it', 'plugging him', 'knocking him off'. It's small wonder people are shy of describing the deed properly. We were going to kill him.

With a jolt the car pulled up.

Kit turned round from the wheel, 'OK to get out lads?' No one answered.

It seemed a hundred years before I nudged Ellis. 'Come on, get out.'

A death sentence—that's what it was—and I saw that he realised it.

I flashed my torch on him. His jaw dropped but he obeyed.

We brought him in about fifteen yards off the road. He didn't murmur.

Gerry Dolan shook my arm, his face was white in the moon-light. His lips grinned as he struggled to find words; he said something about an Act of Contrition. His fancy 9mm shook in his hand. I nodded.

All was in readiness. The handles of the shovels were dimly outlined behind a bush. We stood at the spot. Kit was lighting a cigarette, his hand cupping the flame.

Ellis looked round him, just a little wildly. 'Not yet, lads,' he moaned. He began to cry not wildly but softly, the way a child cries. The tears streamed down his cheeks.

Kit Whelan patted his shoulder.

I wondered what to say to comfort him.

I could hardly tell him it was quite painless, we'd be sure to get the heart. After all he wasn't having a tooth out.

He knelt down and began to pray.

We knelt down with him.

I tried to pray for his soul. I couldn't. It seemed awful to think of souls just then.

We arose and he bent his head close to his body, as if to avoid a blow.

I raised my revolver close to his head, not too close.

If I put it against his head maybe the muzzle would get blood on it, blood and hair, hair with brilliantine on it.

The five guns were levelled at him.

I cocked mine and pressed slowly on the trigger. It seemed to take all my strength.

There was a deafening roar and he pitched wildly forward. I heard more shots and he lay still.

As if in a dream I saw Connie eject the empty shells. Kit was picking them off the ground from his Auto.

'Finished, the poor divil,' he murmured.

We put him in the grave. He felt quite warm. I told the lads to be careful not to get bloodstains on their clothes. We began to shovel in earth. I moved a big stone off my shovel—it might smash in his face.

ON THE BOG

Patrick O'Brian

Murder is not the sole preserve of those involved in terrorism or organised crime. It can become a part of the lives of petty criminals, too, as Patrick O'Brian (1914–) demonstrates in this next story of two poachers going about their nefarious business. Despite the differences in their temperament—Meagher, nervous and uncertain; Boyle, calculating and cruel—the events during their excursions seem to move inexorably towards a violent finale for one or the other.

O'Brian is undoubtedly best known for his hugely successful series of historical novels about Jack Aubrey RN, the captain of HMS Surprise, *and his exploits during the time of Nelson, but he has also written a number of stories inspired by events during his childhood in County Clare. A novel,* Testimonies, *recently republished, provides an insight into his fascination with mystery when the three narrators telling the story of the love affair between an academic and a hill farmer's young wife all prove to be ghosts.*

It was while he was recovering from a debilitating childhood illness that Patrick O'Brian took literally his doctor's advice to get as much sea air as possible in order to speed his recovery and in so doing developed his love of the sea and ships which later became the staple ingredient of his best-selling novels. He also found inspiration in the valleys of the countryside and some of its less law-abiding people, as he reveals in the atmospheric and tension-laden pages of 'On the Bog', written in 1974.

*　　*　　*

'It is time to be moving,' said Boyle.

'What? What?' cried Meagher, starting wildly out of his sleep—a cry of alarm.

Boyle made no reply, but flashed his lighter to look for the leg of the tall thigh-boots beside him; indeed there was no need for a reply, since the momentary gleam showed the whole scene at once, the interior of a reed-walled butt, guns, a game-bag, duck-boarded floor, the wooden bench. The flame also lit Boyle's handsome face, exaggerating its high arrogant nose and the morning beard; and in this brief flash Meagher's being fell back into its present context.

They had lain out on the bog all night, so that they could get out to the far end for the geese, for the dawn flighting, well before daybreak and well before any keepers were moving.

Of course it had been Boyle's idea entirely. In Jammet's a man was prating about geese, great skeins of greylags brought down by the hard weather, and turning to Meagher Boyle said, 'How should you like to have a shot in the morning? I know a capital place, and you are the great wildfowler, I believe.'

Meagher was pleased, flattered with the notice and the preference—particularly the preference, because toad-eating Clancy was there, eager for any invitation that might be going; and although he had been up at a party all night before he said he would be very happy indeed—'wildfowling is meat and drink to me'. They left at once, walked over the river to Boyle's place—Meagher was one of the few who had been there—and loaded gun-cases, cartridge-bags and tarpaulin into the car.

'It is the devil we have no dog,' said Boyle. 'Clancy spoke of a labrador.'

'Oh, that was only his froth and pride; he has never owned so much as a cat in all his life. I'll act as the dog,' said Meagher, laughing.

Boyle sent him for cartridges with a five-pound note and as soon as he came back they drove straight out of the town. A long drive, too fast for conversation with the hood off, fast along winding lanes and boreens, and Meagher was excited with the rushing air, pleased to be sitting there next to Boyle: then the stop in the lee of a turf-stack and the walk out, a great way across rough pasture as far as a dyke. 'We are not going in there, are we?' asked Meagher, reading a notice in the fading light. It was one of many posted all along the near bank forbidding trespassers, warning of mantraps, stating that dogs should be shot on sight.

'That is the general idea,' said Boyle. He felt for a plank in the rushes, laid it across, lifted the wire the far side, slipped through and stood waiting.

'I don't mind a bit of poaching,' said Meagher, 'but . . .' He could not find an acceptable way of putting 'but only when it is fairly safe', so he said no more. This was certainly far from safe: he did not know which county they were in even, but they had run along two miles of park wall with an enormous house inside it before stopping, and now they stood in flat open country without a bush or a hedge for miles. The notices were fresh and trim; this was obviously a strictly preserved estate.

'Never worry about them,' said Boyle. 'You are only an honorary dog; and in any case geese and duck are not game. They are *ferae naturae*—they have no *animus revertendi*.'

Meagher could hardly reply to that. He walked on over the tussocky forbidden ground, looking as unconscious and confident as he could. They had not gone a hundred yards before a single partridge got up in front of them, a little to the right. Boyle's gun leapt to his shoulder; he fired, and the bird hit the ground so hard it bounced twice. He said, 'I beg pardon, Meagher. That was really your bird. Just pick it up, will you, there's a good fellow.'

Meagher picked it up, glancing round in every direction; and he picked up two rabbits and a snipe as well before they reached downright bog with redshanks in the cuttings and curlews crying high overhead. Looking ahead in the twilight he could see tall reeds, dense cover that would hide their nakedness; but between them and the reeds lay an intricate series of channels, many of them newly dredged. Boyle led the way through, walking casual and easy like a tenant for life and a man who knows his way well.

'You seem to know your way well,' said Meagher.

'I used to come here in the old duke's time,' said Boyle. And some time later, pushing through the innermost reeds, he said, 'The old boy always did himself proud. Just look at this butt, will you? Now that's what I call a truly ducal butt. Benches, duck-boarding. There will be straw in that barrel; but suppose you cut some rushes as well—here is a knife. I will keep an eye lifted in case the duck start to move.'

Meagher could have sworn he had not slept at all that night. Certainly with his prickling eyes and general weariness he felt he had not. The greater part of it (all but the last twenty minutes in fact) he had lain listening to Boyle snoring on his back, listening to the desolate call of marsh-birds he could not put a name to, weird shrieks and groanings, and to the stir of the reeds as ice formed on them. He was not very cold as he lay there in his nest of rushes and straw under a piece of tarpaulin, but he was wet from below and hungry, and as the hours wore by he smoked until he had no more in his packet. He was a heavy smoker, deeply addicted to cigarettes.

It was partly anger that kept him awake, anger and resentment. They had not been in the butt half an hour before the duck began flighting, mallard, wigeon, teal, pintail, great numbers of them, and Boyle set up a fusillade, a firework display, an artillery battle, that must have been heard five miles off at least in this deathly calm air. Every shot made Meagher wretched, and by the time the movement was over and he had searched out a good score of birds he was in such a state of nervous indignation that he almost cried out, 'You invite me to shoot and without a word of warning expose me to this sort of thing—you have no consideration at all.'

The only words that actually passed were Boyle's. He said, 'I think it is over: In any case it is too dark to see. I cannot wait to get at the geese. Good night to you, now.' No jocular or commiserating reference to the few ineffectual half-hearted shots that Meagher had let off: tact, that was the lay, a tact so obvious that it was, if not a studied offence, then at least most unfriendly.

Their acquaintance ran back a considerable way, so far that

Meagher could say of Boyle, 'We are old friends: I have known him for years,' but it had never really matured: there was too little in the way of candid interchange, too much reserve for that. Meagher admired Boyle's undeniable style, his offhand way with people, and his occasional lavish generosity; but he had few illusions; he knew that Boyle liked to have a companion—he had no girl, no permanent judy, preferring temporary drags of the lowest kind—and as Meagher was generally available so he was the most frequently chosen. Then again he knew that although Boyle could talk freely about Stockhausen, Schwitters, Brecht, he was virtually illiterate: none of the things that interested Meagher concerned Boyle in the least: he would see the National Library, the Gallery and the Abbey go up in flames with cheerful indifference. Occasionally a wild, unpredictable gaiety would come over him and then he would lay aside his reserve, horsing around in Mother Daly's like a boy; but on the whole he was elusive—there was no coming close to him at all— and rather than friendship between them there was a kind of exasperated love on Meagher's side alone, a love not only for Boyle's thoroughbred grace, his elegance, his ability to cope with guns, rods, horses, waiters and girls, but also for his vulnerability. Boyle was a man who had to be on top: he had to excel in every field. Humiliation would destroy him—if a girl were to turn him down or if he were to scrape a bus as he shot his car one-handed through the whirlpool of College Green he would be undone. In some fields—in talk—Meagher could protect him; and to protect such a creature was a privilege, an infinite superiority. Boyle walked a perpetual tightrope, and although up until now he had never stumbled badly to Meagher's knowledge he was continually in danger of doing so, in danger deliberately created by himself. Blazing away as though he owned creation on preserved land stuffed with keepers: a perfect example.

As though he owned creation . . . he must own quite a share of it, however. How much nobody knew, but certainly more than most of their circle, certainly very much more than Meagher, who lived by expedients—small journalism, a little reviewing, the occasional grant. Once he had taken Meagher and a couple of dreadful little bus-stop tarts to a house behind Enniskerry, letting himself in with his key: half had been ruined so long ago that trees grew twenty feet out of it, but the rest was deeply uncomfortable, though dusty—carpets, huge leather chairs, mahogany—and the drive was kept up. He also had a tower in the County Clare, where he fished: but many of them claimed to have towers in the County Clare and what really impressed them was this visible car, the sight of him coming out of the Kildare Street Club, and his beautiful cigarette-case, made of gold. The car might be uninsured, the tower a myth, but the case was there all the time.

Money: that was the great trouble. When they went out, who picked up the restaurant bill? Who paid for the drinks, the petrol, the tickets? Usually Boyle was delicate, but he had a sadistic streak in him and sometimes he could make Meagher feel all the difference between a man with fifty pounds in his pocket and one with a packet of pawn-tickets done up with an elastic band. There were times when instead of offering a lift, a dinner-jacket, a loan, he would compel Meagher to make the direct request; once or twice he had casually borrowed one of Meagher's precious pounds and had forgotten to repay. Odd little meannesses too, such as disappearing for a moment and coming back with a freshly-lit cigarette. No doubt they arose from a dislike of being sponged on, of being manipulated; and fellows like Clancy were shameless at sponging.

Yet in spite of all this they laughed at many of the same things; they enjoyed the same films; they could be companionable enough; they had fun; and surely, said Meagher, fundamentally Boyle had a liking for him, and respected his parts.

The liking was not apparent on either side at this moment, however. Something seemed to have happened to their relationship during the night, as though Meagher's resentment and silent injurious expressions had conveyed themselves into the other's sleeping mind; or as though Boyle had reflected upon Meagher's 'I do not mind poaching but . . .' and had filled in the gap, or upon his ignominious performance with the gun (Meagher was a countryman only by theory). While for his part Meagher could not see why he made all this coil about a mere dilettante, a sciolist, a dabbler. 'I am far more intelligent than he is, far better educated,' he reflected, plucking straw and rushes from his clothes. 'He may have a bodily, an animal intelligence—he is good at killing things—but surely to God a man is above a brute. He has read nothing at all.'

Here Boyle finished buckling his thigh-boots and walked out of the butt, leaving the game-bag for Meagher to carry: in the reeds outside he lit a cigarette, and at the smell of the returning waft Meagher's stomach gave an avid craving heave. He remembered not only that his packet was empty but that he had had neither dinner nor tea. To be sure, Boyle had eaten nothing either; but Boyle was well padded, whereas Meagher, who lived by his wits, was painfully thin. The gap of a meal told on him at once.

'Perhaps that is why I am feeling so very brittle all over,' he thought. 'That and two sleepless nights. And I dare say I have a cold coming on—to lie out all night in the wet, what a notion!—a bad go of flu.'

He followed Boyle through the reeds: they walked without speaking to one another, as though there were an acknowledged breach. Through the reeds round the lake and out on the far side; and here, stretching infinitely far beyond them, was the landscape of a dream, perfectly silent, perfectly still; the whole bog, with every rush and clump of grass upon it, was white with hoar-frost, and it gleamed gently in a suffused shadowless light that came dropping from the frozen air together with minute crystals of ice: no visible source for the light, no stars, no moon, only this high luminous mist. A world before the creation. An enormous flatness with no details in it, for the impression of light was illusory and at any distance everything merged into uncertainty; there was no one object that could be seized and defined apart from the sea-wall away to their left, the single firm line in this universal vagueness, a line that ran curving away for ever.

Boyle was screwing himself up to see his watch, to make the hands show in the darkness of his bosom. 'Just hold my gun, will you?' he said. A beautiful short-barrelled hammerless ejector, lighter by far than the old-fashioned brown keeper's gun allotted to Meagher.

'Can you make out the time?' asked Meagher, and to his shame he heard a placating note in his voice.

Boyle did not answer directly. In a cold impersonal tone he said, 'Only two hours to go. We shall have to step out if—oh for Christ's sake don't hold your gun like that, you silly whore! Don't you know you must never point your gun at anything you don't mean to kill?'

Meagher was on the edge of crying out that it was not pointed, that it was not loaded; but the shocking brutality of the assault, quite outside their habitual intercourse, choked back his lies and he followed Boyle in silence.

Two hours, he had said. Surely they had been walking more than two hours? The night seemed a hundred years old. The sea-wall was unchanged, the one firm thread in a shifting interminable dream; it stretched before and behind, a broad ten-foot earthwork with sluices here and there and every few hundred yards a set of posts, startlingly upright in a world so flat, like black exclamation marks signalling danger: each one might be an armed keeper. The idea of running away from a keeper, of labouring over the bog with a gun pointing at his back, was horrible to Meagher: and who could tell what Boyle might do, in such an encounter out here at the far end of the world with no one to see? He was a deeply bloody man. 'A whore, a pillar of ignorance,' said Meagher.

But although the sea-wall was still the same it no longer ran through the same country: now they had primaeval saltings on their left hand and the deep mud of a tidal river, while on the right the sweet-water marsh shone and glittered with creeping water. A landscape even more inhuman, desolate and unearthly than before: vaster too, for now an increase in the light had brought the indeterminate sea into its farther rim. The falling aerial crystals had turned to penetrating wet, but so far this had not affected the whiteness of the ground. The frost still struck upwards.

The mud seemed deeper underfoot, however—it had long since filled Meagher's inadequate shoes; and certainly his sick hunger and abject craving for tobacco had grown immeasurably. He felt even more brittle and his lack of sleep had got into his red-rimmed bleared watering eyes, so that when he concentrated on a post it flickered and even waved its arms; his sense of smell and his hearing had become unnaturally sharp. He heard the whistle of a flight of duck before Boyle, as they passed high overhead. These must be the first birds of the dawn flighting; so surely the day could not be very far off, and release from this nightmarish entertainment?

Certainly there was more light, even if it was only the rising of the moon; but at the next set of posts this did not prevent him from catching his leg in the barbed wire slung between them. He gave a strong kick to be free of it: the wire broke from the post and snarled right round his leg, the barbs running deep. It nearly had him down: he staggered on one foot, his loaded gun swinging in an arc, pointing now at Boyle's head, now at his loins as he walked steadily on. Meagher recovered his balance, laid down the gun, laid down the game-bag (it weighed forty pounds), and knelt to wrestle with the wire. Wet with drizzle and mud, his numbed hands merely fumbled, and in a sudden flare of anger and resentment he tore at the wire with all his force. It was no good. He was still held fast, ignominiously kneeling there with the mud soaking into his knees; and in a sudden collapse of spirit he crouched against the post, watching Boyle stride away. He knew Boyle was aware—it was a conscious back—and he knew Boyle would not turn unless he were called upon for help.

Meagher did nothing until he saw the small leap of a flame: Boyle had lit a cigarette and was waiting for him. Meagher forced his mind to be cold, followed the pattern of the barbs and disentangled them one by one, tearing the cloth as he did so. He picked up the bag and followed, limping: as he got under way so the glow of the cigarette moved on.

Long before he caught up, the cord of the bag was biting into his shoulder again and the weight of the gun was a torment: he was wet through and through; he was full of yellow rancour and spleen; but with something of the cunning of fever he said 'I shall keep up with him: even Boyle has not the face to smoke without offering me one if I am right by him—a guest, for all love!'

He could feel the paper cylinder between his two fingers and his thumb, the glowing end sheltered in his palm from the drizzle, the deep inhalation, the yielding of the tube at the very end, the red arc and the hiss as he threw it into the water.

Still the old night faded and little by little the marsh came to life—heart-broken cries as dim birds fleeted away; rails grunting and squealing in a reed-bed; far over the devilish yell of a vixen. 'Do come along,' said Boyle once or twice. 'We shall never get there in time.'

A little while after they had passed a patch of black quaking bog with a dead bullock in the middle, its peeling horns and part of its head showing above the mud, a brace of teal sprung from a flash of water to the right of the wall, rising fast, almost vertically. Boyle missed them right and left. He walked on, saying nothing, faster than ever; and Meagher could tell from the set of his back that he was bitterly crossed.

'Do come on,' he said again, and now the light was spreading fast from the east, showing the white carcass of a boat on the far bank of the river. 'All I ask is a couple of shots at the geese. Just one pitiful shot; and we shall not get even that at this pace.'

On, faster still: Meagher did not give a damn in hell for the geese or the prospect of shooting at them, but Boyle's failure had revived his spirits a little and he walked along with his resentment somewhat appeased. Yet at the same time the sense of unreality—this unearthly landscape, his own light-headed fatigue—grew on him: his mind wandered off to other places and times, to odd, disconnected fantasies of triumph, and when he returned to the present he found he had dropped behind. He also found that his anger was dead: weary tolerance had replaced indignation.

Boyle had left the sea-wall some way before the point where it turned right-handed, and he was making his way cautiously through the mud towards a plank that led to a dense screen of reeds. Meagher did notice a soft gabbling in the distance, but it meant nothing to him. He only saw that by going straight along the wall he would avoid the mud and come to the bridge as soon as Boyle, thus making up for lost time. He did not catch Boyle's backward signal—the flash of his hand he would have used to a dog—and he hurried along with a sudden quick softening and a resolution to ask Boyle openly for a cigarette, to accept the humiliation of doing so, to gratify him. This was to be an offering, a reconciliation, and he called out 'Boyle, I say, Boyle.' As he called he saw the furious gesture and ducked; but it was too late. There was a monstrous threshing of wings on the far side of the reeds and the geese, hundreds, even thousands of geese, lifted high out of range.

As if he were alone Boyle walked on through the screen, taking no precautions now, and he went along the edge of the turlough where the smell of geese lay heavy, looking at the droppings and feathers: after some time he emerged, much farther round the bend, and came back along the wall. Meagher ran to meet him: his apologies died in his throat at the look, not of intense dislike or anger nor even fury but of utter contempt. A frigid, objective, dismissing contempt like a blow, breaking even the most rudimentary social contract. And while Meagher was uttering the few words he could force out, Boyle's eyes wandered off, bored, uninterested: he reached for his case, opened it—it gleamed like a chalice inside—deliberately chose and lit a cigarette.

Beside them, lower than the wall itself, a huge pale-blue bird came gliding through the frozen air, shadowless over the white ground, never moving its wings: behind and a little higher came its mate, even larger, dark and forbidding. They turned their heads to look at the men but they never deviated from their course; and as they flew a silence spread over the marsh—duck and small birds had been stirring; now they were mute. Not a sound, not a movement. Meagher's sense of the world was so altered that he saw them with no surprise: in this universe huge pale sinister birds might very well pass within handsreach.

Boyle's gaze followed them, and then as he turned to go he glanced at Meagher again, noticed that he was still speaking, moved his mouth into a civil, well-bred rictus, and walked off.

Meagher walked along behind him: the distress of this look, so much more fundamental than the rough words at their setting-out, combined with the unreality of the scene, with the monstrous birds, the silence, the unbelievable final severing of their relationship and with his own state of physical wretchedness to shake him so that he hardly knew what he was at.

He walked on a mile, close at heel, the general pain separating into its various components. Rage predominated, and the extreme of humiliation—ultimate humiliation: the rage made him tremble; it knotted his throat and his stomach. The expression on his very pale face was strange to him, like a mask imposed from outside. Yet he still thought he was indulging in fantasy when he said 'But it is you are the fool, Boyle, to go out no one knows where with a man you humiliate: it is you are the fool to put a gun in his hands and turn your back on him and walk where he can push you down into the slime for ever, you whore.' And even when he had the brown gun up and quivering behind Boyle's head it still seemed only unreal show and mime, part of the abiding nightmare all round; but his finger curled on the trigger and squeezed as he cried 'Like that!' and the gun shot out an orange flame.

The unexpected bang and the recoil quite stunned him: it was not until the slow smoke cleared that he saw Boyle in the water, motionless now. Meagher slid down the wall and stood up to his knees, straddling the body and bowed as though to heave it out. Blood flowed from the shattered head, pouring and turning like smoke in the water, and through the eddies rose an enormous eel.

Silence returned: only the raucous panting of his animal breath. Then from far away on the motionless air over the bog came a sound. He looked up—the sky had turned pale—but there was nothing above him. The sound grew stronger, a rhythmic singing beat, and turning his appalled staring face still higher he saw three swans. The first light of the sun touched them from below and they flashed pure against the blue, flying straight and fast from the north with their long necks stretched out before them.

The rhythm changed a little, sighing and poignant: changed still more, and as they passed high overhead their wings sang in unison, bearing his spirit away and far, far away.

TRIO

Jennifer Johnston

There is an interesting topicality about this story of two men lying in wait to murder an unsuspecting Irish businessman, although it was written more than twenty years ago, in 1977. The parallel between the assassination and the fate that awaited Veronica Guerin, the award-winning Dublin Sunday Independent *reporter who was murdered by unknown assailants in her car in June 1996 while engaged in exposing the city's drug barons, will be immediately apparent. But what Jennifer Johnston has done in 'Trio' is to give the reader an insight into the emotions of the very different characters involved, demonstrating how difficult it is to comprehend such dreadful events.*

Jennifer Johnston (1930–   ) was born in Dublin, the daughter of the distinguished Irish barrister, Denis Johnston, who made the transition from the law to become one of the nation's major dramatists for the stage and television. Her mother was the Abbey Theatre actress Shelagh Richards, and both parents instilled in her a love of literature and drama. Among her most popular novels, several of which have been filmed, are The Captains and the Kings *(1972),* How Many Miles to Babylon? *(1974),* Shadows on Our Skin *(1977) and* The Railway Station Man *(1984). Her work has earned wide critical acclaim and in 1972 she won the Robert Pitman award. Today, Jennifer Johnston lives far away from the strife-torn city setting of her story in peaceful Donegal.*

*   *   *

In spite of the brilliant, sliding sun the evening was cold. Frank pushed his hands deep down into his pockets and stamped his feet uselessly.

'What a wind.'

Dust and an empty cigarette-box skeltered past their feet, down the hill past the waiting gateways and the neat hedges.

'West. It's from the west. That means rain. More rain. God, I'll be glad when this winter's over.'

Murphy pulled on his cigarette and let the smoke trickle slowly out through his nose. He was wearing a knitted hat pulled well down over his ears.

Frank shuffled his feet on the pavement again.

'I get chilblains,' he complained. 'Every bloody winter. There's nothing you can do about it. There was one year I didn't, that was the time I was working in London. It's the damp. So they say. Drive you crazy sometimes, so they would. Just that one year I didn't get them.'

Murphy sighed. Talkers. He was always lumbered with a talker. Voices always nagging away, nudging their way into his head, never letting him be at peace with his own thoughts. Silence was good. Golden, his mother used to say. He turned and squinted his eyes towards the setting sun. Golden, but you couldn't see with it dazzling in your eyes, even when you turned your head away again you couldn't focus for a moment or two. He walked back up the street towards the main road. With a bit of luck the sun would be behind the hill in about ten minutes.

'Did you ever suffer with chilblains?' asked Frank behind him.

'No.'

'You wouldn't know then what it's like at all.'

'No.'

They stood at the corner for a few moments, watching the cars go by. Behind them, below where they had been standing, a man sat, reading a book, in a parked car. Murphy dropped the butt of his cigarette on the pavement and then put his foot on it.

'What's the time?'

Murphy looked at his watch.

'Ten to.'

'He's late.'

They stared across the valley at the distant hills, the glitter.

'It'd be a great evening if it wasn't so cold. Maybe he'll not come.'

They turned and strolled back down the road again.

'He'll come all right.'

Patrick opened the door of his car and threw his briefcase over onto the back seat. Late. He got into the car and slammed the door. Meticulously he placed his thin white hands on the steering-wheel and stared at them. What does it matter anyway? Late or early. Nobody else worries. No one gets agitated. We all have our own obsessions. I like to treat time with care. He started the engine and sat listening to the comfortable sound of it. Like a cat by the fire. What precisely do I consider myself to be late for? The small preoccupations of domestic life. The kiss on the cheek. The careful arrangement of glasses on a tray. Clink, clink across the hall, taking care not to slip on the Persian carpet. Last shafts of sun and then pull the curtains, keep our privacy to ourselves. No dreams. No time for dreams. The stir and tumult of defeated dreams ... who could have said that? From those years when I read books and nervously brooded on the meanings of things. I must tidy things up and have a break. I'm tired. He laughed and moved the car slowly forward across the yard. A break indeed. What happens I wonder when you, for a moment, realise the emptiness of the future, oh and God the past. The dreamlessness even of the past. Forget it. Impeccable safety.

'Good evening, sir.'

George, the security man, opened the gate into the street.

Patrick smiled and nodded.

'You're late tonight, sir. It's ten to.'

'Telephones should never have been invented.'

'Goodnight.'

'Goodnight, George. See you in the morning.'

'Of course he'll come.'

'But if he doesn't? What do we do?'

'We come back tomorrow.'

Murphy's voice was exasperated.

The wind was banging at their backs, pushing them firmly down the hill.

'I suppose we would.' Frank sighed. 'My sister's just been took into the hospital. Just, there a few minutes before I came out. Her first. Ay. I know she'll be expecting me up to see her tomorrow.'

The way of the world, thought Murphy, one goes, another comes. Apart from his own somewhat amazed arrival into the world, he had no close, touching experiences of either birth or death. It didn't do to look at the whole thing in a broad, emotional way. Achievement was what mattered.

'That is, if he comes . . .'

Murphy's cap had worked its way up on to the top of his head. He pulled it firmly, warmly down over his ears again.

The gate closed behind him. The traffic was edging slowly along between the high warehouses. Time, as usual, being wasted, mal-treated. Then suppose, just suppose that I treated time as if it belonged to me. I am no longer time's servant. What then? It becomes at once a precious commodity. The only one worth having. Will I turn on the radio and listen to the news? Drown the sound of my own thoughts? I hate this street, the unpainted windows and the dirty walls. Hate is a word I haven't used since I was a child, and now, having used it, I feel myself filling with it, feel it burning inside me. It feels good. I must be having a little madness of some sort. I don't want to hold things together any longer. Not even at home. In the words of the immortal Greta Garbo, I want to be alone. Free. Me and my servant Time. Unobtainable, before it is too late. Christ. To have to watch yet again the great triumphal renewal of the earth as we ourselves decay. Break. I must break. My life in shreds.

'It's her first.'

'So you said.'

'Mam went with her in the ambulance. Just to give her a bit

of . . . well you know . . . moral support like. Sean's in England. That's her husband. She thought she'd like to have it here. At home. I suppose you're nervous with the first one. Mam went with her. I'd say she'd be all right, wouldn't you?'

'You're to cover me. That's all you're to do.'

'I'll try and get to see her tomorrow. That is . . .'

'Did you hear me?'

A small girl with a dog on a lead walked past them down the hill. She walked past the gate and the parked car and then crossed the road and went into a garden on the other side. Inside the gate she stooped and let her dog free. Huge clouds were beginning to pile up in the sky. The sun was almost gone. The hedge beside them smelt sweet.

'Whose child is that?'

'How the hell would I know whose child it is.'

They turned and walked slowly up towards the corner again. The man in the car put down his book and switched on the engine. Down the road a door banged. Frank groped in his pocket.

'Would you like a fag?'

'No. Did you hear what I said? You are to cover me. Nothing more. Just keep your eyes skinned.'

'I wonder will it be a boy or a girl.'

Only a golden line of sun. Rain was blowing from the west. It was going to be a stormy night.

So many wrong decisions I have made all the way down the line. I never searched for courage, never realised the possible need for it. Can I summon that neglected asset now, before it is too late? If . . . It's just nerves Mary would say. The situation is getting you down. You should take a break . . . pull yourself together. That's what I'll do. I'll go home and have a large drink and pull myself together. Face whatever it is she has arranged for me to face. It is unkind and totally unrealistic to throw the blame on her. Face my own music. Or else I could do the other thing.

He slowed down the car and pulled in to the side of the road.

I could. There is nothing to stop me. I could fill the car with petrol, I could . . . Commitments, aged commitments. Lack of courage. Worse, of hope. They would bring me back. I would blow it. He moved back into the mainstream of traffic.

'I wouldn't mind what it was really. She'd like a wee boy. You want it to be all right. That's what really matters. You know, all right. One of my aunties had one that was . . . well . . . not quite right. That'd be always in your mind. He's grown up now. He's not too bad, just a bit soft, you know . . . but nice enough.'

Paining my head, all this talk. But maybe he's right, time is getting on. Maybe he's not coming.

Several large drops of rain, blown by the wind, scattered themselves on the ground.

Frank ducked his head into the collar of his coat.

'What did I tell you? Rain.'

Behind the clouds the sky was stained pink now.

'Red sky at night . . .'

'Oh, for Jesus' sake . . .'

'What's up, Murphy?'

They stood for a moment and then turned their backs on the west.

'Nerves?'

Slowly they moved down the street once more. Murphy felt in his pocket for a cigarette.

'Nerves got you?'

He put the cigarette into his mouth.

'I'd say you're right. He's not coming,' he said at last. His hand fumbled for the matches.

'It's late now. Too late.'

The car down the street revved its engine. Murphy dropped the cigarette on the ground.

'Just cover me,' he said. 'Don't do another bloody thing.'

Patrick slowed down and turned into the street. There was a car moving towards him and then past him as he swung the wheel to turn in the gate.

The spring will come and then the summer. I have no energy,

no will. I will put on my smile. I will resume my role. I will wait.

He became aware of the two men walking down the path towards him. Quite casually they seemed to come, the guns raised in their hands.

How strange, how very, very strange . . .

There was no more time.

The echoing frightened some birds, who flew uneasily into the air. Far away a dog barked. The car accelerated and was gone. It was almost dark.

WESLEY

Carlo Gebler

*'All histories are really murder stories,' Carlo Gebler (1954–)
writes at the start of* How to Murder a Man *(1998), one of the
most highly acclaimed murder-mystery novels to come out of
Ireland in recent years. This story of the secret society, the
Ribbonmen, who pursued merciless violence in County Monaghan in 1854 in the name of strongly held beliefs, is based on
historical fact like William Carleton's short story 'Wildgoose
Lodge' about the same group of men. It was enthusiastically
reviewed in a number of newspapers,* The Daily Telegraph, *for
example, finding it 'powerfully memorable' but a work that should
perhaps carry a publisher's warning: 'This book contains explicit
scenes of mutilation, torture and killing: read only if accompanied by a stiff drink.' Indeed, Carlo Gebler has a talent for
choosing little-known incidents of Irish history and 'letting loose
vast terrors with dazzling adroitness', as* The Sunday Times
put it.

*Gebler was born in Dublin and, after graduating at York Uni-
versity and the National Film and Television School, became a
playwright, broadcaster and novelist. He has directed a number
of documentaries for British television which have shown his
penchant for controversial subjects. He now lives in Enniskillen
in County Fermanagh where he continues to write, demonstrating
his versatile talent with books on travel ranging from Greenland
to Morocco, with children's fiction and with short stories which
often feature what has been called 'the underbelly of Irish life'.
'Wesley', a brilliant* conte cruel *about a very uncomfortable
taxi-ride through the 'killing streets' of Belfast, was originally*

published in Fortnight *in 1993 as 'The Driver's Story' and contains enough menace to make your spine prickle.*

*   *   *

The taxi driver whizzes through Belfast. It is early morning. Talk is of cars and babies and the new car I bought—this was years ago—and how I was never able to get the milk smell of the baby's sick off the back seat.

'I know where you're coming from,' the driver says.

He has a pleasant face and wears a chunky identity bracelet.

'A couple of years back now . . .' he continues.

I feel a confidence looming.

'Pre-ceasefire?' I ask.

'Yep,' he says. 'Pick up two suits on the street—we're not meant to pick up on the street but they look okay; one goes in the back, other in the front; he says, "Town centre".

'Off we go. Then the one in the back, he says, "Driver, look between the front seats!" I think, new car—she was new then—and the eejit's been sick. Then I look down and I can't believe it.'

'What?'

'It's a gun. "Republican Army," he says, then the one in the front, he flaps the sun-visor down and takes my licence from behind. I keep it there; you know, handy for checkpoints.

'He opens it and he says, "Hello Wesley." And I think, oh God! why am I called Wesley? Couldn't I be John or Tom? But it's Wesley and that's like having Prod tattooed right across my forehead.'

' "This is your home address, Wesley?" he asks.

'But I can't speak, the words won't come out.

' "Just nod," he says.

'Thank God, I think, at least he's a pro, and he isn't shitting himself because it's his first time out. So I'm not going to get killed by accident anyway.

'I nod and they tell me where to go. It's in west Belfast. I drive there very slowly, and all the time I keep praying, please, no checkpoint, I'll be killed in the crossfire. And God hears me. No checkpoints. Then at last we arrive, I hand over the keys, we go into a house.

'There are two others there and oh, my heart sinks when I see this! They're in balaclavas. Armed too. ''This is Wesley,'' says one of the suits. Oh Wesley, that name.

' ''Go and stand over there,'' says the other suit. ''Look at the wallpaper. These two will look after you.''

' ''Of course, anything you say.'' I'm over to that wallpaper quicker than Roger Bannister ran the mile.

'The suits leave and the old cogs start turning. The guards are going to shoot me. That's the plan. It'll be on the news, Wesley X, well known Loyalist, executed by ASU, blah, blah. I start to sweat. I want to pee. I think I'm going mad. I'm a cert for Purdysburn—I know it.

'Then I say, whoa, Wesley! Hold on. You've got to stop this.

'So I look at that wallpaper. It's beige with red pictures— woman on a swing, sedan chair, a guy on a horse—and I look at that wallpaper like it's a woman, or I put it up myself.

'Then I hear the door opening. The suits are back.

' ''All right Wesley. Car's outside, key in the ignition. You just count a hundred and go. But don't go to the cops, Wesley. We know where you live, and you don't want a home visit, do you, Wesley?''

'They leave. The door closes. I count. I get to a hundred. Then I think, my hundred might only be their ten. I do two hundred. I do five hundred. I do a thousand.

'Then I say goodbye to that wallpaper and I get out of the house. And you know what? No fucking car.

'Then the fear kicks back. It's dark by now, it's west Belfast and I'm a Wesley.

'I run and run and just as I hit the top of the Grosvenor Road, I see the Police Land-Rovers. I start to wave but they don't see me. But some guys on the street, they see me waving to the cops all right. Oh no, I think, that's it, I'm in for a kicking.

'So I have no choice. I just run right out in front of the first

Land-Rover and it screeches to a stop just two feet in front of me.

'The policeman gets out and I explain what's happened and that's it. He takes me to the police station. I hadn't smoked for ten years but I had eight fags then, in a row.'

'What about your car?' I wondered.

'It was up in Poleglass.'

'How did it get there?'

'It's a mystery. Someone stole it while I was counting, or the Provos never left it outside. I don't know.'

'Had it been used?' I asked.

'Yes, they had someone in the boot, drove him quite a few miles. That's what the cops told me.'

Wesley looked around his car interior, then jiggled the pine freshener dangling from the mirror.

'She's a good runner', he said, 'good mileage, but I never open that boot, you know, but I get this really strong smell. I've sprayed it, I've washed it, I've even hung up one of these pine tree thingies—but nothing shifts it.

'You talked about a milk smell from your baby earlier; well, in that boot, my friend, I've got the smell of human fear.'

SHE

Neil Jordan

Now something of a wunderkind *in the Hollywood film business as a result of the success of* The Crying Game *(1992),* Interview with the Vampire *(1994) and the controversial* Michael Collins *(1996), Neil Jordan (1950–) is also a very accomplished novelist and short-story writer. His novels* The Past *(1980),* The Dream of a Beast *(1983) and* Sunrise with Sea Monster *(1995) have marked him out as one of Ireland's best modern novelists, while his short stories display a command of language and character-building that is in the very best Irish tradition. Jordan's fascination with his native land, its bloody history and intriguing mysteries is often evident in these stories, even though the majority have contemporary settings.*

Jordan was born in Sligo and studied at University College, Dublin. He worked briefly as a labourer, then as a teacher, before his love of literature and the theatre inspired him to write and direct a number of his own plays. He also helped to found the Irish Writers' Co-operative to publish the work of unknown authors, including his own early short stories. The critical acclaim for the low-budget Oscar-winning movie The Crying Game, *starring Stephen Rea, helped him to realise his ambition to get into films, and it has also enabled him to tackle other Irish themes, notably* Michael Collins *and the adaptation of Patrick McCabe's novel* The Butcher Boy. *Both have, of course, attracted their fair share of notoriety, especially* Michael Collins *which starred Liam Neeson and was condemned in some quarters as a propagandist vehicle for the Provisional IRA. Jordan defended the film fiercely against this charge in a number of newspaper articles and interviews. In* Sunrise with Sea Monster *he returned again to the theme of Republicanism with a story of a young Irishman who returns from the Spanish Civil War only to become involved with an IRA cell and is drawn into a dangerous case of espionage. 'She', written in 1980, is quite different and reflects Jordan's interest in movie-making, in particular the filming of a murder scene.*

*   *   *

The director is walking around in circles talking about the last scene. He takes the last scene first for a reason I don't understand. He's trying to explain to them the key to the whole thing, which is at the point where the girl walks to the cross-roads to meet the young priest, all ready to tell him she won't go with him after all, but the priest doesn't turn up so the girl says her message to a man she doesn't know, a man that's just passing by. She repeats it over and over but the man just stares at her. Then the man walks off and the girl is left just standing there saying nothing and at this point, the director says the light should fade just a little and the film is to be about the light fading more than about anything else. My father nods his head and agrees and says the film is about the light fading and the knife the priest used in the third scene, not about the girl or the schoolteacher or the priest. He says the director should film it backwards is just as break-up-able as space, that that's such a cliché now it shouldn't need to be repeated. His hair has gone grey now, not all grey, just grey at the sides. I think he likes it grey, I think if it wasn't grey he would dye it grey anyway. I think he has wanted to have grey hair ever since I knew him and now that he has it he is more pleased than he has ever been, which is not much. He wanted to be grey like that, to talk like that, to be thin and distinguished like that so when he talked everybody would listen. He wanted to be like that since he was born because he knew then people would look at him, and listen to him without turning round and talking to someone else.

I walk away from the set and lie down beside the caravan that is used as a canteen. The grass is flattened here by the tyres of the camera trucks, it is flattened like a bed, I stretch out my legs on this straw bed and roll my Levis up over my knees. My knees are like big dimples, my legs are slim and brown with the sun of the last few days with spines of tiny hairs all along the shinbones. I think of those hairs, I think of my father's hairs, I think how pleasant the sun is.

They tell me I have a peculiar quality of lightness, he says he wants to capture it, the lightness in the way I walk, the way I say lines without moving my face or my body. I think of this and I feel light, as if the grass is not really bent underneath me but each blade is just tensed lightly, holding me who am so light. And we have waited three days now for the sun to fade to just that quality of light that he says the scene demands, since he can't afford false light and the film is about the light fading more than anything else. So we rehearse it during the day for the evening take, we go through it falsely, waiting for the perfect falsity of when the light fades. I am a girl who sits in the glass cabin of a petrol-filling station somewhere in the country on an empty road between two towns. I was picked up by a traveller who later deserted me and in the scene, the last-but-one, I sit in the cabin again waiting for a man to pass, my hand round the butt of a heavy German Mauser pistol, in an open drawer and when the arbitrary man passes I raise it and shoot through the glass panel of the cabin and the glass windscreen at his astonished face, shattering all three. Then I drop the gun and stare with a deadened blankness at the road I have always stared at, the cars coming down it from one town, going to the other, their dimmed lights coming on now. And I stare at the lights as if they were messages I am beyond reading.

I get up from the grass, I take out a *Gauloise* from my pocket, the packet is crushed, the sun is covered by one of those white cumulus clouds so the heat is gone. I light the cigarette as I walk back over to them, the man who could be my father with the grey sidelocks, the youngish Londoner who's directing, short and perceptive with cropped hair, boyish clothes. He has that London quality I've always admired, a kind of tired, wry decadence, affluent and beyond affluence. He sees the world through opaque lenses, is universally and meaninglessly polite, gives an impression of being constantly engrossed in some personal tragedy that probably doesn't exist. I suspect he's homosexual but so far he's shown no antipathy to me. And so I tell myself I like him, I tell myself I like them both, my sympathy amazes me.

2

BODY OF EVIDENCE

Cases of Mystery

THE MAN IN THE MIDDLE

Nigel Fitzgerald

Nigel Fitzgerald (1906–85) was in my view a rather underrated mystery novelist and certainly among the best Irish writers in the genre. His cases of the resourceful Inspector (later Superintendent) Duffy, including The Rosy Pastor *(1954),* Suffer a Witch *(1958),* Black Welcome *(1961) and* The Day of the Adder *(1963) are models of their kind. Fitzgerald used his home country to provide highly effective backgrounds for many of his intricate mysteries. 'Deft characterisation, some ingenious murder methods, and an accomplished atmospheric touch are key features in his work', according to one of his great admirers, the detective novelist H. R. F. Keating, who described Fitzgerald as being very much in the classic tradition of crime writing.*

Born in County Cork, Nigel Fitzgerald was intended for a career in the law, but according to his version of events, 'After getting my luggage mixed up with a celebrated actor manager's while on my way to study, I became sidetracked to the stage.' His career as an actor was itself interrupted by the Second World War when he served with the British Army in Africa, Sicily and Italy, and then again when the idea for his first novel, Midsummer Malice *(1953), actually came to him while appearing in a thriller. Apart from the successful Duffy novels, Fitzgerald created a second series character in Alan Russell who tackled mysteries such as* Ghost in the Making *(1960) and* The Candles Are All Out *(1961). Sadly, he wrote very few short stories, but 'The Man in the Middle', which appeared in* Suspense *magazine in March 1960, is a fine example of his ability to combine an Irish setting with a mystery tale of mounting terror.*

*   *   *

Fintan stopped his car at the top of the hill and looked down at the village; he might have been seeing it for the first time.

When had he been last in Clarinbridge? Two years ago? Three? It scarcely mattered, for then he had come as a friend; now he came as an enemy.

He had given Cressida his promise in Dublin ten days ago, and the glamour had faded from the project with every minute that separated him from his last glimpse of her face.

Down below the houses clustered about the bridge under the dominance of the church; the river ran straight past the quay and then curved round the walls of the old castle, while water and window-glass shimmered in the light of the spring sun. All this, he supposed, was unchanged, but now Clarinbridge seemed to him no longer a straggle of houses along a funnel-shaped Main Street, but a fortress to be attacked. He glanced uneasily at his watch.

Twelve-fifteen. He was perhaps a little early; the midday drinkers at Martin Fogarty's pub would not yet be in session. The man who had been Cressida's husband would still be limping around about his business, holding his small son by the hand, saluting his friends with a wave of his stick and calling, 'See you in the Gluepot.' Here the pattern of Saturdays did not change. Fintan slipped the car into gear and began to coast slowly down the hill.

As he came into the village everything was unbelievably the same: the red lorry on-loading flour-sacks at the mill, the cars, station-wagons and vans parked haphazardly along the Main Street, the sober clothes of the country people—all were as he remembered them. And most familiar of all was the sight of the tall soldierly figure limping into the bank, in one hand a stout stick and, holding on to the other, an erect little boy in grey flannel shorts. The child, Fintan thought, was like a tiny image of Rollo already. Gripping the wheel more tightly, Fintan drove on towards the bridge.

He had no need to drive along the quay; he could see all that he wanted to see from the bridge. The boat was there. Cressida had not failed to keep her part of the bargain, as he had begun to hope that she might. He turned and went slowly back towards the Main Street, passing Tobin's Garage without remembering to get petrol. The pumps at Carty's were busy, so he drove up the street where the cars were parked more thinly, near the bottle-neck at the top.

He needed a drink for what he had to do, and automatically his feet carried him to Fogarty's Gluepot. It would be thought strange if he were seen going into any other pub, and he did not want to set a pattern of strangeness so soon. He did not want to meet Rollo either, but Rollo's business would probably detain him at the bank for a few minutes yet, and it was a long pull up the street for a man with an unserviceable leg. Fintan pushed through the doors into the untidy bar, where a group of farmers made way for him to reach the counter.

'Why, if it isn't Mr Fintan!' exclaimed Fogarty, holding out a hand, retracting it, wiping it on a towel and extending it again to be shaken. 'Welcome, Mr Fintan. What a grand surprise for Mr Rollo when he comes in! Is it a glass of the usual you'll be having?' He was already pouring the drink.

'Is it down for the fishing you are, sir?' asked one of the farmers. 'Lough Lahan's been great this year.'

'No—unfortunately. Just passing through. But I couldn't pass without dropping in at Fogarty's.'

'Ah! Mr Rollo will be sorry to hear that—but you must stop and have a drink with him anyway.' Fogarty placed the glass of whisky on the bar and put a jug of water beside it. 'He'll be in by one o'clock.'

Fogarty filled up his own glass and hid it behind a row of bottles. 'In case the wife comes in,' he explained. 'Young Billy will be five years old tomorrow,' he went on, 'and Mr Rollo's got a little Connemara pony for his birthday. She's above in Murphy's stable now, waiting for the morning.'

'I wonder will the mother send him anything? 'Tis that one has the money now,' said someone on the outskirts of the group; the remark was evidently thought to be in poor taste, for many voices tried to drown it.

It was a big man beside Fintan who suddenly observed, 'I seen a fine motor yacht alongside the quay, in front of the doctor's house, an' I coming into town.'

'I hear tell 'tis a wealthy Brazilian millionaire owns her. They're all foreigners in the crew whatever.'

'She looks to have speed by the cut of her—and there'll be fast goings-on below decks too, I wouldn't be surprised. Them fellas take a bevy of fillum stars around with them wherever they go.'

'Whoever piloted her in must have known the estuary,' said the publican thoughtfully. 'Are you off, Mr Fintan? Will you not wait to see himself—and the little fellow?'

'I'll be back. Must get some petrol. My tank's practically dry.'

In the street he ran into a trio of Rollo's friends, obviously heading for the Gluepot; he could not remember their names, nor, apparently, they his. He got away from them on the promise of returning when he had filled up with petrol.

'What's your hurry? The stuff won't run away,' one of them protested.

Fintan merely smiled and went on towards his car; he had no intention of lingering after he had done what he had come to do, and he had been running on his reserve tank for the last few miles into Clarinbridge. But he changed his mind when he saw the parish priest coming down the street, and realised that if each of them kept to his present course they would meet abreast of the car; he turned down a lane that led circuitously to the quay. Here, he was walking between the back walls of gardens, cut off at once from the limited modernity of the Main Street; traffic noises gave way to the murmur of bees, and the air was heavy with the scent of wallflowers.

'Hurray, Fintan, hurray! Hello!' He heard the patter of feet and saw a small grey-clad figure come running towards him and leap to a halt at his feet. Rollo's son was beaming up at him with a smile of anticipated pleasure.

'Good lord, Billy! What are you doing down here by yourself?'

'Mrs Ryan always gives me a peach on Saturday.' The little boy waved towards one of the garden-doors; a half-eaten peach was in his hand. He did not inquire why Fintan should be in Clarinbridge but accepted his presence joyfully.

'Won't Daddy be looking for you?'

'Pop's going to the Gluepot when he's finished in the bank, and he'll bring me a Coke out to the car.'

Fintan licked his lips which had suddenly gone dry; the opportunity was too good to miss. 'I'm going down to the quay to have a look at the big boat that's come in. Would you—' He cleared his throat and started again—'Would you like to come with me? She's a lovely ship—all the way from Italy.'

'A pirate ship?'

'Well—yes, in a way.'

They were already walking down the lane towards the quay; at least Fintan was walking, and Billy was bounding along, sometimes beside him, holding his hand, sometimes ahead, making a noise like a machine-gun. In the whole length of the lane they encountered no living thing other than a cat.

On the quay passers-by were few; the strange boat had lost its initial interest for the villagers, and anyone who still gaped at it did so from the polite distance of the bridge. The occasion was tailor-made for Fintan's purpose.

The little boy sped down the road, to come to a halt, straddle-legged, hands clasped behind his back, gazing in complete absorption at the boat, an ocean-going motor cruiser with shining brass and gleaming paint-work. Suddenly he threw back his head and laughed derisively.

'That's not a pirate ship,' he said. 'There's no skull and crossbones.'

'Would you like to go aboard?' Fintan was impatient.

'May I?'

'Of course.'

There was no sign of life aboard and the child reached for

Fintan's hand, leading the way up the gang-plank as one who starts upon high adventure. From the shadow of a tree, where they had been lounging unseen, two bronzed men in white jerseys and slacks strolled casually after them.

'This boat would have to give way to Pop's,' Billy pronounced authoritatively. 'Engines must give way to sail.'

A face appeared in the hatchway, a face with too red lips and anxious eyes, Cressida's face; she had been drinking again. All Fintan's pity for her came flooding back. For all her wealth, for all her power over men, she was at a crisis of her life, dependent upon the approval of a little boy who would be five years old tomorrow. He had not yet seen her. She gazed at him with a wild longing in her eyes.

'Billy. Billy, my darling.' Her voice shook with emotion.

The child swung round. He shouted—' 'Mummy! Mummy!' and jumped up and down; but he did not run to throw himself into her arms. He showed no more excitement than he had shown at meeting Fintan, and part of what he felt now must be eagerness to investigate the boat. Cressida's outstretched arms dropped.

'Would you like to see the cabins, Billy?' she asked, her voice almost casual.

'The cabins! Oh, yes! Yippee!' He reached the companionway in a series of hops and disappeared from Fintan's sight.

Well, it was over. Fintan had done what he had promised. He felt confused, sick with distrust of his own judgement.

He had known Cressida and Rollo since his childhood: they were his oldest friends, and when Cressida left Rollo it had shaken his world. Since then he had met Rollo and Billy from time to time in Dublin, but he had seen more of Cressida—had been disturbed by the deterioration in so short a time, the fevered dissolution of her once lovely face.

'A short while is all I ask,' she had told Fintan. 'Just a visit— a week or two weeks. I'll bring him back. And it might even be the means of Rollo and me—' Her voice had trailed off and recklessly, impulsively, Fintan had agreed. Cressida was pampered, spoiled, but after all her life was empty. Full of misgivings now, he turned away to go ashore.

It was as he set foot on the gang-plank that he found himself looking into the window of the doctor's surgery, separated from him only by the width of the quay and the narrow road. The doctor was staring out, an expression of astonishment on his face, a hypodermic syringe poised in his hand. As Fintan watched, the doctor put down the syringe and lifted a telephone receiver. He began to speak urgently, his head turned towards the boat.

Fintan glanced at his watch. It was only twelve-fifty, exactly ten minutes since he had left the Gluepot; five minutes to reach his car, another five to fill up with petrol, and he could shake the dust of Clarinbridge from his feet and from his tyres. Behind him he could hear the seamen taking in the gang-plank, but he did not look back; for better or for worse the episode was finished.

Thrusting it from his mind, he turned into the lane by which he had come. It made a detour to the Main Street, so there was little likelihood of meeting in it anyone that he knew. Its loneliness now, however, was not reassuring; absurdly, he felt that he was being spied on from behind ivy-covered walls and that the garden were murmurous not with bees, but with low-voiced comments on what he had done.

He met no one on the way; a cat interrupted her ablutions to gaze at him sombrely as he passed. That was all.

Where the lane joined the Main Street he hesitated, but there was nobody in sight that he knew, so after a moment he went on to his car. Strangely, parking space was now available opposite Fogarty's, which suggested that the pub-crawlers had hurried away to look for Billy, or to shake threatening fists from the quay. Fintan had thought at the time that the doctor was probably ringing up the pub.

He got into his car and drove slowly down the street. Carty's Garage was between the Gluepot and the quay, so he passed it and went on to Tobin's at the other side of the bridge. Passing the entrance to the quay, he glimpsed activity at the water-side, then the high wall of the bridge cut off his view of the river; a moment later he pulled up at the petrol pumps. An overalled youth was pouring oil into a station-wagon's engine, and the other visible attendant was changing a wheel on a Hillman saloon;

Peter Tobin came out of the office, his big face void of recognition.

'Yes?' he asked sourly.

'Fill her up, please.'

Tobin slapped the pump with a ham-like hand. 'Empty,' he said. 'Not a drop in her.'

'All right. I'll move on to the next pump.'

'She's dry too. They all are. We're waiting on the tanker this minute. Try Carty's in the Main Street.'

'I'll do that.' Fintan wondered if Tobin were suffering from the effects of a binge; it was notorious that alcohol made him surly. On the other hand the lack of fuel suggested that he might be in financial difficulties. The important thing for Fintan, however, was to get his tank filled; there was nothing for it but to go to Carty's and run the risk of meeting Rollo.

At the end of the bridge Fintan slowed down to walking pace. He heard an outboard motor pulse into life; a small boat was putting out into the stream with three men aboard her, one of whom might have been Rollo. Pursuit could be no more than a gesture—there was not a boat in the estuary that could catch Cressida's motor cruiser with its two thousand horse-power engine, but at least it served to distract attention that might otherwise have been turned to Fintan. He pulled in to the side of the road just short of Carty's, and waited for one of the pumps to be free.

Carty was standing before his door, a sturdy compact man with iron-grey hair and the face of a bronzed angel; a smile crinkled the corners of his mouth and eyes as he saw Fintan.

'Fine day. Nice to see you in these parts again,' he said. 'Are you stopping with Mr Rollo?'

Fintan was relieved to see the smile. He knew that Carty had been Rollo's second in command in the old IRA, and he knew that he would not have been so amicably received if the news had already reached the garage. 'Just passing through,' he explained. 'I may have time for a couple of drinks before I move on though.'

'I'd be up in the Gluepot myself now only that I'm waiting

on a man that says he's thinking of buying a Jaguar. I'll probably take him there to make the deal.'

From the dim interior of the garage a voice shouted—'Hey, boss! Telephone.'

'Excuse me a minute.' Carty disappeared into the gloom.

The car in front moved on, and Fintan took up his position beside the pump. 'Fill her up,' he told the boy in charge. 'She'll take eight.'

'Right you be, sir.' The boy vanished towards the back of the car.

Fintan relaxed; he took out a cigarette and lighted it, gazing composedly up the street to where a big green bus was pausing on its journey from Clarin Head to Tully, the county town. In two minutes he too would be on his way; he wondered what sort of a lunch he would be likely to get in Tully.

A tap on the glass of his near side window recalled him to the present. It was not the boy who had started to fulfil his order, but a larger and more formidable person in oil-stained overalls.

'What do I owe you?' Fintan asked.

'Nothing. You didn't get anything.'

'But a lad was giving me eight gallons. Are you sure—?' He switched on the ignition; the fuel indicator remained at empty. 'Damn! He must have forgotten about me. Give me eight gallons, please. I'm in a hurry.'

'There's no petrol.'

'What's that?'

'There's no petrol, only for customers. We want the space here. Move along, please.'

'But I must get some juice—if only a couple of gallons to get me to Tully. I want to see Mr Carty; he's a friend of mine.'

The man shrugged and turned away just as Carty came out of the garage. The bronzed face still looked like that of an angel, the archangel Michael perhaps, but Fintan felt that he was getting rather a Satan's-eye-view of it.

'There's nothing here for you, not now nor ever,' said the garage proprietor in a cold level voice. 'Get on about your business.'

Fumbling, as if he had never driven a car, Fintan turned out into the street and went slowly up the hill.

He had to have petrol; it was an emotional need now as well as a practical one. He had to drive out of this village before he met anyone else that he knew, before he read in any other eyes the contempt that he had seen in Carty's. The car was facing towards the poor part of the village that bordered the first hundred yards or more of the road to Clarin Head; somewhere there, amongst the clutter of small shops and pubs, must be a place where he could get petrol. He kept going slowly, glancing down each turning, and at last his patience was rewarded by the sight of a pump outside a dingy little shop.

No one appeared when he stopped the car, and he had no desire to attract unwelcome attention by using the horn. The locality indeed had a deserted look, but the door of the shop was open, and the cigarettes and 'fancy goods' in its window were reasonably free from dust. Fintan got out of the car and entered the shop.

Behind the counter an elderly bright-eyed little man in a brown suit and rimless pince-nez smiled a greeting, shaking hands with himself unctuously the while.

'Good afternoon, sir. What can I have the pleasure of doing for you?' he asked in a flute-like voice. The glass-topped counter before him displayed studs, cigarette-holders, brooches and knitting-needles; china dogs and Spanish shawls were arranged behind his head.

'I want some petrol, please.'

'Petrol? Now isn't that too bad. 'Tis the nephew that runs the pump, and he's away to his lunch at the present, and the key with him. I never learnt to use these modern-fangled contrivances. Are you going on to Clarin Head, sir, might one ask?'

Fintan wanted to be directed to some source of supply that he had not yet tried, so he said, 'Yes. I am.'

'It will save you turning back into the town if you can make a couple of miles along the road.'

'I can—just about, I think—if it's no more than that.'

'Oh, less if anything, sir. Can I interest you in any little memento of your visit to the town? What about a nice cigarette-case or—'

'No, thanks. Ah—some lighter fuel, perhaps.'

'Lighter fuel? Now, isn't that too bad, sir? I don't seem to have anything you want. Would a little pen and pencil set—?'

Fintan was gone. He was speeding down the road towards Clarin Head. It was ten to one that a roadside filling station in the middle of a bog would have no telephone, and there had been no traffic on the road to carry the news ahead of him. This time he was safe.

It was when he topped a rise, exactly two miles farther on, and saw the road stretching straight and bare before him that a small seed of doubt began rapidly to grow. He hailed a prim-looking woman who was wheeling a bicycle towards him.

'Where can I get petrol?' he asked.

'I believe there's a place in Clarin Head.'

'How far is that, for goodness sake?'

'About eleven Irish miles from here—fourteen English.'

'The bastard,' said Fintan viciously, as the perfidy of the old man in the shop became plain to him. 'The sneaking little old bastard. I ought to wring his neck.' He took no further notice of his informant, who climbed on to her bicycle and pedalled unsteadily away, occasionally throwing anxious glances over her shoulder.

The situation called for a new appreciation. Clarinbridge was two miles behind him, on his way home; he must return through it, unless he intended to spend the rest of his life on the desolate peninsula that ended in Clarin Head. In Clarinbridge there were Civic Guards and a hotel and telephones—telephones! That was it! They might deny him petrol, but they could not debar him from the use of a public telephone. He turned the car and headed back towards the village, hoping that his fuel would last until he got there.

It did—just. In the widest part of the Main Street, right in the centre, midway between the Gluepot and Carty's Garage, the engine spluttered, coughed once, and was still. The crowd of shoppers had thinned considerably; those who remained in the street regarded the occurrence sardonically. No rush of volunteers came to help Fintan to push the car in to the side of the road; he left it where it was stopped, and walked on to the Post Office.

The spinster sisters who ran the Post Office presided over the sale of stamps and postal orders in a ladylike manner; raised voices were unknown in their domain and unseemly haste was frowned on. For all his sense of urgency, Fintan knew better than to show that he was in a hurry; he looked up the number of a garage in Tully, then patiently awaited his turn to be served.

When he had asked for his number over the counter he could both see and hear the spinsters' niece putting the call through in the tiny exchange which was a part of the office itself. He heard her say 'Hold the line,' and he saw her nod towards one of the two telephone boxes; he went in and closed the door.

'Hello,' he said.

There was no reply. The line was dead. The operator said that she would try again; she got on to the Tully exchange, asked for the number, got an acknowledgement from Tully, and the line became dead. This was repeated three times with, as a variant, a little polite buck-passing between Tully and the local operator. It was only when Fintan by chance noticed the expressions of the waiting customers that he realised at last that he had as much chance of getting his connection as he had of finding petrol. Without a word he shouldered his way out of the dimness into the afternoon sunlight.

He could not get through from the Post Office but he might from an outside telephone, if he disguised his voice—and he could do with a drink. He crossed over to the side door of the hotel and went into the bar.

In spite of its lavishness and comfort, the bar of Moore's Hotel had never become popular with the residents. It was early in the season for tourists, so Fintan was not surprised to find the stools before the counter untenanted, although he could hear the murmur of voices from the alcoves that opened from the darker part of the room. The presence of unseen customers was confirmed by the sight of the bartender carrying a tray of empty glasses back to his automatic washer. The boy set down his burden and looked politely at Fintan.

'Yes, sir?' he asked.

'A large Vat 69 and soda, please.'

The boy turned to the well-stocked shelves and lifted down a fat green bottle; he inspected it lugubriously against the light. 'I'm afraid we're a little low in Vat 69 just now, sir.'

'All right then—any standard Scotch will do.'

'Well, we're a bit short on all Scotch at present.'

'Do you mean you haven't any at all?'

'Yes, sir.'

'Why on earth couldn't you say so? I'll take Irish then.'

The boy shook his head and looked uncomfortable.

'I'm not going to believe you've no Irish. That's too tall a story.' Fintan was conscious of a listening silence behind him but he did not care. 'Damn it, I can see a dozen bottles behind your head—yes, and I can see Scotch, too. Do you realise that you can get into serious trouble for this, my lad?'

The boy flushed; he swallowed a couple of times. 'They're all dummies, sir.'

Fintan gripped the counter. All his frustration had become concentrated into an overwhelming desire for a drink; he would have his whisky, if he had to tear Clarinbridge apart to get it. Into the tense silence broke a remembered voice.

'The poor gentleman is unfortunate. Nobody in the place has anything at all that he requires.' It was the voice of the 'fancy goods' merchant who had sent Fintan on his wild goose chase after a non-existent petrol-pump; it came from an alcove in the far corner of the room.

Fintan followed the sound until he came face to face with the speaker across a table on which stood two tumblers liberally charged with whisky. He was vaguely aware of the presence of a fat man whom he had not seen before, but he had eyes only for his misinformant.

'I suppose you think it's funny,' he said.

The little man had a pipe in his mouth and was preparing a fill of tobacco; he regarded Fintan dispassionately through his pince-nez. ' 'Tis no wonder the gentleman is upset. He must have had a disappointing day,' he observed.

Fintan leaned menacingly over the table. 'You seem to know how to get whisky in this place. If you don't persuade that half-witted creature behind the bar to bring me what I want within two minutes, I propose to push that pipe down your neck.'

The man seemed unimpressed; his hands stopped working on the plug of tobacco that they had been paring, and their stillness emphasised that they had been doing it with a pruning-knife. The blade looked sharp, but none too clean.

'Is that so?' the man inquired gently.

For a moment Fintan hesitated; he wanted to sweep the glasses from the table, to wipe the superciliousness off the little man's face, to break something, anything in this town which was boycotting him with such uncanny effectiveness, but he had heard from an adjoining alcove a voice that he knew. The sound had sobered him. Carty was there, selling a Jaguar over a drink; the memory of the coldly contemptuous eyes in Carty's angelic face was too much for Fintan. He strode out of the room without a word.

Where was he to go? There must be some corner of Clarinbridge that had not yet heard of the boycott, but how was he to find it? And what ultimate good would it do him, if he could not get petrol? His question was answered on his way out of the hotel; a local bus timetable was pinned to a notice-board.

The bus! What a fool not to have thought of it! The route from Clarin Head through Clarinbridge to Tully connected with trains to Dublin. With trembling fingers he found the place; the last bus for Tully on Saturdays left at two-twenty. His watch made it now two-eighteen. The stop was no more than a minute's walk from the hotel; nevertheless he began to run, panting in his eagerness.

He stopped running when he came to the corner. He must keep out of sight until the last moment. He leaned against the side wall of the hotel, strangely exhausted, waiting for the bus driver to start up his engine.

At last the welcome sound came. Fintan strolled round the

corner, saw the big green vehicle throbbing to the rhythm of its engine, saw the conductor raise his hand towards the bell, and sprinted to get aboard.

'Wait a minute now. Where's your hurry?'

Fintan's hand was already on the rail; without letting go, he turned to see who had spoken, for there was undeniable authority in the voice. An enormous red-faced Civic Guard was gazing at him suspiciously.

'Is that your car in the middle of the road?'

'Yes, it is.' Fintan's first sensation was of relief. Parking was preferable to kidnapping as a topic.

'What made you leave it in a place like that?'

'She's stuck fast there—won't move. She'll have to be towed away.'

'Is that a fact? Show me your papers.'

With both hands Fintan searched for his driving licence and insurance certificate. 'Here you are.'

The Guard unfolded the papers and examined them with meticulous care before handing them back. 'Get your car out of there as soon as you can.' He nodded and sedately took his departure.

With tears of rage starting to his eyes, Fintan looked after the bus; he was in time to see it turn the corner at the end of the Main Street and disappear in the direction of Tully.

He was at the end of his tether. As the word came to his mind he realised its appositeness; they thought they had him tethered, but he would show them their mistake, if he had to walk all of the twenty-five miles to Tully. He opened his cigarette-case and found that it was empty; automatically he started for a shop before he remembered that money could buy nothing in the village for him. He must get out of Clarinbridge to get so much as a drink of water.

With the recollection of the knife in the little fancy goods-merchant's hand came realisation of the urgency of the need to get away before dark. He must set out to walk; that was the only solution. He began to stroll in apparently aimless fashion up the road towards the church.

The church was on the outskirts of the village; from it a foot-path led to the main road to Tully. He found the path deserted and stepped out along it purposefully, reaching the junction with the main road unobserved. Rhododendrons were coming into flower on either side of the way, and there was a feeling of peace in the air that he was as yet far from sharing. But he was no longer desperate; roadside pubs lay ahead, where he could at least get something to eat and drink, and he might be able to hire a car, or to telephone.

He began to tire on the first hill. At the point where he had stopped his car on the way to Clarinbridge he sat on a bank to rest, and opened his cigarette-case; he had forgotten its emptiness. In a flash of rage he hurled it across the road, then picked it up and continued on his way, cursing silently but steadily. It was as he rounded the next corner that he saw the man with the scythe.

He was an enormous man with a craggy inscrutable face; he leaned on the scythe, staring straight in front of him as if deep in thought.

'Are you going far?' he asked. He had not moved; he still seemed to be looking over Fintan's head, out towards the sea. His voice was soft and dispassionate.

'Why?'

'The road might be dangerous.'

'There's such a thing as the Law in this country.'

' 'Tis a slow thing—the Law.'

'I can look after myself.'

'All right. Try it so.'

Still the man did not move, but continued to lean statuesquely on his scythe. There was no sign that he had been using it; nothing in the immediate vicinity required to be cut. The scythe then was to be accepted as a weapon, or as a threat—a supererogatory threat, for the man unarmed looked to be more than a match for Fintan. His impassivity made him doubly formidable; here was a man confident not merely of what he could but of what he would do. In the bright still afternoon the road beyond him seemed less inviting for walking.

Fintan turned on his heel and went slowly back towards the village; after he had taken a few paces, a sound behind him made him look round. Scythe on shoulder, the man was stolidly following him down the hill.

The ignominy of Fintan's return to Clarinbridge was a thousand times more galling than the furtiveness of his departure. It seemed that behind every eye lay the knowledge not only of what he had done, but of what he had not had the courage to do. He got into his car and hid behind the morning paper.

Time passed, marked by the chimes from the church steeple; four o'clock, then five o'clock came, and still Fintan sat on, ignored by and trying to ignore the villagers. The street seemed to him to grow wider and the buildings on either side to recede, leaving him remote and defenceless on a beleaguered island. At five-thirty a man on a chestnut mare rode up from the bridge, leading a little Connemara pony. Abreast of Fintan's car, somebody hailed the rider from a shop doorway.

'Are you going up to the great house?'

'I am so—taking the pony up for the little lad's birthday.'

'Then you haven't heard the bad news?'

'Of course I have. Haven't Mr Murphy taken his boat out like the rest?'

'Ah, sure, but what's the use of sails, or auxiliary engines, against the like of that motor yacht?'

'The doctor thought of that, more power to him; he got Clarin Head to contact the fishing fleet by wireless. The mouth of the bay isn't so wide but what they'll have been able to block it.'

'Why isn't there news by this, so?'

'They may be playing tag around the islands. If the child isn't brought back anyway, there'll be murder done in this town tonight.'

With this parting thought the rider pulled gently on the leading-rein, kneed the mare into motion and continued on his way up the street, Billy's birthday-present trotting alongside. Fintan followed their progress in the driving-mirror until they were out of sight.

By six o'clock no more than half a dozen cars remained in the whole length of the street, and the crowds had thinned almost to vanishing point. Fintan, however, derived no comfort from the apparent lessening of the number of his enemies; round the doorways of pubs and at street-corners had formed silent groups of young men, who propped their backs against walls and stared at Fintan—or so he imagined—as cats might stare at a goldfish in a bowl. The departure of the country people had only made his isolation more marked.

The church clock measured the half hour; in the silence that followed the single note the sound of regular footfalls became audible as two Civic Guards paced imperturbably up to the top of the street and down to the bridge, ignoring alike the watchers and the watched. Did rural Guards stay up all night, Fintan wondered. What would happen if they went to bed?

But that was nonsense. He must be gone long before then. But how? Slip away in the first darkness, that was it. He must crawl in the shadows, slink behind hedges, swim the river, anything— so long as he was clear of Clarinbridge before Rollo came back without his child. He was hungry and thirsty and his whole being ached for a cigarette, but he must wait for darkness to make his attempt to slip away with his jack-handle as a weapon, leaving the sinister young men to watch an empty car. This time he must succeed.

The sun had gone down when the clock struck seven. At the same moment the street lamps came on, making the encroaching night more apparent. Fintan had forgotten about the lamps; their light was focused mainly on the roadway, leaving the pavements in shadow. Fintan could now see the faces of the watchers only as an actor glimpses blurred faces from a flood-lit stage. His chance was gone.

A little after eight there came a scurry of movement in the dark opening of a lane; a stone crashed against the car like the first shot of a bombardment. It was the only shot. A voice spoke angrily, and another answered in more subdued tones. A waiting silence returned to the street.

No noise came even from the pubs. Every now and then a door opened and closed; sometimes an audible question was asked, to be met with the invariable reply—'Not yet.' Once a woman's voice demanded—'What in the name of God is keeping them?' Nothing else was to be heard but the footfalls of the Guards, regular as a metronome's beat, as they passed up and down the street. Fintan began to measure time by the sound of their passing, once up and once down to each quarter of an hour as proclaimed by the church clock.

Fintan was hungry. He was sick and cold and miserably afraid. The few cars that passed through the village left him with a bitter envy for those who could so easily and thoughtlessly get out of Clarinbridge. It was after the passing of a noisy truck that he felt rather than heard some difference in the quality of the silence.

It was a quarter past ten, and the light no longer showed from the Gluepot lounge; but something else was missing, something that had been audible. Panic clutched his heart as he realised what it was that he should have heard and did not hear. Almost he held his breath for minute after minute, straining to hear, telling himself that there was yet time. The clock struck half past ten. The Guards were no longer on their beat.

He listened now with a difference. He had the nightmare feeling that just beyond the angle of his vision stealthy attackers were closing in, but he could hear nothing—nothing but the noises in his own head. His blood was pounding rhythmically, but too fast, and too loud, drumming insistently and maddeningly in his ears. Then suddenly the motionless watchers began to move; they swept in a great wave across the street, silent no longer.

' 'Tis the boats,' they shouted. ' 'Tis the boats.'

Doors opened. Windows were thrown up; question and answer were shouted across the width of the street. Feet rushed past the car, down towards the bridge, round the corner on to the quay; then after a few moments of pandemonium the street was deserted. The shouting died away; all Clarinbridge waited in silence as the throbbing of the boats' engines came more clearly over the water. Gripping the handle of his jack, Fintan climbed furtively out of the car.

He listened; he heard neither footstep nor voice. He peered

into the shadows; they did not move. He began to run down into
the shadows; they did not move. He began to run down the road
as the others had done. He must get across the bridge; they would
not look for him there.

'Are you going down to welcome your friend?'

Carty was standing outside his garage, still as one of his own
petrol pumps and as solid-looking.

'Damn you to hell,' said Fintan.

He tried to lift the jack-handle, but the strength had gone out
of his arm. He could only stand and stare and will himself to
strike.

'It won't be long now,' Carty said softly.

The engines were very near; one of them spluttered and
stopped. Suddenly the unseen crowd lifted up its voice, one great
voice, which as suddenly was silent. Then nothing could be heard
but the sound of hurrying feet. Back around the corner they swept,
a limping man in the lead.

Again Fintan was in the toils of a nightmare. Immovable, he
watched the crowd approach, silent and purposeful, up the long
hill. Nearer they came, and nearer; then they swept past him as
if he had not been there. At their head, Rollo looked neither to
right nor left; he carried a sleeping child in his arms.

Before Fintan realised what had happened the crowd had
melted away, into pubs and houses and cars. Through the open
door of the Gluepot he had a momentary glimpse of happy faces.
Then, as Rollo's car drove away into the night, no one was left
in the street but Fintan and Carty.

Then Carty, too, was gone. The slam of his door seemed to
put a full stop to the night's activity. Sobbing with mingled relief
and frustration, Fintan crept back to his car.

A few minutes later Carty reappeared, carrying a can of petrol;
he set it down on the road in front of the car, then turned and
went home.

THE SWORD OF YUNG LO

Maurice Walsh

There is a tiny corner of Ireland, the little village of Cong in County Mayo between Loughs Mask and Corrib, which is forever associated with the classic short story 'The Quiet Man' by Maurice Walsh (1879–1964), because it was there in 1952 that the story was made into an equally famous film by John Ford, starring John Wayne. Shooting the picture there also represented a landmark in American film-making, for previously virtually all films with foreign backgrounds had been recreated on Hollywood backlots. Ford brought his entire cast and crew to Cong, and the memory of their stay lingers on in the shape of souvenir postcards, a heritage shop and coffee room named after the film, and a pub, 'The Quiet Man Hostel', once run by Joe Mellotte, the local man who was John Wayne's stand-in. The movie was a huge box-office success and also earned Maurice Walsh first prize from the Screenwriters' Guild in Hollywood, considerably enhancing his literary standing—although none of his subsequent works achieved quite the same legendary status.

Walsh was born the son of a farmer in Ballydonoghue, County Kerry. He was educated at Lisselton and St Michael's College in Listowel and then worked in Scotland with the Customs and Excise service which, he said. 'gave me a pretty good insight into villainy of all kinds.' His first novel, The Key Above the Door *(1926), was followed by several other titles in which murder and mystery featured, including* The Small Dark Man *(1929),* Son of the Swordmaker *(1938) and* Danger Under the Moon *(1954). Walsh's contribution to Celtic literature was recognised in 1938 when he was made President of Irish PEN. When 'The*

Sword of Yung Lo', with its story of two brothers and their fierce love for the same woman, was published in Fantastic *magazine in April 1953, the editor prefaced it with this remark: 'It seemed no human agency could resolve their problem . . . which left it up to a hunk of cold steel.' Maurice Walsh's ability to blend a mystery with raw human passions is seen at its best in the narrative that follows . . . complete with its truly chilling finale.*

*   *   *

Brothers they were, the two of them. And what is more, they were twin brothers; but not similar twins, or identical twins, or whatever the term is. That is an outward appearance; and whether they were sib or not below the surface we shall be seeing if the Lord spares me the use of my tongue.

Larry, the elder by a split minute, was a big, lean, swank lad, with a curly wave of black hair, a face of dark comeliness, and a pair of black eyes with the devil behind them when they set on a shapely woman—or a shapelier bottle of Irish whiskey; and he'd choose the bottle most times. He was good with his hands, and good at games, and the best company in the world, drunk or sober, whether in a saloon bar or a lady's boudoir; a devil to tell a story on the far edge of decency, and with a mellow baritone voice to charm a bird off a bough. And look! he had brains to burn; and could extract the meat out of a text book same as you'd extract a periwinkle out of its shell on the point of a pin.

Timothy—Timmy for short—the other twin, was small by comparison: under middle height, slim and neat in build, fair in the skin and fair in the hair, and grey eyes diffident when any woman at all turned her head to look at him. As a student he was a steady worker, but slow, and in his leisure hours—not so many— he was given to day-dreaming and versification, save the mark, probably seeing himself a mile high and a mile wide playing the lute to his own song under his lady's window—or inside it.

Their father was a fairly strong farmer away down on the Kerry border, and the only fortune for them was the sort of education that would fit them for the Civil Service. And Civil Service it was.

At the age of eighteen, or it might be twenty, the two of them sat the entrance examination to a certain Department, and as luck would have it they were successful the first time of asking. Big Larry, after a two months' intensive grind, took the first place in all Ireland; and Timmy, after years of plodding, took the nineteenth, which was not the last successful place, but the second last.

In Dublin, they took their humble places in a big office among a score or two of their subhuman species. They went into digs on a quiet street off the Circular Road, and in their own opinion they were on top of the world, the ball at their feet, the field open before them, and the goal of a Secretaryship in the not-too-far distance.

For a beginning, you could not see Larry for dust, with Timmy lost in it far behind. At the end of five or seven years Timmy had a desk of his own in the big office, and a fourth share of a lady typist; but by that time Larry had a room to himself, and a typist and a couple of clericals to jump to his beck and call.

Listen, now! Timmy had a fourth share of a typist, as I said, and, in process of time and propinquity, he wanted more, and then more, for she fitted his dreams to a nicety; and fine dreams he had: his own fire-corner and his slippers warming on the hob, a chess problem at hand, and his lady-of-the-house on the other side of the fire.

Her name was Emer, and she had her share of good looks, with green eyes alive under copper hair; and, besides, she was gay and gallant, with a bit of pleasant devilment at heart. And, mind you, she was liking Timmy, and warming a corner of her heart for him, and warming it a bit more, and a bit more, until—

Ay, until! Until big Larry set eyes on her, and approved of what he saw. By a bit of office manoeuvring Larry shifted his own typist, and got Emer promoted into her place. There he had her under his hand and eye, and loosed all his charm on her.

To make a long story short, Emer fell for Larry good and hard, but not hard enough to suit him. For she was a girl of character and integrity, and the only invitation she would accept, and there were many, was an invitation to the marriage rails. This astounded Larry of the easy conquests, and nettled him too, and put him on his mettle, and made Emer all the more desirable, and finally blinded him into taking the plunge into matrimony.

So Larry and Emer were married. And Timmy, his face calm but desolate, was best man. And Timmy, under instructions, acquired a house for the young couple and, what is more, he went to live with them. He did not want to live with them, desperately he did not want that; and Emer did not want it either, for she knew how Timmy felt, and was sorry for him—and a bit ashamed of herself. But Larry was his usual dominant self, and had his own way—as usual.

'Sure, Timmy boy,' said he, 'haven't we been together all our lives, sharing everything together, and why should we change now?' He slapped Timmy on the back. 'Begod sir! there is nothing I would not share with you—nothing at all, and that's flat.'

Emer had three children—two sons and a daughter—in ten years. And in the same ten years her husband, big Larry, went all to hell—but eternal hell not yet.

He was a brilliant devil, and his superiors were slow in finding out his shortcomings, but they got round to them in time. Larry was a hard drinker on the road to dipsomania; he was a gambler prepared to cheat; he was a philanderer without morals. He made reckless mistakes that even his ability could not cover; he was demoted from his grade, pulled himself together, was promoted again, and again lapsed; and at the end of ten years he was ignominiously dismissed.

It did not worry Larry. His disgrace slipped off him like water off a duck's back, for he was become a depraved man, and morals no longer had any meaning for him—if they ever had. He lived unashamedly and shamelessly, smugly and boastingly, like—like a deposed monarch—on his brother and on his own wife.

There was nothing the two could do about it. Indeed, there was nothing they wanted to do; for, if the truth must be told, the sort of equilibrium that was achieved at the Sandymount villa suited Timmy and Emer well enough. The house was by no means unhappy, and don't think it was—apart from a natural frustration.

Big Larry was seldom at home, maybe twice in a month to replenish the exchequer, a thing Timmy was ever ready to do to be rid of him. And once he was three months away, in Mountjoy Jail, for driving off and wrecking another man's car.

Timmy, who had taken charge of household affairs from the very beginning, merely went on with the job. He was fond of Emer in his own steadfast way, and he grew fond of Emer's children. He played about with them, took them to the zoo on a frequent Sunday in summer, took their mother to the pictures or a play at the Abbey once a week, and on an occasion stood her a slap-up dinner in Jaminet's Restaurant. Begod sir! it looked like an ordinary, unromantic married establishment in suburbia, with husband and wife living amicably together, and the black sheep of the family turning up occasionally with a hard-luck story.

No doubt certain scandalous tongues went awagging, but without reason.

Timmy's worth in his Department was slowly recognised, but then wholeheartedly. From nine to five, five days a week, he was the perfect administrator: exploring every avenue, reaching a conclusion slowly, altering a decision like a mountain in travail and then bringing forth the mouse like a clap o' thunder. He could devise, create and promulgate an official form to be signed three times in triplicate, with a questionnaire that no taxpayer could fill in short of one brainstorm—maybe two. He could keep a file alive longer than any other official anywhere; and there was one famous file, pride of the service, that took four messengers and a wheelbarrow to get borne into the Presence on ceremonial occasions.

Timmy went on and on, and up and up: from Junior to Higher Executive, to Principal, with an Assistant Secretaryship within his grasp, and a Secretaryship in the offing.

Outside office hours, you would take him for a staid and law-abiding denizen of one of the deserts of suburbia. But you wouldn't be too sure if you knew the two little hobbies he was proclivated to. Ay! Two hobbies, but you might call one of them a vice.

That doubtful hobby was drink. And the king of all drinks for male men: ten-year-old Irish whiskey. Ah-ha! you will say, the twin in him! Maybe so. But there one twin was a profligate dipsomaniac, the other was a continent imbiber, regulating his drink as he regulated his work.

Once a month, no more and no less, on a certain Saturday evening after tea, Timmy depraved his neat little body by investing it in the shabbiest, shapelessest old suit o' tweeds ever handed down from a secondhand shelf; twisted a blue bird's-eye muffler round his collarless neck; stuck a dirty-shiny peaked stevedore cap over one eye, and disappeared from respectable purlieus for thirty hours.

Where did he go? I'll tell you that too. He went into town, he crossed the Liffey, he went down by the Quays, he took two turns to the left and one to the right, and slipped in by the lounge door of a certain hotel and hostelry.

Maybe it was a fourth-rate hotel; maybe it was a low pub; but it was not a mean one. Good order was kept, as gentlemen to gentlemen, and the liquor was the best, and the best only. No woman, virtuous or spendthrift, was allowed inside the door of bar or lounge. Men only, and not every man either, had a right to put a foot on the brass rod or wallop an emphatic fist on a scarred table-top; sea-worthy men, writing Johnnies on the make, and those wonderful working men of Dublin who could out-talk Dillon, and down pints of Guinness to the confoundment of biologists who hold that the capacity of the human stomach is only a quart-and-a-half. One of them, one time, on a bet, drank five pints in five minutes, a thing contrary to nature.

'You did it, Jerry,' says his backer, 'but it was a dam' close thing.' 'It was so,' agreed Jerry through the high tide in his thrapple, 'but I knew I could do it. Sure, I tried it up at the Red Cow before coming along here. Yes, sir!'

Timmy would slip in quietly looking at no one, take the same chair in the same quiet corner, and lift one finger.

And to the lift of Timmy's finger a barman would bring across a ball o' malt, a glass of ten-year-old Irish, pale-straw in colour; and Timmy, slowly and meticulously, would add a modicum of ten drops of water, and toss the mixture straight down on the pit of his stomach; and again lift the one finger. He would do the same thing with the second ball o' malt, and the identical same thing with the third one. But not with the fourth—never with the fourth.

He would look at the fourth on the table-top, and smile at it in a friendly fashion, and sit up as if waking out of a day-dream. And after a while he'd rise slowly to his feet, move with slow dignity to the long bar where a place was waiting for him, put a foot on the brass rod and an elbow on the zinc, and in a voice resonant as a clarion enunciate something like this.

'Ned Keogh yonder, usually accurate, was holding forth last month that the mongoose fighting the king cobra owes its safety entirely to its activity. That is not so, Edward my friend. Mongooses—not mongeese you will note—mongooses in the death-struggle with their inveterate enemy are frequently wounded, but possess a large degree of immunity to the deadly venom. I recall an incident that I personally observed an Ahmednugger in the Province of Bombay . . .'

Ay, begad! And the furthest he ever was outside Ireland was the Kish Light off Dublin Bay—in a rowboat.

I'm telling you: when Timmy got to his fourth drink he began to be the grandest company within the four seas of Erin. He had an extraordinary volume of tone, and could shake the cobwebs off the ceiling with ballads like *Behold Phelim Broady* and the *Battle of Keimeneigh*; he would stand a drink here and take a drink there, and propose a toast with humour and felicitation; he would enter into a learned discussion of any subject under the sun, listening to another man's points with impatient courtesy and producing his own with courteous authority. And, invariably, he illustrated his theses with some outrageous incidents that had befallen him in foreign parts: the Headwaters of the Nile, the

Cordilleras of Patagonia, or any dam' place so long as it was far enough off. Ay faith! the finest company in all Dublin while the bout lasted . . . But let a veil be drawn . . .

Thirty hours was his dead limit. At midnight on Sunday he slipped away like the Arab of old, steady as a rock on his feet; took the three turns on to the Quays wide and easy; crossed the Liffey by the Butt Bridge; perambulated the three miles out to Sandymount; and so to bed.

And on Monday morning he shaved and bathed, clothed himself in official buckram, and sedately proceeded to his devastating pursuit of useless ratiocination for another month.

But take note of this: from the time that he had reached his fourth drink on Saturday evening until he waked up on Monday morning he suffered a complete blackout: a blankness like a wall where no faintest shadow of memory was ever cast. Let it be.

Timmy's other little proclivity was a real hobby. He was a hoplologist. Hoplology! There is a Society, with world-wide correspondents, called *The Right Worshipful Company of Hoplologists*. The word hoplologist is from the Greek, of course, and it means a collector of weapons—not firearms, but swords and similar instruments of evil: every class of weapon to slit a throat, cleave a head or pierce a wame.

Up in the double-attic of the house at Sandymount, Timmy had a sample of every blame weapon you could put a name to, and some you never heard of: broadsword, claymore, sabre, cutlass, rapier, small-sword, falchion, scimitar, yataghan, talwar, kukri, kvis, sumarai halberd, battle-axe, assegai, and I don't know how many more, arranged in patterns on the wall, catalogued and cross-indexed in Civil Service fashion, and with a history attached, where possible.

He had a rust-eaten iron sword that Sigurd of Caithness bore at the battle of Clontarf in 1014 before Murrough slew him; he had a Dervish spear that had killed a 21st Lancer in the gorge at Omdurman, and had gone within an ace—Ochone, the day!— of killing Winston Churchill, who was a war correspondent at the time; he had an Andrea Ferrara that had flashed down the line at Fontenoy and fallen from the dead hand of a clansman on Culloden Moor; he had—I don't know all he had, but they were a bloodthirsty collection sure enough; and Timmy used to handle and gloat over them in blood-thirsty day-dreams.

There was, however, one notorious weapon that he had not got, and that he, or any hoplologist the world over, would give half his collection to possess. That was the personal sword of one of the Chinese Emperors—the Doom Sword—the Blade of a Thousand Cuts—the sword that was never drawn except to destroy evil.

There is mention of thirteen of these all down history and tradition. Four of them have never been identified; eight of them are in museums or private collections; the thirteenth—the sword of Yung Lo, the son of Chu Yuan-Chang of the Ming Dynasty— was looted from a palace in Peking that time Chinese Gordon set out to show the Oriental the benefits of opium and Western Civilisation.

Timmy's notion was that the sword had been swiped by a British solder and, ultimately, it might be found hanging about in some old manor house of military tradition anywhere in England, Scotland, Wales or Ireland—and Ireland for choice; for sure an Irish soldier would loot the cross off an ass's back in foreign parts.

That is why Timmy took a day off to visit every auction of old houses and old furnishings within reach of Dublin.

Now we are coming to the crux. On a certain Saturday. Timmy caught a bus that took him down to view an old house and furniture up for auction on the Wexford border. The forefathers of that old house had been with Cromwell at Clonnel, and William at Steenkirk, and Marlborough at Malplaquet—and, finally, with Chinese Gordon in the opium wars. And, of course, there was a bundle of old weapons tied with a piece of rope.

You know well what happened. Dambut! the Sword of Doom was in that careless bundle of old iron.

The bundle was propped in a corner of the big hall amongst a lot of old junk. At the back of the bundle a tall hilt stood up from the other hilts: a two-handed hilt without a guard, and it was that hilt-without-a-guard that gave Timmy his first flaming hint of the prize. He couldn't believe his eyes.

Was it too good to be true? But true it was, and in two minutes Timmy made sure, his heart beating hard and high.

He knew all there was to be known about Yung Lo's sword: the guardless hilt, with the two little ivory household gods of the Emperor caught under the gilt wrapping, the Emperor's sign-writing bitten deep on the back of the blade just below the hilt, the shallow channel at each side of the heavy back, the half-inch of curvature on the lower half of the blade, the square-cut tip: they were all there.

Timmy drew eighteen inches of the blade from its sheath, gave the hilt a little jerk, and listened for a dulled tinkle. He heard it. That was the final proof, for the tinkle came from a sealed, longitudinal chamber in the back of the blade below the point of balance, where steel pellets ran free in a ball-race, so as to add power to the slash.

As usual, the junk was kept for the end, and the bundle of swords was the final item put up for sale. The auctioneer would have put up the bundle at any time if Timmy had approached him, but Timmy did not, for he was afraid of attracting attention to his find.

About dusk the auctioneer made a washing motion with his hands. Devil the thing he knew about hoplology, but he would be facetious after the manner of his tribe.

'The final item, ladies and gents, and someone is due for a bargain.' His voice rang clear but hoarse, and no wonder. 'Here now is a historic set of bone-breakers: the sword of Brian Boru, who knows! or the slasher of our noble Sarsfield, or Wolfe Tone's stainless blade! Who'll bid me twenty pounds the lot?'

Some dealer chuckled.

'Come on! I'm not waiting. Start the ball rolling with fifteen quid? Ten? Five then? No! Very well then! I'll not waste any more time. Who'll bid me a pound?'

Timmy lifted a quiet forefinger.

'A pound, sir!' The auctioneer smashed down his mallet. 'A

bargain I said, and a bargain it is. They are yours for a pound. Take them away, sir—and kill your man with any of them.'

Timmy paid his pound, and wrestled the bundle of swords. They weighed like the very devil too, but the bus stop was at the lodge gates only a hundred yards away. However, before he got there he came on a thick clump of shrubbery. Without hesitation he dodged round to the back of it, extracted his royal sword carefully, and carelessly tossed its humble companions under the overhang of a bush. Then he fitted his sword of doom under the wing of his overcoat, with the long hilt standing up by his ear, and away with him back to Dublin, exultation bubbling in him.

It was six o'clock on a rainy October evening when he got there, but the high spirit in him did not mind the rain. The occasion surely called for a bit of a celebration, and for a start he treated himself to a slap-up meal in Jaminet's: milk-fed chicken and Limerick ham, washed down by a tall bottle of Liebfraumilch 1934, a good year and a heady wine.

At first he had intended to ring up Emer to join him; and then he decided not to; and after a while he was glad he hadn't. And I'll tell you why.

It had been his intention, also, to go straight home after his meal, and bestow his precious sword in a safe place. But, as I said, Liebfraumilch is a heady wine and, already, the revived little maggots of desire were wriggling in Timmy's brain and spinal column. And as is the way with men in the early stages of thirst, he made excuses to himself. He wanted the boys to see and admire his find, and he'd stay only one hour anyway.

So he went down to the wash-room in Jaminet's, removed his gent's collar, twisted a silk handkerchief loosely about his neck, knocked a dent in his respectable bowler hat; and hied himself down by the Quays, his sword under his coat and the hilt by his cheek. And begod, sir! already the little idol gods under the lacing were beginning to whisper: queer, guttural little mutterings right into the drum of his ear.

Timmy took his three turns as usual, slipped through a lounge door, and took his seat in his usual quiet corner. He laid his sword on the scarred board, and lifted one finger.

Timmy did not reach his fourth ball o' malt tonight. At the third he rose majestically to his feet, reached for the two-handed hilt. The rich voice resounded.

'Gentlemen, behold the Doom Sword of Yung Lo, son of Chu Yuan-Chang, Emperor of China! Let me demonstrate.'

The great sword came swooping out of its broken sheath, and every man there got out from under.

One thing is certain: that night will not be soon forgotten in that low pub. By a miracle, no blood was shed. There was harangue that went back and forth over ten centuries; there were recountings of strange and bloody incidents, and there were demonstrations to the risk of life and limb. The only neck that suffered was the neck of a Gold Label whiskey bottle, and that went clean as a whistle through a mirror at a cost to Timmy of thirty bob. Bedad sir! it was an ignoble performance for a sword that had never been wielded but for the extirpation of evil.

The pledged hour went by, and ten more with it. Indeed, the usual time went by, and at midnight Timmy slipped away as usual, still biled as an owl, but as steady as an archbishop on his feet.

The rain was coming down heavens-hard; and Timmy pulled his coat collar about his ears and snuggled his cheek against the sword hilt. And again he heard little guttural murmurings in his ear.

You will not believe this. It might only have been the drink talking in Timmy but, as sure as death, the mutterings of the idol-gods were no longer indistinct; he could pick out words and phrases.

Chang in one blow—Kuo-Sing, and a thousand cuts—still I thirst—all knots I cut—give me air and a neck of evil—air and a neck of evil. Over and over again. And it might be possible, if only dimly, that there came to Timmy the thought of a neck of evil . . .

He came round by the long façade of the Customs House, where the tall lamps glistered on the pavements and glistered on the roily waters of the turbid and turgid Liffey. One of Guinness' steamboats, piled high with porter barrels, was moored close to the quay wall ready to go out with the morning tide. The rain was still pouring, and no one, not even a cat, moved on the glaring asphalt.

Wrong. Two men moved. Timmy was one, and another man also. As Timmy faced towards the parapet, another man came round it from the bridge. And that man was his twin brother, Larry.

Larry was bareheaded, and his black hair gleamed wetly under the lamp. However drink had besotted his mind, it had never coarsened his body. He was a lean limb of Satan, with gleaming black eyes and a strangely austere mouth: a distinguished-looking devil, as many devils are.

The two brothers, the big and the little, stopped and faced each other. The only sounds were the quiet sough of the falling rain, and a thin, cold tinkle of raindrops from the railway bridge high overhead. And in that waiting hush, Timmy heard an urgent whisper in his ear: *The evil neck only! Give me the air.* That was the whisper.

Then Larry spoke, throwing up his hands in pleased surprise, and there was pleasure and surprise in his voice too: 'Well, oh well! My lucky night, and no doubt about it—brother Tim on the loose, and myself in need of him.'

Ay, his lucky night! Timmy said nothing, for he was trying to draw his mind away from the alluring whisper in his ear: *For the neck of evil I take the air.*

'Sure I ought to have known you were my twin under the skin,' said Larry. 'Mandear, have you anything good in mind?'

'Good or evil—I do not know,' said Timmy deeply.

'A matter of outlook, the same good or evil,' said Larry agreeably, and his hand moved invitingly. 'There's a place I know not far from here, and you can make your own choice. Come along with me, you gay devil!'

'I will not come with you.' Timmy's voice was strong and definite, and then low and urgent. 'Go your own road, you blind fool—and go now.'

'Ah-ha! You're on a trail of your own, are you? Very well

so!' Larry was still agreeable, but now came promptly to his own need, one hand out confidently. 'Would you have the loan of a fiver for me, Timmy boy?'

'I have not,' said Timmy, shaking his head against the insidious murmur that would not be silent.

'Murder alive!' cried Larry. 'But surely you'll have a quid or two to help me over the night?'

'I have no money on me,' said Timmy, and that was true. And some small, sane inner self was crying desperately: *Oh God! if I only had a pound for him he would go away.*

'You're a bloody liar!' said Larry warmly. 'You were never short of a fiver in all your born days.'

'Tonight I am,' said Timmy, and his voice lifted. 'Get out of my road!'

Quickly he took two paces aside, but alas! Larry was just as quick; and again the two brothers faced each other, almost breast to breast.

Timmy drew in his breath hissingly, and his hands came up towards the long hilt. But at the last moment sanity flashed again; his hands dropped, and he took two paces backwards. Behind him was the Liffey, and the edge of the quay not three yards away.

Larry thrust his head forward, and put his hands on his hips. Here was threat of rebellion. Poor Timeen! All the times he had threatened revolt, and all the times he had caved in—as he would cave in now.

'You haven't drink taken, Timeen?' he inquired half-mockingly.

'Buckets,' said Timmy. And buckets was right.

Larry laughed unbelievingly. He had never seen Timmy under the influence, in that queer, insanely sober state beyond the far edge of mere drunkenness.

'Wherever you got the courage,' said Larry, 'you will not deny your brother for the first time in your life.'

'Ten years ago I should have denied you,' said Timmy. And in a flash he realised what a desolation those ten years had been, a desolation where two frustrated lives had moved forlornly on broken wings, and where he himself had been driven to drinking for the surcease of misery.

Is he going to be troublesome—I don't want to manhandle the little tomcat, said Larry to himself. He took a quick glance up and down the quays to see if the coast was clear, and it was. Unluckily for someone, the coast was clear. Then he turned to Timmy and took a stride forward.

'Take one other step,' said Timmy warningly. He braced his legs, and his hands came up chin high. And the whisper in his ear: *'The air now—now—now!'*

'You and your foolish old gut-sticker!' sneered Larry, anger rising in him. 'Very well then! You go your way, and I go mine, a fiver in my pocket.' He voice snarled. 'Out with it!'

'Go your own road, you doomed fool!' said Timmy throatily.

And then, a flame of insane rage leaped in Larry, as it will leap in a man long soaked in alcohol. His hands and his voice lifted, and the power of words came to him.

'You ungrateful pup dog, that I cherished in my bosom all your useless days! You destroyer of house and home, that set me wandering the streets, a damn'd soul! You hanger-on to the apron strings of another man's wife! You twin-brother to a cuckold! Do you know what I am going to do to you now? Shake the last farthing out of you, and pitch your miserable carcass into the Liffey tide.'

'You foul-mouthed liar—'

That is all that Timmy had time to say, for Larry launched forward, his hands out to clutch and wrench.

But Timmy was not there. Timmy side-stepped lithe as an eel, and Larry stopped himself a stride from the edge of the quay, unbalanced for a moment, head and hands thrown forward.

Something flashed in the air; something gave an exultant double-cry; something, of its own volition, swooped and checked and swooped on. The force of that terrific swoop whirled Timmy round, and round again. He staggered, balanced precariously, and steadied himself on the very edge of the quay. He was looking down into the water. The water flowed sternly, turbidly, and heaved itself sullenly against the stern of the steamer moored against the quay wall. And the only thing that moved was the water.

Timmy straightened up and turned round. He was alone. Up and down the wide quay nothing moved.

'My God! what mad vision was that?' he said aloud.

On Monday morning Timmy awoke out of a dreamless sleep; and, as usual, his mind was a blank wall where no faintest shadow was cast of anything that had befallen since his third whiskey on Saturday; nor did any weight of gloom press on him from the unconscious.

But he remembered his Sword of Doom all right. There it was laid carefully along the top of his dressing table. He got out of bed, and examined it with growing satisfaction. The veritable article, as he could prove to any envious hoplologist who dared to challenge. And no damn'd Communist government could claim the sword either.

The hilt and the devilish little gods were still damp from the night's rain; so was the broken sheath; so was the blade when he drew it; and one faint, pinkish-orange stain was drying in one of the grooves. Timmy did not even speculate as to what that stain might be. He went to the bathroom, cleaned and polished the sword, and hung it in the hot-press so that it would dry out thoroughly.

Thereafter he shaved and bathed, attired himself in official buckram, ate a hearty breakfast, told Emer of his find, glanced at the morning paper, and proceeded decorously to his devastating, many-branched, but fruitless labours.

Listen now, you remember that Guinness boat by the quay wall. It cast off that morning to take Dublin stout to thirsty Anglo-Saxons. The propeller blades threshed for two seconds, checked and stuck, and stayed stuck. So they sent an investigator down to see what the trouble was. Within an hour a diver discovered the gruesome cause of the stoppage. Within another hour the poor mangled remains were on the quay wall. The threshing scoop of a propeller blade was not merciful to frail humanity. An arm was torn away, so was a foot. *The head was also missing.*

A nameless body? No. A few sodden papers and an envelope or two gave name and address. And so, early that afternoon Emer and Timmy identified the remains. That was not so difficult. There was a broken finger badly set, and there was a characteristic mole below the left shoulder blade. Timmy, the twin, had a similar mole in the same place. And Timmy, the twin, had no inkling as to how his brother had died.

He had no inkling then. And he has no inkling now. And he has not taken a single ball o' malt since that fateful weekend. He no longer feels the craving for one. But if ever he downs four balls o' malt one on top of the other . . . ? I wonder!

DEATH

Brian Cleeve

Few Irish writers have tackled the themes of murder and mystery with greater variety than Brian Cleeve (1921–), best-selling novelist and former broadcaster on Radio Telefís Eireann. Ranging from vivid portraits of city underworld crime to comic tales of bungling criminals, his books and short stories invariably make for entertaining reading and it is always a personal pleasure for me to use something by him in an anthology.

Brian Talbot Cleeve was born in Essex of Irish parents, served in the merchant navy for some years, and then lived in South Africa for a while before settling in Ireland. He wrote his first novel, The Far Hills, *in 1952, but it was not until 1961 that he created his first mystery thriller,* Assignment to Vengeance, *which became an immediate best-seller, was translated into several languages, and introduced his name to an international readership who have continued to admire his fertile and unmistakably Irish imagination ever since. Recently he has been writing a series of books featuring Sean Ryan, described as 'one of the most forceful and convincing secret agents in contemporary fiction.'*

'Death', Cleeve's contribution to this book, is an authentic story of prison life which originally appeared in London Mystery Magazine *in September 1953. He introduced it with these intriguing remarks: 'I have always felt prisons contain the essence of all mysteries; perhaps because I have been inside a number of them ''on business''! But which sort of uniform my business called for, I leave to your conjecture and my discretion.'*

*　　*　　*

We used to call him Death. Of course, that wasn't his real name. Outside the prison he was someone else, but inside he was Death. We never thought of him as ever being outside the walls, and I don't think he did go out much. It was going outside that got him called Death. A bunch of roughs waited for him one night when he was off duty and beat the daylights out of him. They tied him up to a railing, and stripped him and slogged him with his own truncheon until he nearly snuffed it. When a copper found him at four o'clock in the morning he thought that he *had* snuffed it, and got the ambulance to drive straight to the morgue; but Death came to on the slab, and that's how he got the name.

Of course, it wasn't only that. There was another screw got tossed off the fourth landing on the Moor, before they had nets, and the only thing that didn't get broken was the chain on his whistle. He's a humpy now, but we didn't give him a name. It was the way Death looked more than the story that made him something special. He was small and shapeless, and you never heard him move. You just saw him there when it was too late. You could be having a drag at a cigarette or passing a note, and you'd see a shadow on your hands, and that was Death. He'd be standing there with his eyes like little wet stones behind his spectacles, playing with the strap of his truncheon. You'd look at him, and he'd flip the strap up and down, up and down, and you knew he was just waiting for you to move too quickly.

We were scared of Death. We'd see him creeping round, with his little pot-belly and his short legs and his spectacles, and I tell you straight, I used to shudder. I'd sit there straining my ears like a damn rabbit, waiting for him to get to my cell, but I'd never hear him coming. There'd just be the shadow, and I'd stand up stiff, with my thumbs to the seams of my trousers and my eyes straight ahead, while he looked round the cell. Even if he had his back to you, he'd know if you moved. He'd know if you looked at him. 'Eyes front,' he'd say, and the strap of his truncheon would go 'tap, tap', against his trouser leg. He never upset everything, the way the other screws did. He never turned the bedding over or moved anything, but if there was something to find, he'd find it. When he'd gone it was as though someone had taken a tight rope off your chest and you could breathe properly. I know how that feels, because Manny's gang hung me up like that all night once; but I never hated Manny the way I hated Death.

I didn't mind the other screws so much. When one of them pushed me round a bit, I knew it was because I was class and he wasn't. I'd lived in the big hotels with French tarts, whilst he had cocoa for supper and a wife with bad breath. Half of them would have been on our lay if they'd had the guts; but Death was different. He didn't hate us because he was jealous of what we'd got or because he'd been beaten up. He just hated us because we were crooks. When we did anything wrong he nailed us, and when we didn't he didn't believe it. He just thought he hadn't watched close enough. That was the way he saw his job—not to trust us, to catch us out, to get our remission stopped; not out of spite, but because he thought it was the right thing to do. There was nothing human about him. Nothing you could lay hold of and tell yourself you'd scored over him there. Even his little, short legs and his pot-belly weren't a score, because he didn't want to be different. It was like being guarded by a toad.

I got to hating Death so much I couldn't sleep. I'd lie awake hating him, and thinking about Zoe and Rita, and the 'Splendide', and what a crummy little runt Death would look if he ever got into a place like that; but it didn't do any good. He wouldn't want to go there. He'd stay here, in his uniform and his regulation boots, waiting for me to come back. I used to beat my hands on the wall when I thought of that. When I did get to sleep, I'd dream about it.

I'd dream about the court-room the way it was when I got this stretch—old Charleston sitting high up, like a parrot, all grey and red, and his big red beak of a nose almost touching his notes, and Manny and his bunch down in the back row, grinning all over their greasy clocks. It was only the end that was different. Instead of giving me all the long spiel and the three-stretch, old Charleston just took out a little black handkerchief and put it on top of his wig. 'The sentence,' he said, 'is Death.' Then the judge and the rest of them disappeared, and I was alone in the dock, waiting. Then I'd hear it. 'Tap, tap', as the strap went up and down, up and down, against his trouser leg, and I'd stand like a waxwork, with my thumbs to the seams of my trousers and my eyes looking straight ahead. I couldn't look round. Not if you'd paid me, I couldn't have looked round; because I knew he was standing there, waiting to take me down.

A couple of dozen times I must have had that dream, until it began to seem as if it was real, and the only way out was to kill the little slob, so that he couldn't be standing there waiting to take me down to the drop. Even by daylight it began to seem like that. He wouldn't look so clever then. He might not want a drape-cut and a fancy French bit, but he'd want something that I had when he was lying there on the slab. He'd want to be alive.

There were a lot of others felt the same way about knocking him off. The difference was I meant it. I didn't talk. I let the others do that, and they talked a lot, especially a little punk that used to carry a cosh for Manny's gang. He'd been there the time they hung me up to find out who'd slashed a couple of Manny's girls. He'd talk about all the fancy razor work he'd do on Death down a dark alleyway some night, and I'd act impressed and ask him to tell us how. With a bit of a prod from me in the right places he finally got it doped out, and when he did there was quite a few of us listening.

It seemed that the only time Death went outside was to visit his mother every Thursday night. Whatever trouble he took to steer clear of dark alleyways, there was one place he'd relax, and that was inside his mother's front door. If an alec was waiting there with a razor . . . The little tramp stuck his chest out like a dog waiting for a bone.

'How about an alibi?' I said.

'S'easy. I get sprung on a Thursday morning. I take the ten-thirty for the Smoke, and they notice me at the station because they know I'm a con. I get off at the first stop and I walk back. I do the job, and I jump the milk train at four in the morning. I'm at the labour at nine o'clock, and if anyone wants to know where I was last night, I was with the boys. Ask 'em. Am I smart, or am I smart?'

'You're smart all right,' I told him, and I nearly got a rupture trying not to laugh. I knew it was only blow. The little rat wouldn't dare swipe a packet of fags unless Manny was there to help him. He'd no more knock off a screw than he'd knock off Carnera, but there were six people had heard him say he would and describe how he'd do it. I was going out a couple of days before he was, and the next time Death opened his mother's door, I'd be there. I'd turn on the light, so he'd know it was me, and then I'd give it to him. It wouldn't take long. Not long enough for the neighbours to come or for the old woman to get down the stairs; but it'd seem like a long time to Death.

I was in the court when they brought it in guilty for Manny's punk. He stood like I'd stood in the dream, only instead of looking at old Charleston, he looked at me, and when the judge said 'Death,' he looked over my shoulder like he'd seen somebody he knew. I know it's crazy, but just for a second I heard something going 'tap, tap', like a strap against a trouser leg. I know it's crazy and I never heard it since, but I've started listening for it and I've started getting careful—about crossing the street, and train journeys, and things like that. The insurance people tell me I ought to last another thirty years, and I don't know if that's good or bad. It's a long time to wait. They think I'm going screwy. Everyone has to die sometime, they say, and not to worry about it. It's all right for them to talk. He's not waiting for them, with his strap going 'tap, tap', up and down against his trouser leg. Death is waiting for me.

THE SIGHT

Brian Moore

It is not generally known that Brian Moore (1921–99), one of Ireland's most distinguished literary novelists although he was a Canadian citizen for much of his life, started his career in the Fifties writing 'hardboiled' murder mysteries which were all published in paperback. The titles of these rare books with their exotic covers, now much sought after by collectors, speak for themselves: Wreath for a Redhead *(1951),* French for Murder *(1954),* Bullet for my Lady *(1955) and* This Gun for Gloria *(1957). After this 'apprenticeship', Moore moved to Hollywood where he wrote the screenplay for Alfred Hitchcock's famous murder film* Torn Curtain *(1966) in which Paul Newman starred as a killer. Despite his self-imposed exile, he never forgot his Irish roots and several of his most successful novels had Irish themes, among them* The Emperor of Ice-Cream *(1965),* The Mangan Inheritance *(1979) and* Lies of Silence *(1990), a Booker-nominated psychological thriller set in his native Northern Ireland, which focuses on the dilemma faced by a man wondering whether he should plant an IRA bomb and slaughter dozens of innocent people or let the terrorists murder the wife whom he is about to leave.*

Brian Moore was born in Belfast, one of nine children in a family of fervent Republicans. His father was a surgeon and his uncle was Eoin McNeill, founder of the Irish Volunteers. Not wanting to get drawn into the troubles, Moore joined the British Army in 1943 and, after serving in North Africa, Italy and France, crossed the Atlantic and began working as a journalist in Montreal. Over nearly fifty years he produced an amazingly varied body of novels, from Victorian fantasy to crime thrillers, including some violently anti-Republican and anti-clerical works which were banned in Ireland. Despite the realistic nature of much of his fiction, Moore was deeply interested in the history and legends of Ireland and, not surprisingly, quite a few of his stories spilled over into the realms of fabulism. Such is the case with 'The Sight', written in 1977. It is set in the heart of New York, but deals with the mysteries of prevision which have been an enduring preoccupation with the people of Ireland for many centuries . . .

*   *   *

Benedict Chipman never took a drink before five and never drank after midnight. He ate only a light lunch, avoided bread and potatoes, and drank decaffeinated coffee. These self-regulations were, he sometimes thought, the only set rules he observed. Otherwise, he did as he liked.

Yet on the morning he returned to his eight-room apartment on Fifth Avenue after four days in hospital, his first act was to tell his housekeeper to bring some Scotch and ice into the library. When she brought it, he was standing by the window, looking out at Central Park. He did not turn round.

'Will that be all, sir?'

'Yes, thanks, Mrs Leahy.'

Chipman was fifty-two and a partner in a New York law firm. A few weeks ago, during his annual medical check-up, his doctor had noticed a large mole on his back and had recommended its removal. The operation was minor but, for Chipman who had never been in hospital before, the invasion of his bodily privacy by doctors, nurses and attendants had been humiliating and vaguely upsetting. Then, to complicate matters, while the biopsy showed the mole to be probably benign, the pathologist advised that 'to be completely sure', the surgeon should repeat the procedure but, this time, make a wider incision. The second biopsy had been scheduled for the end of the month. 'There's nothing to worry about,' the surgeon said. 'Just relax and come back ten days from now.'

But Chipman did not feel like relaxing. He felt nervous and

irritable. As he poured the Scotch, he looked at the tray containing his mail. The first letter on the pile was postmarked Bishopsgate, NH. He had been born in Bishopsgate and for some reason he could not explain the sight of the postmark disturbed him. The letter was from his brother, Blake, who wrote that he and his wife were coming to New York to visit their son Buddy, a journalism major at Columbia. Buddy, it seemed, had learned that his uncle had been in hospital and Blake wrote that all three of them would like to call tomorrow afternoon. The letter irritated Chipman. He had no wish to see Blake and his family. He thought of his brother as a man who had never in his life owned a hundred dollars he didn't know about and whose relations with himself were sycophantic rather than fraternal, largely because of loans which Blake had not repaid.

At the library door, Mrs Leahy announced herself with a small prefatory cough. 'Mrs Kirwen is here, sir.'

'Show her in. And ask if she'd like something to drink.'

As he put his brother's letter down and rose to greet Geraldine, he heard her chatting with Mrs Leahy in the front hall.

'Is *he* having one? Oh, well then, a sherry, I think. By the way, how's your nephew, Mrs Leahy?'

'He still has the pleurisy, ma'am. But he'll be all right.'

'Good, that's good news.'

'Thank you, Mrs Kirwen.'

I never knew Mrs Leahy had a nephew, Chipman said to himself. But, come to think of it, he didn't know much about Mrs Leahy, although she had been with him for almost ten years. Lately, he had decided that his interest in other people was limited to the extent of their contributions to his purse, his pleasure, or his self-esteem. He had a weakness for such aphoristic judgements. But in this instance he also remembered another aphorist's warning: lack of interest in others is a first sign of age.

'Ben, darling, how are you? Shouldn't you have your feet up or something? You mustn't overdo it on your first day home.'

'Stop fussing.'

'I'm not fussing. Dr Wilking told me you should take it easy.'

'When was Wilking talking to *you*?'

'I met him in the corridor yesterday. Remember, he thinks I'm your wife.'

The surgeon, who did not know Chipman, had come in on them unexpectedly the night after the biopsy and found Geraldine, the buttons of her dress undone, lying on the hospital bed with Chipman. The surgeon had tactfully assumed she was Chipman's wife and had addressed her as such in the subsequent conversation. No one had contradicted him. 'That was a mistake,' Chipman said now, remembering. 'I should have said something.'

'Oh, what's it matter?'

'Well, my own doctor, Dr Loeb, knows I'm not married.'

'Oh, Ben. Who cares nowadays?'

At that point Mrs Leahy brought Geraldine's sherry. Geraldine, sipping it, put her long legs up on a yellow silk footstool. In this posture her skirt fell back, revealing her elegant thighs. Although impromptu erotic views normally pleased Chipman, this morning he was not pleased: he was irritated. 'Why can't you sit properly?'

'That's not a very nice thing to say when I've given up an important job to be with you today.'

'What job?'

'Remember I tried out for the Phil Lewis show last week? Well, my agent called and said they want me for a second audition this afternoon. He says that usually means you've got the job. But, I'm not going.'

'Why not?'

'Because if I got the job it would mean I'd be on the coast for the next seven weeks. I'm not going to be three thousand miles away while you're in and out of hospital.'

'I'm not in and out of hospital. I'm just going back for a couple of days, that's all. Now, be a good girl. Phone and say you'll be glad to audition this afternoon.'

'No,' she said, suddenly looking as though she might begin to cry.

'But why not?'

'Because I've realised something, Ben. I'm in love with you. I don't want to be separated from you.'

In love with him? He remembered La Rochefoucauld's maxim

that nothing is more natural or more mistaken than to suppose that we are loved. He knew Geraldine did not love him. She was an unsuccessful young actress, divorced from a television producer and in receipt of a reasonable alimony. His own role in her life was that of a suitable escort, an older man capable of providing presents and a good time, a friend who was good for a small loan and might not expect to see his money again. This sudden protestation of love was, he decided, no more than the familiar feminine need to justify having gone to bed with him. Geraldine would not give up her alimony: he did not want her to. The present arrangement suited him perfectly.

Nevertheless when she said that she loved him, for one moment he felt strangely elated. Then put his glass back on the silver tray and in its surface saw his face, which seemed distorted, white, old. This foolishness must stop. 'Now, don't talk nonsense. Go and phone those people.'

'Are you trying to get rid of me?'

'Of course not. But if you go out to Hollywood this week it might work out very well. I was thinking of going to Puerto Rico. I thought I'd take a vacation. Lie in the sun until I have to go back into hospital.'

'Do you know people in Puerto Rico, is that it?'

'No. No. Look, Geraldine, you're *not* in love with me. My God, I'm twenty years older than you.'

'Age has nothing to do with being in love with someone.'

'Maybe not at your age. But at my age it has everything to do with it. Now go and make that phone call. Then I'll take you out and buy you lunch.'

She stood and picked up the otter coat he had helped pay for, trailing it behind her on the carpet as she moved across the room. At the door, she turned. 'So that's what you want? To go to Puerto Rico alone?'

'Yes.'

'OK.'

She went into the hall. He listened to hear the tinkle as she picked up the phone, but instead heard the front door slam. He started across the room, thinking to go after her and bring her back, but stopped. He realised that he was close to the almost forgotten sensation of tears. Dammit, he'd just invented Puerto Rico to help her make up her mind about the audition. But now, as he felt himself tremble with anger—or was it weakness?—he decided a short vacation in the sun might be the ideal way to wait out the next ten days. Maybe with Geraldine. He decided to suggest it at the office when he went in tomorrow.

There might be a little ill-feeling, though. He had already had a long vacation this summer. But what could they do? In the seventeen years he had been a member of the firm he had frequently demonstrated that his interests were not the law or the success of the partnership, but women, music, and his collection of paintings. However, on the day he joined the partnership he brought with him, as a wedding present from his father-in-law, an insurance company which dwarfed all other clients the firm did business with. And although his marriage had subsequently broken up (his wife died eight years later in an alcoholic clinic, driven there, some said, by Chipman's behaviour with other women) his father-in-law had not held it against him. He still represented the insurance company and this power, coupled with his disregard for the firm's other clients, had driven his partners to revenge themselves on him in the only way they knew. They no longer invited him to their homes or, indeed, to any social function. Their boycott amused him: they bored him. They knew that he was amused and bored. Their dislike of him, he guessed, had long ago turned to hatred.

Yet on the following morning when he went to the office he was surprised to see George Geddes, the senior partner, come in at his doorway, eager, out of breath, and smiling like a job applicant. 'Ben, how are you, how're you feeling?'

'Hello, George.'

'So, how did it go?'

Directly behind Geddes, Chipman's secretary was at her desk in the outer office. He did not want her to hear what he had to say and so beckoned Geddes in and shut the door. 'Matter of fact, George, I wanted to have a word with you about that. Everything went very well, but they want me to go back, just as a precaution, and have a wider excision made. They've scheduled it for the thirty-first. I don't know. I'm feeling a little knocked out. I thought, if you don't mind, I might go and lie in the sun for a week. Not really come back to the office until next month.'

As he spoke he noticed that Geddes was already nodding agreement as though helping someone with a speech impediment. 'Of course, Ben, of course. No sense sitting around here. Good idea.'

'Well, thanks. Of course there are a few things I can clear up before I go.'

'No, no,' Geddes said. 'Let the juniors do some work for a change. Get on your feet again, that's the main thing.'

After Geddes had left, Chipman phoned a travel agency. He booked a double room with patio and pool in a first-class Puerto Rico resort hotel, starting the following Monday. He called in his juniors and reviewed their current handling of his clients' affairs. At noon he told his secretary that he was leaving and would not be back until the first week in December. Then he took a taxi to his apartment and for the second morning in a row broke his rule and made himself a drink.

But now his reason was celebratory. What a relief it had been to find Geddes agreeable for once. And there was a note saying Geraldine had telephoned. Obviously, her temper tantrum had not lasted. After pouring a Scotch he picked up the phone and dialled her number.

'Geraldine? Ben. First of all, I'm sorry about yesterday.'

'No, darling, it was my fault. Why shouldn't you go on a trip if you want to? When are you going, by the way?'

'No, tell me first, how was your audition?'

'I didn't go. It's a long story, I won't bore you with it.'

'Does that mean you might be free to join me in Puerto Rico?'

'Ben, do you mean it?'

'Of course. I booked a double room with patio and pool in the Caribe Imperial. Or would you rather I got you a room of your own?'

'No, no.'

'Good. And what about the week-end? Are you free?'

'Do you mean now? Yes. Completely.'

'Well, so am I. Or, almost. I have to be here tomorrow after-noon when my brother and his family are coming. But that shouldn't take more than an hour.'

'Are we thinking of the same thing?'

'I hope so.'

'All right, darling. Come on down. I'll be waiting.'

'I'll be right there.'

His brother's hand, tentative at first, went out to finger the Steinway's polished surface, then boldly stroked the wood. His brother's head turned, afternoon sunlight merciless on the thin grey hair, the pink skull-cap of skin beneath. His brother smiled, ingratiate and falsely intimate. 'Beautiful piano, eh, Ben?' his brother said. 'You must play something for us before we go. I mean, if you feel up to it.'

'Oh yes, Ben, you must,' said his brother's wife who, he knew, did not care at all for music.

If he felt up to it. What would they say if they knew he had come up from the village two hours ago after a night of screwing that would exhaust anyone? Perhaps it would not exhaust Blake's wife, though. One summer, when their son Buddy was still a brat in rompers, Chipman had gone to visit them at their summer cottage on Cape Cod. He was sunbathing in the dunes when Blake's wife came up from the beach, drying her hair on a towel, her shoulder-straps undone, her swimsuit wet from the sea. She did not see him until she stumbled on him and when he reached up and pulled her down she did not say a word. Later they walked hand in hand over the dunes towards the cottage. Blake was sitting on a deck-chair on the lawn, reading a book, and the child was on the porch playing with an inner tube. Man and child looked up and his brother's wife at once let go of his hand and ran to kiss her child. She avoided Chipman for the rest of that evening and the following morning he thought it wise to pretend a business engagement in Boston. He had not been to stay with them since.

'Let Buddy play something,' he said, knowing that Buddy's

atrocious playing would please them much more than his own. And so Buddy obediently flopped down on the piano bench, looked disdainfully at the music scores in front of him, then poised his large hands over the keys. 'What'll it be, Uncle Ben?'

'You choose,' Chipman said. Years ago, prodded by Blake's wistful hints about the child's musical inclinations, he had paid for a series of piano lessons for Buddy. The money had been wasted for Buddy's musical talents were a myth, the first of a long series of efforts on his parents' part to make Chipman feel a special affection for the boy. All had failed. Buddy's only effect on his uncle was to relieve him of any regrets about not having had a son of his own.

But now he pretended to listen as Buddy stumbled through some Cole Porter tunes, noticing as he mimed attention that Buddy's parents seemed nervous as though they had quarrelled before coming and were now trying to cover it up by a surfeit of polite remarks to each other. Chipman was uninterested. He simply wanted them to go and so, when Blake glanced at last in his direction, he pretended drowsiness. It worked. As his son thumped to a pause in the music, Blake stood up. 'Thanks, Bud, but we'd better not overtire your uncle. Besides, your mother and I want to catch that Wyeth show at the Met before our train leaves.'

Then he turned to Chipman. 'Ben, could I have a word with you?'

As on signal both Buddy and his mother left the room. It was, Chipman knew, the usual prelude to Blake's asking for money, but today a loan seemed well worth it to get rid of them. He went to his desk, aware that Blake, if left to his own devices, would take at least five minutes to come to the point. He opened a drawer and took out his cheque-book.

'What's that for?' Blake asked sharply.

'Nothing.'

'Put that away, will you,' Blake said. 'I'm ashamed that I owe you so much. As a matter of fact, Ben, it wasn't that at all. It was just that we wondered if you'd like to come up to Bishopsgate to convalesce until you go back into the hospital.'

'Thanks, but I'm going to Puerto Rico.'

'Oh. Puerto Rico?'

'Yes, I thought I'd like to lie in the sun for a few days.'

'Oh, that's a pity, we were looking forward to the thought of having you. You and I haven't spent much time together these last years.'

'I know. Well, maybe some other time.'

'Any time,' Blake said. 'I'd like us to go for walks around the old place and have talks and all that. I'd like that a lot.'

And then, abruptly, Blake took hold of his hand and squeezed it. 'I'd really like it, Ben.'

'Well, we'll do it,' Chipman said, uneasily, beginning to move towards the hallway where the others waited. As they came out he saw Blake's wife glance at her husband and saw Blake give a small, almost imperceptible shake of his head. Buddy came forward, hand out, smiling. 'Goodbye, sir.'

'Goodbye,' Chipman said. 'Goodbye, Blake.'

His sister-in-law came towards him. He held out his hand. She ignored it and reached up to kiss him on the cheek. He was astonished. 'Goodbye,' his sister-in-law said. 'Take care of yourself.'

The elevator came. They went down.

Confused, Chipman closed the door of his apartment. It was as though he had found an interesting passage in a dull book and had seen it snatched away before he had time to finish it. Why had Blake's wife kissed him, she who had so carefully avoided kissing him ever since that summer on the beach? And why had Blake come up with this unprecedented invitation to visit them at Bishopsgate? Why were they being so kind all of a sudden? Come to think of it, everyone had been abnormally kind these past two days—Geraldine, Geddes, Blake. It was irritating, dammit, to be treated as though, all of a sudden, he were made of glass. How did La Rochefoucauld put it? *Pride does not wish to owe, nor vanity to pay.* He didn't want favours from anyone. So, why did they try?

He had reached the library door before the thought and the answer came to him. He was going to die. That was why they were all being so gentle. They knew something he didn't know. A wider excision, that was what the surgeon said. 'To be completely sure,' the pathologist said. They hadn't told him the truth, that was it. 'Just relax,' the surgeon said.

He must not panic. He must call Dr Loeb, his internist, and put the question to him quite casually, implying that he already knew all about it. He must go to the phone now and clear things up.

He went into his bedroom and closed the door so that Mrs Leahy would not overhear him. He phoned Dr Loeb but the answering service said Dr Loeb was out of town for the weekend and a Dr Slattery was taking his calls. So that was no use. The surgeon's name was Wilking. He looked up the number. The answering service said Dr Wilking wasn't in, but would he leave a message. He left his name and number and lay down on the bed, worrying. After five minutes he telephoned again and said it was an emergency. He must reach Dr Wilking at once. This time, the answering service gave him a number to call. Dr Wilking answered.

'Dr Wilking, this is Benedict Chipman speaking. Now, I know this may sound silly to you, but was there anything about that operation of mine that I should know about?'

'Why do you ask, Mr Chipman?'

'I just want to know the truth. It's important, doctor.'

'Well, look, Mr Chipman, it's pretty much as I told you. I don't think you have anything to worry about.'

'Is that the truth? I want the truth.'

'Yes, what can I say? Look, Mr Chipman. The best thing you can do now is relax. Your wife mentioned you might go off for a short vacation. I think that's a good idea.'

'How the hell can I take it easy? For God's sake, doctor, that's like telling a man to take it easy in the condemned cell while you decide whether or not he's to be reprieved.'

'Oh, come on now, Mr Chipman, I wouldn't say that.'

'Of course you wouldn't,' Chipman shouted. 'And that girl isn't my wife, do you hear? So anything you have to say, just say it to me!'

He put the receiver down without waiting to hear the surgeon's reply. He looked at his bed. This was the bed he might die in. He turned from it and went into his library. Small picture-lights lit his collection of Krieghoff landscapes. When he died these pictures would be sent to the Bishopsgate Art Gallery to be exhibited in a special room with a brass plaque over the door, identifying him as their donor. They would arrive after his body, which would be buried under a plain headstone in the episcopal cemetery, next to his parents' grave. How many people ever read donors' plaques or the names on headstones? A year from now he would be forgotten.

But wasn't that jumping the gun, giving in to a bad case of jitters unsupported by any evidence? How could they know he was going to die when they hadn't even done the second biopsy yet? What were they keeping from him? Whatever it was had frightened Geraldine into suddenly declaring her love. But she doesn't love me, Chipman decided, she pities me. Pity is what everyone feels for me now: Geraldine, Geddes, Blake, Blake's wife. Yet how could they all know this thing about me? Geraldine has never met Geddes. Or Buddy. Who told Buddy, for instance?

Chipman went to his desk, searched it, and then went to the telephone table in the hall. He knew he had a number for Buddy someplace, and when he found it and dialled it, it was a fraternity house. No one answered for a long time and then some boy told him Buddy wasn't in, and that he didn't know when he would be back. As Chipman replaced the receiver, Mrs Leahy passed him in the hall, going down the corridor to her own room. Only one person might have spoken to Buddy, to Geddes, to Geraldine. One person who would answer the phone when people called here to ask how he was. He went down the corridor to the far end of the apartment and stopped outside Mrs Leahy's door. He almost never came into this part of the apartment, near the pantry and wine cellar, and past the kitchen. He stood for a moment and then, without knocking, he opened the door.

He had not seen the inside of Mrs Leahy's room for years. Sometimes he heard the television sound, turned low, and sometimes she would leave the door open, at night, when she went to answer the phone. Now, his eyes went from the television set to the horrid rose and green curtains, the cheap coloured lithograph of some saint, to the crucifix, entwined with fading palm, which hung over what seemed to be a sewing-table. It was the sort of room he used to glimpse through upper-storey windows, years ago, when he still rode the subways, a room which screamed a sudden mockery of all other rooms in his elegant apartment. And its occupant, her back to him, unaware of his presence, was the perfect figure in this interior. In her pudgy fingers, the surprise of a cigarette: on the lap, inevitably, the garish headlines of the *Daily News*.

'Mrs Leahy?'

She turned. Her grey head was that of a stranger's, utterly changed by the absence of her uniform cap. 'Oh, did you ring, sir? Is the bell not working?'

'No, I didn't ring.'

'Can I get you something, sir? Are you all right?'

By this time she had stubbed her cigarette and had pinned on the familiar housemaid's cap. 'A little whisky?' she said. 'Or, are you hungry, sir? Would you like a sandwich?'

'Whisky,' he said. 'And I want to talk to you.'

'Yes, Mr Chipman.' Swiftly she moved past him going down the corridor to the monastic neatness of her kitchen. She did not, of course, expect him to follow her into the kitchen and looked up, surprised, when he did.

'A little water with it, sir? I'll bring it into the library, will I?'

'No. Sit down, Mrs Leahy. Please.'

As she placed the bottle of Scotch, ice, and a glass and pitcher of water on a tray, he drew out one of the chrome and leather kitchen chairs, indicating that she should sit in at the table. As she did, he saw a red rash of embarrassment rise from her neck to her cheeks. They had never been informal together. He sat opposite her and poured himself a Scotch. 'Now,' he said. 'Let me ask you something. Are you the person who's been telling people I have cancer?'

'Me, sir?'

'Yes, you.'

She did not answer him at once. She put her veiny old hands on the table, joined them as in an attitude of prayer, then looked at him with the calculating, ready-to-bolt caution of a rodent. He had never before noticed this animal quality of hers. Why, she's a hedgehog, he decided. She's Mrs Tiggy-winkle.

'Yes, sir. It was me.'

He must keep calm. He must not let her know that he was ignorant of all the facts of his illness. 'I see. And who told *you* that I might have cancer?'

'Mrs Kirwen, sir.'

'And what did she say, exactly?'

'Ah, she didn't say you had cancer, she said they were going to operate on you again just to be sure. There was always the chance, she said. And I said to her I thought I should let Mr Buddy know. On account of your brother, sir. And then Mr Geddes rang up about you. And I told him. To let him know, like.'

'Oh, you did, did you? Well, I like the way you let them know. They think I'm going to die. I could see it on my brother's face this afternoon. He thinks I'm going to die.'

'I'm very sorry, now, Mr Chipman.'

'Mrs Kirwen *didn't* say to you I had cancer, did she? She didn't say the doctors had told her something they hadn't told me. Or, did she?'

'Ah, no, sir. Mrs Kirwen never said you were going to die. 'Tis not Mrs Kirwen's fault at all. 'Tis my fault, and I'm very sorry now.'

'Tell me Mrs Leahy. Do you dislike me?'

'Oh, no, sir.'

'Then why did you tell these people that I'm going to die?'

'Ah, well, sir, that's a long story. And I'm very sorry to be bringing you news like that. But them doctors don't know every-thing, now do they?'

'What do you mean?' He was shouting, but he could not stop himself. 'Just exactly what the hell do you mean, Mrs Leahy?'

Mrs Leahy, avoiding his eye, stared down at her joined hands. 'Well, sir, you see, I have something now, something not many people have. And there's times I wish I didn't, let me tell you.'

'Didn't what? Didn't have what?'

'I have the sight, sir. The second sight.'

'Second sight?' Chipman repeated the words with the joy of a man repeating the punch line of a joke. 'Well. And there I was . . .' Beginning to shake with amusement, he lifted his glass and drank a great swallow of whisky. 'You mean you dreamed it, or something like that?'

'Yes, sir. Last Monday, the night before your operation.'

'Now let me get this straight,' Chipman said. 'Mrs Kirwen told you nothing except what you've told me. The truth is nobody *knows* I have cancer. There's absolutely no proof of it at all.'

'That's right, sir.'

'My God, do you realise the mischief you've caused?'

'I'm very sorry, now. I see I shouldn't have said anything. I beg your pardon, sir.'

'It was a disgraceful thing to do!'

'Yes, sir. I'm sorry, sir. Maybe I should give you my notice?'

'No, no.' Chipman poured himself a second drink. Suddenly, he felt like laughing again. 'Well, now,' he said. Unconsciously, and for the first time in their acquaintance, he found himself slipping into an imitation of her Irish brogue. 'And how long have you had this ''sight''?'

'Ah, a long time, now. I noticed it first when I was only fourteen.'

'You dream about things and then they happen, is that it?'

'In a way, sir.'

'What do you mean? Tell me.'

'I'd rather not, now, sir. I'm sorry about speaking to those people. I only meant it for your sake, sir.'

'Now, wait. I'm just interested in this premonition of yours. Now, what happened in my case? You had a dream?'

'Yes, just the dream, sir. Nothing else.'

'What do you mean, nothing else?'

'Well you see, first there's the dream. And then, later on, you see, there's a second sign.'

'And what's this second sign?'

'It's a look I do see on the person's face.'

'A look?'

'Yes. When the trouble is very close.'

Chipman, in the act of downing his second Scotch, looked at her over the rim of his glass. Ignorant, stupid old creature with her hedgehog eyes and butterfat brogue. Some primitive folk nonsense, typically Irish, he supposed; it was their religion that encouraged these fairy-tales. 'When it's close,' he said. 'What does that mean?'

'When it's close to the time, sir.'

'So, I take it you haven't seen this look on my face. Not yet.'

'That's right, sir.'

'When do you think you'll see it?'

'I don't know that, sir. Better not be asking me things like that. It's no pleasure to me to be seeing the things I do see. That's the God's own truth, sir.'

'But how do you know you'll see it? Do you always see it after you have this dream?'

'I'd say so, sir.'

'Give me an example.'

'Well, I saw it on my own sister, sir, the night before she died. I had a dream and saw her in the dream, and when I woke up she was sleeping in the bed with me and I lit the lamp and looked at her face. I saw it in her face. And the very next night she was killed by a bus on her way home. I was fourteen at the time.'

'Tell me about another time.'

'Ah, now, what's the use, sir?'

'No, you started this, Mrs Leahy. I want to hear more.'

'And I don't want to tell you, sir.'

'But you told Mrs Kirwen and Mr Geddes and my nephew. You weren't afraid to tell them this fairy-tale.'

'Ah, I didn't tell them that at all, sir. Sure they wouldn't believe it. I just said I had information, I couldn't say more. But that the doctors were very worried about you.'

'*Did* you?' Again, he felt furious at her. 'How dare you, Mrs Leahy!'

'I'm sorry, sir. I wanted to be a help to you, sir. I mean I wanted Mrs Kirwen, and your family and all, to be good to you now in your time of trouble.'

I must *not* lose my temper with a servant, Chipman told himself. 'All right,' he said. 'You told me about your sister. Give me another example.'

'My husband, sir, God rest his soul. I dreamed about him June second, 1946, and he was took on the second of November, the same year. And on the first of November I saw the look on his face. I begged him not to go to work the next day, but he didn't heed me. He fell off a scaffolding. He never lived to see a priest.'

'Wait,' Chipman said. 'Both these deaths were from accidents, not illnesses.'

'Yes, sir.'

'Well, have you had any premonitions about deaths from illness?'

'Well, Jimmy, one of the doormen in this building. I saw him in a dream four months before he died of heart disease. And on the day he was taken I went to see him in the hospital. And I saw the look on him.'

'Indeed.' Slowly, Chipman finished his Scotch.

'Of course, 'tis not always departures. Deaths. Sometimes I do see arrivals. Do you remember, sir, the night you came home from Washington, last New Year's it was? I had your dinner waiting for you. I dreamed the night before that you would come at nine, wanting your dinner. And you did.'

As a matter of fact, Chipman thought, I remember it well. I remember thinking she'd prepared that roast lamb for herself and some crony. Extra-sensory perception, premonition: of course all that was only one jump away from teacup reading, table turning, spiritualistic quacks. But she dreamed of my death.

'So, Mrs Leahy. You dreamed of me, again, the other night. But this time it wasn't about my arrival?'

She nodded.

'Tell me the dream.'

'Ah, don't be asking, sir.'

'But I am asking. If you go around telling false stories to people about my death, you have the obligation to tell me the truth about what prompted you to do it. Now, what did you see in this dream?'

'I saw the shroud, sir. You came in the room and you were wearing the shroud.'

'A shroud. That means death.'

'Yes, sir.'

'When?'

'Ah, now, I don't know that, sir.'

'But you will know, as soon as you see this look on my face, is that it?'

'Yes, sir. I'd know the time, then.'

'I see,' Chipman said. 'And now I suppose you'd like me to cross your palm with silver, so that you'll tell me when I must make my funeral arrangements. Well, Mrs Leahy, I'm going to disappoint you. A few minutes ago, when I thought of the mischief you've done and the worry you've caused my family and friends, I was quite prepared to let you go. But, believe me, I wouldn't let you go now for all the gold in Fort Knox. A year from now, Mrs Leahy, you and I will sit here together. We'll have a drink together, this time, this date, one year from now.'

'God willing and we will, sir.'

He stood up, suddenly feeling his drink, his chair making a screeching noise on the linoleum floor. 'And now,' he said, 'I'd better phone Mrs Kirwen and those other people and explain what's really happened.'

'Yes, sir. I'm very sorry.'

He went back into the library. There was no point in being angry with her, it was a joke really. He should be celebrating. The doctors weren't alarmed, and even if they found some malignancy, there are all sorts of treatments, cobalt bombs, chemotherapy and so on. To think that stupid old hedgehog had set all this in motion—Geddes, Buddy, even Geraldine. Poor Geraldine.

He went to his shelves, took down a volume of the *Encyclopaedia Britannica* and read and entry under *cancer*. He then read the entry under *clairvoyance*. When he had finished, he replaced the books and rang the bell.

'Yes, sir.'

She stood at the door, her uniform cap on straight, the perfect housekeeper, a treasure, his women friends said. 'I'd like some ice and water,' he said.

She nodded and smiled. Mrs Tiggy-winkle. When she came back with the tray, he tried to affect a bantering tone. 'Now, just in theory, mind you, just for curiosity's sake. When do you think you'll see that look on my face?'

'I don't know, sir. I hope it will be a long, long time off. Was there anything else, sir?'

'No.'

'Goodnight, sir.'

She bobbed her head in her usual half-curtsey of withdrawal. When she had gone he made himself a fresh drink, then went to the window and stood looking down at Fifth Avenue. People in evening dress were getting out of rental Cadillac limousines in front of his building, laughing and joking, going to some function.

An hour later, he was still standing there. The room behind him was quite dark. He heard no sound in the apartment. He walked into the lighted hallway and went towards the kitchen. She was not there. He went past the kitchen, going towards her room. He stood in front of her door, trembling with excitement. He knocked.

'Yes, sir.'

She was sitting in her armchair, stitching the hem of an apron. The television set had been turned off.

'You were waiting for me, weren't you?'

'No, sir. Would you be wanting dinner, sir?'

'You should know I don't want dinner. I thought knowing things like that was one of your specialities.'

She bent to her sewing.

'Mrs Leahy, I want to ask you something. What if I fired you tonight? You'd never see the look, would you?'

'I suppose not, sir.'

'Then you'd never know if you'd been right. I mean supposing you never saw my death in the paper. You wouldn't know, would you?'

She bit the edge of her thread.

'Well, answer me.'

'Yes, sir, I'd know.'

'Look at me!' Even to himself, his voice sounded strange. 'You haven't looked at me since I came into the room.'

She folded the apron, placed it on the sewing-table and turned round. He went towards her, his face drained. As her eyes met his, he thought again of an animal. An animal does not think: it knows or it does not know. He sat on the edge of a worn sofa, facing her.

'Well?' His voice was hoarse.

'Well what, sir?'

'You know what. Am I still all right?'

'Yes, sir.'

'Mrs Leahy,' he said. 'You wouldn't lie to me, would you? I mean, you'd tell me if you saw it?'

'I suppose so, sir. I might be afraid to worry you, though.'

His hands gripped hers. 'No, no, I want to know. You must tell me. Promise me you'll tell me when the time comes?'

Tears, the unfamiliar tears of dependence, blurred his vision: made the room tremble. Gently, she nodded her head.

HOLY BLOOD

Peter Tremayne

Peter Tremayne (1943–) combines Celtic scholarship with proven story-telling ability in producing works of fiction that often focus on the murderous and mysterious in Irish history. His major fictional creation is undoubtedly Sister Fidelma, a spirited seventh-century Irish dálaigh, or advocate of the law, who has earned the reputation as a skilled solver of mysteries in six novels (which began in 1994 with Absolution by Murder*) and 14 short stories of which 'Holy Blood' is the latest. The cases of Fidelma have been published on both sides of the Atlantic, translated into German, French, Italian and Greek, and it was recently said of her in the* Irish Post, *'Sister Fidelma is fast becoming a world ambassador for ancient Irish culture.'*

Tremayne, whose real name is Peter Berresford Ellis, is the son of a journalist from Cork City, and took a first class honours degree in Celtic Studies followed by a master's degree. Like his father, he worked for some years as a journalist before branching out into the world of books and his first work, A History of the Irish Working Class *(1972) is now regarded as a classic. Tremayne has subsequently utilised his original research material from contemporary Irish sources as the basis of his fiction. In this latest case Sister Fidelma is travelling through what is now modern Belgium, but in AD 665 was the land of the Franks, when she literally walks into the scene of a brutal murder . . .*

*   *   *

'Sister Fidelma! How came you here?'

The Abbess Ballgel, standing at the gate of the Abbey of Nivelles, stared at the dusty figure of the young *religieuse* with open-mouthed surprise.

'I am returning home to Kildare, Ballgel,' replied the tall, slimly built figure, a broad smile of greeting on her travel-stained features. 'I have been in Rome a while, and where else should I come when passing through the land of the Franks on my way to the coast?'

To the surprise of two elderly *religieuses* standing just behind the abbess, Ballgel and Sister Fidelma threw their arms around one another and hugged each other with unconcealed joy.

'It is a long time,' observed the abbess.

'Indeed, a long time. I have not seen you since you departed Kildare and left the shores of Éireann to come to this place. Now I am told that you are the abbess.'

'The community elected me to that honour.'

Sister Fidelma became aware that the two sisters who accompanied the abbess were fretting impatiently. She was surprised at their grim faces and anxiety. Abbess Ballgel caught her swift examination of her companions. The group had been leaving the abbey when Fidelma had come upon them.

'I am afraid that you have chosen a bad moment to arrive, Fidelma. We are on our way to the Forest of Seneffe, a little way down the road there. You didn't come by that route, did you?'

Fidelma shook her head.

'No. I came over the hills from Namur where I arrived by boat along the river.'

'Ah!' The abbess looked serious and then she forced a smile. 'Go in and accept our hospitality, Fidelma. I hope to be back before nightfall and then we will talk and catch up on each other's news.'

Fidelma drew her brows together, sensing a preoccupation in the abbess' voice and manner.

'What is the matter?' she demanded. 'There is something vexing you.'

Ballgel grimaced.

'You had ever a keen eye, Fidelma. A report has just arrived that one of our sisters has been found murdered in the Forest of Seneffe and another member of our community is missing. We are hurrying there now to discover the truth of this report. So go and rest yourself from your travels and I will join you later.'

Fidelma shook her head quickly.

'Mother Abbess,' she said softly, 'it has been a long time and perhaps you have forgotten. I spent eight years studying law under the Brehon Morann. I have an aptitude for solving conundrums and investigating mysteries. Let me come with you and I will lend you what talent I have to resolve this matter.'

Fidelma and Ballgel had been novices together in the Abbey of Kildare.

'I remember your talent well, Fidelma. In fact, I have often heard your name spoken for we receive many travellers from Éireann here. By all means come with us.'

Indeed, Ballgel looked slightly relieved.

'And you may explain the details of this matter as we go,' Fidelma said, putting down her travelling bag within the gate of the abbey before joining the others.

They set off, walking side by side, with the two other *relig-ieuses* bringing up the rear.

'Who has been reported murdered?' Fidelma began.

'I do not know. I know that early this morning Sister Cessair and Sister Della set off for the Abbey of Fosse. It is the seventeenth day of March and so they were taking the phial of the Holy Blood of Blessed Gertrude to the brothers of Fosse for the annual blessing and . . .'

Fidelma laid a hand on her friend's arm.

'You are raising more questions than I can keep pace with, Ballgel. Remember that I am a stranger here.'

The abbess was apologetic.

'Let me start at the beginning then. Twenty-five years ago the ruler of this land, Peppin the Elder of Landen, died. His widow, Itta, decided to devote herself to a religious life and came here, to Nivelles, with her daughter, Gertrude. They built our abbey. When Itta died, the Blessed Gertrude became abbess.

'About that time two brothers from Éireann, Foillan and Ultan, came wandering and preaching the word of God. They decided to stay and Gertrude granted them lands a few miles from here in Fosse, the other side of the Forest of Seneffe. Foillan and Ultan gathered many Irish religious there and some were attracted to our abbey as well. It is said that the Blessed Foillan prophesied that Abbess Gertrude, because she so loved and encouraged the Irish missionaries, would die on the same day that the Blessed Patrick died. And it happened as he said it would seven years ago today.'

Abbess Ballgel grew silent for a while until Fidelma encouraged her to continue.

'So Foillan proved to be a prophet?'

'He did not live to see his prophecy fulfilled for he died four years before his beloved Gertrude. He and his three companions were travelling from his abbey of Fosse though the very same forest that we are entering—the Forest of Seneffe—when they were set upon by robbers and murdered. Their bodies were so well hidden in the forest that it took three months before anyone stumbled across them. Foillan's brother Ultan then became the abbot.

'When the Blessed Gertrude died it was agreed between the two abbeys that, as she was the benefactor of both, each anniversary of her death, a phial of her holy blood, taken from her at death to be held behind the high altar at our abbey, would be taken to the abbey of Fosse and blessed by the abbot in service with his community and returned here. This was the task which Sister Cessair and Sister Della set out to fulfil this morning.'

'How did you hear that a sister had been murdered in the forest?'

'When midday came, the time of the service at Fosse, and no members of our community had arrived with the Holy Blood, Brother Sinsear, a brother from the Fosse abbey, set out to see what delayed them. He found the dead body of one of the sisters by the roadside. He came straight away to us to tell us and then immediately returned to alert the community at Fosse.'

'But you do not know which of the poor sisters was killed?'
The abbess shook her head.

'Brother Sinsear was too agitated to say but merely told our gatekeeper the news before returning.'

By now they had entered the dark and brooding Forest of Seneffe. The track was fairly straight though at times it twisted around rocky outcrops and avoided streams to find a ford in a more accessible place. The afternoon sun was obliterated by the heavy foliage and the day grew cold around them, Fidelma realised that the highway proved an ideal ambush spot for any robbers and it did not surprise her to hear that lives had been lost along this roadway.

Although Irish religious went out into the world unarmed to preach the Faith, most of them were taught the art of *troid-sciathagid* or battle through defence—a method of defending oneself without the use of weapons. Not many religious, thus prepared, fell to bands of marauding thieves and robbers. Clearly, from their names the two sisters had been Irish and must have known some rudiments of the art for it was the custom to have such knowledge before being allowed to take the holy word from the shores of Éireann into the lands of the strangers.

Now they walked silently and swiftly along the forest track, eyes anxiously scanning for any dangers around them.

'Is it not a dangerous path for young sisters to travel?' observed Fidelma after a while.

'Not more so than other places,' her friend replied. 'Do not let the death of Foillan colour your thinking. Since his death a decade ago, the robbers were driven from these parts and there have been no further incidents.'

'Until now,' Fidelma added grimly.

'Until now,' sighed Ballgel.

A moment or so later, they rounded a clump of trees which the path had skirted. Not far away they saw a group of religious. There were four or five and they had a cart with them, harnessed to an ass. They clustered under a gnarled oak whose branches formed a canopy over the pathway, so low that one might almost reach up and grab the lower branches. It made this particular section of the forest path even more gloomy and full of shadows.

A tall, florid man, wearing a large gold cross, and clearly one of authority, saw Abbess Ballgel and came hurrying forward.

'Greetings, Mother Abbess. This is a bad business—a profane business.' He spoke in Latin but Fidelma could hear his Frankish accent.

'Abbot Heribert of Fosse,' Ballgel whispered to Fidelma as he approached.

'Where is the body?' Ballgel came straight to the point, also speaking in Latin.

Abbot Heribert looked uncomfortable.

'I would prepare yourself . . .' he began.

'I have seen death before,' replied Abbess Ballgel quietly.

He turned and indicated the far side of the oak tree.

Ballgel hurried forward in the direction of his hand, followed by Fidelma.

The body was tied to the oak tree on the far side from the path, almost in mockery of a crucifixion. There was blood everywhere. Fidelma screwed her features up in distaste. The woman, who was dressed in the habit of a *religieuse*, had been systematically mutilated about the face .

'Cut her down!' cried the sharp tone of the Abbess Ballgel. 'At once! Do not leave the poor girl hanging there!'

Two of the monks went forward grimly.

'Who is it?' Fidelma asked. 'Do you recognise her?'

'Oh yes. We have only one sister with hair as golden as that. It is young Sister Cessair. God be merciful to her soul.' She genuflected.

Fidelma pursed her lips thoughtfully. She watched as two male religious cut down the body.

'Wait!' she called and, turning to the abbess, said quickly, 'I would examine the body carefully and with some privacy.'

Ballgel raised her eyes in surprise.

'I do not understand.'

'This is a bizarre matter. It might be that she has been . . . brutalised.'

Ballgel passed a hand across her brow as if bewildered but she understood what Fidelma meant.

She called to the monks to set the body down on the ground before the cart and then asked Abbot Heribert to withdraw his men to a respectful distance while Fidelma made her investigation.

Fidelma knelt by the body, noticing that the shade of the oak tree stopped the sun's rays from drying the ground. It was muddy and the mud had been churned by the cart and the footprints of those trampling round. Her attention was momentarily distracted by indentations of two feet at one point, which were far deeper than the others to the extent that water had formed in the hollows. Nevertheless, she ignored the mud and bent over the body. She turned and motioned the Abbess Ballgel to come closer.

'If you will observe and witness my examination, Ballgel,' she called over her shoulder. 'You will observe that the sister's face has been severely mutilated with a knife. The skin has been deliberately marked with a sharp blade, disfiguring it, as if the purpose were to destroy the features of this young girl.'

Ballgel forced herself to look and nodded, suppressing a soft groan of anguish.

Fidelma bent further to her work before pausing, satisfied with her physical examination. Then she turned her attention to the small leather *marsupium* which hung at the dead sister's waist. It was not secured with the leather thong that usually fastened such a purse and it was empty.

Fidelma rose to her feet. Next she went to the tree from which the body had been taken and began to look about. With a gasp of triumph she bent down and picked up a torn scrap of paper. There was no writing but a few curious short lines had been drawn on it. Fidelma frowned and placed it in her *marsupium*.

Her keen eye then caught a round stone on the ground. It was bloody and pieces of hair and skin were stuck to it.

'What is it?' demanded Abbess Ballgel coming forward.

'That is the instrument with which Cessair was killed,' Fidelma explained. 'Her death was caused by her skull being smashed in

and not through the blade of the knife that destroyed her features.
At least this was no attack by robbers.'

'How can you be so certain?'

'We have observed that the girl was not sexually molested in
any way. Yet this was an attack of hate towards the sister.'

Ballgel stared at her friend in amazement.

'How can you say it was an attack of hate?'

'Let us discount the idea of robbers. The purpose of a thief is
to steal. It is true that some thieves have been known to sexually
assault even sisters of the faith. There was no attempt at theft
here. The sister's crucifix of silver still hangs around her neck.
It was not a sexual assault. What is left of the motivation which
would cause someone to smash her skull, tie her to a tree and
mutilate her features? There is surely only hatred left?'

'The Holy Blood of the Blessed Gertrude is not in her *marsupium*,' Ballgel pointed out. 'I have been looking all around for
the phial. That is valuable; but above all, where is Sister Della?'

Fidelma grimaced.

'The Holy Blood may be valuable to you, yes. Not to a thief.
There would be no purpose is stealing that if one wanted money.'

'Do thieves and robbers need a purpose?'

'All people need a purpose, even those whom we deem mad
follow a logic, which may not be our logic but one of their own
creation with its own rules. Once one deciphers the code of that
logic then it is as easy to follow as any.'

'And what of Sister Della?'

Fidelma nodded. 'There is the real mystery. Find her and we
may find the missing phial. Has a search been made for her?'
She asked the question of the abbot.

Abbot Heribert looked sourly at Fidelma.

'Not yet. And who are you?'

'Sister Fidelma is a qualified advocate of our legal courts,'
explained Abbess Ballgel hurriedly.

A look of derision crossed the abbot's face.

'Do women have such a status in your country?' he demanded
in astonishment.

'Is that so strange?' Fidelma replied irritably. 'Anyway, we waste time. We must find Sister Della for she may be in danger. If Sister Cessair was not robbed, and was not attacked for sexual motives, the alternative is that she was killed from some personal motive which, judging from the savagery of the attack, shows a depth of malice that makes me shudder. Who could have been so angered by her that they would attempt to destroy her beauty? It is as if she were attacked by a jealous lover for it is known that hate and love are two sides of the same coin.'

Fidelma suddenly saw Abbot Heribert's eyes widen a fraction. She saw him glance swiftly at Ballgel and then drop his gaze.

'Why does the mention of a lover have some special meaning for you?' she demanded.

It was Abbess Ballgel who answered for him.

'Sister Cessair did have a . . . a liaison,' she said quietly.

'It was disgusting!' grunted Abbot Heribert.

'A curious choice of word?' Fidelma's eyes narrowed. 'Disgusting in what way?'

'Abbot Heribert is a firm believer in the concept of celibacy,' explained Ballgel.

'Celibacy is by no means universally approved of by the Church,' Fidelma pointed out. 'There are many double houses where religious of both sexes live and raise their children to the service of God. What is disgusting about that?'

'Paul of Tarsus spoke firmly in favour of celibacy and many other Church Fathers have done so. There are those of us who argue that only through celibacy do we have the power to spread the Faith.'

'I am not here to discuss theology, Heribert. Are you telling me that Cessair was in love with a religious from your abbey of Fosse?'

'God forgive him,' Heribert lowered his head piously.

'Only him?' Was there sarcasm in Fidelma's voice? 'Surely forgiveness is universal. Who was this monk?'

'Brother Cano,' replied Ballgel. 'He was a young monk who arrived from Éireann only a few weeks ago. It seems that he and Sister Cessair met and were immediately attracted by one another.'

'And this relationship was disapproved of?'

'It did not matter to me,' Ballgel said hastily. 'Our culture does not forbid such relationships as you have pointed out. Even Kildare, where we studied, was a mixed house.'

'But it mattered to Abbot Heribert.' Fidelma swung round on the tall Frankish prelate.

'Of course it mattered. My abbey of Fosse is for men of the Faith only. I follow the strict rule of celibacy and expect all members of my community to do the same. I warned Brother Cano several times to cease this disgusting alliance. Abbess Ballgel knew my views. It does not surprise me that this woman of loose morals has paid a bitter price.'

Fidelma raised her eyebrows in surprise.

'That is also an interesting statement. You seem given to much passion over this matter, Father Abbot.'

Heribert frowned suspiciously at her.

'What do you mean?'

'I merely make an observation. Does it worry you that I comment on the passionate tones in which you denounce this poor sister?'

'I believe in the teachings of Paul of Tarsus.'

'Yet it is not the rule of the Church. Nor, indeed, does the Holy Father denounce those who reject celibacy. It is not even a rule of our Faith.'

'Not yet. But the ranks of those of us who believe in the segregation of men and woman and the rule of celibacy are increasing. One day the Holy Father will have to pay us heed. Already he has suggested that celibacy is the best way forward...'

'Until that happens, it is not a rule. Very well, I understand your position now. But we have a murder to solve. Where is this Brother Cano?'

Abbot Heribert shrugged.

'I understand from brother Sinsear that Brother Cano left the abbey this morning and was last seen heading along this road. Perhaps he came to meet Sister Cessair?'

Abbess Ballgel groaned softly.

'If Cano was coming to meet Sister Cessair . . . if he could do this to her . . . we must find Sister Della!'

Fidelma gave her a reassuring smile.

'No one has said that Cano did this as yet,' she observed quietly. 'However, it seems that, as well as the missing sister, we also have a missing brother to account for. Perhaps we will find one with the other. Can we speak with this Brother Sinsear?'

A religious who was standing nearby coughed nervously and took a hesitant step towards her. He was a pale-faced young man, hardly more than an adolescent youth. His features were taut and he appeared in the grip of strong emotions.

'I am Sinsear.'

Fidelma regarded his flushed, anxious face.

'You appear agitated, brother.'

'I work with Brother Cano in the gardens of our abbey, sister. I am his friend. I knew that he had a . . .' he glanced nervously at his abbot, '. . . a passion for Sister Cessair.'

'A passion? You do not have to bandy words, brother. Was he in love with her?'

'I only knew that they met at regular times in the forest because of Father Abbot's disapproval of their relationship.'

Abbot Heribert's brows drew together in anger but Fidelma held up a hand to silence him.

'Go on, Brother Sinsear. What are you saying?'

'They had a special meeting spot in a glade not far distant from here. A woodman's hut. It occurs to me, in these circumstances, that the hut might be searched.'

'You should have spoken up sooner, brother,' snapped Abbot Heribert. 'Cano may have fled by now. I see no point in seeking him in that hut.'

'You are presuming that he is guilty of this deed, Heribert,' Fidelma rebuked him. 'Yet I think we should investigate this hut. Do you know the way to it, Brother Sinsear?'

'I think so. There is a small path leading off this track about fifty metres in that direction.' He pointed towards Fosse, and on the far side of the track from the oak tree where Cessair had been found.

'How far into the forest?'

'No more than three hundred metres.'

'Then lead the way. Father Abbot, you may send the rest of the brothers of your community to escort the sisters and the body of Cessair back to the abbey of Nivelles.'

Heribert made to object, hesitated and then obeyed.

Brother Sinsear turned pale eyes on Fidelma.

'Could Cano really have done such a terrible deed? Oh God, to maltreat such grace and beauty! Why did she not give her love to one who would appreciate such exquisite . . .'

Abbot Heribert interrupted impatiently.

'Let us get a move on, Brother Sinsear. I expect it will be a waste of time. If Cano killed Cessair then he will not be hiding in a forest hut but will have fled the area by now.'

With the young Brother Sinsear leading the way, they trod a well-worn track through the great forest.

They were soon in a little glade, a pleasant spot through which a small stream meandered. By it stood a woodman's crude hut. The door was shut and there was no sign of life. As they neared the door of the hut, Fidelma's keen eyes surveyed it quickly. The first thing she noticed was bloodstains on the door jamb and there were several palm prints on the door as if someone, with bloodied hands, had pushed it open.

They heard a sobbing sound from within.

'Brother Cano!' Sinsear suddenly called. 'The abbot and I are here.'

There was silence. The sobbing suddenly halted. Fidelma glanced at the impetuous young man in irritation.

'Sinsear?' came a hesitant male voice. 'Thank God! I need help.'

There was another sound now. A feminine cry which sounded as if it were stifled almost immediately.

Fidelma signalled her companions to halt.

'Stay back. I shall go in first.' She turned and raised her voice. 'Brother Cano? I am Fidelma of Kildare. I have come to help you. I am coming in.'

There was no response.

Slowly Fidelma leant forward, placing her hand near the bloodied imprint, and pushed against the door. It swung open easily.

At the far end of the woodman's hut she saw a young man clad in religious robes, kneeling on the floor. His hair was dishevelled, his eyes red and cheeks stained as if from weeping. He held a piece of bloodstained cloth in his hands. Before him lay the prone figure of a girl. Her eyes were open and she appeared conscious but her clothes were covered in blood.

Fidelma felt the others crowding behind her.

'Stay back!' she snapped. There was such a power in her voice that they paused. 'I will speak with Cano and Sister Della first.'

Fidelma took a step into the hut.

'I am Sister Fidelma,' she repeated. 'May I attend to Sister Della?'

'Of course.' the young man seemed bewildered at her question.

Fidelma knelt by his side. He had been trying to cleanse her wounds.

'Lie still,' she said, as she examined the wound of the young *religieuse*. It was to the back of the head. Sister Della had been clubbed there in the same fashion as Sister Cessair. Unlike the blow delivered to Cessair's skull, it had not broken the bone of the skull. There was, however, a nasty swelling.

'Am I dying, sister?' the girl's voice was faint.

'No. In a moment we will get you back to the abbey so that you may be properly attended. What can you tell me about the attack on Sister Cessair and yourself?'

'Little enough.'

'A little in these circumstances may mean a lot,' encouraged Fidelma.

'Alas, the little is nothing. Sister Cessair and I were bringing the phial of the Holy Blood of Blessed Gertrude to the Abbey of Fosse. We were walking through the woods. I remember . . .' she paused and sighed. 'I did not hear anyone behind us for we were talking together and . . .' She held up a hand to her head and groaned. 'There came a sharp blow and then I can remember nothing until I came to, lying on the path with a blinding pain in my head. I thought I was alone. I could see no one. I began to look around and then, then I saw Cessair...'

She gave a heartrending sob.

'What then?' prompted Fidelma gently.

'I could do nothing for her, except try to get help. I came here and...'

'You came here?' Fidelma interrupted quickly. 'Why come to this woodman's hut? Why not go on to the abbey of Fosse or back to Nivelles?'

'I knew Cano would be here.' The girl groaned again.

'She knew that I had arranged to meet Cessair here on the journey from Nivelles to Fosse,' interrupted Cano defiantly. 'I am not ashamed of it.'

Fidelma ignored him and smiled down at the girl.

'Rest a while. It will not be long before we have you safe and your wound properly attended to.'

Only then did she turn to Cano.

'So you were waiting here for Cessair?'

'Cessair and I loved one another. We often met here because Abbot Heribert was vehement against us.'

'Tell me about it.'

'There is not much to tell. I arrived at Fosse about a month ago to join the community. Although there are several Irish religious here and in Nivelles, it is a strange land. They are more inclined to celibacy than we are in Éireann. They do not have the number of mixed houses that we do. Abbot Heribert was fanatical for the rule of celibacy; even though there is no such proscription in the Church, he makes it a rule in his abbey. I think I would have left long ago had I not met Cessair.'

'When did you and Cessair meet?'

'The week after I came here. It was Brother Sinsear who introduced me when we were taking produce from Fosse to Nivelles.'

'Brother Sinsear introduced you?'

'Yes. As a gardener, Sinsear often took produce between the two abbeys. He knew many of the *religieuses* at Nivelles.'

'Did Cessair have any enemies that you knew of?'

'Only Abbot Heribert. That was when he discovered our relationship.' Cano's voice was bitter. From the doorway, Fidelma heard Heribert's suppressed expression of anger.

'Why didn't you leave and move on to a mixed house?'

'We planned to but Abbess Ballgel counselled Cessair against it.'

Fidelma was surprised.

'Why would she be against such a plan?'

Cano shrugged.

'She was . . . protective to Cessair. She felt Cessair was too young.'

'More protective to Cessair than to her other charges?'

'I do not know. All I know is that we were desperate and planning to leave here.'

Fidelma waited a while. Then she said abruptly:

'Did you kill Cessair?'

The young monk raised a tear-stained face to her and there was a haunted look in his eyes.

'How can you ask such a question?'

'Because I am a *dálaigh*, an advocate of the law,' replied Fidelma. 'It is my duty to ask.'

'I did not.'

'Tell me what happened this morning, then.'

'I knew that Cessair and Della were bringing the phial to Fosse for the annual blessing. So we arranged to meet here.'

'Surely that would mean a delay in the bringing of the phial to Fosse? The service was at midday.'

'Cessair was going to persuade Della to take the phial on to Fosse while she joined me here. We only meant to meet briefly to make some arrangements and then the idea was that Cessair would join Della at Fosse, pretending that she had broken her sandal on the road.'

'So you came here . . . ?'

'And here I waited. I thought Cessair was late and was about to go down to the main track to see if there was a sign of her coming when Della came stumbling into the hut. She was almost hysterical and told me what had happened, then she passed out.

I could not leave her alone and have been trying to return her to consciousness ever since. It is only a moment ago that she regained her senses.'

Fidelma turned to Della.

'Do you agree with this account?'

The girl had raised herself on an elbow; she still looked pale and shaken.

'So far as I am able. I do not remember much at all.'

'Very well. Then I think we should get you to the abbey where you may have the wound tended.' Then she remembered the phial.

'Do you have the phial of blood, Sister Della? The Holy Blood of the Blessed Gertrude?'

Della frowned and shook her head.

'Cessair carried it in her *marsupium*.'

'I see,' replied Fidelma thoughtfully. She told Sinsear to help Cano carry Sister Della and suggested that they go to Fosse first.

The church and community of Fosse was not as spectacular as some of the abbeys which Fidelma had encountered in her travels. She reminded herself that it was barely twenty years old. It was no more than a collection of timber houses around a large, rectangular wooden church.

Sister Della was immediately taken to the infirmary while the abbot led the abbess and Fidelma to the refectory for refreshments. Brother Sinsear and Brother Cano were told to go to their cells and await the abbot's call.

Abbess Ballgel was the first to break the uneasy silence that had fallen.

'Well, Fidelma, do you see a solution to this horror? And where is the Holy Blood of Gertrude?'

'Let us summarise what we know. We can eliminate certain things. Firstly, the concept that this action was committed by robbers. I have already given the main reason, that is the mutilation of Cessair. That was done from hate. Secondly, we have the testimony of Della who says that she was walking along talking with Cessair and did not hear or see anything until she was struck from behind.'

'You mean, if there had been robbers waiting in ambush then she would have seen something of them?'

'Just so. The very idea of even a single person creeping up unobserved behind someone walking in a forest is, I find, rather a difficult one to accept.'

Abbess Ballgel frowned quickly.

'You claim that Sister Della is lying?'

'Not necessarily. But think of it in this way: think of a forest path strewn with dead leaves, twigs and the like. An animal might move quietly over such a carpet, but can a human? Could a man or woman creep up so quickly behind someone walking along and strike them before they knew it?'

'Then we must question the girl further,' snapped Heribert, 'and force her to confess.'

Fidelma looked at him in disapproval.

'Confess to what?'

'Why, to the killing of Cessair,' replied Heribert.

Fidelma gave a deep sigh.

'There is another more plausible explanation why Sister Della did not hear her assailant creep up behind her.'

The abbot frowned in anger.

'What game are you playing? First you say one thing and then you say another. I do not follow.'

The Abbess Ballgel intervened as she saw Fidelma's facial muscles go taut and her eyes narrow.

'I suggest we allow Fidelma to follow her path of reasoning.'

The abbot sat back, his face set in a sneer.

'Proceed, then.'

'Let us proceed along another route first. The savagery with which Sister Cessair was attacked, the fact that her features were mutilated, the fact that Sister Della was left unmarked except for the blow that laid her unconscious, all indicate that Cessair was, indeed, singled out particularly. She was, as I said before, attacked out of some great malice towards her.'

'It seems logical, Fidelma,' agreed the abbess.

'Then we must consider who had such a hatred of Cessair.'

She paused and allowed them to consider her proposal in silence.

'Well, we can eliminate almost everyone.' The abbess smiled briefly.

'How so?'

'Cessair made no enemies . . . except . . .'

She suddenly hesitated.

'Except?' encouraged Fidelma gently.

The abbess had dropped her eyes.

It was Abbot Heribert who flushed with anger.

'Except me, you mean?' He rose to his feet. 'What are you implying? Because I uphold the teaching of celibacy? Because I forbid any liaison with women among the members of my community? Because I urged the abbess to forbid Sister Cessair to see Brother Cano as I had also forbidden him to meet with her? Are these things to be thrown at me in accusation that I murdered her?'

'Did you?'

Fidelma asked the question so quietly that for a long time it seemed that the abbot had not heard her.

'How dare you!'

'I dare because I must,' replied Fidelma calmly. 'Keep your bluster to yourself, abbot. We are here to discover the truth, not to engage in games of vanity.'

Heribert was inarticulate with rage.

The Abbess Ballgel leant forward to calm him.

'Abbot Heribert, we are simply intelligent people trying to resolve a problem. Our pride and self-regard should not impinge on that process for we are seeking the truth and only the truth.'

Abbot Heribert blinked.

'I resent being accused . . .'

'I did not accuse you, Heribert,' Fidelma replied. 'Your unthinking pride did so. But, since you have raised this matter yourself, I put it to you that you certainly had no liking for Cessair.'

He stared at her and then shrugged.

'I have made that evident. I disliked her for she was a distraction to Brother Cano. Indeed, she was a distraction to all the young men in my community. I have even seen young men like Brother Sinsear moonstruck in her presence.'

'My mentor, the Brehon Morann of Tara, used to say it is easier to become a monk in one's old age,' sighed Fidelma. 'Anyway, as abbot you were expecting Sisters Cessair and Della to arrive at Fosse at noon, or so I am led to believe?'

'Not precisely. I was expecting two sisters of Abbess Ballgel's community to arrive but I did not know who they would be. Had I known one was going to be Sister Cessair . . .'

'What would you have done?'

'I should have stopped her coming to mislead Brother Cano further into temptation's way.'

'Cano was misled?' queried Fidelma. 'I thought he was in love with Cessair?'

'Women are the temptresses by which the saintly fall from grace.'

Fidelma realised it was impossible to overcome his misogynist prejudice and decided to ignore the remark.

'Ballgel, why did you choose Cessair and Della to bring the phial of blood for the service this morning?'

'Why did I . . . ?'

'Someone knew that Cessair was going to be walking along that forest track.'

The eyes of the abbess widened.

'It was Sister Della who came to me last night and asked if she might be allowed to take the phial for the blessing. She also asked me if she could choose a companion to accompany her.'

'You did not know that she would choose Cessair?'

'As a matter of fact,' confessed the abbess, 'I presumed that she would. They have been inseparable companions.'

'You knew that she would choose Cessair to accompany her through the Forest of Seneffe even though the abbot disapproved of Cessair? Isn't that strange?'

'Not at all. I am like you, Fidelma. I refuse to be dictated to as to whom I can send here or there.'

'So Sister Della was the only other person who knew Cessair would go with her, apart from yourself, Ballgel?'

Abbess Ballgel looked carefully at her friend.

'You will remember, Fidelma,' she said softly, 'that you arrived at Nivelles only a short time after Brother Sinsear had brought us the dreadful news.'

Fidelma smiled sympathetically.

'I do remember. And you need hardly remind me that you would have had no time to do the deed. Besides, it would be very difficult for an abbess to absent herself from her abbey for the time needed to carry out this murder.'

'It would likewise be difficult for an abbot to absent himself from his abbey,' Heribert added.

'I had not forgotten, Heribert,' Fidelma said solemnly. 'Tell us, as a matter of record, where you were about noon.'

Abbot Heribert hesitated and shrugged.

'I will play your game to the end,' he said tightly. 'Today being the anniversary of the death of the Blessed Gertrude, we have a midday angelus followed by a service of remembrance not only for Gertrude but in memory of the Blessed Foillan whom she allowed to build our abbey. The phial of the Holy Blood is brought to the abbey just before the midday angelus bell is sounded.

'At ten minutes before midday I was standing with several brothers awaiting the appearance of the two sisters who usually carry the phial from Nivelles. I did not know who they would be. When midday came and the bell was tolled, I thought that the only thing to do was proceed with the service although without the phial.'

'Did you send anyone to look for the sisters?'

'I was informed that Brother Sinsear had already left to escort the sisters through the forest. So I did not need to.'

'I see. Go on.'

'Well, we performed the service and when it was over there was no sign of the sisters nor of Brother Sinsear.'

'Brother Sinsear had come straight to Nivelles to alert us,' pointed out Ballgel.

'It was some time before Brother Sinsear returned,' agreed Heribert, 'and told us the appalling news, and we immediately set out for the forest. We had barely reached there when you arrived.'

'I see. Will you now send for Brother Sinsear?'

It was moments before they were joined by the young monk. The youth made an effort to overcome the nervous twisting of his hands by placing them behind his back.

'I know that you are upset,' Fidelma smiled gently. 'After all, it is your close friend who stands in some danger. The finger of suspicion points in his direction.'

'Brother Cano might be possessed of a temper but he would never . . . never . . .'

'He was quick-tempered?' Fidelma interrupted.

Brother Sinsear hung his head.

'I should not have said that. I meant . . .'

'I can confirm the truth of this,' observed Abbot Heribert. 'I have rebuked him a couple of times for his turbulent moods.'

'Well, all I want from you, Brother Sinsear, are the details about today. I understand that you left the abbey to go in search of the two sisters bringing the phial of Holy Blood? At what time was this?'

'Some time before midday, I think. Yes, it was half an hour before the midday angelus bell sounded because that was when the phial was due to be at the abbey.'

'Were you instructed to do so?'

Brother Sinsear shook his head.

'No. But knowing Cessair . . . well, I knew she would be in no hurry.'

There was a brief silence.

'You *knew* that one of the two sisters would be Cessair?' pressed Fidelma. 'How did you know?'

'Why, Brother Cano told me. We had few secrets. He left to go to the woodman's hut where he and Cessair usually met. I knew that this would delay them bringing the phial to the abbey. That was why I set off in good time to meet them and encourage them to hurry. Alas, I was too late.'

'You found Cessair dead?'

'I did. She was tied to the tree even as you saw her.'

'And Sister Della?'

'There was no sign of her. So I hurried straight to Nivelles to alert Abbess Ballgel.'

'Why did you do that?' Fidelma asked.

'Why?'

'There were other options. Why not rush back to Fosse and alert the Abbot Heribert?'

Sinsear grimaced.

'It is well know that Nivelles is closer to that point in the forest than is Fosse. Also I thought it more expedient to bring the news to Nivelles and then return to alert Fosse.'

'Have you been friends with Cano from the time he arrived in Fosse?'

'He was assigned to help me in the gardens and we became friends.'

'Yet you knew Cessair before Cano arrived?'

'I have met Cessair and Della as well as many others of the sisters of Nivelles. There is much intercourse between the abbeys. You see, I am employed in the gardens and my job is to take fruit and vegetables to Nivelles once a week.'

'Brother Sinsear is perfectly correct,' interrupted Heribert. 'Members of our community often go to Nivelles to help them with the heavy building work and the upkeep of their fields and crops. In fact, Brother Sinsear took produce to Nivelles only yesterday afternoon. Ah, but didn't Brother Cano accompany you?'

Brother Sinsear flushed and nodded reluctantly.

Fidelma pursed her lips thoughtfully.

'There is a further question that I must now ask Sister Della. Please wait for me here.'

In the infirmary Sister Della, although pale-faced and weak, was looking much improved.

'Sister Della,' Fidelma began without preamble. 'There is only one question I need ask you. Why did you especially ask to be allowed to take the phial of Holy Blood to Fosse today?'

'Sister Cessair asked me to.'

'Cessair, eh? Then it was not your idea?'

'No. Neither was it her idea, to be truthful. She knew that

there would be some argument with the abbot who disliked her, and was reluctant to go. However, Brother Cano had particularly asked her to come . . .'

'How had he asked? Had he not seen her yesterday?'

'No. He sent a note to Cessair asking her to come early to the hut so that he could spend a few moments with her to discuss their future.'

'Did you approve of her meetings with Cano?'

'I was Cessair's friend. I knew that there is no stopping the stupidities that love brings with it. And I thought it was only one question that you wished to ask?'

'So it was. Is this the note?' She pulled out the piece of torn paper from her *marsupium.*

Sister Della glanced at it and shrugged.

'I do not read Ogham,' she said, 'but I think it is part of the note. Cano and Cessair used the ancient form of Irish writing to write cryptic notes to one another.'

Fidelma turned back to the refectory.

'I think I have the solution to this mystery,' she announced as Abbess Ballgel and Abbot Heribert gazed up as she re-entered the room.

'Who then is guilty?' demanded Heribert.

'Ask Brother Cano to come here. You will remain, Brother Sinsear.'

'Brother Cano,' Fidelma began when the young man arrived, 'the future looks bleak for you.'

Cano grimaced in resignation.

'The future is empty for me,' he corrected. 'Without Cessair my life is indeed an abyss filled with pain.'

'Why did you ask Cessair to meet you today?'

'I have told you already. So that we could plan to go away together and find a mixed house where we could live and work together and, God willing, raise our children in his service.'

'Whose ideas was that?'

'Mine.'

'I thought that someone else might have suggested it to you as a solution to your problems,' Fidelma said quietly.

Cano frowned.

'It matters not who suggested it. That was the purpose of our rendezvous.'

'It does matter. Wasn't it Brother Sinsear who suggested that you should plan to leave here?'

'Perhaps. Sinsear has been a good friend. He saw that there was no future for us here.'

'You went with Brother Sinsear to Nivelles last evening to take garden produce. Why didn't you speak with Cessair then?'

'We arrived during the evening service and as there was no excuse to delay at Nivelles, I wrote Cessair a note in Ogham suggesting the meeting. I knew that Cessair could read the ancient Irish writing. I put the instructions in the note and left it with the gatekeeper.'

'Yes. It all fits now,' Fidelma sighed. She turned to the young brother. 'Sinsear, would you mind handing Abbess Ballgel the phial of the Holy Blood from your *marsupium*? The abbess has been fretful about it ever since she realised that it was missing.'

Brother Sinsear started, his face white. As if in a dream he opened his waist purse and handed it over.

'I found it on the ground . . . I meant to give it to you before . . .'

Fidelma's voice was sad.

'One of the most terrible passions is love turned to hatred because of rejection. A lover who sees the object of his love in love with a rival can sometimes be transformed into a fiend incarnate.'

Brother Cano looked astounded.

'Cessair did not reject me,' he exclaimed. 'I tell you again, I did not kill her. We planned to go away together.'

'It is to Sinsear that I refer,' replied Fidelma. 'It was Sinsear here whose love had turned to a rage that wanted to hurt and mutilate Cessair.'

Sinsear was staring at her open-mouthed.

'Sinsear here had been in love with Cessair for a long time. Being young and unable to articulate his love, he worshipped her from afar, dreaming of the day when he could summon up courage to declare himself. Then Cano arrived. At first the two were good friends. Then Sinsear introduced Cano to his love. Horror! Cano and Cessair fell truly in love. Day by day, Sinsear found himself watching their passion and his jealousy grew to such a peak at what he saw as Cessair's rejection of him, that his mind broke with the anguish. He would revenge himself on Cessair with such a vengeance that hell did not possess.'

Sinsear stood with his face drained of all emotion now.

'He suggested to Cano that he invite Cessair to a rendezvous in the hut and gave him the pretext of discussing a means of leaving the abbeys. Then he left Fosse in plenty of time to climb the old oak, hiding among the low-hanging branches, to await the arrival of Cessair and her companion. That was why Sister Della did not hear anyone approach them from behind. He jumped down. I saw the indentation of where he landed. He landed just behind Della and felled her with a blow before she knew it. Am I right?'

Sinsear did not respond.

'Perhaps then he revealed his twisted love to Cessair. Perhaps he begged her to go with him. Did she react in horror, did she laugh? How did she treat this frenzied would-be lover? We only know how it resulted. He struck her several blows on the head and then, in a gruesome ritual, which serves to demonstrate his immaturity, he decided to punish her beauty by which she had beguiled him by mutilating her face with a knife. Whether he tied her first to the tree or not, we do not know unless he tells us. But I have no doubt that she was dead by then.

'At some stage the phial of blood either fell from her purse or Sinsear took it. His religious training got the better of him for, instead of leaving it in Cessair's purse, he put it in his own for safe keeping. Knowing the missing phial was irrelevant to her murder, I could not account for its disappearance until I realised that I was searching for reasons which were not there.

'It may be that Sinsear heard Sister Della coming to. Whatever happened, he ran to Nivelles to raise the alarm. Maybe he thought that Sister Della would come to and hurry on to Fosse to alert the abbot.'

Abbot Heribert was staring at Sinsear, seeing the truth of Fidelma's accusation confirmed in his cold features.

'How did you first suspect him?' he asked.

'Many reasons can be mentioned if you think back over the events. But, according to his story, Sinsear went along the path in search of Cessair and Della. He found Cessair dead and tied to the tree. He claimed that he had reached the point after Della had disappeared. But how could he have seen the body tied to the tree when it was on the far side of the tree from the path he was travelling? It could not have been seen by anyone simply travelling that path.

'Even allowing that he somehow might have spotted something that made him suspicious, gone round the back of the tree, and was so distraught that he did not think to cut down the body or see if he could revive her, why did he run on to Nivelles?'

'He wished to raise the alarm and, as he pointed out when you asked, Nivelles is closer than Fosse to the place,' Abbot Heribert said. 'It is logical.'

'There was an even closer place to seek help,' Fidelma pointed out. 'Why not go there? He knew that Brother Cano was waiting in the woodman's hut just a few hundred metres away. Had he been innocent, he would have rushed to seek Cano and get immediate help.'

The scream made them freeze.

Sinsear had turned and drawn a knife and made a thrust at Brother Cano. He was babbling incoherently.

Cano reacted by striking out in self-defence, felling the young monk with a blow to the jaw.

'Now you can punish him by whatever laws apply here,' Fidelma told Abbot Heribert. She turned to the abbess. 'And we, Ballgel, shall escort poor Sister Della back to Nivelles. We have much to talk about . . .' She paused and glanced sadly at Brother Cano who was now sitting quietly, his head in his hands.

'Even the ancients were acutely aware that strong emotions can cause madness. *Aegra amans*—the lover's disease—can make people lose all reason. Even the most mature people can go insane, and in the young and immature love can destroy the soul as well as the mind. What was it Publilius Syrus once wrote? Ah, yes. *Amare et sapere vix deo conceditur*—even the gods find it hard to love and be wise at the same time.'

BURDEN OF PROOF

Bob Shaw

From the past, when powers of deduction were all that was available to an investigator, this story moves to the near future and a not so far-fetched invention that can solve any mystery— even the perfect crime. Author Bob Shaw (1931–96) was a former Northern Ireland journalist who made a remarkable impact on the world of Science Fiction with his innovative stories. 'Burden of Proof' is one of several he wrote on the concept of 'slow glass', glass that slows down light so much that to look into it is to see the past. So long does it take for light to travel through these panes that they can be sent anywhere for use in the future. Employing this remarkable material for solving even the most impenetrable mystery is obvious. This story, the second in the author's series, was written in 1967 for Analog *magazine and appeared a year after publication of the first, 'Light of Other Days', which made Shaw's name, was nominated for both the Hugo and Nebula awards and was included in the list of the year's 'World's Best Science Fiction'.*

Bob Shaw was born in Belfast and worked as a structural engineer until he was 27. Then, after a period in aircraft design and industrial public relations, he joined the staff of The Belfast Telegraph *as a columnist and science correspondent before becoming a full-time author in 1975. Shaw had been a fan of Science Fiction since his youth—indeed, it is not generally appreciated that Ireland has a rich tradition of writers who have worked in this genre. Among the two dozen and more names that can be cited, the best known are probably 'AE' (George Russell), Robert Cromie, Edward Lester, Ian McDonald, Joseph O'Neill,*

James White and Leonard Wibberley, not forgetting Shaw's namesake, the great GBS. Bob Shaw's first sf novel, Night Walk *(1967), about a man trying to escape from a penal colony, hinted at his remarkable ingenuity, and it was followed by* The Palace of Eternity *(1969), an exceedingly grim tale in which two opposing forces gradually destroy an astonishingly attractive planet. These works were followed by his 'Orbitsville' series, focusing on a vast alien artefact in space (which won the 1976 British Science Fiction Award) and the entertaining 'Ragged Astronauts' and 'Wooden Spaceships' sagas which are infused with a particular Irish feel. 'Burden of Proof' draws on Shaw's experiences of journalism and his remarkable concept of 'slow glass' which, ultimately, provides the answer to a question of murder. Did Judge Harpur make the right decision?*

*   *   *

Harpur peered uncertainly through the streaming windows of his car. There had been no parking space close to the police headquarters, and now the building seemed separated from him by miles of puddled concrete and parading curtains of rain. The sky sagged darkly and heavily between the buildings around the square.

Suddenly aware of his age, he stared for a long moment at the old police block and its cascading gutters, before levering himself stiffly out of the driving seat. It was difficult to believe the sun was shining warmly in a basement room under the west wing. Yet he knew it was, because he had phoned and asked about it before leaving home.

'It's real nice down here today, Judge,' the guard had said, speaking with the respectful familiarity he had developed over the years. 'Not so good outside, of course, but down here it's real nice.'

'Have any reporters shown up yet?'

'Just a few so far, Judge. You coming over?'

'I expect so,' Harpur had replied. 'Save a seat for me, Sam.'

'Yes, *sir!*'

Harpur moved as quickly as he dared, feeling the cool rain penetrate to the backs of his hands in his showerproof's pockets. The lining clung round the knuckles when he moved his fingers. As he climbed the steps to the front entrance a preliminary flutter in the left side of his chest told him he had hurried too much, pushed things too far.

The officer at the door saluted smartly.

Harpur nodded to him. 'Hard to believe this is June, isn't it, Ben?'

'Sure is, sir. I hear it's nice down below, though.'

Harpur waved to the guard, and was moving along the corridor when the pain closed with him. It was very clean, very pure. As though someone had carefully chosen a sterile needle, fitted it into an antiseptic handle, heated it to whiteness and—with the swiftness of compassion—run it into his side. He stopped for a moment and leaned on the tiled wall, trying not to be conspicuous, while perspiration pricked out on his forehead. *I can't give up now*, he thought, *not when there's only another couple of weeks to go . . . but, supposing this is it? Right now!*

Harpur fought the panic, until the entity that was his pain withdrew a short distance. He drew a shuddering breath of relief and began to walk again, slowly, aware that his enemy was watching and following. But he reached the sunshine without any further attacks.

Sam Macnamara, the guard at the inner door, started to give his usual grin and then, seeing the strain on Harpur's face, ushered him quickly into the room. Macnamara was a tall Irishman whose only ambition seemed to be to drink two cups of coffee every hour on the hour, but they had developed a friendship which Harpur found strangely comforting. He shook out a fold-up chair at the back of the room and held it steady while Harpur sat down.

'Thank you, Sam,' Harpur said gratefully, glancing around at the unfamiliar crowd, none of whom had noticed his arrival. They were all staring towards the sunlight.

The smell of the rain-damp clothing worn by the reporters seemed strangely out of place in the dusty, underground room. It was part of the oldest wing of the police headquarters and, until ten years before, had been used to store obsolete records. Since then, except on special press days, its bare concrete walls had housed nothing but a bank of monitoring equipment, two very bored guards, and a pane of glass mounted in a frame at one end of the room.

The glass was of the very special variety through which light took many years to pass. It was the sort people used to capture scenes of exceptional beauty for their homes.

To Harpur's eyes, the view through this piece of slow glass had no particular beauty. It showed a reasonably pretty bay on the Atlantic coast, but the water was cluttered with sports boats, and a garishly-painted service station obtruded in the foreground. A connoisseur of slow glass would have thrown a rock through it, but Emile Bennett, the original owner, had brought it to the city simply because it contained the view from his childhood home. Having it available, he had explained, saved him a two-hundred mile drive any time he felt homesick.

The sheet of glass Bennett had used was ten years thick, which meant that it had had to stand for ten years at his parents' home before the view from there came through. It continued, of course, to transmit the same view for ten years after being brought back to the city, regardless of the fact that it had been confiscated from Bennett by impatient police officers who had a profound disinterest in his parental home. It would report, without fail, everything it ever saw—but only in its own good time.

Slumped tiredly in his seat, Harpur was reminded of the last time he had been to a movie. The only light in the room was that coming from the oblong pane of glass, and the reporters sat fidgeting in orderly rows like a movie audience. Harpur found their presence distracting. It prevented him from slipping into the past as easily as usual.

The shifting waters of the bay scattered sunlight through the otherwise dismal room, the little boats crossed and recrossed, and silent cars occasionally slid into the service station. An attractive girl in the extremely abbreviated dress of a decade ago walked across a garden in the foreground, and Harpur saw several of the reporters jot some personal angle material in their notebooks.

One of the more inquisitive left his seat and walked round behind the pane of glass to see the view from the other side, but came back looking disappointed. Harpur knew a sheet of metal had been welded into the frame at the back, completely covering the glass. The county had ruled that it would have been an invasion of the senior Bennetts' privacy to put on public view all their domestic activities during the time the glass was being charged.

As the minutes began to drag out in the choking atmosphere of the room, the reporters grew noticeably restless, and began loudly swapping yarns. Somewhere near the front, one of them began sneezing monotonously and swearing in between. No smoking was permitted near the monitoring equipment which, on behalf of the state, hungrily scanned the glass, so relays of three and four began to drift out into the corridor to light cigarettes. Harpur heard them complaining about the long wait and he smiled. He had been waiting for ten years, and it seemed even longer.

Today, June 7th, was one of the key days for which he and the rest of the country had been standing by, but it had been impossible to let the press know in advance the exact moment at which they would get their story. The trouble was that Emile Bennett had never been able to remember just what time, on that hot Sunday, he had driven to his parents' home to collect his sheet of slow glass. During the subsequent trial it had not been possible to pin it down to anything more definite than 'about three in the afternoon'.

One of the reporters finally noticed Harpur sitting near the door and came over to him. He was sharply dressed, fair-haired and impossibly young looking.

'Pardon me, sir. Aren't you Judge Harpur?'

Harpur nodded. The boy's eyes widened briefly then narrowed as he assessed the older man's present news value.

'Weren't you the presiding judge in the . . . Raddall case?' He had been going to say the Glass Eye case, but immediately changed his mind.

Harpur nodded again. 'Yes, that's correct. But I no longer give interviews to the press. I'm sorry.'

'That's all right, sir. I understand.' He went on out to the corridor, walking with quicker, springier steps. Harpur guessed the young man had just decided on his angle for today's story. He could have written the copy himself:

Today Judge Kenneth Harpur—the man who ten years ago presided in the controversial 'Glass Eye' case, in which twenty-one-year-old Ewan Raddall was charged with a double slaying—sat on a chair in one of the underground rooms at police head-quarters. An old man now, the Iron Judge has nothing at all to say. He only watches, waits and wonders . . .

Harpur smiled wryly. He no longer felt any bitterness over the newspaper attacks. The only reason he had stopped speaking to journalists was that he had become very, very bored with that aspect of his life. He had reached the age at which a man discards the unimportant stuff and concentrates on essentials. In another two weeks he would be free to sit in the sun and note *exactly* how many shades of blue and green there were in the sea, and just how much time elapsed between the appearance of the first evening star and the second. If his physician allowed it, he would have a little good whiskey, and if his physician refused it, he would still have the whiskey. He would read a few books, and perhaps even write one . . .

As it turned out, the estimated time given by Bennett at the trial had been pretty accurate.

At eight minutes past three Harpur and the waiting newsmen saw Bennett approach the glass from the far side with a screwdriver in his hand. He was wearing the sheepish look people often have when they get in range of slow glass. He worked at the sides for a moment, then the sky flashed crazily into view, showing the glass had been tilted out of its frame. A moment later the room went dark as the image of a brown, army-type blanket unfolded across the glass, blotting out the laggard light.

The monitors at the back of the room produced several faint clicking noises which were drowned out by the sound of the reporters hurrying to telephones.

Harpur got to his feet and slowly walked out behind the reporters. There was no need to hurry now. Police records showed that the glass would remain blanked out for two days, because that was how long it had lain in the trunk of Bennett's car before he had got round to installing it in a window frame at the back of his city home. For a further two weeks after that it would show the casual day-to-day events which took place ten years before in the children's public playground at the rear of the Bennett house.

Those events were of no particular interest to anyone; but the records also showed that in the same playground, on the night of June 21, 1981, a twenty-year-old typist, Joan Calderisi, had been raped and murdered. Her boy friend, a twenty-three-year-old auto mechanic named Edward Jerome Hattie, had also been killed, presumably for trying to defend the girl.

Unknown to the murderer, there had been one witness to the double killing—and now it was getting ready to give its perfect and incontrovertible evidence.

The problem had not been difficult to foresee.

Right from the day slow glass first appeared in a few very expensive stores, people had wondered what would happen if a crime were to be committed in its view. What would be the legal position if there were, say, three suspects and it was known that, five or ten years later, a piece of glass would identify the murderer beyond all doubt? Obviously, the law could not risk punishing the wrong person; but, equally obviously, the guilty one could not be allowed to go free all that time.

This was how tabloid feature writers had summed it up, although to Judge Kenneth Harpur there had been no problem at all. When he read the speculations it took him less than five seconds to make up his mind—and he had been impressively unruffled when the test case came his way.

That part had been a coincidence. Erskine County had no more homicides and no more slow glass than any other comparable area. In fact, Harpur had no recollection of ever seeing the stuff until Holt City's electrical street-lighting system was suddenly replaced by alternating panels of eight-hour glass and sixteen-hour glass slung in continuous lines above the thoroughfares. That was several years after techniques had been developed for the mass production of slow glass, or—as it was officially known—retardite.

It had taken some time for a retardite capable of producing delays measured in years to evolve from the first sheets which held light back by roughly half a second. The original material was developed by a glass manufacturer trying to produce a transparency which was both shatterproof and a really efficient insulator. Its unique properties might never have been noticed but for the fact that it was first used—unfortunately for a number of people—in automobile windscreens.

The auto manufacturer concerned spent upwards of half a million dollars trying to find out why one batch of one model had been involved in a statistically improbable number of accidents involving right-hand turns. Expensive as the investigation was, it paid off because retardite became a major industry in a matter of months.

'Scene-stealing' was one of the prime applications, and slow-glass farms sprang up at beauty spots all over the world. A large part of the commercial success of slow glass lay in the fact that there was absolutely no difference, emotionally, between owning a 'scenedow' and owning the land which had charged it with light. The occupant of the most airless, glove-tight duplex in a city could look out on pine-clad valleys—and in every important respect they were *his*.

It was also discovered that, for many applications, cameras had become obsolete. All planetary expeditions, manned or robotic, carried practically weightless retardite slivers of appropriate periods. In any cinematic field, from industrial recording to bird-watching, where large footages had normally been wasted while waiting for an unpredictable key event, short-period slow glass was used instead. The cameras were turned on it—with comfortable hindsight—at the right moment. Spy cameras became tiny flecks of glass which operatives had been known to push into their pores, like blackheads.

But no matter how varied the purpose, all slow-glass applications had one thing in common. The user had to be absolutely certain of the time delay he wanted—because there was no way of speeding the process up. Had retardite been a 'glass' in the true sense of the word, it might have been possible to plane a piece down to a different thickness and get the information sooner; but, in reality, it was an extremely opaque material. Opaque in the sense that light never actually got *into* it.

Radiations with wavelengths in the order of that of light were absorbed on the face of a retardite panel and their information converted to stress patterns within the material. The piezoluctic effect by which the information worked its way through to the opposite face involved the whole crystalline structure, and anything which disturbed that structure instantaneously randomised the stress patterns.

Infuriating as the discovery was to certain researchers, it had been an important factor in the commercial success of retardite. People would have been reluctant to install scenedows in their homes, knowing that everything they had done behind them was being stored for other eyes to see years later. So the burgeoning piezoluctics industry had been quick to invent an inexpensive 'tickler' by which any piece of slow glass could be cleaned off for reuse, like a cluttered computer program.

This was also the reason why, for ten years, two guards had been on a round-the-clock watch of the scenedow which held the evidence in the Raddall case. There was always the chance that one of Raddall's relatives, or some publicity-seeking screwball, would sneak in and wipe the slate clean before its time came to resolve all doubts.

There had been moments during the ten years when Harpur had been too ill and tired to care very much, times when it would have been a relief to have the perfect witness silenced forever. But usually the existence of the slow glass did not bother him.

He had made his ruling in the Raddall case, and it had been a decision he would have expected any other judge to make. The subsequent controversy, the enmity of sections of the press, the public, and even some of his colleagues, had hurt at first, but he had got over that.

The Law, Harpur had said in his summing up, existed solely because people believed in it. Let that belief be shaken—even once—and the Law would suffer irreparable harm.

As near as could be determined, the killings had taken place about an hour before midnight.

Keeping that in mind, Harpur ate dinner early then showered and shaved for the second time that day. The effort represented a sizeable proportion of his quota for the day, but it had been hot and sticky in the courtroom. His current case was involved and, at the same time, boring. More and more cases were like that lately, he realised. It was a sign he was ready to retire, but there was one more duty to perform—he owed that much to the profession.

Harpur put on a light-weight jacket and stood with his back to the valet-mirror which his wife had bought a few months earlier. It was faced with a sheet of fifteen-second retardite which allowed him, after a slight pause, to turn round and check his appearance from the back. He surveyed his frail, but upright, figure dispassionately, then walked away before the stranger in the glass could turn to look out.

He disliked valet-mirrors almost as much as the equally popular truviewers, which were merely pieces of short-term retardite pivotal on a vertical axis. They served roughly the same function as ordinary mirrors, except that there was no reversal effect. For the first time ever, the makers boasted, you could really see yourself as others saw you. Harpur objected to the idea on grounds he hoped were vaguely philosophical, but which he could not really explain, even to himself.

'You don't look well, Kenneth,' Eva said as he adjusted his tie minutely. 'You haven't *got* to go down there, have you?'

'No, I haven't *got* to go—that's why I've got to go. That's the whole point.'

'Then I'll drive you.'

'You won't. You're going to bed. I'm not going to let you drive around the city in the middle of the night.' He put an arm round her shoulders. At fifty-eight, Eva Harpur was on a seemingly endless plateau of indomitable good health, but they maintained a fiction that it was he who looked after her.

He drove himself into the city, but progress through the traffic was unusually slow and, on impulse, he stopped several blocks from the police headquarters and began to walk. Live dangerously, he thought, but walk slowly—just in case. It was a bright, warm evening and, with the long daylight hours of June, only the sixteen-hour panels slung above the thoroughfare were black. The alternating eight-hour panels were needlessly blazing with light they had absorbed in the afternoon. The system was a compromise with seasonal variations in daylight hours, but it worked reasonably well and, above all, the light was practically free.

An additional advantage was that it provided the law enforcement authorities with perfect evidence about events like road accidents and traffic violations. In fact, it had been the then brand-new slow-glass lighting panels in Fifty-third Avenue which had provided a large part of the evidence in the case against Ewan Raddall.

Evidence on which Harpur had sent Raddall to the electric chair.

The salient facts of the case had not been exactly as in the classic situation proposed by the tabloids, but they had been near enough to arouse public interest. There had been no other known suspect apart from Raddall, but the evidence against him had been largely circumstantial. The bodies had not been found until the next morning, by which time Raddall had been able to get home, clean himself up and have a night's sleep. When he was picked up he was fresh, composed and plausible—and the forensic teams had been able to prove almost nothing.

The cast against Raddall was that he had been seen going towards the public playground at the right time, leaving it at the right time, and that he had bruises and scratches consistent with the crime. Also, between midnight and 9:30 in the morning, when he was taken in for questioning, he had 'lost' the plasticord jacket he had worn on the previous evening, and it was never found.

At the end of Raddall's trial the jury had taken less than an hour to arrive at a verdict of guilty—but during a subsequent appeal his defence claimed the jury was influenced by the knowledge that the crime was recorded in Emile Bennett's rear window. The defence attorney, demanding a retrial, put forward the view that the jury had dismissed their 'reasonable doubt' in the expectation that Harpur would, at the most, impose a life sentence.

But, in Harpur's eyes, the revised legal code drafted in 1977, mainly to give judges greater power in their own courts, made no provision for wait-and-see legislation, especially in cases of first-degree murder. In January 1982 Raddall was duly sentenced to be executed.

Harpur's straightforward contention, which had earned him the name 'Iron Judge', was that a decision reached in a court of law always had been, and still was, sacrosanct. The superhuman entity which was the Law must not be humbled before a fragment of glass. Reduced to its crudest terms, his argument was that if wait-and-see legislation were introduced criminals would carry pieces of fifty-year retardite with them as standard equipment.

Within two years the slow-grinding mills of the Supreme Court had ratified Harpur's decision and the sentence was carried out. The same thing, on a microscopic scale, had occurred many times before in the world of sport; and the only possible, the only workable solution, was that the umpire was always right—no matter what cameras or slow glass might say afterwards.

In spite of his vindication, or perhaps because of it, the tabloids never warmed to Harpur. He began making a point of being indifferent to all that anybody wrote or said. All he had needed during the ten years was the knowledge that he had made a good decision, as distinct from a wrong one—now he was to discover if he had made a good decision, as distinct from a bad one.

Although this night had been looming on his horizon for a decade, Harpur found it difficult to realise that, in a matter of minutes, they would *know* if Raddall was guilty. The thought caused a crescendo of uncomfortable jolts in his chest and he stopped for a moment to snatch air. After all, what difference did it really make? He had not made the law, so why feel personally involved?

The answer came quickly.

He was involved because he was part of the law. The reason he had gone on working, against medical advice, was that it was he, not some abstract embodiment of Webster's 'great interest of man on earth', who had passed sentence on Ewan Raddall. And he was going to be there, personally, to face the music if he had made a mistake.

The realisation was strangely comforting to Harpur as he moved on through the crowded streets. Something in the atmosphere of the late evening struck him as being odd, then he noticed the city centre was jammed tight with out-of-town automobiles. Men and women thronged the sidewalks, and he knew they were strangers by the way their eyes occasionally took in the upper parts of buildings. The smell of grilling hamburger meat drifted on the thick, downy air.

Harpur wondered what the occasion might be, then he noticed the general drift towards the police headquarters. So that was it. People had not changed since the days they were drawn towards arenas, guillotines and gallows. There would be nothing for them to see, but to be close at hand would be sufficient to let them taste the ancient joy of continuing to breathe in the knowledge that someone else has just ceased. The fact that they were ten years out of date, too, made no difference at all.

Even Harpur, had he wanted to, could not have got into the underground room. Apart from the monitors, there would be only six chairs and six pairs of special binoculars with low magnifications and huge, light-hungry objective lenses. They were reserved for the state-appointed observers.

Harper had no interest in viewing the crime with his own eyes—he simply wanted to hear the result; then have a long, long rest. It occurred to him he was being completely irrational in going down to the police building, with all the exertion and lethal tension the trip meant for him, but somehow nothing else would do. *I'm guilty*, he thought suddenly, *guilty as ...*

He reached the plaza in which the building was situated and worked his way through the pliant, strength-draining barriers of people. By the time he was halfway across sweat had bound his clothes so tightly he could hardly raise his feet. At an indeterminate point in the long journey he became aware of another presence following close behind—the sorrowful friend with the white-hot needle.

Reaching the untidy ranks of automobiles belonging to the press, Harpur realised he could not go in too early, and there was at least half an hour left. He turned and began forcing his way back to the opposite side of the plaza. The needle point caught up with him—one precise thrust—and he lurched forward clawing for support.

'What the ... !' A startled voice boomed over his head. 'Take it easy old-timer.' Its owner was a burly giant in a pale blue one-piece, who had been watching a 3-D television broadcast when Harpur fell against him. He snatched off the receiver spectacles, the tiny left and right pictures glowing with movement like distant bonfires. A wisp of music escaped from the earpiece.

'I'm sorry,' Harpur said. 'I tripped. I'm sorry.'

'That's all right. Say! Aren't you Judge ...'

Harpur pushed on by as the big man tugged excitedly on the arm of a woman who was with him. *I mustn't be recognised*, he thought in a panic. He burrowed into the crowd, now beginning to lose his sense of direction. Six more desperate paces and the needle caught him again—right up to its antiseptic hilt this time. He moaned as the plaza tilted ponderously away. Not here, he pleaded, not here, *please*.

Somehow, he saved himself from falling and moved on. Near at hand, but a million miles away, an unseen woman gave a beautiful, carefree laugh. At the edge of the square the pain returned, even more decisively than before—once, twice, three times. Harpur screamed as he felt the life-muscle implode in cramp.

He began to go down, then felt himself gripped by firm hands. Harpur looked up at the swarthy young man who was holding him. The handsome, worry-creased face looming through reddish mists looked strangely familiar. Harpur struggled to speak.

'You . . . you're Ewan Raddall, aren't you?'

The black eyebrows met in puzzlement. 'Raddall? No. Never heard of him. I think we'd better call an ambulance for you.'

Harpur thought hard. 'That's right. You couldn't be Raddall. I killed him ten years ago.' Then he spoke louder. 'But, if you never heard of Raddall, why are you here?'

'I was on my way home from a bowling match when I saw the crowd.'

The boy began getting Harpur out of the crowd, holding him up with one arm, fending uncomprehending bodies away with the other. Harpur tried to help, but was aware of his feet trailing helplessly on the concrete.

'Do you live right here in Holt?'

The boy nodded emphatically.

'Do you know who I am?'

'All I know about you, sir, is you should be in the hospital. I'll call an ambulance on the liquor store phone.'

Harpur felt vaguely that there was some tremendous significance in what they had been saying, but had no time to pursue the matter.

'Listen,' he said, forcing himself to stand upright for a moment, 'I don't want an ambulance. I'll be fine if I can just get home. Can you help me get a cab?'

The boy looked uncertain, then he shrugged. 'It's your funeral.'

Harpur opened his door carefully and entered the friendly darkness of the big, old house, During the ride out of town his sweat-soaked clothes had become clammy cold, and he shivered uncontrollably as he felt for the light switch.

With the light on, he sat down beside the telephone and looked at his watch. Almost midnight—by this time there would be no mystery, no doubt, about exactly what had happened in the Fifty-third Avenue playground ten years earlier. He picked up the handset, and at the same moment heard his wife begin to move around upstairs. There were several numbers he could ring to ask what the slow glass had revealed, but the thought of talking to any police executive or someone in City Hall was too much. He called Sam Macnamara.

As a guard, Sam would not know the result officially, but he would have the answer just the same. Harpur tried to punch out the number of the direct line to the guard kiosk but his finger joints kept buckling on impact with the buttons, and he gave up.

Eva Harpur came down the stairs in her dressing-gown and approached him apprehensively.

'Oh, Kenneth!' Her hand went to her mouth. 'What have you done? You look . . . I'll have to call Dr Sherman.'

Harpur smiled weakly. *I do a lot of smiling these days*, he thought irrelevantly, *it's the only response an old man can make to so many situations.*

'All I want you to do is make me some coffee and help me up to my bed; but first of all get me a number on this contraption.' Eva opened her mouth to protest, then closed it as their eyes met.

When Sam came to the phone Harpur worked to keep his own voice level.

'Hello, Sam. Judge Harpur here. Is the fun all over yet?'

'Yes, sir. There was a press conference afterwards and that's over, too. I guess you heard the result on the radio.'

'As a matter of fact, I haven't, Sam. I was . . . out until a little while ago. Decided to ring someone about it before I went to bed, and your number just came into my head.'

Sam laughed uncertainly. 'Well, they were able to make a positive identification. It was Raddall, all right—but I guess you knew that all along.'

'I guess I did, Sam.' Harpur felt his eyes grow hot with tears.

'It'll be a load off your mind all the same, Judge.'

Harpur nodded tiredly, but into the phone he said, 'Well, naturally I'm glad there was no miscarriage of justice—but judges don't make the laws, Sam. They don't even decide who's guilty and who isn't. As far as I'm concerned, the presence of a peculiar piece of glass makes very little difference, one way or the other.'

It was a good speech for the Iron Judge.

There was a long silence on the line then, with a note of something like desperation in his voice, Sam persisted , 'I know all that, Judge ... but, all the same, it must have been a big load off your mind.'

Harpur realised, with a warm surprise, that the big Irishman was pleading with him. *It doesn't matter any more*, he thought. *In the morning I'm going to retire and rejoin the human race.*

'All right, Sam,' he said finally. 'Let's put it this way—I'll sleep well tonight. All right?'

'Thank you, Judge. Good night.'

Harpur set the phone down and, with his eyes tight-closed, waited for peace.

3

MALICE DOMESTIC

Stories of Vengeance

THE INHERITANCE

Frank Delaney

'The Master of the Irish Saga' is just one of several accolades that have been bestowed on Frank Delaney (1942–), a man as well known as a broadcaster as for his best-selling novels. His stories of Irish life have frequently blended elements of mystery and murder with everyday events—a pattern that he established with his first novel, The Sins of the Mothers *(1992), which vividly captured the mood of the Irish countryside after the 1922–23 Civil War. In it, a pious young woman marries a former gunman and then has her world turned upside down when her husband is himself gunned down. The book was number one on the Irish best-seller lists for nine weeks and has resulted in four more novels in the series in which Delaney has shown an intimate knowledge of setting and characterisation and earned an international following.*

Frank Delaney was born in Tipperary and, after working in a bank for a time, obtained a job with RTE in Dublin as a newscaster. During the Seventies he worked as a BBC correspondent in Dublin and in 1978 launched the very successful BBC radio programme, Bookshelf. *Since then he has made a number of documentaries, hosted his own late-night chat show interviewing celebrities from the arts, and been described by* The Times *as 'one of the best-loved broadcasters in Britain'. His first published work was* James Joyce's Odyssey—a Guide to the Dublin of Ulysses *(1982), written to celebrate the centenary of Joyce's birth, and most recently he has followed his best-selling Irish series with an out-and-out thriller,* The Amethysts *(1997), a powerful and sinister story about a series of contemporary murders rooted in the Holocaust of the Second World War. 'The Inheritance', which he wrote for* The Mail on Sunday *magazine in 1996, is also about calculated murder, but on a domestic scale.*

*   *   *

He knew—I am certain now—that I had come to kill him. Nothing in his face or hands said so: his head told that he knew—he leaned back and opened his mouth as if at a sudden loss of breath. Hands on the steering wheel suddenly not going anywhere, he sat in his car on his gravelled drive. Long ago he had possessed laugh lines round his eyes, and now only traces of them could be seen, as if someone had ironed the skin not quite successfully. Skin like linen and beautiful hands, exquisite hands for a man, and considering how he had used them.

After that first shock at my silent appearance, he asked me, 'Do you know exactly how old I am?'

I shook my head.

'This morning . . .' He stopped and blew a puff of resignation. 'I am 76. You should have known that. Shouldn't you?'

I never took my eyes off his head, and still he could not look at me.

'And this morning.' He sighed. 'This morning—I knew. I knew I was likely to have a visitor. I mean, that's you. Or, I mean, it turned out to be you.'

He was not gabbling, yet spoke faster than usual and then he caught himself doing so and stopped, retrenching by means of a deep breath—always the self-disciplinarian.

'That is why I, well, I was going out anyway, but I waited. D'you see?'

Liar. But I did not say it. I said nothing. He glanced at my hands. Did he notice the fraying of my cuffs? I cannot afford better now—Beatrix's medical bills. He must have recognised at least the favoured type of shirt, the wool check.

It seemed that the heat stiffened moment by moment. At the bridge of his nose a single bead of sweat formed like a teardrop of clear gel. He coughed a small and dry cough. I rapped my hand on the car door.

He started—and asked, 'Shall we go for—a drive? Can we ... what is it, where do you want to speak, if that's what you want? To speak? Is that it? Shall we go for—a drive?'

I gestured and he got out, much smaller nowadays. With a hand movement I directed him around to the passenger door, followed him, held it open for him and like a chauffeur supervised him to the seat. He seemed to whimper as he clicked the seat belt and I returned to the driver's side.

The beautiful car crunched the gravel.

'If we—if you, if you turn right. And then you turn left, immediate left, you could get on to the autobahn. If that's what you want. You can see the signs.' He sighed after each sentence.

I pressed the button and my window rolled down.

He said, 'I had, I had some ah'm, some Respighi, some—d'you know Respighi?—I have a cassette here. His *Ancient Airs and Dances*? I think you'd like them. It's odd to think, when you listen, that he only died in 1936—someone I knew met him. But Respighi, I mean his name sounds as if he were Venetian, like Vivaldi . . .' His voice declined.

Even now—and you may think this callous beyond imagination—I have no difficulty in understanding the dynamics of what I had come to do. Have you ever watched someone you love—someone you love as you love the bright air before your face, as you love the blue of sky—have you ever watched such a loved one endure true torment in an agony caused by someone else? And that someone else still living? Night after night I held her and night after night I failed to console her and yesterday I looked again at the scars on her arms and legs and face where again she had self-mutilated. Nor did she recognise me any more, she who so often traced the shape of my lips with her little finger.

I have some blame in the matter. Should I not have left the documents behind in Moscow? In mitigation I plead that she suggested it, and it is true that she did suffer an obsessive desire to know what had happened to her family.

I looked at him. He was 23 at the time he did all those 'things', as I too now called them in my head. Could I find any trace in his face of the 'things' he had done to her family? 'Things,' she cried, 'things,' with that new, high, uneasable anguish in her voice. Specifically and methodically, using his proud attention to detail, he had behaved unspeakably.

Perhaps I too have behaved wrongly. I allowed Beatrix to read the papers, I trusted my 'judgement', my famed 'accuracy', the 'character assessment' of which I felt so capable. Only death or madness releases people from such knowledge.

He spoke. 'There is an especially pleasant view. Not far from here.'

His intonation had grown formal and I remembered that I had heard this of some people who know they face death. They speak slowly as if seeking control; they fight for some dignity. I looked at his smooth and creamy hands again. See his cuffs? Perfect, and (was this significant?) cuff links made of silver pistols. In one incident, he had fired bullets along the soft edges of a woman's thighs and breasts, burning and scoring her with red flesh wounds. Think of her undeserved terror.

I left the road that would have taken us to the autobahn and entered the woods beyond the empty, silent village. The grassy banks were dotted with the milky yellow of flowers. Climbing, we passed a small wayside shrine and he made a gesture with his right hand.

'I have become a Catholic,' he said. 'You didn't know that?'

This is what happens when someone you love is rendered mad and rent apart by her past: you become the avenger not only of her and her family but of all others. One night in the Altstadt in Düsseldorf a young Irishman, working for a season in the municipal theatre, asked several of us whether we knew what had occurred in our own, native German, non-Jewish families during the war. He received three types of response. Some turned away in discomfort. Others made angry remarks and told him to avoid the past. Two, including me, engaged with the idea. But we reached no conclusion other than a vague, unattached remorse and in me this gave rise to a relentless curiosity that would now damage.

The top of the hill proved to be a plateau and in a forest road I stopped, pressed buttons to open all the car windows.

He said, 'Look.' A small shape sang high above us. 'A lark,' he remarked. 'Always here, larks.' He unclipped his seat belt. 'Did you come here especially? Or were you in the region?' He looked at me directly this time.

No, I would not tell him anything—not about the shock, nor the agony, that sudden sobbing explosion of tears which overtakes and overcomes even the most controlled of men. When Beatrix went mad, I went back to Moscow to find, if I could, the names of the perpetrators. At first I did not believe: denial. Then I laughed: refusal. Next I raged: rebellion. Then I wept: acceptance. Then I took my decision: resignation. Just like the stages of being told you have cancer. Which, in a sense, I had.

I snapped the key from the ignition and stepped outside. The lark whup-whuppered upwards, singing and singing. Far below, a few low-headed cattle mooched near a timbered house.

He climbed from the car as if aching all over.

'I come and stand here. Often. Sometimes . . . the view.' He looked closely at me now, then he paused and frowned, disturbed in his thought. Finally he gathered his mind.

'Sometimes the view inspires me. But I can't write. Or anything like that. Or play music. I listen, though.'

The bleached slash of an old small scar glowed white on the bone of his cheek. He stood square and clamped hands behind his back.

The supplementary decision I had taken—to remain silent—sustained me. In extreme circumstances, speech deflects purpose. But I needed such strength, though, not to ask him teeming questions. If he had been given a gift by which to expiate—what might he have written? An atonement? A requiem? Were he an instrumentalist, what would he have played? A Chopin for his soul? A Schubert Impromptu to calm his bewilderment? Or— like to like—Wagner? I directed him to a small patch of grass, then indicated that he should stand with his back to the valley and face me. He could not run because he was too infirm, and he could not grapple because he was too old and weak. For a moment he closed his eyes.

When I first met Beatrix she was dancing in the street to illustrate to her friends some point she had been arguing about Ginger Rogers and Fred Astaire.

'But you don't play dance music,' she teased me. 'What use are you?'

When I could not remember the precise details of her face that night, I knew I was locked to her and probably lost, and my heart was merry at the thought. No sign of her anguish materialised then, not for a year, perhaps 18 months. She came to each concert and then she toured with me and the other three loved her. Do you know Limburg? It has an ugly cathedral and any antique beauty the town once had has been almost overwhelmed by new business premises. In Limburg, where she first showed the signs of melancholia, Edward Anderson, our English cellist, a man of intuition, asked me softly, 'Is Bea Jewish?'

On principle I had never asked; she had never spoken: we are all the children of our parents.

After this first collapse, Bea and I talked and talked and talked, and out of it arose my mistaken offer to trace her family's fate. But she descended rapidly after my misjudgement. I had believed that the revelations, the Truth, might prove a therapy. I was wrong. I went further, found out what I found out, and therefore my huge, unendurable self-accusation had to be converted to something manageable. The bleakness seemed to require a comparable size of something else, some other form of expression—and here we now stood on this forest hillside.

I looked at him closely to inspect—as if I could—his genetic pathway. Classic, really: the blue eyes, the hard forehead, the long, strong ears. As I have no children of my own and now never will, I can use the rest of my life to contemplate what this inspection of him produced in me.

Not that I faltered: I, too, have an unwavering man in me. Beware of those who cannot waver.

Turning my back, I walked to the car and removed my jacket.

From the inner pocket I lifted the weighted leather package and turned back towards him, opening the flap. I knew that he watched: I felt his eyes. The holster dropped to the grass.

'In memoriam,' I said, words that I had rehearsed and rehearsed, 'in memoriam. This is for Joanna Lichterman whose dear daughter Beatrix I love and who is now mad.'

He looked at me and I think he remembered or did he? 'I did my duty,' he said.

I then forgot the limits I had placed on the words I was going to speak—or perhaps I needed to provoke myself.

'But a self-imposed duty. Who gave the orders that ordered you to fire bullets along Joanna Lichterman's body, burning her flesh night after night? I have read all the reports.'

'The reports are untrue.' He rallied. 'And there is a word for what you are contemplating. Patricide. That's what it is called.'

He was ever a man who liked wordplay so I replied, 'I am not contemplating. I am executing. Avenging things destroyed. Think of the blood lines and intellectual inheritances and artistic strains you and your final-solution comrades denied us all.'

'This is not your business.'

'You are wrong.'

I knelt on one knee: fingers that play Mozart can also squeeze a trigger. For a heavy man he fell quickly—and, exactly as I had predicted to myself, a kind of primal love overcame me and I wept. Then I knelt and embraced him and kissed his face. In his wallet I found a photograph of me aged five with him and Mother, and I have this photograph now, here on this table. I have since discovered that he had always taken the radio to his study alone during broadcasts of our recitals.

When I went to see Bea and told her what I had done, she did not comprehend one word I said and kept fingering her hacked hair and talking about chocolate.

AN INFRINGEMENT OF THE DECALOGUE

Donn Byrne

Once referred to by Ellery Queen, the doyen of murder and mystery fiction, as 'that wild, extravagant, swashbuckling Irish-American', Donn Byrne (1889–1928), or Brian Oswald Donn-Byrne, was born in New York and brought up in South Armagh and Antrim where the developing unrest was to have a profound effect upon him and his work. After studying at University College, Dublin, and in Paris and Leipzig, he returned to New York in 1911. In 1915, his first book, Stories Without Women, *appeared, but only 639 copies were sold—of which the author himself bought the ill-omened number thirteen! Today copies of this book, which earned Byrne less than £50, are worth more than three times that on the very rare occasions when they appear on the second-hand market. He finally struck gold when one of his short stories was accepted by Hearst Publications. So impressed were the company with his work that Byrne was given a contract to supply one new story per month for the whole of 1919. Within three years he had become one of the highest paid magazine writers in the United States and simultaneously started writing the novels that established his literary reputation, includ-ing* Messer Marco Polo *(1921) and* Hangman's House *(1925), both of which drew on his dual interests in travel and mystery fiction. Tragically, he died in a car accident aged 39, shortly after returning to Ireland to settle.*

Stories of murder and mystery are to be found in several of the posthumous collections of Donn Byrne's stories which were assembled by Dorothea Donn-Byrne at Kilbrittain in County Cork. 'Triangle', about Detective Thomas Denihan, appears in Sargasso Sea *(1932); the hardboiled tale of 'The Colleen Rue' is in* Rivers of Damascus *(1935); and, perhaps most impressive of all, 'An Infringement of the Decalogue' written for* Smart Set *magazine, is collected in* A Woman of the Shee *(1932). Ellery Queen reprinted the tale as his 'star story' in the May 1950 issue of the mystery magazine which bears his name and there referred to it as 'one of [Donn Byrne's] most heart-warming and human tales.' To that I should add that it is also a graphic story of brutality and, ultimately, revenge.*

*   *   *

When Bertrand Lacy, gambler, wastrel, and blackguard generally, deserted his wife Nan, aged eighteen, and his son Norman, aged three weeks, in New York, there was no limit to the pity people extended to her.

'And he left her without a cent in the world!' they whispered in the boarding-house. 'He even pawned her jewellery!'

'Of course she will go back to her people in Ireland,' the wiseacres decided for her. 'She has them to fall back on.'

But here the wise erred. She had not them to fall back on. When Bertrand Lacy had come to Galway, hardly over a year before, and when he and Nan Burke-Keogh met, fell in love with each other, and courted, they had done everything surreptitiously. From New York had Lacy come, according to him, in a haze of glory. His business in New York was vague and his pedigree vaguer. The man knew horses. He knew the points of flat and steeplechase racing, of hunting, of harriers. These things he might have picked up about race-courses and about dog-shows, to be sure, but the impression he gave was that he had been accustomed to them as a sportsman, not as a hanger-on.

At Baldoyle he had met some of the newer generation of gentility, honest tradesfolk who should have been harvesting the fruits of commerce in place of squandering it on a sport they could neither afford nor understand. His knowledge of horses stood him in good stead. It provided him with a comfortable sum for summer expenses, some introductions, and an invitation to spend a month in Galway.

'We'll show you sport the like of which you never saw in America, when we get you after the harriers,' his host, a wealthy brewer, told him. And so Lacy went.

In Dublin it would have been impossible for him to meet, without a proper investigation of his antecedents, Nan, daughter of Sir Michael Burke-Keogh, that fierce old fox-hunter with the most terrible temper in Ireland. But Galway is a sleepy city, basking like a kitten in the sun, with boats drowsing along the stone quays, and strange, silent country people coming in from the purple Connaught hills. Life is empty there, and social barriers are not strictly kept. At the hunt Lacy met her, and later at the houses around, where he had secured a casual entry. Her father he never met, nor wished to meet. The old man's bushy eyebrows and granite eyes beneath, as he saw them in the distance, warned him that here was an examiner who could probe like a lancer.

The very surreptitiousness of it all captured her, as well as Lacy's appearance and his potent way with women. Not a tall man, by any means, but stocky and well built; a clear face, with waving ruddy hair and chestnut eyes; a cleft chin and a voice that was soothing like music. And there was an eternal quizzing smile on his face that hinted at superior knowledge of the world, of women, of life.

I think he must have been very much in love with her, or taken with her, as the case might be better put. She was a very small and lithe woman, with quick, incisive gestures. Her hair was misty black, and her eyes were nearly too large for her face, and very grey. Her nose and nostrils had the clean cut of race. Her mouth might have been cut by a sculptor's scalpel, so well shaped and firm it seemed; and she was only seventeen. She was a very beautiful woman then, was Nan Burke-Keogh of Galway, and she is now, twenty-three years later, and she will be until the day she dies.

They met. They rode and boated together. They danced together at the hunt balls. He swept her off her feet by the impetuousness of his love-making.

'I love you, Nan, little Nan,' he told her. They were on the terrace of the club, and from where they stood they could see the glistening Atlantic waves shimmering under the harvest moon. The dancers within were waltzing rhythmically, a delicate kaleidoscope of frocks and uniforms and red hunting-coats. The band breathed out a dreamy waltz of Strauss, and mingling with the rippling music came the languorous murmur of the waves.

'Little Nan, will you come away with me to America? Will you marry me, and fly over? Will you, little Nan?'

'What will Father say?' She was fearful.

'Listen, little Nan,' he pressed eagerly. 'We won't tell him until everything is over. Let's not have a wedding with a crowd at church. Let's go off. I want to sweep you away. I want to carry you off in my arms, right here, right now.'

'But Father . . .' She hesitated.

'Your father will come round!' he told her. 'Don't fear. Come, little Nan, little Nan!'

She thought for an instant, and by some measure of intuition she knew that her father would never give his consent to her marriage with this man; and that if she loved him and wanted him she must listen to his wooing now.

'My father will never come round,' she said simply. She swept about to him, and her hands went out. 'But I will come with you and follow you to the end of the world. And you will be good to me and take care of me, won't you, Bertrand, won't you?'

'I will take care of you and cherish you until the end of the world!'

'Then I will come,' she decided.

That very night she came, and on the morrow they were married in Dublin, and on the next day were flying towards America. There was not much reason to fly, however, for Sir Michael Burke-Keogh had no intention of following them. He contented himself with a terrible outburst of temper, in which he cursed her solemnly by bell, book and candle; disinherited her; erased her name from the family records. Then his mouth closed forever into a grim, thin line. When a priest came to inform him of the marriage, he turned on the father with a roar as of a maddened bull.

'My daughter married!' he shouted. 'My daughter! If you mean the slut who ran away with somebody's cast-off groom, let me tell you, sir, that she is no daughter of mine. No woman of our house has ever done a thing like that before; and when she does, she is dead!'

Little by little she came to understand the manner of man she had married, and, loyal heart that she was, might have condoned his way of livelihood had he kept up his love for her. Imperceptibly it waned until it was no longer there. They travelled about the race-tracks of the South and West for nearly a year. Luck deserted him, and he grew irritable. They were in New York when their son was about to be born, and at their lowest ebb for money.

'Cable to your father, Nan,' was his eternal plea. 'If he knows, he'll be glad to help you out.'

He reasoned, he cajoled, he threatened, and about this time her lips began to curl into a faint sneer as she heard him whine. She could have borne much in him—his dissoluteness, his dishonesty even—but one thing she could not bear, and that was the whine, the cowardice of him.

Their son was born, and as he lay in her arms a few days after, the father made an attempt to bluster.

'Now, look here, Nan!' he told her. 'You've got to be sensible. You'll send that cable. Tell him he has a grandson. That will soften him.'

She said nothing. She looked at him searchingly, probingly, with her great blue-lined eyes standing out in her wan white face like dead stars. At last he saw the futility of it. He paced about the room.

'Curse you!' he raved. 'If it hadn't been for you, I'd have never been in this mess. If I hadn't married you, I'd have been having a good time now, instead of being broke in this dump.' He paced about more and suddenly he quailed before the glance in the haggard, shadowy eyes. 'What are you looking at me like that for?' he ended weakly. 'Take your eyes off me!'

A fortnight after that he left her. He had gone out in the morning, and returned about eleven—two hours later. He walked into the dingy room, carelessly humming a tune, but there was something tense and nervous about him. He glanced at her, and he glanced at the child sleeping on the bed.

'I think I'll drop round to the corner for a couple of minutes before lunch,' he hazarded. He opened the bureau drawer and extracted the last few dollars from it. 'Ahum! Yes! I think I'll drop round.' And he sauntered out.

And that was the last Nan saw of Bertrand Lacy, living or dead.

Her heart was broken. It had been broken long before this, although she had said nothing. But if her heart was broken, her spirit wasn't. It was as vital in her at that moment as it had been in any of the Burke-Keoghs who had sailed out of Galway into Spain, resilient as whalebone, strong as steel.

She sat and she thought for a while in that grim and sordid room, with the child sleeping peacefully on the bed; and her brain operated as clearly then as it has ever operated since, more clearly than it had ever done before. Here she was, an abandoned wife, with a child not a month old, with not a cent of money, and with little that was pawnable. What was she to do? She couldn't go back to her father: he would have her whipped from the gates. And what was more, she wouldn't if she could, for she had made her own bed and she would lie on it! Below, the people of the house might extend her charity, but she suspected shrewdly how impatient and overbearing charity can be. Besides, she would have none of it were it the kindest thing in the world.

She put her coat on with quick decision. She put her hat on. She requested a fellow-lodger—a hard-faced little circus woman whose heart belied the aggressive glint in her eyes—to mind the baby until she returned.

'I'll be a half-hour at most,' she said, and she went down the dingy brownstone steps with her head high, as a queen might descend the steps of a throne.

There was a great department store around the corner, and she swept into it. Because she was a lady, and because she had that firm, commanding way of the Burke-Keoghs, when she asked to see the manager she was led to him. A kindly, shrewd-eyed, fleshy man, he took in every detail about her, from the well-worn but well-brushed suit to the proud tilt of her head and the firm command in her eyes. He noticed too, in an impersonal way, how beautiful she was, even with her features as wan and haggard as they now were.

'What can I do for you, madam?' he asked courteously.

'You can give me something to do,' she told him. 'I want work.'

'Yes,' he said, without apparent surprise. 'Is there any particular thing you could do?'

'I know a great deal about lace,' she answered. 'I was once told I knew more about it than any person in Europe.'

Which was true, large as it sounds. As far back as Nan Burke-Keogh's mind could go, she could remember her mother's pride in it, and how the dear lady had tried to instil a love into her for the filmy, web-like fabrics. At the convent in Malines the sisters had encouraged her in the study of it. When other children were deep in the delights of innocuous love-stories, she was following with an appreciative eye the stars and circles, the whorls, the lunes, the bars, the arabesques of laces done by the delicate fingers of noblewomen now dead, and the fresh products of patient peasants. Those were Nan's two accomplishments—her knowledge of laces and her horsemanship.

'Would you mind telling me,' she was asked, 'why you want to work?'

'A very private matter,' she answered proudly, 'and because I have to.'

He sent for a silent, dapper man, who talked to her of work, questioning her minutely, without seeming to do so, about what she knew. The fleshy manager rose.

'I think we might arrange something,' he decided.

This is not the chronicle of Nan Lacy's success in the business world. I know nothing about business and I care less. I am not interested in the various steps by which she rose from a twenty-dollar-a-week position to a salary of fifteen thousand a year. It suffices me that she did so. She rose to danger like a thing of race, and smashed all obstacles aside, like a blooded hunter at the touch of the spur.

And this was not the only obstacle in her way. There was the question of Norman Lacy, aged one month. What was to become of him, now that she was earning her own living? She could not keep him by her. In that one electric day of clear thought she accomplished everything. She found a pair of ladies in Sheepshead Bay who were delighted to take care of him, for a nominal board bill, so empty their lives were. For two years she lived out there with him, looking after him at night, and leaving him in the morning, to come in to her business. At the age of two he began to show signs of wilfulness that filled the old ladies' hearts with dread, much as they loved him.

'God grant he won't be a heart-sore to her when he grows up!' they prayed fervently.

There came the time later when her rise had been such as to warrant the leasing of an apartment and the hire of cook and nurse. At five the qualities the child had shown at two had strengthened and diversified. He seemed full of ebullient, uncontrollable spirits that nearly always resulted in mischief. He was ready with fists and feet. He had a mania for breaking things.

She was twenty-five now, and yet, except for the quietness of her eyes that should have been sparkling with laughter, she seemed little older than the day she left Galway. The colour had never gone from her cheeks, and she took an honest, womanly pride in her beauty, though the thought of another husband had never entered her mind; and, moreover, there was always the possibility of the first turning up again, and claiming her. If he did—her eyes glinted with sudden savageness—she would thrash him with her riding-crop until he screamed for mercy, and she would cast him out into the street, like the most unfaithful of mongrel dogs!

So, unmindful of any man save the first, for whom she had nothing but the utmost loathing, she went her way, sufficient unto herself. She took care of her beauty, and took care of her health. She could ride now that the yoke of want had been raised from her neck, and Saturday afternoon and Sunday would see her whirling through Westchester country on a great hunter, like an Amazon going into battle. She walked through the streets with her head high, her shoulders straight, her stride swinging and rhythmic. And there was no man she knew who did not admire her, and there were many who loved her, but there were none who dared speak to her of it, because of that aloof and magnificently chaste expression of her eyes.

'My Lord!' Bahr, the advertising manager, used to mutter to himself. 'To think that that woman was married, and had a child by a scoundrel! She looks like one of Diana's attendants; like Diana herself, begad!'

She understood the boy, and she felt, intuitively, that the boy understood her. There were very few demonstrations of affection between them, but there was a bond, a sort of friendliness, a manner of comradeship. Those about her did not understand this. At eight he was sent to a military school in the South. He shook hands with her in a manly way, and blushed when she stooped to kiss him. Then he was off.

'And not a tear in his eye!' a woman friend thought to herself. 'The hard-hearted little beast! She need never depend on him when she grows old.'

And so years slipped onward. For her they went by like one mellow day after another, sunset verging into sunrise, and the sands of the hour-glass rippling silverly until the sun dropped again. More intent still she became on her work, until there was nothing of space left in her time which was not taken up by business, and her riding and swimming, and the reading of letters from and reports of her boy at school.

From an educational point of view these reports were not very encouraging. 'He is the sturdiest lad in the school,' so they went, 'honest and honourable, but nearly beyond control. His knowledge of books is disgraceful. The only interest he has is athletics. A great pity!' But she only smiled.

He would come home at the end of the year laden with athletic trophies, with cups and medals. These he distributed about the apartment. He never formally gave them to her or mentioned them, but she knew they were for her.

At eighteen she broached to him the subject of college. He shook his head.

'I'm not keen on it,' he said casually. 'I've been casting about for something to do. A man I know has a place down in Ecuador—a sort of mine or something. Thought I'd like to have a go at that.'

She looked at him a little wistfully, but she smiled. So he was a man now, eager for adventure and life! How like his father he looked in feature, she thought. The same rippling chestnut hair; the light-brown eyes; the straight nose; the cleft chin. There the resemblance ceased. Where his father had been short and stocky, with small, delicate hands, the son was well over six feet, with hands that seemed gigantic, broadened and hardened by glove contests, by hockey stick and polo mallet. Other people were shocked by his prowess in the amateur ring: it was said he could knock an opponent out with the ease of a professional heavyweight, but somehow she was glad. There were other things of his father's he did not inherit. He had not his father's uneasy eyes; he had not his father's flow of speech and musical voice. His speech was casual; his voice rough.

'If you think that's the best thing,' she told him, 'then go.'

He did think so, and he went. But the fortune at the end of the rainbow did not reveal itself to him. For four years he tramped up and down the world, returning home at intervals of six months—except for fifteen months in Africa—and bringing with him sufficient money to tide him over a month at home and to pay his fare overseas again. He had never any luck in his ventures. Once it was the mine in Ecuador, and once a banana plantation partnership in Colombia, and once a game-capturing expedition in the Congo, but none of them came to anything. Yet he never complained. He would come back with weird presents for his mother; spears and arrows from the Congo; a compressed human head from the waters of the Maranon; fifty aigrette feathers from Colombia. He was arrested for attempting to smuggle in these last, and it took the combined influence of fifty million dollars' worth of money to have him released on the ground that he was a harmless lunatic.

And every time he returned she watched him with continuously growing pride. He was only twenty-two now, but he had broadened and filled, and he might have been thirty, so self-reliant he seemed, and so firm and challenging was his eye. His face was tanned to the colour of leather, and the huge hands had become clubs of brown sinew and muscle.

When they stood side by side they seemed like sister and brother. It would have been impossible for anyone not aware of the facts to suppose them mother and son. She was forty now, and she looked not a day over thirty years old. Her black massy hair shone as brightly as ever, and she was as lissom as she had ever been. The only difference was a certain maturity to her frame, and that look of patience and understanding in her great grey eyes.

Even the marriage with Lacy, the terrible year spent with him, had faded from her memory until it had taken on the proportions of some ancient tragic romance she had read in a book.

She had been getting a little lonely of late, and after she passed her fortieth birthday, a week before, she had begun wondering what life would be like ten, or even twenty years from now. She would cry a little in the evenings, for she knew she could not work forever, and she knew too that she could not expect her harum-scarum son to settle down, and marry, and have children she could unload her heart upon in her old age. He was not that kind, she knew. As soon think of changing a gerfalcon into a twittering pigeon, or a leopard into a house cat. She did not blame him. Had she been a man she would have had exactly the same vision of life as he—a restless, roving one. There was no place for her to return to in Ireland; the entail of the estate was broken and the property had descended to a nephew. She had friends in New York, to be sure, but to impose on a friendship the burden of a restless, homeless woman of middle age was something she, with her sportsmanlike blood, could not do. For the first time in her life her seemingly indomitable courage failed her. It was then she met John Hunter—Colonel John Hunter—and she fell in love with him, and he with her.

She was a big woman now, a power in business circles, but she had never forgotten the hobbies of her girlhood. She could still lift a hunter over a six-foot-six-inch gate, and she still thrilled to the intricacies of fine lace. An exhibition of Philippine industries was held somewhere on Forty-second Street and she went there to see the lace that had been brought over. She asked some technical questions of the little *mestiza* attendant. The girl, at a loss, appealed to a great bent pillar of a man, who was carefully selecting some cigars.

'My name is Hunter, John Hunter,' he explained embarrassedly. 'If there's any way I can help?'

And in this wise she met Colonel John Hunter—General now, of the Philippine Scouts. A gigantic frame of man, lean nearly to the point of emaciation; a great, sweeping line of jaw, with an embarrassedly smiling mouth; grizzled at the temples; great-nosed; with black eyes that seemed to pierce and to smile good-naturedly at the same time.

He had a long and honourable record, had John Hunter—in Cuba, in Porto Rico, and in the Philippines. He was very deadly in warfare and very kindly in peace, but the most marked characteristic about him was his shyness where women were concerned. He could never find anything to say to them, and he fidgeted so much in their company that they were as glad to be rid of him as he to get away. He was forty-five now, and unmarried, though it was not for lack of women who would have been glad to be wife to him had he been interested in them or had they been able to interest him.

There is a chemical affinity, which we can prove meticulously by the action of acids on salts, or gases on molten metal; by quantitative and qualitative analyses that leave no whit of doubt. There is a spiritual affinity, too, which we cannot prove, but which is evidenced by such occurrences as John Hunter, shyest of men, babbling over tea at the Ritz to Nan Lacy, most guarded of women, whom he had met a bare half-hour before—and she as conversationally enthusiastic as he. It was evidenced by her parting from him blushingly, having made an appointment to ride with him in the park next morning; and by the cock of his head and the swing of his stride as he walked up the avenue, and by the lightest expression of his heart he had experienced since he had received his first command. They rode together next morning and had lunch. They met the next day. A week whirled by in a vortex, and the end naturally came.

It came at the most unromantic of places, at the most unromantic of times. It came while they were sitting on a bench in Central Park on a Saturday afternoon. Beside them horses clumped painfully along the bridle-paths, their mouths sawed by clumsy riders. Nearby, motors snarled past with a raucous barking of horns. A few urchins chased one another loudly about. Hunter moved his head away.

'There's something I wanted to say,' he announced haltingly. He stopped for a few instants. 'There's something I wanted to say, and I don't know how to put it. I had it all worked out a while ago.

'You see,' he went on lamely, 'I've never been married.'

He felt a wild panic then, as if he wanted to rise up and flee away. He summoned up enough courage to look at her face, to see if she were shocked, insulted, hurt. She was smiling at him tenderly, and her eyes were full of tears.

There was no wild embrace in the middle of the public park. There was no torrent of love-making. He simply put out his hand and took hers, and patted it gently. Thus they were affianced.

She was very much in love. It tingled in every nerve in her body and filled every crevice of her brain, and set her spirit singing tunefully.

She was happy now, utterly happy. No longer would she look in terror towards the barren years. There was a goodly stretch of life and health before them both, and then they would drift imperceptibly into the quietness of age, as on the breast of a singing river.

There were two fears before her: One was the husband unheard from for twenty-two years. She was certain he was dead, but it seemed wrong to contract a marriage with another man while there was this uncertainty.

'I know he's dead!' she told Hunter, 'but somehow I . . .'

'I understand,' the soldier told her. 'You don't feel a widow. At any rate, he's legally dead, and you're free. We can get out the legal papers.'

So that was settled. But something that disturbed her more was the attitude her son might adopt. She felt towards him as she might have felt towards a parent whose consent she was uncertain of—a great shyness, a modesty, a sort of unreasonable fear. Very timidly in a dimmed light, she told her son about it. He listened to her, and when he raised his face, he saw her features glowing, and the minute, gemlike dimness in her eyes. He went over and, putting his arm about her, kissed her silently, unadroitly. Then he straightened up, and his voice was gruff, as though he were ashamed of giving way.

'I think I'll take a little stroll,' he said.

She smiled to herself, for she knew well where he was going on his stroll. He was going out to call on Colonel Hunter, and to size him up, as the lad's saying was. It warmed her heart to feel that she had him looking after her, even in that undemonstrative, casual way of his. She went singing about the apartment until he returned, stopping at times to try to guess what he would say when he returned.

When he came in, his face was puzzled, and a certain line of disgust ran across his features. She started up in fear.

'What is it, Norman!' she cried. 'What's wrong?'

'Nothing,' he said, 'I was thinking of the Gold Coast. A Galla there wanted to sell me a diamond stolen from the Kimberley mines. Big as the Kohinoor! Offered him six hundred bones for it, but he wanted a thousand and I hadn't it. And if I had just belted him one on the jaw I could have got it for nothing. I wish to Heaven I had! It would have made a corking wedding present for you!'

He looked across the dingy table in the back room of the saloon at the grey-haired, furtive man in front of him. Detail by detail he went over the man's appearance—the livid skin and manner of speaking with half-closed lips, which denoted the man had known jails; the furtive, cowardly, and overwise look in the eyes, that told of evil learned and done; the shabby but well-brushed clothes, the last stand of the old dandy.

'So you're my dad!' he said acidly.

'Yes, I'm your dad,' the old man agreed nervously.

'So you thought you'd look us up, Dad,' the son went on. 'Why didn't you do it before?'

'I thought you were all dead,' Bertrand Lacy explained nervously. 'It was only when I saw that article about your mother in the paper—how successful she had been, and how she was going to marry this colonel—that I knew she was alive. I found out where she was, from the people in New York, and I came on.'

They had come down for a few weeks to a little New England watering-place, Nan Lacy and John Hunter, and Norman came also with them, by way of a chaperon. They had not been married yet, and they were not to be for a month. This was not to be a hole-in-the-corner affair like her first venture, Hunter had decided in his generous way. She was to have everything she missed then, and more—a reverend cleric and a crowded church, an organ reverberating through the chancel, ushers in dress-uniform.

And so her son, who was more at home in any other line of endeavour, found himself in the profession of chaperon. To his credit or discredit, as the case may be, he was lax in the performance of his duties, leaving his mother and the colonel severely alone while they went riding or walking. It was due to this that he had been in the hotel when the furtive man was making inquiries about Mrs Lacy, Norman discovered him trying to extract some information from the porter of the hotel.

'Mrs Lacy is out,' he went forward and told him, 'but I am Norman Lacy, her son, and if there is anything I can do for you . . .'

He had steered the furtive man into a quiet saloon, and had listened, expressionless, to the information that his companion was his father.

'And now that you are back,' the son went on warily, 'this wedding is off?'

'I don't know,' the father sparred. 'It seems a pity!'

'Come through!' The son had dropped his caustic manner and his voice grated with menace. 'What do you want?'

'I've got my rights,' the father laughed.

'You've got no rights,' the son retorted hotly. 'You're legally dead.'

The elder Lacy smiled. Of all the subtle weapons that Satan had placed in his hand, the subtlest was his understanding of women. He might be legally dead. He might be a scoundrel and a blackguard. But he knew that Nan Lacy would marry no man if she were confronted with her first husband. He knew that to marry Hunter, with Lacy about, would appear to her a monstrous immodesty, a thing that she would shrink from as the blackest of mortal sins. Even her own high sense of chastity he would turn against her as a weapon. He knew women well. And from that mocking smile the son glimpsed something of the danger in which his mother's happiness stood.

'Well?' he snapped. 'What is it? What do you want? Money?'

The older man was on sure ground now. His nervousness had worn off.

'Yes, you pup!' he answered boldly. 'That's what I want, and that's what I'm going to get, and get quick. And I want a lot of it. I want five thousand.'

'I haven't got it,' the son answered. 'It's out of the question.'

'If you haven't got it, your mother has, and you can get it from her, or you and her new friend can fix it up between you. I don't care what you do. But I'm going to get it.'

The son rose in a passion of fury, but his four years in the jungle had taught him something. It had taught him the value of cunning as well as the value of strength. To strike the man now would be as dangerous as to strike a fanged snake.

'I'll give you until tomorrow at this hour,' the father dictated, 'and if it isn't fixed—then blooey! Understand? Now go home and have a family party. Regards from Pop!'

The son rose and went off. At the door he turned.

'Until tomorrow!' he said quietly. 'And if, in the meantime, you dare speak to my mother, or to Colonel Hunter, then God help you!'

It occurred to him more than once that day, with a sense of ridiculousness, that in all his life he had never thought as much as in those ten hours. What could he do? he asked himself in panic. Should he go to the colonel and tell him everything? The man would understand. That was a last resort. He had friends in New York, rich men—men he had met abroad—who might help. Might, he repeated to himself. What could he do? He would give his right hand, his right eye, his life even, to preserve that look of happiness on his mother's face.

He had been lax in his duties as chaperon until now, but today he never let his charges out of his sight for an instant. He had a vague dread that his mother might meet the man in the street, or that the father himself, in his impatience to make a killing, might disclose himself to Hunter. From noon until ten at night he thrust himself upon the lovers. Even when, at that hour, they decided to stroll down the pier, he insisted upon walking along with them.

They walked down the street and onto the deserted quay. There was the cold quality of a May night in the air, and no moon. Outside the circles of light cast by the dim street lamps was a purple darkness like velvet, like some sort of opaque liquid through which one walked. They passed a garish picture house, with its posters of black and red. They skirted a ship-building yard, the white population of whose slips were invisible in the dark. Their feet struck hollowly on the wooden planks of the pier, and they passed along slowly through the black air towards the violet nimbus of the great incandescent light in the middle of the pier.

To the right of them the harbour lay, the tiny lights of the opposite shore mirrored faintly on its surface. To the left of them the wooded country rose, and there was a faint *shush* to the boughs of the trees as a quiet and unseen wind moved them.

The colonel and Nan Lacy stopped under the bluish shower

of incandescent light and gazed silently across the dark space. The son looked vacantly over the waters. He was standing lazily, his hands in his pockets, when he stiffened into attention suddenly, like a bird-dog pointing. His ear caught the shuffle of careful footsteps, and as he threw his head around to catch a glimpse of the passer-by, he saw a furtive, rapid figure slip into the shadows past him.

'Hum!' he said to himself. He had recognised his father. So the man was stalking them. He was afraid, perhaps, that the son would have bundled the party off to some other place and have the wedding celebrated before he could act. He was taking no chances on that. He was as much on guard as his son was.

The boy turned to his mother.

'I think I'll stroll to the end of the dock,' he said.

'Be careful,' she warned him, 'be careful, Norman. It is pitch-dark.'

'Oh, I'll be all right,' he laughed. He made his way down the pier sure-footedly through the darkness until he came to the crouching figure in the shadows.

'I want to have that thing out,' he whispered. 'Come along with me.'

He walked along until they came to the end of the pier, picking out his steps with the certainty of a cat in the dark. His father followed him haltingly. He stopped at the edge and turned on the man.

'So you've been following them about all day!' he sneered. 'Probably telling your business to everyone too!'

'No such fool,' his father laughed. 'Nobody knows my business and nobody knows I'm following you around. Well, did you get that money?'

'I didn't get that money,' the boy told him; 'and, what's more, I'm not going to get it. Now, listen to me. Your game's up. There's nothing you can get out of us. You're lucky you're not in jail for blackmail. One word to you: you'd better clear.'

There was an instant's silence. The faint, invisible wind continued to rustle tree branches in a harmonious, swinging minor, and the outgoing tide swirled against the pier supports and choked in the little whirlpools. There was an unpleasant, dangerous laugh from the elder man.

'So that's the lay, eh?' he sneered. 'Well, you've got something coming to all of you. I'll give you scandal if you like. I'll put the lid on this little party.

'Here I am. There's my wife, up there—' he was pointing to the figures beneath the arc-light—'snuggling to another man's side, and planning to marry him, the shameless—'

'You had better clear,' the son warned.

'Clear!' Again the laugh came. 'I'm going right up there and take a hand in the game. I'm going to get my rights.'

'I'll give you a chance,' the son said grimly. 'Will you get out and stay out?'

The father had come round in front of the son, between him and the water. He looked at the boy. Dimly, from looking at each other, they could see each other's features in the pitch-dark.

'No!' he said. 'I'm going to face them. I'll have my rights. I want justice!'

'Justice!' his son repeated.

'Yes, justice!'

'Very well,' the boy said calmly. He balanced himself easily on his feet, and pushed out his left arm as a range-finder. He drew back his sledgehammer right hand. 'God forgive you,' he muttered, and he drove it home.

He heard the dull, thudding crack as it reached the jaw, and the heavy splash that followed. He stood alone on the pier-head for a minute, listening for other sounds, but all that came to his ears was the restless movement of the pine trees, and the rush of hurrying water.

He turned and sauntered up the pier easily. His mother was looking for him anxiously.

'I was afraid,' she said. 'I heard a splash.'

'It wasn't I,' he laughed. 'Probably some fish or other.' He stood and looked at the pair of them. 'Listen,' he said quizzically. 'I've been playing chaperon all day, and I'm a bit tired of it. I'm going off to shoot a game of pool. Good night.'

His mother's eyes sparkled with pride as she watched his loose swinging stride, and Hunter's dimmed a little as he watched her. 'She cares so much for him,' the soldier thought. 'I wonder does he appreciate it?'

THE FLOWER OF KILTYMORE

Brian Friel

The Sally Gap in Wicklow is perhaps the wildest and bleakest spot close to Dublin, and it was here that the film version of Dancing at Lughnasa, *by the country's internationally acclaimed playwright, Brian Friel (1929–), was filmed in the autumn of 1997. An abandoned cottage in this isolated part of the Liffey Valley was restored by the production company who had to make special allowances for some bats living in the roof space as they were protected by law. The resulting picture, which starred Meryl Streep, Michael Gambon, Kathy Burke and Sophie Thompson, satisfied Friel as much as the rave reviews which had greeted the original stage production at the Abbey Theatre in Dublin in 1990, and the three Tony Awards it won on Broadway. It was yet another of the author's brilliant studies in small lives and domestic tensions which began with his first international success,* Philadelphia, Here I Come! *(1964), filmed in 1970, and* The Loves of Cass Maguire *(1966) and have continued ever since including, most recently,* Give Me Your Answer, Do! *(1998). All of them focus on his native Ireland.*

Brien Friel was born in Omagh, County Tyrone, the son of a schoolmaster, and for ten years in the Fifties followed his father's profession as a primary and intermediary teacher in Derry. His early writing took the form of short stories about the rigid social and religious codes to be found in the small communities of Ireland, and these were published in a number of prestigious magazines on both sides of the Atlantic. Fame came when he concentrated on writing for the theatre and the only regret of some of his admirers is that he has not occasionally returned to the short-story genre. 'The Flower of Kiltymore', published in 1966, is the story of Sergeant Burke and his run-ins with the Blue Boys, a gang of yokels who vengefully play tricks on him with tales of imaginary fires, drownings and even murder. But when an unexploded mine is washed up on the tide, the repercussions go far beyond anything the boys or the old policeman could possibly imagine . . .

*   *   *

The calm and peace that the death of Lily, his wife, brought to Sergeant Burke's life were an experience so new and so strange to him that the only explanation he could imagine was that he must be ill himself, the unnatural tranquillity he had often heard about that frequently forebodes the end. And this knowledge was a vague comfort. Not that he wanted to die—he was, after all, only sixty-two, as strong as a bull, and within sight of retiring from the police force—but he felt guilty at having her lying all alone up there for the past four weeks in the new graveyard, the only grave in the cemetery, with not even a wall around it yet to keep the wandering sheep out. Still, it was where she had wished to be buried. Even on her death-bed, the doubtful distinction of being the first tenant in the new cemetery had tickled her vanity. Immediately before the second, and final, stroke had silenced her she had said to him,

'Where will they lay me, Burkey?'

On those rare occasions when she was not taunting him she addressed him as Burkey; otherwise it was Burke, a sharp command. She had been a sergeant's daughter herself, and anybody below the rank of superintendent was a nobody.

'Quit talking about dying, will you?' he whimpered.

'Ask the Canon to put me in the new graveyard,' she said. 'Away from all the riff-raff.' And she screwed up the side of her face over which she still had control in a coquettish grin so horrible that he averted his eyes.

'Surely, Lily, love. Anything you say.'

That was the last conversation they had. She died that evening,

and two days later was buried in the top right corner of the green
field that had borne wheat last year.

He confessed his premonition to Guard Finlin, his assistant,
on the first Monday in August when they had finished breakfast.

'Ill?' said Finlin solicitously. 'What way ill, Sergeant?'

'I'm damned if I know,' said Burke. He was a slow, heavy man,
unpractised in self-analysis. 'It's just as if the whole bloody inside
of me was—you know there—aw, by God, it's terrible, terrible.'

'It's a pain, is it? A soreness?'

Finlin, a Kerryman, was young and keen and cunning. The
countryside loved him for his stock of hilarious Lily-and-Burke
stories. He had made even the Canon laugh.

'No, no, no soreness. Just this big—this big bastard of nothing
inside my belly. Christ, man, it's horrible!'

Involuntarily Finlin glanced over his shoulder to acknowledge
Lily's conspiratorial wink. So often together they had made a
butt of the Sergeant, Lily bluntly and savagely, Finlin slyly and
with apparently innocence.

'D'you know what you'll do, Sergeant? You'll hop on the bike
and away into the town to see the doctor. I wouldn't like the
sound of that at all. O, God, no!'

'You wouldn't, eh?'

'There may be nothing to it, Sergeant. But then on the other
hand . . .'

His eyes were troubled.

'Off you go, Sergeant,' he said briskly. 'I'll hold the fort till
you get back.'

'Maybe I should, Finlin, eh? You think I should?'

'I'm sure of it. A thing like that isn't natural. I remember once,
when I was stationed outside Dublin, the superintendent was
always getting this feeling—'

'What was it like?'

'Sort of as if he was full and empty at the same time—if you
know what I mean.'

'And what?'

Finlin examined his fingers before he answered.

'The third attack was the sorest,' he said softly.

'Attack?'

'The first two, you see, they only paralysed the poor bugger. But the third one, Sergeant, it turned him purple.' His stomach fluttered with delight at the Sergeant's expression. 'And when they laid him out he glowed in the dark.'

The Sergeant did not speak.

'Of course, that was a long time ago,' Finlin went on. 'Things like that don't happen nowadays.' He began piling the dishes. 'But just in case. So away off with you, Sergeant, and I'll keep an eye on things till you get back.'

'Thanks, Finlin.'

'As a matter of interest, Sergeant,' said Finlin, lowering his voice, 'did you notice how quiet the Blue Boys have been since Mrs B. went to her reward?'

The Sergeant grunted. The self-styled Blue Boys were a group of about a dozen local yokels whose sole purpose in life was to torment the old policeman.

'But it's true, Sergeant!' said Finlin earnestly. 'Now, I know what you think of them—'

'Scamps! Bloody scamps!'

'True. True. But nevertheless, it's a nice mark of respect all the same, a tribute to herself.'

This had not occurred to the Sergeant. Indeed, he had not noticed that the Blue Boys had not played a prank on him for the past four weeks.

'Maybe,' he said guardedly. 'Maybe.' He rose and buttoned his tunic.

'It's in here,' he said, tapping his sagging stomach.

'The doctor's the man,' said Finlin. 'He'll see you right.'

'I'll try him anyway,' Burke replied in a voice already weary with resignation.

He was out in the turf shed, pumping his bicycle, when the phone rang.

'Is that the barracks?' a voice asked.

'It is,' said Finlin.

'I want to speak to Sergeant Burke.'

'The Sergeant's not here. Could I take a message?'

'Tell him there's something coming in on the tide. It's halfway between the islands and the slip.'

'What's coming in? Who's speaking?'

'A big, round, iron thing. It looks like a mine.'

The Blue Boys!

'A mine? And how do you know it's a mine? Who's—?'

'There are spikes sticking out of it.'

'Hello. Hello. Have you seen this thing yourself? What's your name? Hello?'

The line went dead. Just as Finlin hung up the phone the Sergeant went past the window.

'Sergeant!'

The old policeman did not hear. His assistant rapped on the glass.

'Sergeant Burke!'

Burke went slowly down the path that led to the road.

Finlin shrugged his shoulders. Then, he took off his heavy boots and his socks and went upstairs to bed in his bare feet.

The doctor just laughed when Burke told him that he thought he was finished.

'Take off that uniform, and we'll have a look at you,' he said, and only then did the Sergeant remember that he had not changed his underclothes. He lay on the doctor's couch and perspired with embarrassment as the short, white fingers prodded and probed and crept inquisitively over his naked body that had not been touched in thirty years. Throughout the examination he lay perfectly still, panting like an animal, his eyes roving over the ceiling, not wanting to see what was being done to him. But as the doctor's hands moved from the neck to the chest and down to the stomach the emptiness within him melted away, and he felt whole again.

To indicate that the inspection was over the doctor slapped his bare rump with the flat of his hand.

'If all my patients were as strong as you, Burke,' he said, 'I'd be out of business in the morning. Dress yourself, man, and away out of my sight. Damn the thing wrong with you.'

Burke dressed, and paid his two guineas, and went out into the early afternoon sun. And even before he could find a low wall from which to climb on to his bicycle he felt his inside drain of substance again, and the dull discomfort that was like a cramp entered into him and settled in him. Two good guineas down the drain, he thought.

Throughout the five-mile journey back to the barrack Lily sat on the handlebars, her face inches from his, as if he were seeing her through binoculars. Now she was as he remembered her on their wedding morning, her red hair limp about her head, her eyes wide and alert (she was forty-two then, he remembered, and he thirty-one). Now she was dressed for golf and striding towards a waiting taxi. Now her features were blunt with pregnancy; she was sitting in a wicker chair outside the barrack door, knitting. Now she was coming down the steps of the hospital, pale after the miscarriage, her cardboard case in her hand, a cigarette dangling from her lips, her eyes flat. Now she was standing in the day-room, her bitter laughter echoing throughout the whole ground floor, on the day the Blue Boys took his uniform from the clothes-line in the garden, soaked it in whitewash, and hung it up again. Now her face was pinched with fury, and she was screaming at him, 'For God's sake, I'm not going to rot away here for the rest of my life!' Now, in slacks and turban, smoking incessantly, quick with excitement, she was supervising the removal of their tired furniture from Kiltymore to Culdreivne, from Culdreivne to Ballybeg, from Ballybeg to Beannafreaghan, from Beannafreaghan back to Kiltymore where they had begun their married life. And as he pushed his bike up the last incline before he dropped down into the valley of Kiltymore that was his kingdom, her face was wet with tears, and she was sobbing, 'Are you not going to help me, Burkey? Are you not going to take me away from Mayo? I'm dying of loneliness, Burkey, dying of loneliness.'

Finlin was in the day-room, busily checking over applications for farm-fuel grants. He gave the Sergeant his honest smile.

'Well? What's the good news?'

Burke told him.

'Man, that's powerful!' Finlin exclaimed. 'That's the best bit of news I've heard in weeks! Heart, liver, pressure—all perfect, eh?'

The Sergeant sank into a chair and grunted.

'Lord, but that's a great relief,' Finlin went on, 'to know that you're hale and hearty and you about to go out on pension.'

'You know damn well I've three more years to go, Finlin.'

'But it'll fly, Sergeant, fly.' He began to gather up his papers.

'And what did he say about the shortness of breath?'

'The what?'

'Maybe you didn't mention it to him. And maybe you were wise. The less you tell them bucks the better. But it's a wonder he didn't notice it himself, Sergeant, isn't it?'

'Notice what?'

'You know—the way you puff and pant when you climb the stairs, Sergeant. Like an aunt of mine, God have mercy on her, but she was as contrary as a tinker's goat, she had that trouble, too. Not that it killed her, mind you—it was the cancer that took her at the heel of the hunt—but the noise of her going about the house was something fierce. As my father used to say—'

'Any messages while I was away?'

'Messages? Damnit, I almost forgot! The Blue Boys are back on the warpath!'

The Sergeant sat up ins his seat. Another prank, he knew; another practical joke at his expense. Within the past twelve months alone they had sent him to two imaginary fires, three car crashes, one murder, and two drownings. But for no reason that he could understand he welcomed the news that they had resumed their tricks.

'They phoned three times,' Finlin went on, 'looking for you. Their story is that there's a mine washed up on the beach beside the slip!'

'A mine?'

'Aye. A mine—boom! Whoever sees them now, they're dodging behind the rocks there, waiting to see you arrive in a lather of sweat. And me after saying only this morning that they seemed to have quietened down. Ah, a low crowd, Sergeant! A gang of toughs!'

'Which of them phoned?'

'You don't think he gave me his name and address, do you? A born actor, whoever he was, shouting his message as if the thing was going to explode under his tail! It might have been young Crerand, or one of the Thompson twins. You couldn't tell.'

'And what did he say?'

The Sergeant felt a sudden spurt of energy. He wanted to jump on his bicycle, and cycle over to the pier, and—what the hell was wrong with him? Had the journey into the town been too much for him?—yes, and hear the mocking laughter echoing through the rocks. That was what he wanted most of all: to hear the whooping laughter.

'Say? The first story was that the mine was floating in past the Stags. Then, it was supposed to be drifting towards the slip. The last message—it came about an hour ago—was that it was sitting on the beach. ''If the Sergeant's not there,'' says the bucko to me, ''you'd better come yourself.'' ''And who'd look after the station?'' says I. ''It's a matter of live and death,'' says he. ''Fair enough,'' says I, cool as you like. ''I'll make a note of it in the book.'' A mine, no less! Well, at least it's original.'

The Sergeant jumped to his feet.

'I'm going over there,' he said impetuously. 'It's a policeman's job to answer every call, even if it is a false alarm.'

'Sergeant!'

He avoided Finlin's incredulous stare.

'Duty, Finlin. A man must do his duty.'

'God, man, are you out of your mind?' Finlin blurted. Then, recovering, 'And what about the Canon, Sergeant?'

'What about the Canon?'

'Have you forgotten that he wants me to put a new light in the paybox in the hall this afternoon?'

Burke had forgotten.

'The Canon can wait,' he snapped.

'There's a harvest dance there tonight,' said Finn softly. 'And, as you know, the Canon waits for no man.'

'Damn him!' said Burke. 'You're a policeman, not an

electrician. If he weren't so bloody mean—Go on! Go on! Fix his wee light for him and hurry back! And in future, Finlin, you can do your parochial jobs outside duty hours.'

'Very well, Sergeant.'

'And you can tell him that from me.'

As soon as he said it he regretted it because he knew that Finlin would do just that.

'That's one thing I'd never do, Sergeant.'

'Clear out to hell!' Burke roared, for the surge of sudden energy had soured to temper. 'This bloody place is run like a bloody boy scout outfit!'

'I'm away, Sergeant,' said Finlin meekly.

He slipped out the door, stopped, and stuck his head back in again.

'What about the bastard, Sergeant?'

'The what?'

'The big bastard of nothing in your stomach—what did the doctor say about it?'

'Clear out to hell!' Burke said again, but softly this time, because Finlin made no effort to conceal the humour in his eyes, and he was, after all, only a boy, young enough to be the Sergeant's son. 'You have my heart broke.'

'Good luck,' said Finlin, disappearing.

He pulled the door after him, lifted a golf club and a ball from the hall-stand, hid them under his top coat, and went off whistling.

The afternoon was warm and rich and yellow. The Sergeant took off his tunic, and rolled up his shirt sleeves, and undid the top button of his trousers for comfort. He thought of lunch, went into the kitchen, made himself a cup of tea, and did not finish it. He came back into the day-room, and sat at the trestle table, and fingered papers, and felt the vacuum grow until it was a throbbing pressure that pushed against his chest, and then, as soon as he was certain of its location, shifted suddenly to his stomach and nibbled at his groin. He shuffled out to the garden, and stood irresolutely among the weeds that had taken control in the last month of good weather.

There was a pine tree at the foot of the garden. When he had come first to Kiltymore his intention had been to plant forty or fifty trees along the bottom of the garden to act as a shelter-belt against the hard Atlantic winds. But Lily had mocked at his plan—'Spend your good money on trees? Sure nothing grows here, you clown you! And besides, even if they did grow, we'll be gone long before they'd be any height'—and he had dropped it. But when he was sent back to County Mayo there was a single tree growing exactly where he had hoped to plant the shelter-belt, a single pine tree with a frail trunk and agonised, leafless branches that leaned away from the Atlantic and towards the barracks, as if they were appealing for comfort. Now, he lowered himself clumsily to the ground beneath it, and let his bulk relax against it. He closed hie eyes. So this was peace, this terrible emptiness. So this was what, in those odd moments of treachery when Lily flogged him with her tongue, he had dreamed of, this vacuity that was a pain within him. Sweet God, he prayed, sweet God, if this is what I wanted, take it away from me.

There was only one explosion, a hollow, muted thunder, but there seemed to be five or six, because the drowsy air enveloped the sound and bounced it leisurely against the surrounding hills again and again until the countryside ached with a dull, throbbing spasm. He knew immediately that it was the mine, but he did not stir until the third echo broke and spilled over him; and even then, as he scrambled to his feet and automatically tensed his flabby girth and buttoned his trousers and his shirt, there was no intimation of disaster in his mind. The Blue Boys had laid a trap for him. He had avoided it by accident. Now, dutifully, he must go and investigate, because that was his duty, if only to give them the satisfaction of a belated laugh.

In the day-room, when he was putting on his tunic, the phone rang. He ignored it. He left a note for Finlin, got out his bicycle, and headed towards the harbour.

He was half-way there when the Canon's car, travelling even more recklessly than ever, passed him without the usual toot of acknowledgement, and was lost in a cloud of white dust. Then

he remembered that the Canon never blew his horn when he was
going on a sick call (as Willie Long's cow and Hanna Brennan's
donkey foal could testify, if they were alive). But who was sick,
he wondered; nobody that he knew of in the west side of the
parish. A mile further on it occurred to him that there was no
one working in the fields; and that was strange, because the closer
you got to the sea the slower the harvest was; there were still
lots of patches of hay that had not been cut. Then, when he
reached the cross-roads where the track to the harbour left the
main road, he met young Crerand running blindly towards him.
They may snigger at me in private, he thought, but, by God, I'm
damned if they're going to make a public joke of me!

'Well, Crerand, and what's the hurry for—'

'A slaughter,' Crerand gasped. 'O, God, terrible! Terrible!
They're lying all over the beach, dying and dead! All the boys—
O, God!—terrible!'

Burke looked beyond Crerand and down to the slip. There was
only half a slip now, a cement path that ended abruptly in shallow
water. The beach nearby was crowded with people.

'What happened?' he asked.

'We were fooling about with the mine—trying to lasso it with
ropes—and then—and then—the Thompson twins were throwing
rocks at it—and then—'

Annie Murtagh, the mad crone who lived in a hovel beside
the beach, leaped from behind a stone ditch and pulled at the
Sergeant's elbow.

'They're all gone!' she screamed in her wild voice. 'All gone—
the flower of Kiltymore!'

The Sergeant looked at her, at Crerand, down to where the
slip had been.

'How many?' he said to Crerand. But the youth did not hear
him. He was kneeling on the ground, his forehead resting on the
white dust, sobbing.

'The flower of Kiltymore!' chanted Annie Murtagh in exultation. 'The flower of Kiltymore—all gone!'

Very carefully, very slowly the Sergeant rested his bicycle
against the stone wall. 'Now,' he said to himself, aloud, and

again. 'Now.' Then, gripping his hands behind his back, and his mind still saying Now, Now. Now, he walked the hundred yards down to the edge of the sea.

He was there until late that night. Two had been blown to pieces, one of the Thompson twins, and a fourteen-year-old boy from the neighbouring parish of Crockbeg; seven had been seriously injured; and four others were suffering from shock. There were no scenes, no panic, indeed scarcely any tears—they came later, in the homes. On the golden sand the injured boys lay side by side and stared up at the sky. Beside them knelt their families, too grieved or too relieved to talk. Groups of helpers waded in the water or searched the bent for pieces of the dead youths, and when they found something that looked like a limb they brought it silently over to the rocks and left it beside the two sets of parents who still tried to believe that their sons had gone for the day to the town, or to the bog, or to the trout lake beyond the church. The Canon moved from group to group, praying, whispering, consoling.

Then, when the two ambulances came just before dusk, the noise of their engines shattered the unnatural quiet. Someone began the rosary. The searchers in the water and among the bent called out triumphantly when they found something. The Thompson grandmother, too old for grief, lost her reason and wandered from group to group, lilting bits of randy Gaelic songs. Everybody started to talk, at first in subdued tones, then aloud so as to be heard above the sea and the cold dusk. Then, when it was known that the ambulances could take only four boys each at a time, there was jostling to see who would be taken away first. At this point the Sergeant would have asserted his authority, but the Canon took over and was obeyed meekly. Burke stood at his elbow and held the ambulance door open; it was the only useful thing he had done since he arrived. It was then that he noticed Finlin for the first time, stripped to the waist, carrying a stretcher.

In the interval before the ambulances returned the rosary was said again. After that, families and friends intermingled and talked urgently in undertones. Blackness closed in on them. The sea hissed. Burke took off his tunic and spread it over a boy who groaned in his sleep. Then he joined the doctor and the Canon and listened to them discussing the sinking of the *Titanic*. The doctor was saying, 'They sang a hymn, Canon, didn't they— *God Bless Our Pope*, wasn't that it?' when suddenly Burke felt wet lips against his ear and heard a man's voice say with intense threat, 'You'll pay for this day, Burke! You'll pay for it!' He wheeled round and saw a figure disappear into the gloom. It looked like Billy Thompson, the father of the twins.

He was the last to leave the beach. When the ambulances came the second time, their four piercing headlights searching out white, drawn faces, he turned his back so that they would not identify him. And when the stretchers were being loaded there were hands enough without his. Then, the ambulance drove off, and after them the doctor's and the priest's cars; and then the stragglers, uneasy with vague loneliness, went quickly up the track that led to the main road.

Now that he was alone the Sergeant wanted to accomplish something. He would make another search—perhaps someone had been left behind—had all the Blue Boys been accounted for?—had anyone counted them? He walked the beach from end to end. He climbed up the sandbanks and groped about in the bent. He came down to the water's edge and walked along it and then—O God—was it!—still another? No, it was only his tunic, wet through. He held it out from him, took another look around, and went up to where he had left his bicycle.

He found it lying in the middle of the road, a tangled mess of metal. The tyres had been slashed, the spokes pulled out, the handlebars bent and knotted. He examined it carefully. Surely this was no time for another prank, he puzzled. Or was there something more than horse-play in their tricks? Did they really hate him? He dropped the tangled steel behind the stone hedge and set off on foot.

Every window in the barrack was lit up, as if a party were being held, or a home-coming reception. As he got closer he saw three strange cars sitting at the front door. But they prodded no curiosity in him; he was too weary to care any more. All he wanted was a bed and sleep, a full night's sleep. He felt more than old, almost patriarchal, the oldest man in the world, the weariest, the most battered. Rest; that was what he needed.

Finlin must have heard his steps on the gravel because he came running out to meet him. His eyes shone with excitement.

'God, man, where were you? What kept you? We thought you had drowned yourself or something!'

He put an arm round the Sergeant's shoulder and urged him towards the station to get him inside the quicker.

'Do you know who's here, Sergeant? The Superintendent! *The Superintendent!* And four bucks from head office! And Sergeant, Sergeant, do you know who's coming tomorrow? The Commissioner! *The bloody Commissioner!*'

'What for?' said Burke, not because he cared, but because he knew Finlin wanted to be asked.

'What for?' Finlin's voice cracked with disbelief. 'God, man, what do you think? For the enquiry! They've begun already in there! Why did you not answer the first phone call? Why were you not on duty? How many phone calls were there? What time did they come? Oh, my God, wait till you see them! They're rearing to savage you, man, savage you!'

'Why, Finlin?'

'Why? Sergeant, you weren't drinking, were you? And what happened to your tunic? O, Sergeant, Sergeant, what'll you say to them? They're out to nail you, man! They won't leave an inch of you whole!'

They were now at the front door.

'One wee thing, Sergeant—you won't mention about me going off to fix the light in the hall, will you? I mean to say, you wouldn't want the Canon to get mixed up in this, would you?'

'I won't mention it, Finlin.'

'God bless you, Sergeant! You're a right skin!' He now saw his superior in the light of the passage. 'You're sure you're feeling all right, man? You're not sick or nothing?'

'I'm fine, Finlin, fine.'

'Go up and straighten yourself a bit. Those fellows are going to grill you for the rest of the night.' He paused. 'And Sergeant, stand up to them, man. Don't take too much lip from them.'

'Right, Finlin.'

'I'll tell them you'll be down in a minute. O, my God, such a day!'

Burke climbed the stairs to his bedroom. He could hear the hum of voices from the day-room below, and could imagine the five solemn faces ranged around the trestle table. He sat on the edge of his bed and felt his body tremble with exhaustion. He could not even begin to assess how serious his position was or to prepare a defence for himself. They might dismiss him right away; or they might question him for hours, for days, and then dismiss him; or they might make a 'case' of him, compile a file on him, keep him on tenterhooks for months, and then demote him, and send him to the back of beyond. It must be a terrible offence, he thought, that would bring the Commissioner all the way from Dublin tomorrow.

And yet, although he knew that his future was in the balance, he was neither afraid, nor even anxious. Because for the first time in four weeks he felt normal again. There was the fatigue, yes; but it was a healthy exhaustion. But the emptiness in his stomach had evaporated, and his head was clear, and his heart— his heart was gay, sure, vibrant. So many familiar things had happened to him today: the Canon had ignored him; his bicycle had been wrecked; a voice had hissed, 'You'll pay for this, Burke!'—incidents that assured him he was still in the centre of the pushing stream of life, and not floating, as he had been since Lily's death, in the peace and calm of some stagnant backwater. But even more important, in a few days' time Lily would be alone no longer; she would have company in the new cemetery, the eternal company of the two Blue Boys, and that was a great relief to him. It might not have been the company she would have chosen, but they would have a lot in common, he felt. At last he had been instrumental in making her happy, even once.

He got up from the bed, put on his Sunday uniform and his good boots, combed his hair, and straightened his tie. As he went down the stairs to meet his judges the wretchedness of the last four weeks was forgotten, and he knew again the only joy he had ever known. The month of ghostly isolation was over. His prayer in the garden had been answered. Let the Superintendent and the Commissioner do their damnedest to him! He knew now he had the capacity to survive it, because his life had suddenly, happily, slipped back into its old groove.

THE YELLOW BERET

Mary Lavin

Mary Lavin (1912–96) received a very early grounding in the mysteries of Ireland. Born in Massachusetts, she grew up in County Meath, close to the estate of Lord Dunsany, the writer of weird fiction who is credited with originating fantasy fiction in short story form. Her interest in writing about the traditions of old Ireland was fostered by the nobleman, but in much of her work she endeavoured to combine the past with the present in a wholly new style. Her work, primarily short stories, has since been ranked alongside that of Sean O'Faolain and Frank O'Connor to whom she was introduced by Lord Dunsany. Although she lived in America for many years, her affection for Ireland never grew any less, nor did her desire to use Irish backgrounds in many of her stories. Regarded as one of the greatest Irish writers of her generation, she received many honours, including the Katherine Mansfield Prize (1961), several Guggenheim Fellowships and the Gregory Medal (1975) which W. B. Yeats considered Ireland's supreme literary award. She was President of the Irish Academy of Letters from 1972 to 1974.

'The Yellow Beret', written in 1974, is the stark account of a double murder on a single night in Dublin and more than justifies Joyce Carol Oates' description of Mary Lavin as 'one of the finest short-story writers'.

*   *   *

'Two murders in the one night? In Dublin? Nonsense! Maybe it's the same one they're talking about?' Mag looked at her husband in mild disbelief.

'How could it be the same?' Don said. 'Wasn't the other one down at the docks? Do you never read the papers?'

'But two murders in the one night!' Mag knew that the note of doubt in her voice would annoy him, but she couldn't help it, so, to please him, she peered across the breakfast table at the newspaper in his hand. But without her glasses the sun made one blur of everything on the table—plates, napery, and newsprint—and waywardly her mind went back to her own concerns. She'd soon have to call Donny. She glanced up at the mantelpiece to see if the entrance card for his examination was still propped in front of the clock, so he couldn't possibly forget it when he was going out. Then she looked around the room to make sure there was nothing else he was likely to forget—his fountain-pen, or the key of his locker in the College.

But all the time she was vaguely aware that Don was critical of her lack of attention. She'd have to make some comment.

'I hope we're not going to have a wave of crime!' she said.

Exactly the wrong thing to say. She had only revealed the full extent of her heedlessness.

'Wave of crime!' he scoffed. 'I told you there was no connection between the two crimes. You're as bad as the newspapers.' He sounded irritated. But as he read on down the long columns devoted to the two crimes he became more amiable. 'It's a disturbing business,' he conceded. 'It will have a very upsetting effect on the public, I'm afraid!'

Well, here was something Mag could discuss with a genuine interest and liveliness.

'I don't see why! Why anyone should be upset—ordinary people like us, I mean. There's always a reason for these murders! Don't tell me they come out of a clear sky! I see no reason why anyone should be concerned at all about them—beyond feeling sorry for those involved, of course! Take that girl at the docks. I'm sure what happened to her was only the end of a long story!'

'Not necessarily,' Don said curtly. 'As a matter of fact they're looking for a Dutch sailor who only went ashore a few hours before the murder—'

'But he knew her from another time, I suppose? And—'

'Not necessarily,' said Don again.

Mag reddened. She hadn't understood that it might all have happened in that doorway: not only the murder, but . . . well . . . it all.

'Oh!' she said, repulsed. Then her voice quickened. 'Oh, Don. Let's not talk about it. Let's not even think about it. You know how I feel about that kind of thing.'

It was not so much a feeling as an attitude. She had made it a point to draw a circle, as it were, around their home, and keep out all talk of violence and crime. She had always tried to let their son feel he lived in a totally different world from the world where such things happened. Don't talk about it. Don't think about it. That was her counsel to him—and to herself as well.

It wasn't as easy to practise as to preach, though. Last evening, although she had only caught a word or two about that girl who was strangled on the docks, yet she could not get the thing out of her mind all night. Although she had never been out to the Pigeon House where it happened, and had only seen the long sea wall from the deck of the B. & I. Boat—seen it sliding past as the ship pulled out past the Alexandra Basin into the bay—yet she kept picturing the place as if it were a place she knew well.

Through the cranes and ships' rigging one could see the wide wharf narrowing into a place with no human habitation; nothing but coal-yards, and warehouses, and the Power Station of Pigeon House itself, its windows lit by day as well as night with a cold inimical light. Then the wharf narrowed again until it seemed only a promenade for birds, with bollards here and there splattered with glaring white droppings; and where in places steps led down into the water they seemed senseless, more than half of them under water, wobbly-looking and pale, and when a wash of water went over the top steps it lay on them thin as ice.

It was here the pictured it happening. Not at the edge near the steps, but back from them, where, in an abortive bit of wall, an iron gate stood giving entrance or egress to nowhere. She could distinctly picture that gate, reinforced top and bottom with rusty corrugated iron—cut in jags along the top as if with giant pinking-shears.

How could a gateway she had never seen be so vivid in her mind? Even now, in the sunny breakfast-room, with Don across the table from her, she felt the picture forming again in her mind. But this time there was a man in the picture. A Dutch sailor. It was him: the murderer! Who else could it be? Bending downward, in the gateway, with his back to her, she saw him, as clearly as she saw the gate in which he stood. His clothes—a faded blue shirt—his hair—a carroty red—were as plain as if he were standing in front of her in the flesh. She could not see his face, but he could not stand there for ever. In a minute he would have to straighten up and turn and get back to the densely-peopled streets and lose himself in the crowds, and she would be forced to look at him face to face. And when she saw his face—ah, this was the terror—it would, she felt certain, be a face well known to her.

What was the meaning of this vision? There had never been anything psychic about her.

Desperately she closed her eyes to blot it all out—the wharf, the gateway, the figure—but against her closed lids they formed again, more clearly. And then—as she knew he must—the man turned, or half-turned rather, because only his eyes turned towards her; his face and head remained partly averted. His head, indeed, seemed fixed in an implacable pose as if he had no power to move it, and yet in another sense it was all movement, a strange and terrible inner motion. Every cell of skin and hair and membrane seemed to vibrate. His coarse orange hair quivered, and his fibrous beard, while the enormous white whorl of the one ear visible to her seemed as if it was still evolving from its first convolution. And not only the face but the very air around him seemed to whirl and spin until it, too, was all spirals and oscillations. She went rigid with tension.

Then the white whorl of that ear brought her back to her senses. Van Gogh! The self-portrait! Relief left her so limp she slumped down in her chair. What a fool she was! She glanced at Don, glad he was not always able to read her mind. Yet—wait! Why did Van Gogh come into her mind? Could there be any reason? And what did the real murderer look like?

To think that he might at that moment be walking the streets of Dublin! Oh heavens! she could see him again. This time he was standing on Butt Bridge, leaning over the parapet and staring down the river. Terror swept over her.

'Did you say the other murder was in Dublin, too, Don?' she asked sharply.

'Still trying to link the two? I tell you, there was no connection between them, Mag. The other poor creature—' he nodded down at the paper—'the other poor creature was the soul of respectability—'

'The other victim was a woman too? You didn't tell me!'

'And elderly spinster,' said Don, as if not altogether corroborating her statement. 'A school-teacher, I think it said.' He bent and looked for verity to the paper. 'Yes, a school-teacher living in Sandford Road. Respectable enough address! Over fifty, too!'

But Mag rushed over and grabbed the paper out of his hand.

'Over fifty! Oh, no, Don! No! Why didn't you tell me? That's terribly sad. I didn't realise. I thought it was another of those ugly businesses. Why didn't you tell me it was so sad? The poor creature!'

Don stared at her.

'What's sadder about her than the girl on the docks?' he asked.

But Mag had got her glasses and was gathering up the pages of the paper. 'Where is the front page? Was there a picture of the poor thing?'

'I don't think so,' said Don. 'There was a picture of that girl, though! She was only seventeen. A lovely looking girl. Now that was what you might call sad! Oh, I know the sort she was, and all that, but she was so young. She had her whole life ahead of her. There's no knowing but she might somehow have been influenced for good before it was too late. And anyhow,' he said limply, 'the other poor thing—' he shrugged his shoulders, not bothering to finish the sentence. 'She can't have had much of a life. Can't have had much to look forward to in the future! Lived alone. Kept herself to herself. An odd sort apparently. Say what you like—it wasn't the same as being seventeen!'

'Oh, stop it, Don. I can't bear it. You don't understand. To come to such an end after a lifetime of service.' Mag was poring over the paper. 'Yes! she was a teacher. To make it worse she was a kindergarten teacher—oh, the poor thing. I can't bear to think of it. The head was battered in—with a stone, they think—and bruises on the neck and back.'

'Not a sex crime, anyway,' Don said, facetiously Mag thought.

'Oh, Don, how can you? There's no question of anything like that! She was over fifty! Fifty-four. And several people have already come forward, voluntarily, to testify to her character. She led the most normal, the most regular life and—'

'Nothing very normal or regular about wandering the streets in the small hours!'

'Oh, you didn't read it properly.' Mag consulted the paper again. 'She was found in the small hours, but it was done before midnight. They haven't given the pathologist's report yet, but the police put the time between eleven and twelve. She wasn't found earlier because the body was dragged into someone's front garden.'

'Nice for those people!' Don said.

'Oh, Don, how can you joke about it? Do you realise that if she had been left in the street there might have been a spark of life in her when she was found? As things were it seems she wouldn't have been found at all until daylight only a couple coming home from a dance happened to step inside the garden hedge.'

'Nice for them too!' Don said irrepressibly. 'Sorry, Mag, sorry! I feel as bad as you do about it, but you never take any interest in murders, and to hear you carrying on about these women—'

She pulled him up short.

'Don't speak of them in the same breath!' she said coldly.

But he was looking down at the paper again.

'Oh, look, there's more about it in the late-news column. They're looking for any information that may lead to the recovery of a yellow beret believed to have been worn by the victim earlier in the evening.'

Mag pressed her lips together.

'The unfortunate girl! She little thought when she was putting on that beret—'

'It wasn't the girl! It was the other woman.'

'The elderly woman? Are you sure? A yellow beret? It sounds more like what a young girl would wear, surely?'

'The old girl must have fancied herself a bit, it seems.'

'Oh, Don, I ask you not to take that tone again, please. Please! I'm certain it was simply a case of some thug attacking her in the hope that she might have money on her. He probably didn't intend anything more than to stun her, but maybe she screamed, the poor thing, and he got frightened and hit her again to keep her quiet. Maybe he didn't realise he'd killed her at all.'

'Then why did he drag her into that garden?'

'Oh, I forgot about that.'

But Don had had enough of it. He glanced at the clock. 'You forgot something else! How about calling Donny?' he said, and he went out, got his hat and coat in the hall, and where he stood put them on.

'Oh, he has plenty of time yet,' Mag said, and she followed him out into the hall. But she looked up the stairs. 'All the same, I'll go up and call him before I do anything else.' At the bottom of the stairs, however, she turned. 'Don't go till I come down,' she said, quite without reason. Or was it, she thought afterwards, that even then, at the foot of the stairs, a vague uneasiness had already taken possession of her? Had she, all morning, been unconsciously aware of a sort of absolute silence upstairs, different altogether from the merely relative silence when the boy was up there, but asleep? Certainly half-way up the stairs when she looked through the banister rail she was outrageously relieved to see that her son's bed had been slept in, although he was not in it.

'Oh, you're up?' she cried, talking to him, although she wasn't sure whether he was in his room or not. He could be behind the door, perhaps, taking down his clothes from the clothes hook? Or in the bathroom? 'Where are you?' she called, when she saw he wasn't in his room. She went to the door of the bathroom. 'Are you in there, Donny?' she asked from outside the bathroom

door. 'Where are you?' she called out then sharply, still address-
ing herself to him. But when she leaned over the banisters to see
if he could have gone downstairs—to the kitchen perhaps—
without their noticing him—it was to Don she called. 'Is he down
there, Don?'

'Why would he be down here?' Don had come to the foot of
the stairs. She thought there was an uneasy note in his voice.
Then he too started up the stairs.

'Why are you coming up?' she cried.

She must have begun to cry at this point, because Don shouted
at her.

'Stop that noise, for God's sake, Mag! The boy probably stayed
out last night. But what of it? I wish I had a pound note for every
time I stayed out all night when I was his age. I'd be a rich man
now if I had! He has you spoiled; that's all! There's some perfectly reasonable explanation for his staying out!'

'But he didn't stay out. He was in bed when I brought up his
hot jar last night!'

Don seemed taken aback by being reminded of this.

'He's gone out somewhere then, I expect,' he said, 'that's all.'

'Where? And when? I was down early. There wasn't a stir in
the house. I didn't hear a sound till I heard you!'

Together they stood stupidly, one above the other, in the middle
of the stairs.

'He must have gone out during the night then,' Don insisted.

'But why? And why didn't he tell us he was going out?' Mag
demanded. 'He knows I'm a light sleeper. He knows I never
mind being wakened. Many a night, before his other exams, he
came into my room and sat on the end of the bed to talk for a
while if he couldn't get to sleep.'

'Well, come downstairs anyway, Mag,' Don said, more gently.
'There's no use standing up here in the cold. He hasn't done this
before, has he? No! You'd have told me, of course. And he didn't
have a sign of drink on him last night, I suppose?'

'Has he ever had?' she flashed.

In spite of the anxiety that was creeping over him too, she saw
that Don was irritated by her righteous tone.

'Look here, Mag,' he said, 'it wouldn't be the end of the world, you know, if he did take a drink! We can't expect to keep him off it for ever. Moderation is all we can demand from him at his age.'

But Mag set her face tight.

'I'll never believe it of him,' she said. 'Not Donny!'

'Well, how else are you going to account for his behaviour now?'

'Maybe he thought of something he wanted to look up before the exam,' she said desperately. 'You know Donny! If it was anything important—anything for his exam—he'd think nothing of getting up and dressing and going out to quiz some of his pals about it. Not like other fellows that would be too lazy and would chance leaving it to the morning! Donny would never chance anything.'

That was true. She saw Don had to acknowledge it.

'Yes,' he said, 'but in that case he'd have been back in an hour or so.'

'Unless he stayed talking, wherever he went!'

'He would have telephoned!'

'In the middle of the night?'

They looked at each other dully.

'You don't suppose . . . that he might have met with an accident or something?'

'Funny, I never thought of that,' his father said.

Yet, now, to both of them it seemed an obvious thought.

'Hadn't we better do something?' said Mag.

'Like ring the hospitals?' Don went over to the hall table where the 'phone stood. There, he hesitated.

'Which hospital ought I to ring? Street accidents are usually brought to Jervis Street Hospital, I think, but I don't suppose they are brought there from all parts of the city. I suppose all hospitals have casualty wards. I wonder where I ought to try first?' Suddenly his hesitancy left him, and confidently he put out his hand to take up the receiver. 'I know what I'll do, I'll ring the police. That's the thing to do. They must get reports from every hospital.' He turned to her. 'Did he have his name on him, I wonder? Or any form of identification?'

When she didn't answer he looked up. Her face had gone white. He put down the 'phone. 'Don't look like that, Mag,' he said. 'I'm sure he's all right. It was only to reassure you that I was 'phoning at all. We've got a bit hysterical, if you ask me. I think we should wait a while longer before doing anything. He'll breeze in here any minute, I bet. Wait till you see. And look here, Mag, let me give you a bit of advice. When he does come back . . .'

But he saw that she was in no condition for taking advice.

'Don't ring the police anyway,' she said.

It was the way she said it, dully and flatly, that made him feel suddenly that whatever had come into her mind to trouble her was out of all proportion to his own vague fears.

'You're not keeping anything from me, are you, Mag?' he asked, sharply.

'Oh, no,' she cried. 'It's just that I don't think we ought to draw attention to him in case—'

'—in case he got himself into some scrape or other? Is that it? What scrape would he get into?' he asked, stupidly.

'Oh, I don't know,' she said, 'but it seems a bad time to draw attention to him—with all this going on . . .'

It was an exceedingly vague and formless reference to what they had been discussing at breakfast, but he got her meaning at once, and his face flushed angrily.

'You can't mean that! You just don't know what you're saying!' he said. 'Your own son!'

'Oh, don't go on that way,' she cried. 'You didn't wait for me to finish. Listen to me!'

But he wasn't listening then, either. He was just staring at her.

'Oh please! Please!' Mag said wearily. 'I only meant that he might be innocently involved, drawn into something against his will, or even accidentally, and afterwards perhaps been afraid of the consequences. That was all I meant!' Then she looked sharply at him. 'What did you think I meant?'

In sudden enmity each probed the other's eyes for a fear worse than his own.

'Might I ask one thing?' said Don at last bitterly. 'Which of these killings is the one in which you think my son is involved? Battering in the head of an old woman? Or the other one?'

'You know right well the one I mean!' Mag snapped. 'How could he be involved in the other? Nothing on earth could justify killing that poor old creature.'

Don gave a kind of laugh.

'Well! You women are unbelievable. So you consider the poor girl on the docks was fair game for any kind of treatment! Bad luck if it should end as it did—bad luck for the man, that is to say!' He turned away as if in disgust, but the next minute he swung back vindictively. 'Tell me one thing,' he said. 'Just how did you think that anyone could be innocently implicated in a business like that? Your son, for instance!'

'I don't know,' cried Mag. 'It's not fair to take me up like that. I didn't say I thought anything of the kind. I was only frightened, that's all. Any woman would be the same. Many a time when we were first married, if you were late coming home, I'd be looking at the clock every minute and imagining all kinds of things.'

'About me?'

'Oh, you don't understand! What comes into one's mind at a time like this has nothing at all to do with the other person. It doesn't mean one thinks any the less of him. It's as if all the badness of the world—all the badness in oneself—rushes into one's mind, and starts up a terrible reasonless fear. I know Donny is a good boy. And I know he wouldn't harm anyone. But he might have been passing that doorway—'

'Down at the docks, on a dark night? It was raining too, the paper said.'

'Well, how do we know what might have brought him down there? How do we know where he is any night he's out, if it comes to that? He could have been passing that way just at the wrong moment, and maybe seen something. Then, who knows what might have happened!'

'But you forget he came home last night, Mag. You saw him yourself, or so you said. You said you went up and said good night to him like you always do, and gave him his hot bottle?'

Mag said nothing for a minute.

'Don,' she said in a low voice. 'There's something I didn't tell you because it seemed silly, but last night wasn't quite like other nights. His light went out as I went up the stairs. He had put it out although he heard me coming. I didn't mind it at the time—well, not much—and I tried not to be hurt—I told myself his eyes might be giving him trouble after studying so hard all the week. So I said nothing but went into the room without putting on the light and he put out his hand and took the hot bottle from me—in the dark. It wasn't quite like always.'

'Oh, now you're splitting hairs,' Don said, impatiently. Yet, Mag could see he was carefully considering what she'd told him. 'I think there's something you ought to get straight in your mind, Mag,' he said then, slowly, 'even if he were to walk right in the door this minute. You've got things wrong. It's just possible that a young fellow like our Donny might on occasion have some truck with a girl like that poor girl that was strangled without its being necessarily taken that he'd be mixed up in her murder, but he couldn't be mixed up in her murder without it necessarily being taken that he had some sort of truck with her! Get clear on that!'

Mag's mind, however, had unexpectedly cleared itself not only of that, but of all her other senseless fears as well.

'Oh, I'm sure we are being ridiculous,' she cried. 'There's bound to be some simple explanation. Look, Don! If it makes you feel better, dear, go ahead and ring the police.' But when he said nothing she put out her hand timidly and laid it on his sleeve. 'What do you really think, Don?' she said.

'I don't know what to think, now,' Don said, roughly. 'You've succeeded in getting me into a fine state.' He moved over and stood at the window. Then all of a sudden he gave a loud guffaw. 'Well, well,' he said, in an altogether new tone of voice. 'They didn't hang him yet anyway: he's coming down the road!'

'Oh thank God. Let me look. Where is he?'

Mag ran to the window, and then, when she had seen her son with her own two eyes, she ran towards the door.

'Mag!' Don's voice was so strident she turned back, but when their eyes met they were instantly at one again and could seek counsel from each other.

'What will I say to him?' she asked quickly.

'Let him speak first,' Don said, authoritatively.

What they didn't realise, either of them, was that it would be Donny who, with his sunny smile, would speak first as always— with his smile that was always so open, and had such a peculiar sweetness in it.

'I suppose I'm in for it!' he said, light-heartedly. 'Or perhaps you didn't miss me? I thought I'd be back before you woke up.' When they didn't answer, he reddened slightly. 'I meant you to come down and find me as fresh as a lark instead of like most mornings, trying to get my eyes unstuck.' He turned to Mag. 'Were you worried, Mother? I'm sorry. I'll tell you how it happened. I hope you weren't too upset?'

Mag was flustered.

'Well, it was mostly on account of your exam, Donny—' she said, vaguely, glancing at the pink card. 'If it was an ordinary morning . . .'

Donny glanced at the card too, and also at the clock. He went over and took up the card and put it in his pocket. 'I mustn't forget this. It's a good job I came home. I'd have forgotten it. I wasn't going to come home at all, but go right on to the College, only for thinking about you and how you might worry.'

'It was a bit late in the day to be worrying about us then,' said Don.

'I know,' cried Donny. 'But I ought to have been home hours ago, only I got a blister on my heel. It hurts like hell still. I ought to bathe my foot, but I don't suppose I've time. If it wasn't for thinking you'd have been in a state about me I could have washed my foot in the lavatory down at the examination hall. But then I'd have had nothing to eat, and I'm starving.' Seeing some unbuttered toast, he picked it up and rammed it into his mouth.

'Oh, that toast is cold,' cried Mag. 'Let me make some more.'

But Don brought his fist down on the table.

'Toast be damned,' he said, and he turned to Mag. 'Where the hell was he? Isn't that what we want to know?' He swung back towards his son again. 'Where were you? You don't seem to realise—your mother was nearly out of her mind.'

'Oh, Don, what does it matter now!' cried Mag—'as long as he's back, and everything is all right.'

For everything was more than all right now. The absent son had been unknowable and capable of—well—capable of anything. The real Donny, standing in their midst, was once more enclosed within the limits of their loving concept of him.

But Don could be stubborn.

'How are we so sure everything is all right?' he snapped. 'My God, Mag, but you have a short memory!' He turned to Donny. 'It's a queer thing to find a person has got up out of his bed in the middle of the night, and taken himself off somewhere—God knows where—without as much as a word of explanation. Why didn't you tell your mother where you were going? You know she's a light sleeper. And you knew you needn't have been afraid of waking me. I never hear a sound once I finally drop off. Why didn't you do that? Why didn't you come in and tell us what was going on?'

'Oh, Don, don't upset him,' Mag cried. 'Look at the clock. He can tell us at supper tonight, and—'

'But there's nothing to tell!' Donny cried. 'It'll all sound foolish now. I only meant to go out for a few minutes in the first place, but the night was so fine—'

'Are you trying to tell us you just went out for a nice little walk?' said Don. 'In the middle of the night?'

Missing the ironic note in his father's voice, Donny turned round eagerly.

'Not a walk! I had no notion of taking a walk. At that hour of the night! I only intended stepping outside to get a breath of air.' He turned back to Mag. 'I couldn't sleep after I went to bed. You know how it is before an exam! Well, after I was a while tossing about, I knew I'd never sleep. I knew the state I'd be in for the exam, so I got up and dressed. I thought that after a mouthful of fresh air I might look over my notes again for a bit. But as I said—when I stepped outside I was tempted to take a few steps down the road. It was such a night! You've no idea. I just kept walking on and on, till I found myself nearly in Goatstown! I was actually standing on Milltown Bridge before I realised how far I'd walked! And there were the hills across from me when I leant over the bridge—and somehow they seemed so near and—'

'You didn't go up the hills?' Mag couldn't conceal her astonishment.

'Well, as far as the Lamb Doyle's,' Donny said proudly. 'I'd have liked to go on further, up by Ticknock, but it was beginning to get bright—not that it was really dark at all, but day was breaking—you should have seen the sky—I'd like to have stayed up there. But I had the old exam to think about, so I had to start coming down again. Oh, it was great up there: I felt wonderful. I'd been going a bit hard at the work in the last few weeks and everything was sort of bunged up in my brain. Up there, though, I could feel my mind clearing and everything falling into place. But I don't suppose you understand?' he said, suddenly aware of their lack of comment.

'If only you'd come to my door, son,' his mother said.

'As if you'd have let me go out if I did, Mother! You know you'd have got up and come downstairs, and insisted on cups of tea, and re-heating jars and re-making beds. You'd never have let me out! But that breath of air, and the exercise, was just what I needed. I felt great! The good is well taken out of it now though, by all this fuss!' He looked accusingly from one to the other of them.

Mag turned to Don.

'Now! What did I tell you! He could have explained everything at supper.'

'Let's have no more of it so,' said her husband, and he took up his brief-case. 'All I'll say is, it's a pity he didn't cut short his capers by an hour or so, and save us all this commotion.'

'I told you, I got a blister on my heel,' said Donny, indignantly. 'I would have been back hours ago only for that.'

Mag had forgotten the blister. 'Oh! Let me look at it, son,' she cried. 'The dye of your sock might get into it. You could get an infection. We'll have to see that it's clean and put a bandage on it. Sit down, Donny, son,' she said, and as he sat down she sank down on her knees in front of him like she used to do when he was a little boy and she had to tie his shoe-laces for him.

'Wait till you see the bandage that's on it now,' said Donny. 'I came down part way in my bare feet—as far as Sandyford, where the bungalows begin—but people were stirring—milkmen, bus conductors, and that class of person—going to work, and I had to put on the shoes, but I wouldn't have got far in them only I found something to pad my heel. This!' he cried, and he rolled down his sock and pulled it up—a bit of sweat-stained, blood-soaked felt. 'What's the matter?' he cried, as he saw Mag's face. Then he saw Don's. 'What's the matter with you two?' he cried.

Was it the texture of the cloth? Was it the colour? What was it that made his parents know, instantly, that the bit of felt had once been part of a woman's beret?

'Why are you staring at me?' Donny cried. He looked down at the bit of stuff. At the same time he shoved his hand down into his pocket and brought up the rest of the beret. 'I felt bad about cutting it up,' he said, 'it looked brand new, but I told myself that—as the old proverb goes—somebody's loss is somebody else's gain.'

Mag and Don were staring stupidly at him.

'I suppose it wasn't all a yarn you were spinning us, was it?' Don asked at last. But he answered his own question. 'I suppose it wasn't,' he said, dejectedly. And he walked over and took up the paper. 'There's something you'd better know, boy,' he said, quietly. 'You evidently didn't see the morning paper.' He held it out to him, pointing to one paragraph only.

Donny read quickly—a line or two.

'Is this it, do you think?' he asked then, with a dazed look at the bit of yellow felt.

'That's what we want to know,' Don said. 'Where did you get it?'

'I told you! I picked it up in the gutter, somewhere about

Sandyford Road. Oh, do you think it's it?' he cried again, and letting the pieces fall he ran his hands down the sides of his trouser legs, as if wiping them. 'Why didn't you tell me when I came in first?' he said, looking so pathetically young and stupid. Mag began to laugh, odd, gulping laughs.

'Don't mind me, son,' she said, between the gulps. 'I can't help it.' She didn't see the warning look Don gave her. 'It's from relief,' she said.

Donny looked at her. He had not missed his father's look. Ignoring her he turned to Don.

'What did she mean?'

'Nothing, boy, nothing,' said Don. 'We were a bit alarmed, you must realise that. You wouldn't understand, I suppose. Some day you may. Parenthood isn't easy—it induces all kinds of hysterical states in people at times—men as well as women!' he added, staunchly, taking Mag's arm and linking them together for a minute. 'I mean—' he said, but suddenly irritation got the better of him. 'Anyway you've only yourself to blame,' he snapped. 'We were beside ourselves with anxiety—almost out of our minds. We were ready to think anything.'

Donny said nothing for a moment.

'You were ready to think anything? But not anything bad?' He turned to Mag. 'Not you, Mother? You didn't think anything bad about me? Why, you know me through and through, don't you, like—like as if I were made of glass. How could you think anything bad about me?'

'Oh, of course I couldn't,' Mag cried. And she longed to deny everything—words, thoughts, feelings, everything—but all she could do was show contrition. 'I was nearly crazy, Donny,' she cried. 'You don't understand.'

'You're right there! I don't understand,' said Donny, and he slumped down on a chair. After a minute, apathetically, he began to pull his sock on over his grimy foot. 'I'd better go to my exam,' he said.

'Your exam!' Don shouted. 'Are you joking? Well, let me tell you, you can kiss good-bye to your exam. Don't you know you'll have to account for that beret being in your possession, you young fool? You don't think you can walk into the house with a thing like that—like a dog'd drag in a bone—and when you've dropped it at our feet walk off unconcerned about your business?' Suddenly Don, too, slumped down on a chair. 'Oh, weren't you the fool to get us into this mess! You and your rambles! If you were safe in your bed where you ought to have been we'd have been spared all this shame and humiliation.'

Shame? Humiliation? Mag thought all that at least was over. Don gave her a withering look.

'We'll be a nice laughing-stock!' he said. 'I can just see them reading about this in the office. There'll be queer smirks.' He looked at Donny. 'And I'd say your pals in the University will have many a good snigger at you too. To say nothing of what view the University authorities may take of it. And they might be nearer the mark. It's not such a laughing matter at all. It's no joke being implicated in a thing like this. There's no end to the echoes a thing like this could have—all through your life! People have queer, twisted memories. They won't remember that you were innocent: they'll only remember that your name was mentioned in connection with a murder—no matter how innocently. I'd take my oath that from this day you're liable to be pointed out as the fellow that had something to do with the murder of a woman.' In a flash of involuntary malice he turned to Mag. 'They'll probably get things mixed up, seeing both murders were the same night, and think it was in the other one he was involved.'

Donny didn't catch the last reference. He was thinking over what Don had first said.

'God help innocence, if everyone is as good at distorting things as you!' he said angrily.

'Well, it's no harm for you to be shown what can be done in that line,' said Don, a bit shamefaced, but still stubborn. 'I'd be prepared to swear you'll want your wits about you when you're telling the police about it. They'll need a lot of convincing before they believe in your innocence—or your foolishness, as I'd be more inclined to call it. It isn't as if you only saw the thing, or picked it up and hung it on the spike of a railing, as many a one would have done—as I'd have done, if it was me! It isn't even as if you picked it up and put it in your pocket and forgot about it, as maybe another might have done. But oh no! You had to cut it up in pieces! How will that appear in the eyes of the police? And I must say I wouldn't like to be you when it comes to telling them about the blister on your heel! As if you were a young girl with feet as tender as a flower! Those detectives have powerful feet. You couldn't blister them with a firing iron! I tell you, you'll wear out the tongue in your head before you'll satisfy those fellows' questions.' He put his head in his hands. 'Oh, how did this happen to us?'

Mag ran over to him.

'Don! I can't understand you!' she cried. 'You didn't take on this bad when we thought—'

Don glared at her. 'It wasn't me thought it, but you,' he cried. 'And if it was now, I'd know better what to think. He's only a fool—that's clear.'

But Donny stood up.

'I may be a fool, but I'm not one all the way through,' he said quietly, calmly. 'How is anyone to know—about this? It was hardly light when I picked it up. There wasn't a soul in sight. And if no one knows, why should I go out of my way to tell about it? It was up to the police to find it anyway. Isn't that what they're paid for—paid for by us and people like us? Whose fault is it if they don't do their job properly? There must have been any number of them in that vicinity last night, with flashlights and car-lights and the rest of it. If the beret was so important, why didn't they make it their business to find it? Why was it left for me to find? And why should I neglect my business because they don't do their business right? Here—I'm going out to my exam!'

'Oh, but, son.' cried Mag, 'you could call at the station—or 'phone them—yes, that would be quicker—'phone them—and tell them you found the beret, but that you have to go to your exam.'

Donny sneered.

'A lot they'd care about my exam. They'd keep me half the day questioning me, like Dad said.'

'Not if you explained, son. You could say you'd be available in the afternoon.'

'As if they'd wait till then for their information, Mother! No— I'm going to the exam.'

'Oh, son! Time might be of the greatest importance!' She ran over to him. 'Oh, Donny! You don't understand. Even if you were to miss your exam—think of what this might mean—it might lead to their finding whoever did it!'

'It could as easily lead them astray,' Don said quietly. 'I know them—they could lose more time probing Donny than would find twenty murderers in another country. It might not be as bad as it seemed at first, Mag, for him to do as he says: keep his mouth shut!' He stooped and picked up the two pieces of felt and stared at them.

Donny put out his hand.

'Give them to me,' he said. 'I've got to go.' Almost absently, he fitted the two pieces together for a minute till they made a whole. 'I'll see later what I'll do,' he said. Then he looked his father in the face. 'But I think I know already,' he said.

Hastily, Don took up his brief-case again.

'I'll be down the street with you, son,' he said. 'We have to consider this from every angle.' At the door he turned. 'Are you all right, Mag?' he asked.

Mag wasn't looking at him. She was looking at Donny.

'Don't look at me like that, Mother!' Donny said. 'Nobody's made of glass, anyway. Nobody!'

A BIT OF BUSINESS

William Trevor

Domestic violence is a feature to be found in a number of the short stories of William Trevor (1928–) who still vividly remembers from his childhood in Youghal the events when a deeply unhappy man shot himself in a henhouse. At much the same time he also discovered what has proved to be a life-long enjoyment of crime fiction when his mother introduced him to the novels of Agatha Christie, borrowed from a local library. The Christie stories, along with those by other well-known crime and detection writers of the time, such as Edgar Wallace and Sapper, were his main reading-matter for years and have made him something of an expert on the mystery genre. However, what makes his own short stories on the same themes so special is their attention to the minutiae of crime. In one story, for example, a psychopathic killer living at home with his mother is described eating Mr Kipling cakes, while in another a thug quotes Milton as he tries to score with a girl. It is such sinister oddities that make his stories so unforgettable.

William Trevor was born in Mitchelstown, County Cork, the son of a bank manager who was constantly being moved to new branches. This gave his son a rather itinerant view of Ireland as the family moved from Youghal to Skibbereen, to Tipperary Town, Enniscorthy and Port Laoighise; and he also developed a profound fascination with the human condition. His parents were an ill-matched pair and he recalls many arguments before he left home to take a degree at Trinity College in Dublin. His first novel, A Standard of Behaviour, *was published in 1958 and his subsequent work as a novelist, scriptwriter for radio and television, and his masterly short stories have won him numerous literary awards. He is the only writer to have twice won the Whitbread Prize—for* The Children of Dynmouth *(1976) and* Fools of Fortune *(1983)—and has many times been short-listed for the Booker Prize. His most recent novel is* Death in Summer *(1998).*

'A Bit of Business' (1966) tells the story of two petty thieves who fancy themselves as gangsters and go on a spree breaking into unoccupied houses during a visit of the Pope to Dublin— with unexpected consequences.

*   *   *

On a warm Saturday morning the city was deserted. Its suburbs dozed, its streets had acquired a tranquillity that did not belong to the hour. Shops and cafés were unexpectedly closed. Where there were people, they sat in front of television sets, or listened to transistors.

In Westmoreland Street two youths hurried, their progress marked by a businesslike air. They did not speak until they reached St Stephen's Green. 'No. On ahead,' one said when his companion paused. 'Off to the left in Harcourt Street.' His companion did not argue.

They had been friends since childhood; and today, their purpose being what it was, they knew better than to argue. Argument wasted time, and would distract them. The one who'd given the instruction, the older and taller of the two, was Mangan. The other was a pock-marked, sallow youth known as Lout Gallagher, the sobriquet an expression of scorn on the part of a Christian Bother ten or so years ago. Mangan had gelled short hair, nondescript as to colour, and small eyes that squinted slightly, and a flat, broad nose. 'Here,' he commanded at the end of Harcourt Street, and the two veered off in the direction he indicated.

A marmalade cat sauntered across the street they were in now; no one was about. 'The blue Ford,' Mangan said. Gallagher, within seconds, forced upon the driver's door. As swiftly, the bonnet of the car was raised. Work was done with wire; the engine started easily.

*

In the suburb of Rathgar, in Cavendish Road, Mr Livingston watched the red helicopter touch down behind the vesting tents in Phoenix Park. Earlier, at the airport, the Pope's right hand had been raised in blessing, lowered, and then raised again and again, a benign smile accompanying each gesture. In Phoenix Park the crowds knelt in their corrals, and sang 'Holy God, We Praise Thy Name'. Now and again the cameras caught the black dress of clergymen and nuns, but for the most part the crowds were composed of the kind of people Mr Livingston met every day on the streets or noticed going to Mass on a Sunday. The crowds were orderly, awed by the occasion. The yellow and white papal flags fluttered everywhere; occasionally a degree of shoving developed in an effort to gain a better view. Four times already the cameras had shown women fainting—from marvelling, so Mr Livingston was given to understand, rather than heat or congestion. Somewhere in Phoenix Park were the Herlihys, but so far Mr Livingston had failed to identify them. 'I'll wave,' the Herlihy twins had promised, speaking in unison as they always did. Mr Livingston knew they'd forget; in all the excitement they wouldn't even know that a camera had skimmed over them. It was Herlihy himself who would be noticeable, being so big and his red hair easy to pick out. Monica, of course, you could miss.

Mr Livingston, attired now in a dark-blue suit, was a thin man in his sixties, only just beginning to go grey. His lean features, handsome in youth, were affected by wrinkles, his cheeks a little flushed. He had been a widower for a year.

Preceded by Cardinal Ó Fiaich and Archbishop Ryan, the Pope emerged from the papal vesting chamber under the podium. Cheering began in the corrals. Twice the Pope stopped and extended his arms. There was cheering then such as Mr Livingston had never in his life heard before. The Pope approached the altar.

Mangan and Gallagher worked quickly, though with no great skill. They pulled open drawers and scattered their contents. They rooted among clothes, and wrenched at the locks of cupboards. Jewellery was not examined, since its worth could not be even roughly estimated. All they found they pocketed, with loose change and notes. A transistor radio was secreted beneath Gallagher's jacket.

'Nothing else,' Mangan said. 'Useless damn place.'

They left the house that they had entered, through a kitchen window. They strolled towards the parked blue Ford, Mangan shaking his head as though, having arrived at the house on legitimate business, they disappointedly failed to find anyone at home. Gallagher drove, slowly in the road where the house was, and then more rapidly. 'Off to the left,' Mangan said, and when the opportunity came Gallagher did as he was bidden. The car drew up again; the two remained seated, both their glances fixed on the driving mirror. 'OK,' Mangan said.

Mr Livingston heard a noise and paid it no attention. Although his presence in the Herlihys' house was, officially, to keep an eye on it, he believed that the Herlihys had invited him because he had no television himself. It was their way to invent a reason; their way to want to thank him whenever it was possible for all the baby-sitting he did—not that there wasn't full and adequate payment at the time, the 'going rate' as Monica called it. Earlier that morning, as he'd risen and dressed himself, it had not occurred to him that Herlihy might have been serious when he said it was nice to have someone about the place on a day like this, when the Guards were all out at Phoenix Park. The sound of the television, Herlihy suggested, was as good as a dog.

'A new kind of confrontation,' stated the Pope, 'with values and trends which, up to now, have been unknown and alien to Irish society.'

Mr Livingston nodded in agreement. It would have been nice for Rosie, he thought; she'd have appreciated all this, the way she'd appreciated the royal weddings. When his wife was alive Mr Livingston had hired a television set like everyone else, but later he'd ceased to do so because he found he never watched it on his own. It made him miss her more, sitting there with the same programmes coming on, her voice not commenting any more. They would certainly have watched the whole of the ceremony today, but naturally they wouldn't have attended it in person, being Protestants.

'The sacredness of life,' urged the Pope, 'the indissolubility of marriage, the true sense of human sexuality, the right attitude towards the material goods that progress has to offer.' He advocated the Sacraments, especially the Sacrament of Penance.

Applause broke out, and again Mr Livingston nodded his agreement.

Gallagher had wanted to stop, but Mangan said one more house. So they went for the one at the end of the avenue, having noticed that no dog was kept. 'They've left that on,' Mangan whispered in the kitchen when they heard the sound of the television. 'Check it, though, while I'm up there.'

In the Herlihys' main bedroom he slipped the drawers out softly, and eased open anything that was locked. They'd been right to come. This place was the best yet.

Suddenly the sound of the television was louder, and Mangan knew that Gallagher had opened the door of the room it came from. He glanced towards the windows in case he should have to hurry away, but no sound of protest came from downstairs. They'd drive the car to Milltown and get on to the first bus going out of the city. Later on they'd pick up a bus to Bray. It was always worth making the journey to Bray because Cohen gave you better prices.

'Hey,' Gallagher called, not loudly, not panicking in any way whatsoever. At once Mangan knew there was a bit of trouble. He knew, by the sound of the television, that the door Gallagher had opened hadn't been closed again. Once, in a house at night, a young girl had walked across a landing with nothing on her except a sanitary thing. He and Gallagher had been in the shadows, alerted by the flush of a lavatory. She hadn't seen them.

He stuffed a couple of ties into his pockets and closed the bedroom door behind him. On the way downstairs he heard Gallagher's voice before he saw him.

'There's an old fellow here,' Gallagher said, making no effort to speak privately, 'watching His Holiness.'

Gallagher was as cool as a cucumber. You had to admire that in him. The time Mangan had gone with Ossie Power it had been nerves that landed them in it. You couldn't do a job with shaking hands, he'd told Power before they began, but it hadn't been any use. He should have known, of course.

'He's staying quiet,' Gallagher said in a low voice. 'Like I told him, he's keeping his trap tight.'

The youth in the doorway was wearing a crushed imitation suede jacket and dark trousers. His white T-shirt was dirty; his chin and cheeks were pitted with the remains of acne. For an instant Mr Livingston received an impression of a second face: a flat, wide nose between two bead-like eyes. Then both intruders stepped back into the hall. Whispering took place but Livingston couldn't hear what was said. On the screen the Popemobile moved slowly through the vast crowd. Hands reached out to touch it.

'Keep your eyes on your man,' a voice commanded, and Mr Livingston knew it belonged to the one he had seen less of because it was gruffer than the other voice. 'Keep company with His Holiness.'

Mr Livingston did not attempt to disobey. Something was placed over his eyes and knotted at the back of his head. The material was rough, like tweed. With something similar his wrists were tied in his lap. Each ankle was tied to a leg of the chair he occupied. His wallet was slipped out of the inside pocket of his jacket.

He had failed the Herlihys; even though it was a pretence, he had agreed to perform a small and simple task; the family would return to disappointment. Mr Livingston had been angry as soon as he realised what was happening, as soon as the first youth appeared. He'd wanted to get up, to look around for something to use as a weapon, but only just in time he'd realised it would be foolish to do that. Helpless in his chair, he felt ashamed.

On the television the cheering continued, and voices described what was happening. 'Ave! Ave!' people sang.

*

'Pull up,' Mangan said in the car. 'Go down that road and pull up at the bottom.'

Lout Gallagher did so, halting the car at the opening to a half-built estate. They had driven further than they'd intended, anxious to move swiftly from the neighbourhood of their morning's work. 'If there's ever a squawk out of you,' Mangan had threatened before they parted from Mr Livingston, 'you'll rue the bloody day, mister.' Taking the third of the ties he'd picked up in the bedroom, he had placed it round the old man's neck. He had crossed the two ends and pulled them tight, watching while Mr Livingston's face and neck became flushed. He released them in good time in case anything went wrong.

'You never know with a geezer like that,' he said now. He turned his head and glanced out of the back window of the car. They were both still edgy. It was the worst thing that could happen, being seen.

'Wouldn't we dump the wagon?' Gallagher said.

'Drive it in on the site.'

They left the car behind the back wall of one of the new houses, and since the place was secluded they counted the money they'd trawled. 'Forty-two pound fifty-four,' Mangan said. As well, there were various pieces of jewellery and the transistor radio. 'You could be caught with that,' Mangan advised, and the transistor was thrown into a cement-mixer.

'He'll issue descriptions,' Mangan said before they turned away from the car. 'He'll squawk his bloody guts out.'

They both knew that. In spite of the ugliness Mangan had injected into his voice, in spite of the old man's face going purple, he would recall the details of the occasion. In the glimpse Mangan had caught of him there was anger in his eyes and his forehead was puckered in a frown.

'I'm going back there,' Mangan said.

'The car's hot.'

Mangan didn't answer, but swore instead, repeatedly and furiously; then they lit cigarettes and both felt calmer. Mangan led the way from the car, through the half-built site and out on to a lane. Within five minutes they reached a main road and came eventually to a public house. High up on the wall above the bar a large television set continued to record the Pope's presence in Ireland. No one took any notice of the two youths who ordered glasses of Smithwick's, and crisps.

The people who had been robbed returned to their houses and counted the cost of the Pope's personal blessing. The Herlihys returned and found Mr Livingston tied up with neck-ties, and the television still on. A doctor was summoned, though against Mr Livingston's wishes. The police came later.

That afternoon in Bray, after they'd been to see Cohen, Mangan and Gallagher picked up two girls. 'Jaysus, I could do with a mott,' Lout Gallagher had said the night before, which was how the whole thing began, Mangan realising he could do with one too. 'Thirty,' Cohen had offered that afternoon, and they'd pushed him up to thirty-five.

They felt better after the few drinks. Today of all days a bit of fecking wouldn't interest the police, with the headaches they'd have when the crowds headed back to the city. 'Why'd they be bothered with an old geezer like that?' Mangan said, and they felt better still.

In the Esplanade Ice-cream Parlour the girls requested a Peach Melba and a sundae. One was called Carmel, the other Marie. They said they were nurses, but in fact they worked in a paper mill.

'Bray's quiet,' Mangan said.

The girls agreed it was. They'd been intending to go to see the Pope themselves, but they'd slept it out. A quarter past twelve it was before Carmel opened her eyes, and Marie was even worse. She wouldn't like to tell you, she said.

'We seen it on the television,' Mangan said. 'Your man's in great form.'

'What line are you in?' Carmel asked.

'Gangsters,' said Mangan, and everyone laughed.

Gallagher wagged his head in admiration. Mangan always gave the same response when asked that question by girls. You might have thought he'd restrain himself today, but that was Mangan all over. Gallagher lit a cigarette, thinking he should have hit the old fellow before he had a chance to turn round. He should have rushed into the room and struck him a blow on the back of the skull with whatever there was to hand, hell take the consequences.

'What's it mean, gangsters?' Marie asked, still giggling, glancing at Carmel and giggling even more.

'Banks,' Mangan said, 'is our business.'

The girls thought of Butch Cassidy and the Sundance Kid and the adventures of Bonnie and Clyde, and laughed again. They knew that if they pressed their question it wouldn't be any good. They knew it was a kind of flirtation, their asking and Mangan teasing with his replies. Mangan was a wag. Both girls were drawn to him.

'Are the ices to our ladyships' satisfaction?' he enquired, causing a further outbreak of giggling.

Gallagher had ordered a banana split. Years ago he used to think that if you filled a room with banana splits he could eat them all. He'd been about five then. He used to think the same thing about fruitcake.

'Are the flicks on today?' Mangan asked, and the girls said on account of the Pope they mightn't be. It might be like Christmas Day, they didn't know.

'We seen what's showing in Bray,' Marie said. 'In any case.'

'We'll go dancing later on,' Mangan promised. He winked at Gallagher, and Gallagher thought the day they made a killing you wouldn't see him for dust. The mail boat and Spain, posh Cockney girls who called you Mr Big. Never lift a finger again.

'Will we sport ourselves on the prom?' Mangan suggested, and the girls laughed again. They said they didn't mind. Each wanted to be Mangan's. He sensed it, so he walked between them on the promenade, linking their arms. Gallagher walked on the outside, linking Carmel.

'Spot of the ozone,' Mangan said. He pressed his forearm against Marie's breast. She was the one, he thought.

'D'you like the nursing?' Gallagher asked, and Carmel said it was all right. A sharp breeze was darting in from the sea, stinging their faces, blowing the girls' hair about. Gallagher saw himself stretched out by a blue swimming-pool, smoking and sipping at a drink. There was a cherry in the drink, and a little stick with an umbrella on the end of it. A girl with one whole side of her bikini open was sharing it with him.

'Bray's a great place,' Mangan said.

'The pits,' Carmel corrected.

You could always tell by the feel of a girl on your arm, Mangan said to himself. Full of sauce the fat one was, no more a nurse than he was. Gallagher wondered if they had a flat, if there'd be anywhere to go when the moment came.

'We could go into the bar of the hotel,' the other one was saying, the way girls did when they wanted to extract their due.

'What hotel's this?' he asked.

'The International.'

'Oh, listen to Miss Ritzy!'

They turned and walked back along the promenade, guided by the girls to the bar in question. Gin and tonic the girls had. Gallagher and Mangan had Smithwick's.

'We could go into town later,' Carmel casually suggested. 'There'll be celebrations on.'

'We'll give the matter thought,' Mangan said.

Another couple of pulls of the tie, Mangan said to himself, and who'd have been the wiser? You get to that age, you'd had your life anyway. As it was, the old geezer had probably conked it on his own, tied up like that. Most likely he was stiffening already.

'Isn't there a disco on in Bray?' he suggested. 'What's wrong with a slap-up meal and then the light fantastic?'

The girls were again amused at his way of putting it. Gallagher was glad to hear the proposal that they should stay where they were. If they went into town the whole opportunity could fall asunder. If you didn't end up near a mott's accommodation you were back where you started.

'You'd die of the pace of it in Bray,' Marie said, and Mangan thought a couple more gins and a dollop of barley wine with their grill and chips. He edged his knee against Marie's. She didn't take hers away.

'Have you a flat or rooms or something?' Gallagher asked, and the girls said they hadn't. They lived at home, they said. They'd give anything for a flat.

A few minutes later, engaged at the urinals in the lavatory, the two youths discussed the implications of that. Mangan had stood up immediately on hearing the news. He'd given a jerk of his head when the girls weren't looking.

'No bloody go,' Gallagher said.

'The fat one's on for it.'

'Where though, man?'

Mangan reminded his companion of other occasions, in car parks and derelict buildings, of the time they propped up the bar of the emergency exit of the Adelphi cinema and went back in afterwards, of the time in the garden shed in Drumcondra.

Gallagher laughed, feeling more optimistic when he remembered all that. He winked to himself, the way he did when he was beginning to feel drunk. He spat into the urinal, another habit at this particular juncture. The seashore was the place; he'd forgotten about the seashore.

'Game ball,' Mangan said.

The memory of the day that had passed seemed rosy now—the empty streets they had hurried through, the quiet houses where their business had been, the red blotchiness in the old man's face and neck, the procession on the television screen. Get a couple more gins into them, Mangan thought again, and then the barley wine. Stretch the fat one out on the soft bloody sand.

'Oh, lovely,' the fat one said when more drinks were offered.

Gallagher imagined the wife of a businessman pleading down a telephone, reporting that her captors intended to slice off the tips of her little fingers unless the money was forthcoming. The money was a package in a telephone booth, stashed under the seat. The pictures of Spain began again.

'Hi,' Carmel said.

She'd been to put her lipstick on, but she didn't look any different.

'What d'you do really?' she asked on the promenade.

'Unemployed.'

'You're loaded for an unemployed.' Her tone was suspicious. He watched her trying to focus her eyes. Vaguely, he wondered if she liked him.

'A man's car needed an overhaul,' he said.

Ahead of them, Mangan and Marie were laughing, the sound drifting lightly back above the swish of the sea.

'He's great sport, isn't he?' Carmel said.

'Oh, great all right.'

Mangan turned round before they went down the steps to the shingle. Gallagher imagined his fancy talk and the fat one giggling at it. He wished he was good at talk like that.

'We had plans made to go into town,' Carmel said. 'There'll be great gas in town tonight.'

When they began to cross the shingle she said it hurt her feet, so Gallagher led her back to the concrete wall of the promenade and they sat down with their backs to it. It wasn't quite dark. Cigarette packets and chocolate wrappings were scattered on the sand and pebbles. Gallagher put his arm round Carmel's shoulders. She let him kiss her. She didn't mind when he twisted her sideways so that she no longer had her back to the wall. She felt limp in his arms, and for a moment Gallagher thought she'd passed out, but then she kissed him back. She murmured something and her arms pulled him down on top of her. He realised it didn't matter about the fancy talk.

'When then?' Marie whispered, pulling down her clothes. Five minutes ago Mangan had promised they would meet again; he'd sworn there was nothing he wanted more; the sooner the better, he'd said.

'Monday night,' he added now. 'Outside the railway station. Six.' It was where they'd picked the two girls up. Mangan could think of nowhere else and it didn't matter anyway since he had no intention of being anywhere near Bray on Monday night.

'Geez, you're great,' Marie said.

*

On the bus to Dublin they did not say much. Carmel had spewed up a couple of mouthfuls, and in Gallagher's nostrils the sour odour persisted. Marie in the end had been a nag, going on about Monday evening, making sure Mangan wouldn't forget. What both of them were thinking was that Cohen, as usual, had done best out of the bit of business there'd been.

Then the lean features of Mr Livingston were recalled by Mangan, the angry eyes, the frown. They'd made a mess of it, letting him see them, they'd bollocksed the whole thing. That moment in the doorway when the old man's glance had lighted on his face he had hardly been able to control his bowels. 'I'm going back there,' his own voice echoed from a later moment, but he'd known, even as he spoke, that if he returned he would do no more than he had done already.

Beside him, on the inside seat, Gallagher experienced similar recollections. He stared out into the summery night, thinking that if he'd hit the old man on the back of the skull he could have finished him. The thought of that had pleased him when they were with the girls. It made him shiver now.

'God, she was great,' Mangan said, dragging out of himself a single snigger.

His bravado obscured a longing to be still with the girls, ordering gins at the bar and talking fancy. He would have paid what remained in his pocket still to taste her lipstick on the seashore, or to hear her gasp as he touched her for the first time.

Gallagher tried for his dream of Mr Big, but it would not come to him. 'Yeah,' he said, replying to his friend's observation.

The day was over; there was nowhere left to hide from the error that had been made. As they had at the time, they sensed the old man's shame and the hurt to his pride, as animals sense fear or resolution. Privately, each calculated how long it would be before the danger they'd left behind in the house caught up with them.

They stepped off the bus on the quays. The crowds that had celebrated in the city during their absence had dwindled, but people who were on the streets spoke with a continuing excitement about the Pope's presence in Ireland and the great Mass there had been in the sunshine. The two youths walked the way they'd come that morning, both of them wondering if the nerve to kill was something you acquired.

THE KILLING OF MRS NUGENT

Patrick McCabe

The Butcher Boy, written in 1992 by Patrick McCabe (1955–), has been called 'a disturbing masterpiece'; its author 'Ireland's great unsung novelist'; and the film version by Neil Jordan hailed as a 'clever, quirky, dark and at times emotionally violent movie'. Although the story of Francie Brady, who lives in a self-contained world full of cowboys and gangsters, was at first thought to be unfilmable, Jordan and his cast, led by Stephen Rea, Aisling O'Sullivan and Eamonn Owens as the Brady family, successfully shot the picture in 1997 in the small border town of Clones in County Monaghan, with McCabe himself appearing in a small role as Jimmy the Skite. Some viewers of the movie saw Francie as an unbalanced version of Tom Sawyer or Just William, while others found it difficult to understand how they could feel sympathy for such a foul-mouthed murderer. For that is what Francie Brady ultimately becomes.

Patrick McCabe was born in Clones, the second of five children, and among his earliest memories are visits to the local cinema, the Luxor, where he would watch as many as six films a week. He also had a passion for comics—his favourite characters were Roger the Dodger, Green Lantern, The Smasher and the border collie, Black Bob—and he and his friends endlessly played out their heroes from the comic pages and cinema screen. Like a number of other Irish writers in this book, McCabe became a primary school teacher, writing in his spare time. Several of his short stories were published in The Irish Times *and* Cork Examiner, *and in 1979 he received the Hennessy Award for one of them. His first novel,* Music on Clinton Street, *appeared in*

1968, to be followed by Carn *in 1989 and* The Butcher Boy *(1992) which he has described as 'a burlesque grand guignol', adding 'It is the duty of the novelist to subvert, to deliver the unexpected.' McCabe's two subsequent works, a play for television about a pyromaniac,* Old Flames, *and a novel,* Breakfast on Pluto *(1998), featuring an Ulster priest's son who thinks he is Dusty Springfield, have certainly reaffirmed this intention.*

'The Killing of Mrs Nugent' is an extract from The Butcher Boy *in which Francie, who believes that the silly, stuck-up Mrs Nugent and her son Philip have combined to separate him from his great friend, Joe Purcell, plots his revenge . . .*

*   *   *

The black road twisted in and out of the curly countryside like a ribbon at the end of it was Joe's school and what was he going to say then: For fuck's sake Francie, you've done it again! Hey Joe! I'd shout. Saddle up! We're riding out! Yee-haa!

I was getting as bad as ma. Whiz this way then whiz the other way. I'll do this no I'll do that. The whiz again. I know—I'll think some more about Joe and the old days. And then, more laughing. Big whorly clouds made of ink powder riding the sky and the music book stuck in my back pocket. Then the school rising up out of the fields with all its yellow windows gleaming— another house of a hundred windows. But this time it was different, behind one of them windows was Joe and when I thought that I leaped so high I could have headed the moon like a football. Francie Brady plays for the town he's forty yards out thirty yards out twenty ten yards out its a long ball and the goalie's missed it and yes Francie Brady has scored a goal for the town Francie has scored a goal the moon is at the back of the net!

I have been tramping for over an hour before I seen it and then soon as I turn the corner what happens. Out go the lights. Phut!, every last one. Hey—what the hell do you think you're at up there, turning off them lights? Leave them on! How am I supposed to find Joe Purcell! Hey! Did you not hear me!

Then all of a sudden I thought: This is something to do with Mrs Nugent. She's heard about me going to see Joe and she has some plan up her sleeve. She's told the priests to switch off all the lights so they can lie in wait for me and when I'm finished running round the place like an eejit looking for him, she'll appear out of the shadows standing there with them, smiling: So you couldn't find him could you not? That's a pity Francis isn't it and then I knew that would be the end I'd never find him then. But then I started breaking my arse laughing it was such a stupid idea. *Oh no*, I said, *this is one thing that Mrs Nugent isn't going to spoil!*

I'd thought some things but that was the daftest yet.

I went round the back and nearly walked into a big bin full of brock you'd think with me being King of The Brock I'd have been able to see that! I was in behind the kitchens. Grr says a dog.

Fuck up I said but I managed to get past him all right. I could hear the toilets hissing. Hiss hiss, we can see you Francie. I kept checking the book to see that I still had it in my back pocket. Where did I end up only in a room full of football boots and the smell of sweaty oxters. Curse of fuck on this and I had to start again. Dant-a-dan! Along the wall. Don't move! Six soldiers out of nowhere cocking rifles, up against the wall so we have you at last Mr Brady! No, none of that, only snoring priests and bogmen but where were they? Not in here nothing only an empty bed and a cupboard full of medicine bottles. I think I'll have a look at these I said and shovelled a few coloured pills into my hand out of a little brown bottle. Gulp down the hatch they went. I wonder what they were. I don't know. Whee, I thought I heard someone shouting from the other end of the corridor you take a left then the next right Francie and you'll find him no problem. I turned round to thank him whoever it was but there was no one there. Then the pill said: Oh that was just me Francie. Pill, I said, you bastard! Now now Francie said the pill for that I'll just have to turn your feet to sponge. Squish squeesh along the tiles. What's this the biggest bell in the world sitting under the stairs. I said: Mrs Nugent if you're in behind that bell you had better come out. I know you're in there Mrs Nugent you can't fool me.

Then I started laughing I couldn't stop myself. It wasn't an ordinary laugh either it was a bogman laugh the way they laugh at nothing with snots coming out of their noses still laughing long after the joke is over. I says I know what I'll do I'll give this bell a whack and see what happens. I'd say it'd make enough noise to waken every boarding school bogman in the world even the ones who are completely deaf. Ready steady—fuck off! If I did that they'd be down on me like a ton of bricks and maybe give Joe the boot into the bargain. Oh no you don't pill you'll not make a cod of old Francie that easy. Pill, I said—have manners!

I was in a right state now with all this laughing I couldn't stop. Hmm I says I wonder what tricks Joe gets up to in this place. Sliding down the knotted sheets out of the dormitory and away off to midnight feasts in the boatshed I'll be bound! I say Purcell you bounder! You are a perfect cad! For fuck's sake! I wonder is there any secret passageways I said. Fall against the knob of a banister next thing aaaaaaaaaaah! and away off down a black corridor full of cobwebs and the skeletons of dead bogmen boys.

Up the stairs I went what's this, a wooden door creak creak Our Lord Jesus appearing out of nowhere in the dark, hanging on the cross–hello yes what can I do for you? I'm looking for Joe Purcell Jesus. Straight on up to the top of the stairs. Right so Jesus thank you.

What's all this I said, a hundred sleeping bogmen! But not for long. Wait till they seen me and Joe in action!

Da-dan!

Flick—on goes the light blazes away and them all gone chinky-eyed and pulling the clothes round them: What's goin' on who's puttin' on the lights? I nearly said: why its me—Algernon Carruthers of course!

When I thought that I doubled up again and all I could see was them staring at me. They were all saying to the prefect who is he you do something about it its your job and all this but he wasn't going to do anything he had the blankets pulled up the same as the rest of them.

I thumped my thigh with the rolled up music book: *Joe! Where are you Joe Boy? I'm here! saddle up! We're ridin' out!*

I shouted it for all I was worth and then I shouted it again in case he didn't hear me. As soon as I said that all the things I had ever worried about floated away like silk scarves in the breeze and I knew all I had to do now was wait for Joe and we were off and this time we'd be gone for good. It made me feel so good I shouted again: Joe. Yamma yamma yamma! Yamma yamma yamma!

Then I said: Yee haa! Take 'em to Missouri men!

We'll ride out to the mountains Joe and there we can track for days. We can listen to the coyotes in the night. The coyotes baying at the moon because it makes them feel food they howl out anything they ever worried about. Then I did it. A-woo! A-woo! I closed my eyes and cried out across the prairie.

Then I looked up and who's coming the priest. It was Father Fox not because his real name was Fox but because he had a long snout and a hmm I wonder how could I trick this fellow face? Hello Father Fox I said, I'm looking for Joe Purcell. You're *what!* he says and I could see that Father Fox he wasn't such a nice old fox at all his face went all dark and his eyes didn't say I wonder how could I trick this fellow any more they said one more word out of you my friend and I'll take this collar off and I'll floor you by Christ I will and don't think for one second that I wouldn't. Father Fox I'm surprised at you! Don't say such things!

That's what Algernon Carruthers would have said. But I didn't say it.

I just said I'm looking for Joe can you help me please?

What did Fox say half to himself and half to the bogmen I

can not believe it I just can *not* believe it! He shook his head and when the bogmen seen him doing that they did it too. I could hear doors banging and all this commotion and running on the stairs. Then two more priests came in and who had they with them only Joe Purcell.

Joe! I shouted. *Fuck!*

I knew I shouldn't have shouted that, but I did. Fox made a wind at me but I ducked. He tried again but that was no use either I sidestepped it he was only making a cod of himself. All I had to do now was walk right over to Joe and that's what I would have done only for what happened then who was standing right behind him only Philip Nugent. He was taller now a bit tougher looking but it was him all right with the hair hanging down in his eyes. He was staring at me in a way he never did before straight at me. As soon as I seen him everything started to go wrong because he wasn't supposed to be there. All the things I was going to say I couldn't remember what they were now then the priest brought Joe over and the way he looked at me my stomach turned over it wasn't Joe. Philip was still standing over by the door with his arms folded. I knew when it was all over that he would be telling them. That I had wanted to be one of them and had turned my back on my own mother. He'd laugh then and say: Imagine him thinking he could be one of us!

Joe said to me: What do you want?

No he didn't. He said: 'What do *you* want?

It was no use me trying to say I wanted us to ride out Joe I wanted us to talk about the old days and what we'd do if we won a hundred million trillion dollars maybe go tracking in the mountains I don't know Joe, it was no use me saying that for I knew it wouldn't come out right so I said nothing I just stood there looking at him.

He asked me again: What do you want me for? Are you deaf or something?

Then he said: Do you hear me. What do you want me for?

I never thought Joe would ask that I never thought he would *have* to ask that but he did didn't he and when I heard him say it that was when I started to feel myself draining away and I couldn't stop it the more I tried the worse it got I could have floated to the ceiling like a fag paper please Joe come with me that was all I wanted to say dumb people have holes in the pit of their stomachs and that's the way I was now the dumbest person in the whole world who had no words left for anything at all. All I had now was one thing and that was the music book. It had got all twisted up with sweat marks all over it I says don't worry Francie its going to be all right I smoothed it out a bit and handed it to him some way or other I dropped it and the next thing the priest came in between us and says: *Look this has gone far enough! Is this fellow a friend of yours or is he not Purcell?*

I looked at Joe please Joe I was saying but he wasn't looking at me he was just saying I'm tired and I want to get back to my bed its three in the morning.

Then Joe just shook his head and said: No.

Then he left he said something to Philip on the way out and Philip smiled. I stayed there for a minute I was still twisting the book then the priest said I think its time you were leaving Mr Brady. I said yes, yes Father and they brought me to the gate they said I was lucky they didn't call the police I said yes it was then I went off into the dark I had left the bike somewhere but I didn't know where. It didn't matter anyway I just walked I felt like walking that wasn't Joe I said I don't know who that was but it wasn't Joe, Joe is gone they took him away from me and all I could see was a pair of thin lips saying that's right we did and there's nothing you can do that will ever bring him back again isn't that true Francis Pig you little piggy baby pig and I says yes Mrs Nugent it is.

When I got to the town they were all running round saying the world is going to end. The first thing I seen was Mickey Traynor wheeling a statue of Our Lady up the street in a barrow did you not hear he says the world is going to end it was on the news last night its all over he says oh I know says I I know that all right you don't have to tell me *that!*

What do we care he says let them to their worst we have the Blessed Virgin Mary to protect us she spoke to my daughter she says she's going to come with a sign. For the love of God go along and listen to her young Brady in these times every man must look after his immortal soul!

He got a grip of me by the shoulder and says: Will you do that for me Francie I knew your father.

I know you did I says he was supposed to go up to you about the television but he didn't that's why I had to go and watch the octopus in Nugents. right says Mickey I'd better be making tracks good luck now and off he went with the barrow.

I shouted after him: I don't suppose you'd be able to fix it now Mickey would you?

He didn't look round I knew he wouldn't be able to anyway it was too far gone after the kick da gave it. It was finished, that television. I should have thrown it on the dump by right for what was it doing in the coalhouse only taking up space. I went on up the street and who did I meet only the drunk lad. Come on into the Tower I says but he shook his head. I says what are you talking about and he says did you not hear about Traynor's daughter? I says I did but what the fuck do I care about Traynor's daughter come on in and I pulled out a fiver. No he says no I have to go on about my business the priest was down to see me he says I've to get into no more trouble. I've got into enough trouble through going about with you I have to go on up to see Father Dominic he says he might have a job for me. Excuse me he says pushing past me and away he goes with the raggy coat flapping behind him. Go on you humpy bastard! I shouted after him, you were glad enough of it when it was going!

I went in and bought a packet of fags and something to clean my jacket all they had was shampoo that'll do I says. When I came out I seen Mrs Connolly going past on the far side of the street with a basin full of flowers. I waved to her but she got all red and stuck down her head and never let on she seen me. A loudspeaker whistled and screeched then a hymn started up. It was called Faith of Our Fathers. I listened for a while but it was only a fuck up of a hymn. I stood outside the home bakery and sang my own. It was about Matt Talbot, my old friend from the Father Tiddly days. This is more like it, I said, this is a real hymn!

> I love my planks the best of all
> In spite of cold and frost and rain
> And I love my cat I give him kipper teas
> But most of all I love my chains.

I sang a few more verses all about them saying to him: Do you want us to buy you a drink Matt? Fuck off with yourself!

I had a good laugh at that, sitting on the wall and shouting at them going by: Matt Talbot for president!

Then I sang more. I pasted back my hair and sang into a lollystick.

> *Well its one for the money!*
> *Two for the show!*

I sang that one. Then I sang:

> *When you move in right up close to me*
> *That's when I get the shakes all over me!*

I sang more. I shouted:

> *Francie Brady on Radio Luxembourg!*

Then I got fed up singing fuck this I said, fucking singing. I went into the cafe its you he says what do you want I says sausages rashers beans chips eggs all that. I'm sorry we're closing sorry but we got to close now. I bought a bag of Tayto crisps and went out to the hide. I tried to clean the jacket up with the shampoo but it was no use I used half the bottle all it did was make it worse then I fell asleep.

I woke up the next morning and went round to the slaughterhouse but it was too early I was waiting for near two hours before Leddy came how long are you here he says a good while Mr Leddy I said. Its near time you'd show your face around here or where in the hell were you! Oh I says I was off rambling. Rambling he says, you'll do well to ramble in your own time Brady I've a mind to kick you rambling down that road. Well says I you won't have to worry for that's the end of it it'll be all over now shortly. He pulled on his apron and says they have a half ton of shite round at that hotel you were supposed to collect it and they have my heart scalded now get round there today and fuckingwell see about it. Right so Mr Leddy I said.

Then we started into the killing and we were working right through till dinnertime. Then he wiped his hands on his apron and says I'm away to my dinner take that cart round now. And make sure and tell them tell them you'll collect on time next week. I will indeed Mr Leddy I says. When he was gone off down the town I took the captive bolt pistol down off the nail where it was hanging and got the butcher's steel and the knife out of the drawer. There was a bucket of old slops and pig meal or something lying by the door so I just stuck them into that and went away off with the cart whistling. So Traynor's daughter had been talking to Our Lady again, eh? They were all talk about her going to appear on the Diamond. I heard two old women on about it. We should be very proud says one of them its not every town the Mother Of God comes to visit. Indeed it is not says the other one I wonder missus will there be angels. I wouldn't know about that now but sure what odds whether there is or not so long as she saves us from the end of the world what do we care? Now you said it missus now you said it. Everywhere you went: Not long now.

I went by Doctor Roche's house it was all painted up with big blue cardboard letters spread out on the grass: AVE MARIA WELCOME TO OUR TOWN. I was wondering could I mix them up to make THIS IS DOCTOR ROCHE THE BASTARD'S HOUSE, but I counted them and there wasn't enough letters and anyway they were the wrong ones.

Tell Leddy to collect this brock on time or its the last he'll get from us says the kitchen man and stands there looking at me like I was stealing something off him. I will indeed I said and started shovelling it into the cart. I shovelled and whistled away and made sure there wasn't a scrap left so there'd be no more complaining. Then off I went again on my travels. Everybody was all holy now, we're all in this together people of the town, bogmen taking off their caps to women, looking into prams and everything. This is the holiest town in the world they should have put that up on a banner.

There was a nice altar on the Diamond. There was three angels flying over it just in front of the door of the Ulster Bank.

I never saw the town looking so well. It looked like the brightest, happiest town in the whole world.

I went round the back swinging my meal bucket. I could see the neighbour's curtain twitching whistle whistle hello there Mr Neighbour its me Francie with my special delivery for Mrs Nugent. Then away she went from the window so I knocked on Mrs Nugent's door and out she came wearing her blue housecoat. Hello Mrs Nugent I said is Mr Nugent in I have a message for him from Mr Leddy. She went all white and stood there just stuttering I'm sorry she said my husband isn't here he's gone to work oh I said that's all right and with one quick shove I pushed her inside she fell back against something. I twisted the key in the lock behind me. She had a white mask of a face on her and her mouth a small o now you know what its like for dumb people who have holes in their stomachs Mrs Nugent. They try to cry out and they can't they don't know how. She stumbled trying to get to the phone or the door and when I smelt the scones and seen Philip's picture I started to shake and kicked her I don't know how many times. She groaned and said please I didn't care if she groaned or said please or what she said. I caught her round the neck and I said: You did two bad things Mrs Nugent. You made me turn my back on my ma and you took Joe away from me. Why did you do that Mrs Nugent? She didn't answer I didn't want to hear any answer I smacked her against the wall a few times there was a smear of blood at the corner of her mouth and her hand was reaching out trying to touch me when I cocked the captive bolt. I lifted her off the floor with one hand and shot the bolt right into her head *thlok* was the sound it made, like a goldfish dropping into a bowl. If you ask anyone how you kill a pig they will tell you cut its throat across but you don't you do it longways. Then she just lay there with her chin sticking up and I opened her then I stuck my hand in her stomach and wrote PIGS all over the walls of the upstairs room.

I made sure to cover her over good and proper with the brock there was plenty of it they wouldn't be too pleased if they saw me with Mrs Nugent in the bottom of the cart then I lifted the shafts and off I went on my travels again there was more hymns and streams of people up and down Church Hill with prayerbooks. Who did I meet then only your man with the bicycle and the raincoat thrown over the handlebars. He was all friendly this time he was a happy man Our Lady was coming he said. I haven't seen you this long time he says are you still collecting the tax? No I said that's all finished I'm wheeling carts now. You never thought you'd see the day the Mother of God would be coming to this town, eh? he says and looked at me as much as to say it was me arranged the whole thing. No, I did not, I said, its a happy time for the town and no mistake. A happy happy time he says and reached in his pocket to take out his tobacco puff puff what will we talk about now nothing I said the best of luck now I'm away off round to the yard right he says no rest for the wicked that's right I says no rest for anyone only Mrs Nugent in the bottom of this cart. But he didn't hear me saying that.

I left down the cart for a minute and went in to buy some fags the women were there over by the sugar only without Mrs Connolly. I got the fags and I says to the women its a pity Mrs Connolly isn't here I wanted to talk to her about what I said sure I was only codding! I said. What would I go and say the like of that to her for! Me and Mrs Connolly are old friends! Didn't I get a prize off her for doing a dance! A lovely juicy apple! I lit up a fag and puffed it ha ha they said ah sure don't be worrying your head Francie they said we all do things we regret don't we ladies. Yes I said especially Mrs Nugent and laughed through the smoke. Then they said: What? But I said: Oh nothing.

One of them twisted the strap of her handbag round her little finger and said there was no use in people bearing grudges at a special time like this. Now you said it I said, you never spoke a truer word.

Well ladies, I said, I must be off about my business there's no rest for the wicked indeed there is not Francie said the woman with three heads laughing away like in the old days. I had gone through that fag already and the shop was full of smoke I was puffing it all out that fast so what did I do only light another one. Francie Brady—I smoke one hundred cigarettes a day! Yes it's true! Francie Brady says! No, it isn't. Only when I'm wheeling Mrs Nooge around. I stuck a little finger in the air and pulled on the fag like something out of the pictures. I say ladies—good day, I said and that started them off into the laughing again. Master Algernon Carruthers and his Nugent cart. OK Nooge let's ride I said, the Francie Brady Deadwood stage is pulling out. The drunk lad went by with another saint in a barrow and ducked down when he seen me.

Stop thief! Come back with that saint! I says and started into the laughing again. Stop that man! He's going to sell that poor saint for drink! Whistling away on I went my old man's a dustman he wears a dustman's hat. I don't know where all the songs came out of. Well its one for the money. I am a little baby pig I'll have you all to know. Yes this is the Baby Pig Show broadcasting on Raydeeoh Lux-em-Bourg!

Hello my good man. Fine weather we're having. What did you order? Two pounds of chump steak?

Or was it a half pound of Mrs Nugent?

Sorry folks, Mrs Nugent's not for sale! She's off on her travels with her old pal Francie Brady. I was passing by Mary's sweet-shop so in I went and got a quarter of sweets clove drops. I came in to say hello to my old friend Mary I said will you ever forget them old days Mary! Twenty years in Camden Town! What about that! What do you say we go inside and you can give us a song on the piano!

I lit another fag and went on talking away but Mary said

nothing just scooped the sweets into the bag with a silver shovel and then twisted it the way she did spin twist and there it was a little knobbly bag of best clove drops yes indeed. Then she went and sat down by the window again looking out across the square. Look at that Mary! The same old clove drops! I said but she still didn't say anything just smiled if you could call it a smile. I knew who she was thinking about. She was thinking about Alo that's who she was thinking about. Don't worry Mary I said, your troubles are over Mary—Francie Brady the Time Lord is here!

But soon as I said it I felt stupid and I tried to think of something completely different to say but I could think of nothing so I just put the sweets in my pocket and went out the bell jingle jingle and the door closing behind me. Mary had the same face as ma used to have sitting staring into the ashes it was funny that face it slowly grew over the other one until one day you looked and the person you knew was gone. And instead there was a half-ghost sitting there who had only one thing to say: All the beautiful things of this world are lies. They count for nothing in the end.

Even if that was true I still went round the lane where the kids were this might be my last chance I said. Sure enough there they were setting toy tea-things on an orange box and clumping around in the enormous shoes. Can I play I said. How can you play if you're big one of them said, clear off! There was a young lad sailing lollystick rafts out into the middle of a puddle. I said to him: What would you do if you won a hundred million billion trillion dollars?

Without thinking he looked at me and said: I'd buy a million Flash Bars. Well fuck me, I laughed, then off I went again and left him churning up the water with his stick and whistling some tune he was making up as he went along.

Where the hell were you says Leddy when I got back to the slaughterhouse yard. Oh, tricking about I says, well trick about in your own time he says I have to go on up to the shop, you take over here. Right, I said, that suits me, and I left down the barrow beside the Pit of Guts and asked Leddy where he'd put the lime. Clear off Grouse! I shouted and he tore off through the gate with a string of intestines. I got the shovel and slit open the bag of lime there was warm tears in my eyes because I could do nothing for Mary.

I'd say it was a good laugh when Mr Nugent Ready Rubbed came home that evening. Brr that's a cold one yoo-hoo! I'm home what's for tea dear? Dear oh dear that wife of mine she's so busy she hears nothing. The smell of scones and the black and white tiles polished so you could see your face in them. O she's probably just gone out to the shop for something never mind let's see what's on the telly. Here is The News. News. Mm, isn't it quiet around here since Philip went to boarding school? Mm, isn't it quiet around here since my Mrs went to heaven he'd soon be saying but he didn't know that. I wonder what it will be—rashers and eggs maybe or one of her special steak and kidney pies! But poor old Mr Nugent he'd have a long wait before he got one of them again. Ah yes, it was sad. And that is the end of the news. Hmm. Tick tock. I wonder where she could be. I wonder where my wife could be? Hello next door neighbour did you see my wife? No, to tell you the God's honest truth now I didn't. Oh dear said Mr Nooge. Tick tick and walking round the kitchen the silence wasn't so nice now over and over again just where is Mrs Nugent the invisible woman? Tick tock and I don't care about Maltan Ready Rubbed, where is my wife! Look at that old Mr Nugent and his big red eyes! Maltan Ready Rubbed—It's The Best Boo Hoo Hoo! That wouldn't look so good on the television. I wonder would she be upstairs? Do you think she might have gone upstairs and fallen asleep next door neighbour? Why yes she could have couldn't she? Let's go and investigate shall we? Good idea says Mr Nugent and off they go taking the stairs two at a time but then when they open the door what do they see all over the walls oh no Mr Nugent hardly able to stand and the next door neighbour don't look don't look!

Well she doesn't seem to be in there anyway ha ha perhaps the police might know why don't we ring up let me do it Mr Nugent. Sweaty fingerprints all over the telephone hello is that Sergeant Sausage I mean is that the police station?

ACKNOWLEDGEMENTS

The editor and publishers are grateful to the following authors, publishers and agents for permission to reprint copyright stories: the Peters, Fraser and Dunlop Group Ltd. for 'The Sniper' by Liam O'Flaherty, 'The Sight' by Brian Moore and 'A Bit of Business' by William Trevor; Constable Ltd. for 'The Death of Stevey Long' by Sean O'Faolain and 'The Yellow Beret' by Mary Lavin; the O'Brien Press for 'The Execution' by Brendan Behan; HarperCollins Publishers for 'On the Bog' by Patrick O'Brian; Marion Boyars Publishers for 'Wesley' by Carlo Gebler; Sheil Land Associates for 'She' by Neil Jordan; Fleetway Publications Ltd. for 'The Man in the Middle' by Nigel Fitzgerald; Davis Publications Inc. for 'The Sword of Yung Lo' by Maurice Walsh and 'An Infringement of the Decalogue' by Donn Byrne; the author for 'Death' by Brian Cleeve; Curtis Brown Literary Agents for 'The Ineritance' by Frank Delaney; A. M. Heath & Co. for 'Aftermath' by Rearden Conner and 'Holy Blood' by Peter Tremayne; Condé Nast Publications Inc. for 'Burden of Proof' by Bob Shaw; Christopher Sinclair-Stevenson for 'Trio' by Jennifer Johnston; Pan Macmillan Publishers Ltd. for 'The Killing of Mrs Nugent' from *The Butcher Boy* by Patrick McCabe; Associated Newspapers and the *Daily Mail* for the account by Mary Kenny reprinted in the Introduction to this book. While every care has been taken to clear permission for the use of stories in this book, in the case of any accidental infringement, copyright holders are asked to write to the editor care of the publishers.